For Diana, the love of my life.

The Map of Ethasar

You can find a more detailed map at bradtowers.com/map-of-ethasar.

A Word from the Author

This book is unlike most books you've read before.

War of the Seven tells the story of a world-spanning war, with the fates of the gods at stake. You'll witness the conflict through the eyes of multiple heroes from rival factions, and some of them will not survive. You may get attached to a few heroes and fear for their fates, or you could choose to watch the great war from a godlike perspective.

I've turned *War of the Seven* into an immersive experience. After each set of chapters, you'll find a Bonus Content section. This section contains a link to a dedicated page on my website, along with a handy QR code. Follow the links to explore an evolving campaign map that tracks each faction, read a summary of the war's current state, view images of Ethasar's heroes, and listen to nine original songs about the story's heroes and events. The songs are all professionally produced, and I had lots of fun writing them and weaving them into the fabric of the story!

You can dive into these experiences at any time, and it will only take a few minutes.

If you'd rather keep reading, no problem! I've included the lyrics of the songs within the book, before each Bonus Content section. You'll also find a link to all the bonus content as you reach the end of the book. But don't skip ahead, as the bonus materials will contain spoilers.

This book is meant to be Big, Fast, and Fun, with plenty of plot twists that keep you guessing. But it's not for everyone's taste. If you're looking for literary prose, a deep and dark style, or romance, I believe there are other excellent books that you will enjoy more.

With that out of the way: if you're seeking a fun ride through a fantasy world that feels fresh yet familiar, with strong heroes, end-of-the-world stakes, shifting alliances, and a touch of humor, then you're in the right place. And if you're into strategy games (PC or tabletop), mythology, historical fiction, Vikings, Romans, Warhammer, Assassin's Creed, or heavy metal, you'll find even more reasons to love this story.

You're about to begin a completed trilogy. Book 2, *Songs of the Heroes*, continues the story, and Book 3, *Last of the Gods*, brings the conflict to its epic conclusion. All three books are available on Amazon in Kindle and paperback versions, and you can read them for free with Kindle Unlimited.

I hope you will enjoy reading this book as much as I enjoyed writing it.

Ready? Let's get started.

Table of Contents

Part 1: A Meeting of the Gods 1
Part 2: Blood and Vengeance 17
Part 3: The Trickster God 97
Part 4: The Three Queens 149
Part 5: Invasion 207
Part 6: The Strength of Blood 291
Part 7: Surprise Attacks 415
Part 8: Of Love and War 459
Epilogue 475

Part 1: A Meeting of the Gods

The Lady

For the first time in two centuries, the seven gods were gathering together on their divine island. It was time to talk about the end of the world.

Or, rather, about what they could do to prevent it.

The Lady strode forward, her bare feet moving gracefully over the hot sand. Fresh tufts of grass sprang up in her wake, along with the occasional flower, but the Lady knew they wouldn't last long. The ruthless sands would soon devour them.

Only one of her peers stood before her: Augustus, the many-faced god of the Julian Empire. For this meeting, he'd chosen his favorite aspect: a tall, wise-looking man in his physical prime. His skin and hair were as orange as the Lady's were green, and his beard was neatly trimmed. His only garment, a white loincloth decorated with orange motifs, reached down to his knees.

He greeted the Lady with a smile. "All of us, coming together again. I never thought I'd see the day."

"You won't, after today," the Lady said. "Not for a thousand years."

"And why is that?" If he'd noticed the sadness in her voice, he didn't show it.

"You've seen the vision, haven't you?"

"I have," Augustus said. "In seven years, the Vengeful One will come."

The Lady shuddered at the memory. The foreign deity from her vision was winged, and black as night. He could breathe fire, shoot storms of ice from the tips of his claws, and topple mountains with a swing of his tail. But, worse than that, he was larger than the world.

"He'll shatter our world into little pieces," Augustus continued. "None of us are strong enough to stop him. And so, the Supreme One told us to gather here, on this beach, and receive his guidance. Which, *of course*, means that there's a way out of this."

"And that is all you know so far?" the Lady asked.

Augustus nodded.

The Lady sighed. She didn't *want* to tell him what she knew. But the path forward had been set, and holding back her words wouldn't change a thing.

"The Supreme One has told me more," she forced herself to say. "He told me of a way to fight the Vengeful One and have a chance at winning. But it requires a great sacrifice."

"We must preserve this world," Augustus said. "Whatever this sacrifice is, we'll make it gladly."

She looked him in the eye. "No, not *gladly*, my friend. To gain enough power to fight the Vengeful One, one of the seven gods must absorb the divine essence of the others. Which means that six of us must die."

The Seven Gods

No, Augustus thought. He didn't want to believe the Lady's words, but her grave tone and her somber demeanor confirmed the truth of her message.

"There must be another way," he said. "What if we asked the Vengeful One to leave our world alone? There must be something we can offer him."

"I asked the Supreme One the same question," the Lady said. "He told me that neither words nor bribes will turn the Vengeful One away. He has his reasons to destroy us, and they are strong."

"And what are those reasons?"

"The Supreme One wouldn't say."

Augustus ran his fingers through his beard. "Then what if we all fought the Vengeful One together?"

The Lady shook her head. "*It is like this,*" she said, flawlessly imitating the Supreme One's voice. "*Seven men armed with sticks cannot defeat a giant in a fight, not if they tried a thousand times. But a man with the strength of seven could, if he had a big sword, and if he fought well enough and kept his wits about him. It is the same with you, my children.*"

Augustus frowned. "That does sound like something our creator would say. Oh, wait. Why doesn't He stop the Vengeful One himself?"

"I asked Him, but He didn't give me a proper answer," the Lady replied. "He only said that we must defeat the Vengeful One ourselves, without His help."

"Then what if—"

"You're grasping at straws, Augustus," the Lady interrupted him. "As I did. I asked Him all the questions you can think of, and, as much as it pains me, there is no other way. If there was one, He would have given it to us. And so, we must move forward."

Augustus gazed into the distance. *If we fail to defeat the Vengeful One, our world will be destroyed. Our followers, the people of the seven realms, whom we've loved and nurtured for centuries. The cities of the Julian Empire, with their great temples and their places of learning. The Lady's castles and her beautiful forests, full of birdsong. Sarab, the golden city of the desert men. The giants' slumber caves. And everything else.*

All will perish. And to have a chance at saving it, six of us must die.

She hadn't said which six.

He turned his gaze upon the Lady, admiring her perfect features, as he had done so many times before. The sadness in her eyes matched his own. "I don't want to lose you, Lady," he found himself saying.

"I don't want to lose you either," she said in a softer voice. "Nor any of the others, save for one."

Augustus nodded. He knew which one she meant.

"But I don't think we have a choice," the Lady continued.

"I understand," Augustus said. "What else did the Supreme One say?"

She brushed a rebel strand of hair away from her face. "I'll tell you when the others join us."

"Tell us what?" came a sharp voice from the right.

"Aljin," Augustus said as he turned.

The desert men's god had arrived soundlessly, as he often did. He stood tall, clad in his resplendent golden armor. The glow surrounding him turned even brighter as he gave Augustus and the Lady a dazzling smile. He tilted his head to the right and frowned, an unspoken way of repeating his question.

"Patience, Aljin," the Lady said. "I expect the others will arrive soon."

A shadow stretched over the beach, making them all look up. High in the sky, a gray creature the size of a ship flapped its enormous bat-like wings. Serya Krov, the god of the vampires and the worst nightmare of countless mortals across the realms of Ethasar.

"If only I could send my arrow into his eye," the Lady muttered.

"If only," Augustus agreed. Yet she could not. The seven gods were bound in an ancient Godly Pact, witnessed by the Supreme One himself. They couldn't hurt each other, not directly.

The vampire god swooped toward the beach, shrinking as he descended, until he landed next to the Lady with a loud shriek, his talons digging deep grooves in the golden sand. Then Serya Krov turned his scaly back to her, his reptilian tail flicking a fistful of sand over her toes.

"I like what you've done to your beach, Aljin," he said. He kept shrinking as he spoke, until he was less than three feet in height, and twice that from his beak to the tip of his tail.

"The Lady helped." Aljin pointed to a clump of tall palm trees with large, intricately shaped leaves. "She gave me these."

The Lady dipped her head at him.

"The cloud was my idea," Aljin continued. He pointed to a small cloud that floated high in the sky. "It's always there, sheltering the trees from the midday sun."

"I like it, too," Augustus said. "As will the others. I sense they're about to arrive."

A whoosh came from the left, and a puff of smoke sprang up from the ground and grew a dozen feet tall. It dissipated into the air, revealing the elder gods.

They were both muscular, bare-chested, and taller than the rest. Malleon, the god of the giants, stood ten feet tall and carried his great hammer. He was white-haired and purple of skin, as were his followers, and his youthful visage belied his status as the oldest of the gods. Grok, the All-Father of the orcs, was at his side; two feet shorter, strong and proud, red of skin and hair. His white tusks jutted upward from the corners of his mouth. His fists were bigger than Augustus's head, and Malleon's fists were bigger still.

Behind them, a majestic blue serpent darted out of the sea. It leaped through the air and turned into Njord, the blue-skinned, blue-haired, and blue-bearded god of the Islanders, who landed gracefully on the beach. Taller and thinner than Augustus, with a more youthful appearance and with his long beard fashioned into four intricate braids, he was as close to his followers' ideal of male beauty as Augustus was for the Julians.

He still hasn't gotten much of a nose, though, Augustus mused. *And it's not like he couldn't change that*. Then again, such trifles didn't matter anymore.

They had all arrived. The seven gods, one for each realm of Ethasar. Augustus, the trickster god of the Julian Empire, which covered the east of Ethasar's mainland. The Lady, goddess of the northern Verdant Kingdom; a land of strong castles and forest magic, whose people valued the virtues of honor and chivalry. Aljin, whose followers roamed the southern desert. Serya Krov, the god of the western Vampire Kingdom, where his vampire nobles ruled over their human servants and drank the blood from their veins. Grok and Malleon, who ruled the great mountains, where orcs and giants dwelled. And Njord, the sea god, whose Islanders lived in the snowy realm of Hemland, far to the north, and dyed their hair and their beards blue to honor him.

Njord sauntered toward the group, seawater dripping from his braided hair. "Here we are, my friends. Together again, after all this time. And what a glorious rainbow we all make."

"A bloody rainbow!" snapped Grok the All-Father. "This is no time for jokes."

"As if you've never thought of us that way," Augustus said. He tapped a finger to his temple. "Oh, but I forgot. You don't *think* that much, do you, Grok?"

The orc god answered with a low growl and a nasty look.

There was no love between them. Their followers had battled countless times across the centuries, and many of them had passed into legend. Many more had simply *passed*, bathing the earth with their blood.

"Hold your tempers, my friends," said Malleon, the purple god of the giants, his voice deep and steady. "We have enough trouble already."

"Let me guess," Augustus said. "You got the vision, too."

"Of course we bloody did!" snapped Grok. "What, did you think I just happened to run into Old Sleepy as I was roaming around the mountainside," he thumped Malleon affectionately on his shoulder, "and he dragged me here, just to see your ugly face?"

"Knowing you, I wouldn't be surprised if that were true," Augustus shot back.

Malleon thumped his hammer on the sand, causing a tremor that rippled across the beach. "We all got the vision. The Vengeful One is coming and we must stop him. The question is how."

"We already have the answer," Augustus said. "Tell them, Lady."

A Contest of Champions

"One of us must fight him," the Lady said. "But first, he or she must absorb the essence of the other six. Which means that six of us must die." She paused, letting the words sink in. "That's what the Supreme One told me. He asked me to share His message with you all."

"I... see," Malleon rumbled.

Njord's face turned a lighter shade of blue.

"What?" snapped Grok. "This — this is nonsense! Why should we believe you?"

She glared at him. "The rules of honor and chivalry bind me, as does my promise to the Supreme One. I swore I'd tell you all the truth."

"Empty words," Serya Krov said.

"Not for *her*," Malleon intervened. "Besides, I expect the Supreme One is watching us. He wouldn't allow her to deceive us. Not now."

The Lady nodded. "There's more. If the last of us defeats the Vengeful One, he or she will rule alone over all of Ethasar for a thousand years. After that, the Supreme One will return to our world. He'll bring the others back and restore the balance."

"So, we won't *really* die," Aljin said. "Not forever. This softens the blow, if only slightly. Yet a thousand years is a long time to be gone."

It was indeed. Most of the gods would reach that age on the eve of the Vengeful One's arrival. Except for Grok the All-Father, who was nearing two thousand, and Malleon, the oldest of them all.

"Well, I, for one," Grok said, "don't feel like dying anytime soon."

"Neither do I," said the Lady. "Neither will any of us. Those who suffer that fate will find the world changed when they return."

She'd thought about it. If Aljin was the last of the gods, he'd turn most of Ethasar into a desert. Serya Krov would subjugate the other realms and force their people to pay the blood price to his vampire nobles, and that, the Lady could not allow. If she was the last one standing, she'd make the vampires pay for their centuries of bloodshed. And the people of four realms hated Njord's followers, who'd been plundering their shores for centuries. There'd be scores to settle, if he perished.

"Even so," Augustus said, "we must choose one of us to stand against the Vengeful One. I say we all vote, here and now."

The Lady sighed. Of course, he'd choose a way that favored *him*.

"Nonsense!" shouted Serya Krov. "We must fight!"

"But we can't hurt each other, *lizard*," said Grok, whose followers had hunted the great lizards into extinction more than fifteen centuries earlier.

"Not directly," Serya Krov conceded. "So, let us have our followers decide our fates. Let us choose a champion each, and have them all fight to the death until only one remains. We could have the fight here, on this beach. Or high up on the World's Peak, if you prefer."

"You must think highly of your Queen Elena to suggest such a contest," Malleon said, "when you *know* that my champion and Grok's would fight side by side until the end, before turning on each other."

Grok raised his fist in the air. "I like it! A contest of champions it is."

"No, it is not," said Augustus, whose warriors would stand no chance in such a clash. Their strength was in their numbers.

"You all bicker like children," Njord said, which earned him a few angry looks. "There's only one proper way to decide this. We must roll dice, as many times as needed, until one of us prevails. And, Augustus? No cheating this time."

"As if you've ever *caught* me cheating," Augustus said. "Either way, I won't agree to such a ridiculous proposal."

"Then let us have a different contest of champions," Serya Krov said. "One that even *you* would assent to, Augustus. One with our world as its arena. Let us choose three champions each—"

"Four," Grok cut in.

"Fine, four," Serya Krov agreed. "Each of us will choose four champions from among our followers. When three of them die, so does their god — and we'll bind ourselves to this in Godly Pact."

"So be it," Grok said.

Njord frowned. "But such a contest will turn into an all-out war."

"With each of our realms fighting for their god," Serya Krov added. "The bloodshed will be *spectacular*."

"And I will grieve for its victims," Augustus said. "Even so, I agree to this contest."

Of course he would, the Lady thought. Among the races of men, the Julians were smaller and weaker than the others, but they were numerous, and their soldiers were loyal and disciplined. Most likely, Augustus thought he'd have the upper hand in such a war.

"I've already seen one world destroyed in a great war of the gods," Aljin said. "I do not wish to see another."

"You won't," Malleon said, "because we won't interfere. We'll keep ourselves and our godly powers out of this fight, and place our fates in our champions' hands."

"But we'll still advise them and help them in small ways," Augustus said.

The Lady spread out her hands. "Are you all agreeing to this?"

"Me, Grok, Augustus, and Malleon," Serya Krov said. "Four out of seven so far."

"I would agree as well," Aljin said, "except for a few things. First, the Islanders have an unfair advantage. They can just sit back in Hemland, or cling to its coasts, and then my warriors can't get to them. Nobody can."

That was true. Njord's followers had the best sailors and the fastest ships, and they were the only ones who had cannons. And none of the other gods could reveal the secret of gunpowder to their followers, or cause it to be revealed. Another Godly Pact that they'd hastily agreed to, decades earlier, and one that many had regretted shortly after. It still drove Njord to giggles at times, even now.

"There's an easy way to make this fair," Augustus said. "Njord will order his fleet to sail toward the mainland the day after tomorrow, with his four champions on board. After that, Njord himself will surround his people's homeland with an enchanted mist that turns ships away. The mist will follow the Islander fleet all the way to the mainland. They won't sail back home, not even if they want to. Not until the Vengeful One is defeated."

"The day after tomorrow?" Njord asked. "That doesn't give me much time to prepare."

"Your warriors have gathered for the yearly celebration," Augustus said. "You'll command them to sail to war, and they'll do your bidding. After they're gone, your mist will protect your people's homeland from invasion."

"Then I agree," Njord said, "though I still think my way was better. But what about the vampires? They can fly away from danger, and we'll never catch them."

"Take Dragos Castle if you can," answered Serya Krov. "Hold it for one month, and I'll be the one to die. I'll bind myself to this in Godly Pact."

"And before anyone asks," Malleon said, "my giants won't just hide in their slumber caves and collapse the entrances. We'll fight, as will everyone else."

"Aye," Grok said. "It is only fair."

The Lady had heard him use those words often over the past decade. He'd taken a liking to them after seeing a vision of Ghaghar the Brute, a legendary orc warrior from the world of Arcadion, the fifth planet that traveled around Ethasar's sun. A gift from the Supreme One, that vision had been.

They were all agreeing to this monstrous idea.

The Lady shook her head. "Is there no other way to decide this?"

"None that Grok, Augustus, and Serya Krov would all agree to," Malleon said. "You must agree as well, Lady." He gave her a small, almost imperceptible nod.

He means for us to be allies, she thought. "Fine," she huffed, hoping the others hadn't noticed Malleon's gesture.

"Then it is decided," Augustus said. "We'll call it the War of the Seven."

None of the gods objected.

Grok raised a hand. "Soon we'll choose our champions. They'll fight for us, and their names will pass into legend. So, let us choose from among those who are worthy of the honor. I reckon the first champion should be our followers' king."

"Or queen," the Lady said.

"Or emperor," Augustus added.

"Any objections?" Malleon asked.

There were none.

"Let us have one of our highest priests as the second champion," Aljin said. "And one of our most powerful wizards as the third. Or a priestess, or witch."

That was quickly agreed to with ayes and nods.

Serya Krov stepped forward. "For the fourth champion, let us choose freely. Even more, let us bind ourselves in Godly Pact, and swear that we will not reveal the fourth champions' names and locations to any of their mortal enemies, as we can do for the other three. It makes the contest more interesting."

"Aye," Aljin said, a little too quickly. Of course, he'd choose one of his assassins.

Malleon shrugged. "Fine with me."

The others agreed as well, with the Lady being the last. She'd choose Sir Galahad, the foremost of her knights.

"Then let us finish discussing the rules," she said, "and bind ourselves in Godly Pact to obey them, and to let our champions' fates decide our own. Once that is done, we'll reveal our champions' names."

Augustus raised a hand. "Speaking of the rules, we agreed not to interfere. But there must be exceptions."

Malleon nodded. "We won't do anything that would kill one of the champions, or place them in a position they cannot escape from, or rescue them from an inescapable fate. We won't destroy an army, save an army from certain doom, or alter the outcome of a battle."

"I see," Augustus said. "For example, Njord. If my Boy Emperor leads an army through a valley, you're not going to flood it."

"And I won't smite him from the sky," Aljin said, "as you won't smite my Desert King."

"And I won't crash a mountain on his head," Malleon added.

Augustus nodded. "However, we can continue to visit our followers and give them our advice. Though not in the midst of battle, and not if that would break the terms of our pact."

"We won't force or compel them to obey our wishes, though," the Lady said, certain of her people's loyalty.

"Nor shall we punish them if they choose another master," Serya Krov added.

Grok huffed. "As if any of our people would fight for *you*, lizard."

"We'll be able to tell the mortals if some of the champions are dead, yes?" Aljin asked.

"Good idea," Augustus said. "As long as telling them doesn't contradict the other terms of the Pact."

They discussed various other details until they were all satisfied. Then each of the gods let seven drops of their divine essence bleed into a cup, which Aljin heated and swirled around until the contents had blended. Each god drank seven drops: one of their own, and one from each of the others. And so, the Godly Pact was sealed.

Bonus Content

Congratulations! You've finished Part One. Now, let's explore some bonus materials. After all, "War of the Seven" is not just a book—it's an immersive experience!

Use the link and the QR code below to reach the bonus content page on my website. Explore an evolving campaign map that tracks each faction, read a brief summary of the war's current state, view images of Ethasar's heroes, and listen to original songs that bring the story to life. Diving into these experiences will only take a few minutes.

To explore the bonus content for Part 1, visit https://bradtowers.com/wots-bonus-1/ **or scan this QR code:**

You'll find links to similar bonus materials after each set of chapters.

If you'd rather keep reading, no problem! You'll find a link to all the bonus content at the end of the book.

Part 2: Blood and Vengeance

The Vampire Queen

Elena Kylareva, the vampire queen, leaned against the railing of her balcony and squinted against the dawn's early light as the winged shape of Serya Krov disappeared into the distance.

She nodded at the rising sun, as she did every morning.

The warm rays touched her skin without causing her harm. Two centuries before her birth, Serya Krov had struck a Godly Pact with Aljin, allowing her kind to live in the light. Before that, a simple touch of sunlight brought with it an agonizing death, as it did in many other worlds.

In this world, they had Serya Krov. A powerful god who cared about his followers and sought to elevate them at every turn. A god worth fighting for.

She hadn't expected his visit, or the news it brought.

A great war was about to begin. A war among the seven kingdoms, with the fates of the gods, and that of the world itself, hanging in the balance.

It would bring death and destruction to the realms of Ethasar. That saddened her, and yet a part of her looked forward to the upcoming contest. *I've been waiting for a chance like this for five hundred years.*

She turned her back to the sun. It gave her light and freedom, but it did not give her pleasure, nor did it melt her loneliness away. Nothing could do that.

She sighed and returned to her stateroom, leaving the balcony doors open. Her guest was about to arrive.

The stateroom of Dragos Castle was vast and square-shaped, with two rows of thick marble columns supporting a high ceiling, fifteen feet above Elena's head. There was no throne, nor any fancy decorations. Dragos had felt no need for such trappings, and Elena had followed in his footsteps. She wore her dark silver crown, as he had, with its twenty-seven yellow sapphires, each worth a small fortune.

She passed one of the sixteen floor-to-ceiling mirrors that lined the walls and favored it with a glance. A vision of beauty and power stared back at her.

She looked young, despite her age, as did many of her kind. A human from another realm wouldn't think her a day past thirty. Not until she showed him her fangs, at least.

Her skin was a light gray color, except for the right side of her face, which was darker than the rest — and that was not a trick of the light. It was a part of the price she'd paid five hundred years earlier. Now, it was a reminder of her sacrifice.

She wore a gray dress that reached all the way to her ankles. It was fastened in a single point, high across her breastbone, and opened down to the front, leaving part of her midriff bare. An intricate red belt, matching the color of her hair and talons, hugged her waist. Six throwing knives hung from it, three on each side, hidden by the folds of her dress. A gray skirt completed her outfit, covering what the dress did not; a fighting skirt that afforded her freedom of movement.

Her god's brand decorated her left forearm, its red color in stark contrast with her skin. The talons on her left hand were outstretched. She closed her fist once, twice, and bathed in the sensation of power as it coursed through her veins.

She bared her fangs in the mirror. *I am the strongest of the champions, fighting for the strongest of the gods. But in this contest, strength is not everything. I need wisdom as well.*

She snarled at the mirror, and it shattered, but that was no concern of hers.

She turned to her head priest, who waited nearby, his head bowed. "Have this replaced by nightfall, Igor. And bring me the Black Ledger of the Bloodriver province. Better yet, have Kirill Skromnik bring it when he arrives."

"As you wish," the man answered. He took two steps back, then looked up. "Is there anything else I may offer you, my queen? My blood, perhaps?"

The thought of drinking human blood repulsed Elena, yet she did not show it. She simply shook her head. "Spend the day with your family, Igor. It may be the last one for a while. A war is coming, and I will have need of you."

The priest bowed again and shuffled backward toward the door. The noble vampire guard pulled it open and waved him onward. He snarled after the priest, his fangs clearly visible.

Elena favored the guard with a look. "My axe, Vladimir."

The guard retrieved Elena's red-bladed, double-headed weapon from where it hung, high on the wall. He threw it to her, and it came spinning, yet she caught it by the handle, without blinking.

Dragos's axe. He'd wielded it in battle many times, as had four other vampire kings before him. Now, it was hers. After five hundred years of training with it and using it to dispense her justice, the axe felt like an extension of her own body.

She whirled it above her head twice, and went through the battle forms Dragos had taught her, as she did on most mornings. She moved as quickly as a cat, darting across the vast room and striking down imaginary foes, yet she did not take to flight.

In mid-twirl, she threw three of her knives at Vladimir with her left hand, one after the other. He caught the first and deflected the second with his wrist, but the third scored a deep gash across his right cheek before it embedded itself into the wall.

She nodded at the young vampire, whose right hand was already pressing against his cheek. "Better than yesterday, Vladimir. But not good enough. Not yet." His wound would heal in minutes; he was barely in his fifties, he came from a second-tier noble family, and he'd already taken his morning drink.

Vladimir's eyes lit at the compliment. "I strive to improve. For you, my queen."

"You've done better than most," she said. "Come now and receive your reward."

He closed the distance, and she sank her fangs into his neck. A groan of pleasure escaped him, but she wouldn't fault him for it. She'd kept him waiting for two years already.

She took a deep draught and savored the taste of noble blood. Fresh and full of power, yet lacking the quiet wisdom of his father's blood, which sharpened her thoughts for hours at a time. *I'll have to send for him later*, she thought.

Throughout her kind's long history, no other vampire had been allowed to use the power of noble blood as she did. Taking more than a few drops was a heinous crime, just as it was for a human to drink another human's blood. Besides, noble blood tasted worse than the human serfs' blood and yielded no benefits to other vampires — only a swift death sentence. But Elena was special, and she'd been made so by Serya Krov himself.

She let go of Vladimir and he staggered backward, averting his eyes. She'd see lust in them, if she looked, but that hunger of his would go unanswered. No one could fill the void Dragos had left behind.

Instead, she gave Vladimir another reward. "You can have Igor's blood tomorrow morning. And every seven days after that, until I change my mind. Have that written into the Red Ledger."

"Thank you, my queen." Vladimir scoffed. "The gall of that man! To offer his blood to you, of all things!"

He wiped the blood off his cheek, but did not offer his palm for her to lick clean. That was a lover's gesture, and it would have earned him a vicious whipping and a year in the holding cells.

"I no longer care for the taste of servants' blood," Elena replied. Priests like Igor were mere humans, promoted from among the serfs for their accomplishments in the nobles' service and for their devotion to the vampire god. In his late forties, Igor had risen faster than most.

"He should know it by now," Vladimir said. The cut from her throwing knife was closing neatly. "Perhaps you should punish him."

"I won't. Igor misbehaves at times, yet he has his uses. But thank you for the suggestion, Vladimir."

The guard bowed his head. "As you wish, my queen."

His eyes widened as he finished speaking, and Elena heard the flapping of wings behind her. She whirled toward the balcony, battle axe in hand, just in time to see the third of Serya Krov's champions land on the railing.

He hopped down and strode into the room, his wings retreating into his back as he advanced. Six foot two and broad-shouldered, Zoltan Barko was a fine specimen. As the duke of the Labor Plains, the Vampire Kingdom's north-western province, he was one of Elena's most prominent nobles. He was one hundred and sixty-five years old and had fathered three daughters and seven sons. His skin was darker than Elena's, as were his wings, and his talons were three times longer than her own.

He was a fearsome warrior and Elena's most skilled wizard. His spells could strike fear into the hearts of his enemies, and weaken their bodies as well.

He advanced, his neat sleeveless shirt highlighting his muscular arms. He'd let his hair and his eyebrows turn gray, as many vampires did in the last third of their lives, but that only enhanced his appearance.

As he reached Elena, he made to kneel.

She stopped him with a look. "You've traveled fast, Zoltan." Behind her, she heard Vladimir take three steps back. She tossed him her weapon, without looking.

"I have," Zoltan said. "As our god commanded."

"Tell me, did you have time to think on your flight?"

"I did. We're attacking the Lady's people first, yes?"

"We are."

"We'll have a hundred thousand serfs at the Verdant Kingdom's border in a month, with sixty thousand more on the way. And seven hundred war-trained vampire nobles to lead them."

"Very well. What else?"

"We have to do something about Bloodriver."

"I've already asked for the Ledger," Elena said. "I expect to be disappointed. Again." Between the desert men's border raids and the unfortunate incident with Njord's followers three years earlier, they'd lost a third of the province's fighting force and a sixth of the war-trained nobles. And though Elena had ordered the duke to draft more serfs into the army, and to train them well, the number of skilled soldiers was slow to recover. The latest numbers wouldn't be much better than the ones she'd seen before.

"Do you think I should replace the duke?" she asked.

Zoltan shook his head, as she hoped he would. "Not now, my queen. Send him help, though. I have a cousin I'd like to recommend for this."

"I know him well," Elena said. She decided to test Zoltan. "He's only half your age."

"And yet he's a gifted leader and an even better strategist."

Elena nodded. "That he is. I'll give him a command, second only to the duke. I'll draft the letter today. What else?"

"Serya Krov's choice of champions. It troubles me."

"You mean Katrina?"

Zoltan shook his head. "I would have chosen her myself. Yes, she's young, and she's… impetuous, but few can match her killer instinct. She'll do her part."

"Then it's Kirill the priest that you're worried about."

"He's a foreigner. He seems capable, yes; but do you think we can trust him?"

"I do," Elena said. "He's about to join us. Watch him closely and set your mind at ease."

The Sea God's Champions

"Feast your eyes, friends," King Knut Haraldsson said as he gazed into the distance. "For we won't see a sight like this for years to come."

Three of his fleet captains stood with him on the deck of his ship. They were the foremost of Njord's priests, along with Frida Gretasdottir, who had yet to arrive, and King Knut himself. They dyed their hair and their beards blue to honor the sea god, and they wore traditional blue garments.

The Bard's Hamlet lay ahead. Over the centuries, the small settlement had grown into a sprawling town, with its wooden longhouses stretching far along the fjord's shores and its two dozen docks bursting with ships. It was the seat of power in Hemland, the Islanders' realm, and it was there that their fleets gathered every year, at the end of the fourth month, to celebrate their god with a week of feasts and games; but things were different this time. Now, on the day after the drunken revelry had ended, King Knut and his warriors were about to sail south and battle the other realms of Ethasar for the fates of their gods.

Beyond the Hamlet, the Iron Mountain stood tall. It was shaped like the head of Njord's trident, with its three snow-covered peaks pointing to the sky. Njord's Spires, they were called, and King Knut had climbed them all at the age of sixteen, with only a short sword strapped to his belt, to help him keep the wolves at bay.

"Aye," said Lothar Bjornsson. "We'll miss Hemland. But when we return, my friend, you'll be high king of all the lands."

"And I'll be even richer," said Sigurd Larsson, whose blue vest was threaded with gold.

Anders Svensson wrapped himself tighter in his bearskin. "Keep your riches, Sigurd. I, for one, am thinking about the battles we must fight."

King Knut slapped Anders on the shoulder. "We'll fight them soon enough, my friend."

He was proud of his fleet captains. Each of them led a fleet of over two dozen ships, and they did it well. Anders was one of his closest childhood friends and a master of surviving against the odds. He and Sigurd had led countless raids across the vampires' coasts and the Verdant Kingdom's provinces, taking plunder and riches in Njord's name, in quantities high enough to rival King Knut himself. Lothar preferred the Julian shores, and could beat nine sailors out of ten in a wrestling match, even now in his early fifties. Anders, Sigurd, and King Knut himself were a decade younger, give or take a few months each.

"At least we won't be fighting each other," Lothar said.

King Knut nodded. The feud between Hemland's two southern provinces had lasted for eight decades, with both factions raiding each other's shores every few years and fighting dozens of minor battles out on the open sea. On his first anniversary as king, he'd brought Sigurd and Anders together and half-convinced, half-coerced them to sign a peace treaty that had brought the conflict to an end.

At the time, Anders demanded three thousand pounds of Sigurd's gold in exchange for peace. King Knut had paid the price himself, out of his own coffers. He'd only told Sigurd about it a month after the treaty's signing, when they were both deep in their cups.

In the end, the grand gesture had cost him nothing. Sigurd was as honorable as he was rich, and had repaid him within the year.

"Before we sail south," Anders commented, "we must gather our champions."

"Aye," King Knut said. "I wonder what's taking them so long."

"I'm here, my king," a woman's voice came from behind.

He turned around, and there she was. Frida Gretasdottir, a fleet captain in her own right, and Njord's second champion.

King Knut looked her up and down. At six foot three, she was as tall as he was, and well-muscled; a warrior first and a woman second, though that did not detract from her appeal. Her twin trident daggers were strapped to her belt. She'd stabbed those daggers through a bear's eyes at the age of sixteen, but only after the bear had carved three deep scars into her upper chest with a swipe of its paw. She wore the scars proudly, and rarely covered them.

She dyed her hair blue and fashioned it into a long, thick braid. Her sleeveless blouse sat tight on her body and revealed the scars on her chest and the tattoos on her arms, a trident dagger on her left bicep and a dolphin on her right. Two more tattoos, an anchor and a teardrop-shaped blue diamond, decorated her shapely thighs.

King Knut had fancied himself between those thighs, more than once. They would have made a good pairing, and she could have given him many strong sons. But he wasn't ready to settle for one woman, not yet — and he didn't think Frida would appreciate his wandering eyes. And hands. And other things.

It's better the way we are now, he thought. Besides, his latest conquest was a hot-blooded northern lass in her early twenties, and she moved better than any woman he'd had before.

"My king?" Frida said, pulling him from his thoughts.

He gave her a smile. "I was thinking Njord has chosen well."

He wasn't speaking about her looks. Though young, Frida was a peer to the three seasoned captains who stood at his side. A capable one, too.

She'd gotten her fleet's command at the age of twenty-five. Her father had been a well-respected fleet captain, and on the day of his death, his men had chosen Frida to succeed him. By then, she'd been in charge of a third of his ships already. In the four years since, she'd been raiding across the coasts of four realms, with great success.

Her men loved her and followed her gladly. She had plenty of suitors, yet entertained none — at least none that King Knut knew of.

Frida beamed at the compliment. "I'll prove myself worthy of the honor."

"Look." Anders pointed to the left. In the distance, a small shape dashed across the waves.

King Knut raised his spyglass to his eye. *Finally*, he thought as he recognized Ursula Gudrunsdottir, the sea witch. The third of Njord's champions was about to arrive.

She rode her dolphin, as she did on most days, her left hand clutching its dorsal fin as her legs straddled its back. It sped through the gentle waves of the Bard's Harbor and stopped abruptly less than five feet from the ship's hull. Then Ursula summoned a column of water that lifted her high into the air, until she was level with the deck.

She jumped aboard, seawater dripping from her clothes and hair, and dipped her head toward King Knut. She muttered a spell, and a few moments later, she was completely dry.

King Knut glanced overboard and watched her dolphin dive beneath the waves.

He looked Ursula up and down. At five foot eight, she was of average height for an Islander woman, yet taller than most Julian men. Even now in her mid-fifties, she was in good shape, no doubt helped by her long daily swims and dolphin rides. Her wooly hair was arranged in several intricate braids, and a golden coronet sat upon her head. Unlike Frida, she painted her lips blue as well.

She wore a form-fitting blue shirt, a long skirt in the same color, and brown leather boots. How she could swim so well in those clothes, only her magic and Njord's favor could explain.

She was a stern woman who frowned more than she smiled, and spoke only when she had something to say. When she did, people listened.

King Knut nodded at her. "You came at last, Ursula. Now we only need Gunnar."

Ursula shook her head. "He's not coming, my king."

"What do you mean, he's not coming?"

"That's what Njord told me. He'll join us later. Njord will make sure of it."

Of course he will, King Knut thought. The old cannoneer was known for defying the sea god, even hurling insults at him when he was deep in his cups. Why Njord hadn't punished him for it yet, King Knut did not know. Why he'd chosen him as a champion was an even bigger mystery.

"Then we must sail without him," Frida said. "The question is where."

"I don't like the Vampire Kingdom," said Sigurd, who'd raided its coastal towns and villages for over two decades. "Those vampires are the stuff of nightmares."

"I thought nothing scared you, Sigurd," Lothar said. "Are you afraid of a few spineless serfs who give their blood to their masters?"

"The serfs may be weak," Sigurd said, "but the vampire nobles are not. And until now, Anders and I took them by surprise. From now on, they'll be on guard at all times."

"We have cannons," Lothar insisted.

"How fast can you reload if you miss, my friend?" Anders came to Sigurd's aid. "We'd take heavy losses. Besides, if we are to survive on the mainland for seven years, we will need new recruits. And we need free-thinking men, not those spineless serfs you were talking about."

Lothar grinned. "Then let us sail to the Julian lands."

King Knut knew he'd planned for that all along.

"No," Frida and Ursula said at once.

King Knut raised his hand, and the others quieted. "I've thought about this all morning. I've looked at all the options. And there's only one thing for us to do."

"Strike at the Verdant Kingdom," Frida said.

"Aye," King Knut replied. "We'll hit the Lady's people first. We'll find plenty of recruits after we win our first battles. Besides, Queen Marion will be too busy with the vampires to put up a proper fight. We'll carve out a stretch of coastline and grow stronger as she grows weaker. And when we're ready, we'll advance further inland."

"Better yet," Anders said, "let's march to the Verdant capital right away, before Queen Marion gathers her army. We'll take the capital, place our cannons upon its walls, and make it our fortress."

"Ha!" Sigurd spat. "We'd have the whole Verdant army at our backs before our cannons break through Hearthstone's walls."

"Not if we move fast," Anders grumbled.

"They'll outnumber us at least three to one," Lothar said. "That's a fight we cannot win."

Anders did not relent. "I've won battles against worse odds before, my friend."

"And if we lose," Lothar said, "Queen Marion will destroy our army, and Njord's fate will be sealed."

"Stop, all of you," King Knut intervened. "It's an audacious idea, Anders. One that would make Njord smile. But Sigurd and Lothar are right. It carries too much risk, and I won't bet Njord's fate on a roll of the dice. We'll start with the coastline, for now."

"Fine." Anders nodded. "You're the king. We'll do as you say."

"Aye," said Ursula, and Lothar, and Sigurd as well.

"We sail with the tide," King Knut said. "Go back to your ships and get your men ready. And now I bid you farewell, for there's something I must do."

He walked away, and soon he was below deck, striding toward his cabin. Torsten Eriksson, the foremost of his guards, waited for him outside the door. He was a bull of a man, quick for his size, and unmatched with both axe and spear.

"The Verdant Kingdom it is, then?" he asked.

"Aye." King Knut slapped Torsten on his shoulder. "And then, the world."

Torsten laughed. "You're in a good mood this morning."

"I'm basking in Njord's favor, my friend. Soon, I'll stand in the shield wall again, with you by my side."

"And our people will cheer your name when victory is near."

As they've done so many times, King Knut thought. "She's here, yes?"

Torsten answered with a nod and a wide grin.

"Good," King Knut said. "We're not to be disturbed, Torsten. Not unless Njord himself wishes to speak to me."

He opened the door to his cabin and found his young northern lass waiting for him.

She stood facing the cabin door, his writing table at her back, and had settled her cloak on the edge of his bed. She wore a short, thin bodice, laced up in the front, which gave him a good view of her breasts. Her shoulders were bare, as was her midriff — and while her long blue skirt reached her ankles, King Knut knew she had to be naked underneath.

She dyed her hair blue, like most of Njord's followers, though she'd colored a couple of streaks red the day before.

She had her own cabin, as King Knut preferred to sleep alone. But she would come when he wanted her. And lately, he'd been wanting her three times a day.

He closed and barred the door, desire already stirring inside him.

"We sail for the Verdant Kingdom," he said as he advanced toward her. "It is agreed."

Her smile was full of promise. "You don't know how much that pleases me, my king. When do we leave?"

"With the tide. I've already given the orders." The journey would take less than a week. Four days, under favorable winds.

She licked her lips. "May I have you for myself before we set sail?"

"You may." He lifted her up with ease and sat her on the table, facing him. She caressed his cheek and pulled his head forward and down, resting his face between her breasts.

He inhaled deeply. "I love your scent."

"I'm glad it pleases you," she answered.

He looked up into her eyes. He placed his hands on the small of her back and pulled her toward him, and suddenly her legs were wrapped around his waist. He kissed her, his desire growing stronger, his tongue exploring her delicious lips, her mouth, her... FANGS??

She's a vampire! An icy chill ran through King Knut's veins, and terror gripped him for the first time in his life. He shoved the woman away, and her back slammed onto the table, though her legs were locked in a death grip around his waist. He reached for the knife at his belt.

And found his sheath empty.

She grabbed his shirt and pulled herself toward him. Her right hand swiped at his face, her outstretched talons tearing into his left cheek.

He roared and rolled to his right, and they fell onto the floor. Outside, Torsten shouted and pounded on the door, but King Knut had barred it himself.

He landed on top of her and clutched her throat with both hands, trying to squeeze the life out of her. She swiped at his face again, tearing into his right cheek and narrowly missing his eye.

He screamed and squeezed harder.

She *laughed* then, a shrill, unnatural sound. Her fangs were longer now, and her skin had lost its rosy color and had taken the gray tone of her kind.

"You fell for my glamor," she said. "Let me show you my true self."

She grabbed his right wrist and pulled his arm to the side, away from her throat, as easily as if it were child's play. He was twice as heavy as she was, and yet he couldn't match her strength.

He twisted, trying to smash his left elbow into her face, but she moved her head to the side. His elbow crashed into the floor.

She shoved him, forcing him to roll over his left shoulder, and suddenly she was on top and her fangs were tearing into his throat. Outside, something thudded into the door. Torsten's axe, perhaps. But King Knut's vision was growing darker, and he knew his end would come in moments.

The vampire leaped to her feet. Dark wings sprouted from her back.

"Katrina," she whispered. "That's my true name. You've pleased me, for a while."

King Knut sighed. *I'm sorry, Njord. I failed you. I hope your other champions do better.*

The last thing he saw, before his eyes closed forever, was a dark, winged shape bursting out through the cabin window and soaring into the sky.

Queen Elena's Plans

"That's him, Zoltan," Elena said as the familiar footsteps drew near.

She turned toward the door. Vladimir, her guard, had already hung her battle axe in its resting place. He opened the door, and the second of Serya Krov's champions walked in.

He was shorter than Elena, though not by much. A bald man in his late fifties, his skin had darkened from the repeated bleedings. His gray beard was neatly trimmed, and he'd dyed a stripe of it black. He wore a dark gray shirt that reached past his waist, with long wide sleeves that concealed various writing instruments. In his right hand he carried a leather-bound book, and Elena didn't have to guess. It had to be the Black Ledger of the Bloodriver province.

He lowered his eyes and bowed to her, and to Duke Zoltan as well.

Elena spoke first. "It's good to see you, Francis."

He recoiled from her words. "That man died three decades ago, my queen."

"Very well, Kirill." She used the name she'd given him. "And are you sure he'll stay that way?"

"I am."

"We're going to strike against your former people and kill their goddess."

"They haven't been my people since I left the Verdant Kingdom behind. And the Lady is not my goddess. Not anymore. I serve Serya

Krov, and when we win, he will rule supreme for a thousand years."

When, he'd said. Not *if*. She liked that about him.

She favored him with a smile. "Yes. And I will finally avenge my lover's death."

There was no mortal left for Elena to take vengeance upon, not anymore. Sir Godric, the Lady's Paladin who'd killed Dragos twice, had been dead for centuries, as had his sons and their sons after them. Yes, she could wipe out their bloodline from the face of the earth, but that held no meaning for her. The prize she longed for was much greater than that.

"When we kill three of her champions," she said, "the Lady dies for a thousand years. I get to kill her, as that Paladin of hers killed the love of my life. My blade won't cut her down, but it will feel just as sweet."

Kirill nodded. "I can't presume to fathom the depths of your hate for the Lady, my queen. But know that I hate her as well. With all my heart."

Heart. She flinched at that word. *He should have known better.* But she couldn't expect perfection, not even from one of Serya Krov's highest priests. Five centuries of ruling had taught her that.

"When we win," she continued without reprimanding him, "the whole world will have peace, if not freedom. They'll have order and justice as well. As our serfs do, as long as they fulfill their tasks. Your kind works hard, yes. But there is always food on your dinner tables, your sick are taken care of, and your deaths, when they come, are quick and painless, as long as you obey our laws. It is a good life, yes?"

"As good as a man could hope for in this world," Kirill agreed.

"You'd do well to remember it, servant," Zoltan said.

Elena gave him a subtle frown, and she made sure Kirill noticed it. He'd admire her even more for that.

"The only threats to us all come from across our borders, Kirill," she said. "And when we win, when the vampire god reigns supreme and our kind rules across all lands, those threats will vanish. There will be order and justice everywhere, more so than even the Julian Empire and their failed gods could ever dream of."

Kirill nodded. "It is a noble desire, my queen."

"First, we must do our duty," Elena continued. "I'll lead the war effort, with Duke Zoltan at my side. Katrina will play her part. And you, Kirill, you'll help us build our army. Tell me, do you long to fly?"

"I've never dared to dream of it," he replied, though his eyes betrayed him.

Elena shot him a piercing gaze.

He bowed his head. "Apologies, my queen. I thought it presumptuous to admit it. I do think of it, at times."

"Apology accepted. You *will* fly tomorrow. One of my guards will take you. Not Vladimir," she added for Vladimir's benefit. "I need him by my side."

Kirill's eyes sparkled. "As you wish, my queen."

"He'll take you from town to town," she continued, "across the northern provinces. You'll tell the serfs of the great injustices committed by the Lady's followers, against you and countless others. You'll rally them to our banners and strengthen their resolve. And when you're done, you'll return to my side and help me lead our forces in battle." She'd seen him study the great tomes of military strategy for hours at a time.

"I will, my queen," Kirill answered. "Thanks to your great foresight, our army will outnumber the Lady's."

Elena nodded at the compliment. After the famine that had marred the final years of Dragos's reign, she had vowed that her subjects would never know hunger again. She'd worked them hard over the years, and she'd had them experiment with various ways to improve the yield of their crops. And so, over the past five centuries, her realm's population of human serfs had grown tremendously. Only the Julians outnumbered them.

Meanwhile, the Lady had refrained from cutting down her forests. And so, though her realm was twice the Vampire Kingdom's size and a large part of her lands were fertile, her kingdom's population was lower.

"She still has her knights and her castles," Zoltan said.

Elena snarled. "We'll kill her knights and take her castles."

"We will, my queen," Zoltan said. "In the meantime, what about the other realms? What do you expect them to do?"

"An excellent question." Elena strode toward a corner of the room, where a map depicting the seven realms hung on the wall. Zoltan and Kirill followed her, as did Vladimir.

The Vampire Kingdom was the westernmost realm, while the vast Julian Empire lay far to the east. Four realms separated them: the Verdant Kingdom in the north; the mountainous Land of the Giants and the Orc Kingdom in the center; and in the south, the Great Desert, where Aljin's followers dwelled. Farther to the north, a few days' sailing from the mainland, lay Hemland, the realm of the blue-haired and blue-bearded Islanders, who worshiped Njord, the sea god.

"The orcs will strike at the Julians." Elena pointed to the map as she spoke. "The giants will either ally themselves with the orcs or seek to crush them. The Julians will fortify their borders and raise more troops from their provinces. We'll march against the Verdant Kingdom, and the Lady's followers will have no choice but to defend themselves. The desert men's plans are harder to guess, but Serya Krov has assured me that they won't move against us, not for a while."

"If they do," Zoltan said, "we'll destroy them easily."

Elena wasn't as certain of it as he was. Aljin's people were few in number, but that did not make them any less dangerous. Their mounted archers favored surprise attacks and retreated swiftly when the tide of battle went against them, only to strike again another day. As for their assassins, they were skilled and deadly. She'd felt the sting of an assassin's blade once, and it had been poisoned. Only Serya Krov's guidance, along with large quantities of noble blood, had enabled her to survive it.

Even so, she did not reply. Her god's assurance was enough for her.

"And what of the Islanders?" Kirill asked. "What if they decide to land on our shores?"

"Then we'll crush them first," Elena said, "and move against the Lady when we're done." She paused. "We don't just need to defeat the Lady's armies, Kirill. We need to have enough strength left after we do, so that we can defeat the others as well. Though I expect every realm's strength to diminish as they fight each other."

"And what if three or four of the other realms move against us at once, my queen?" Kirill asked. "What if they seek to remove the greatest threat first?"

Zoltan scoffed. "I don't see the orcs and the Julians fighting side by side, do you? And our queen has just assured us that the desert men won't attack us, not at first. What are you afraid of, priest?"

Kirill lowered his gaze. "The unknown, my lord."

Elena smiled at him. "Have faith in me, Kirill. We'll march against the Lady, and defeat her, and then we'll win this war. I am certain of it."

Kirill bowed. "As you say, my queen."

"You'll play your part in it. Today, we will look at the Black Ledger together, the three of us, and think of how to set the Bloodriver province right. Tomorrow, you'll fly and help us raise our army. For now, though, Duke Zoltan has flown for hours. He must be tired, if only slightly. Offer him your blood."

"As you command, my queen," Kirill said.

He tilted his head to his right, baring the left side of his neck, and Zoltan stepped forward to claim the blood price from his veins.

Frida Gretasdottir

Frida Gretasdottir, commander of a fifth of the Islander fleet, leaned forward against the railing and watched King Knut's lifeless body disappear beneath the waves.

She sighed. *Farewell, my king. You were the best of us.*

This didn't have to happen. We should have been more cautious. We should have protected you.

No. Not we. I should have protected you.

Then again, his bedroom was the one place where she couldn't.

The funeral rites had been done according to tradition. The prayers had been said, the songs sung, and a cask of ale spilled overboard, for King Knut to enjoy on his final swim. And now, it was time to focus on the fates of those he'd left behind.

They were without a king. Worse, they'd lost the first of Njord's champions — and they hadn't even left the fjord. That left only Frida, Ursula the sea witch, and Gunnar, who hadn't joined them yet.

If another two of us die, then so does Njord. And our people will be ruled by a foreign god for a thousand years. There'll be scores to settle.

"We need to choose a new king," Ursula shouted, jolting Frida from her thoughts.

She turned around. Knut's foremost captains stood at her side, as did Ursula. Facing them were two dozen ships' captains, who had rowed to King Knut's ship to take part in the funeral rites, and a handful of sea witches. All waiting for a decision.

"Don't look at me," Lothar Bjornsson said, though very few were. "I won't call myself king, though I'll follow one gladly."

Frida was not surprised. Lothar was a seasoned captain and fleet leader, and his raids on the Julian coasts had become legend already. Yet even now, in his early fifties, he sought a father figure — and had found one in King Knut. The fact that the king had been more than a decade younger didn't matter.

"I'll do it," Anders Svensson shouted. "I'll be your king, if you'll have me."

As one, his captains raised their fists in the air and roared their approval.

He's too reckless, Frida thought. *He'll have us march straight to the Verdant capital, and Queen Marion's army easily outnumbers us. She'll order her warriors to destroy us, before marching to confront the vampires. Even if we manage to retreat, we'll lose many men. Perhaps our cannons, too.*

Besides, Gunnar doesn't like him. Not the way he liked Father.

She turned to Sigurd, the richest of them all. *Njord's favorite*, her father had called him, more than once. But Sigurd looked away.

He doesn't think he's strong enough to lead us, Frida realized. *Or perhaps he doesn't want to pick a fight with Anders. He thinks that doing so would fracture us.*

Yet letting Anders become king will destroy us all.

There was only one thing for her to do, whether she wanted to or not. The fates of her people, and that of her god, were at stake.

She touched the bear's claw marks on the upper side of her chest and took a step forward. "I will be your queen."

At first, she didn't understand why Anders's captains were cheering. Then Anders placed a hand on her arm and announced, "We'll be wed by nightfall."

She snatched her arm away. "The queen of the Islanders decides who she marries. And it's not you, Anders Svensson."

It was as if she'd slapped him. "You challenge me, girl?" he shouted as he turned to her.

"Gunnar won't come to us if you're king," she said in what she hoped was a pacifying tone, though she bristled at the word 'girl'. "He'll sail away and take his *Floating Castle* with him — and you know you can't take Gunnar's ship, not with five thousand men. He'll die fighting on some faraway beach, and we won't be there to come to his aid. And Njord will lose another champion."

"I have the most sailors," Anders countered. "The biggest fishing fleet, too." Many of his fishermen would join the war effort, though some had to stay behind to feed those left in Hemland. "And many of our strongest warriors."

Frida nodded at him. "There's no denying what you say, Anders. Each of us has their own bragging rights. Lothar is the most experienced, and Sigurd is the richest, and will be richer still when this war is over."

Shouts of approval came from Sigurd's captains. Sigurd himself remained silent.

"And I may be the youngest of us," Frida continued, "and the newest to command a large fleet. But I got my first ship at the age of ten, and I *took* the next one a week later, and since then I've always proven myself a worthy leader." Her eyes scanned the group of captains and sea witches, who were taking in her every word. "And most of all, Njord did not choose you as his second champion, Anders. He chose me."

"I stand with Queen Frida," Ursula said.

"And I," added Lothar Bjornsson. "I thought I'd follow a king, but I'll be glad to follow you."

"And I," said Magnus, one of Frida's trusted captains.

"And I," shouted one of the sea witches.

"And Gunnar," roared one of Sigurd's captains, a distant cousin of Gunnar.

More voices rose from the crowd, shouting ayes and nays. A few of Anders's captains pushed and shoved, trying to make their way to the front. One placed his hand on the dirk at his belt.

"STOP!" Ursula shouted, her voice booming as if the whole fjord had shouted with her.

That silenced them, and the sea witch continued. "We must be united. Rise against Njord's champions and we'll destroy each other for nothing, and this will only benefit our enemies. Besides, you know which side Njord will pick. Or fight for Queen Frida, fight for Njord, and we will rule the world for a thousand years!"

"Njord!" roared Lothar Bjornsson. "Njord! Njord!"

The other captains joined him, Anders among them, though only half-heartedly. After repeating the sea god's name seven times, Lothar raised his hands to silence the others.

"Queen Frida!" he shouted. "Queen Frida! Queen Frida!"

They chanted her name with him. And so, it was done.

When the captains were silent again, Frida grabbed Anders's arm. "Don't be a sour loser, my friend. Come to my ship tonight, with Lothar and Sigurd." She wouldn't take King Knut's ship for herself, not so soon after his death. "You too, Ursula. We'll feast and drink, and honor our fallen king, and speak of the battles to come."

"Aye," Anders grunted. "I fight for Njord, so I'll fight for you. I'll give my life for you if I must, and for our other champions, too. But if you won't marry me, I'll have you name me next in line."

She smiled. "I make no promises. Not yet. Earn my trust first, and then we'll talk. But now we must prepare. We sail in less than an hour."

Ulrika would have been mad, she thought. *If I returned to Hemland in seven years with this one at my side, and with two of his brats hanging from my skirt, she'd give me a good thrashing. She'd say I deserved better.*

She'd left her friend and lover back in the Bard's Hamlet, and it had been the right thing to do. With most of the captains sailing to war, the people left behind needed leaders, and Ulrika was one. Besides, King Knut had left his brother as well.

She'd miss Ulrika, and couldn't return to her for seven years, not with Njord's enchanted mist that would soon bar the way. But she couldn't afford to think of her, not now.

Now she was queen, and she had a war to win.

Kirill's Flight

"Are you ready?"

Kirill touched the leather harness that strapped him to his companion. It would keep him safe, or so he hoped. He couldn't turn around to regard the noble vampire Nikolay, even if he wanted to.

He looked up at a small white cloud that hung high in the sky. It was so much better than gazing ahead. Or worse, *down*, where hundreds of feet of emptiness gaped beneath his dangling feet, a void eager to swallow him whole.

He waited for a wave of dizziness to pass, then gave a shaky nod.

Nikolay's chest heaved with silent laughter. "And we're off."

He pushed off the edge of the plateau and launched into the air with ease, his powerful wings lifting them into the sky so quickly, Kirill felt the contents of his stomach threaten to make their way up.

"Look down," Nikolay urged as he banked sharply to the right. "Really, look. You have to see this."

Kirill did.

When seen from the courtyard below, the four tall spires of Dragos Castle seemed to pierce the sky. Now he and Nikolay soared above them. On the stateroom's balcony, Queen Elena looked up, watching them.

The castle itself was massive and over two hundred feet tall. It stood on the edge of a narrow plateau, six hundred feet above the plains below.

The cliffs were vertical and smooth, as if an enormous sword had sliced off any imperfection.

That was not what had happened, of course. Serya Krov had raised the plateau from the ground below, over five centuries earlier, and King Dragos had built his castle upon it.

On the far side, his serfs had dug a staircase into the rock, nine hundred and ninety-six steps in all. Kirill took those steps every morning, before sunrise, to place himself at his queen's command; and every evening he descended them and returned to his wife and daughters.

There was an elevator, of course. A thing of ropes and counterweights, reserved for the highest levels of the priesthood. Kirill could have used it, and it would have saved him time and effort, yet he preferred the staircase. It kept him in shape and gave him time to think.

Now, Nikolay hovered above the top of the elevator.

"Sooner or later," he said, "we have to get it over with. Take a deep breath."

Kirill did, and hoped it wouldn't be his last.

Nikolay swooped toward the ground below, and Kirill's chest tightened. The ground drew closer and closer.

And closer!

At the last moment, the vampire veered left at a sharp angle, the sudden shift of direction pushing Kirill hard against his harness. Nikolay started gaining height again, and Kirill surprised himself as an exhilarated whoop escaped his lips.

"This is so much better than jumping off Aunt Mary's roof when I was six," he heard himself say.

Nikolay snorted. "It gets even better. You'll see."

He headed north. He showed Kirill a few of his tricks, swirling and swooping, soaring and gliding, and navigating the air currents with ease. Soon, Kirill's apprehension was replaced by youthful joy, the likes of which he hadn't felt in decades.

They flew over Dragos River, which defined the northern border of the Crownlands. After that, the wheat fields and the villages of the Labor

Plains fell swiftly behind, rooftops turning into red dots in a sea of gold.

It was colder up there, and the winds buffeted them at times, making Nikolay rise or descend, or shift his course slightly. Yet they were getting closer to their destination with each passing minute.

They'd land in the main square of Ravensflight, the third largest city in the province. There, Kirill would tell the serfs the story of his sister's ordeal in the Verdant Kingdom, and other such stories he'd learned over the years. He'd tell them how Queen Elena's rule was fair and just, for nobles and serfs alike. And with that, he'd rally them to her banners.

By dinner time, he'd be gone — and his message would spread like wildfire. First to the neighboring villages, then beyond.

Nikolay would fly him from town to town, taking the blood price from the locals to replenish his strength. Once they'd visited the ten largest cities in the Labor Plains, they'd cross over to Serya's Whip, where Queen Elena planned to gather her forces before striking against the Lady's followers. They'd wait for the queen there.

He'd gone through all his stories a hundred times in his head. He was ready.

He took in the sights. They were flying above yet another wheat field. At its far end, a small village nestled in the bend of a stream. Closer and slightly to Kirill's left, a flock of geese glided through the air. They did not notice the noble vampire flying above them.

A few moments later, his heart skipped a beat as Nikolay swooped downward, without warning, straight toward the birds.

The vampire veered right, then left, chasing his prey as the birds scattered. His left hand darted out and snatched one in mid-flight, inches from Kirill's face. It jerked upward and disappeared from his view. Then he heard a crunch, and drops of warm liquid struck his bald head. The lifeless bird spiraled toward the ground as the vampire released it.

Kirill's heart thumped in his chest. "Why?" The word came out of his mouth before he could stop it.

Nikolay growled, sending shivers down Kirill's spine. Then, in a calm voice, he said, "It's not just the blood, priest. It's the joy of the hunt. The thrill of the kill. It's in our nature."

His right arm appeared at the side of Kirill's face, pointing to the village below.

"Better that bird than them," the vampire said.

Before the words sank in, he added, "This is one thing the Lady shares with our kind. She feels the thrill, just like we do, except she hunts with bow and arrow. I like our way better."

The Greatest Storm

Frida Gretasdottir stood at the prow of her flagship, her gaze fixed on the clouds above. The smell of salt and damp wood filled the air, and the darkening sky brought the promise of rain.

"A storm is coming," Captain Magnus said. In his mid-forties, he had a gift for stating the obvious. He was also a peerless sailor, fierce in battle, and an excellent hunter. His wife had remained behind in Hemland, as had his two young daughters.

"Not a big one, I'd wager," Ursula the sea witch said.

Frida nodded. "Even so, I'd have our ships spread out, so they don't crash into each other as the sea grows restless."

Magnus grunted. "Aye. I'll pass your command to the signal man. But I wasn't speaking about *this* storm." He turned to Frida, a somber look on his face. "Soon, we'll be fighting the other six realms. We'll fight for Njord, and for my wife and daughters, and for all those we've left behind. This war will be the greatest storm of our lives. And you, Frida, will have to sail us through it."

He hadn't called her queen, but Frida didn't mind. She had no need for such formalities.

She held his gaze. "I'll do my duty, Magnus. With men like you by my side, we have a good chance to win."

"And with women like us," Ursula said. Two younger sea witches stood at her side.

"Aye." Frida dipped her head. "I'm counting on you, too."

"Good." Ursula caught Frida's gaze. "I'd like to speak to you alone. In your cabin, perhaps?"

"As you wish." With a final glance at the brewing storm, Frida bid Magnus goodbye and led Ursula below deck.

She bent forward as she entered her room, ducking to avoid smashing her forehead against the doorframe. Her twin trident daggers hung on the wall to her right, where she'd left them. Dorgoth Ironcrusher, one of the few orcs in her father's crew, had gifted her the weapons on her tenth birthday. Nineteen years later, the steel had kept its edge, though Dorgoth was long gone, his body burned according to the orcs' tradition.

A map of Ethasar's mainland covered the wall ahead. On the Verdant Kingdom's coastline, a small bay was circled with blue ink: Sapphire Bay, the first destination of the Islander fleet. Frida had marked the spot the day before.

She took a seat at the small table and motioned Ursula to do the same.

"You stepped forward yesterday, at the election," Ursula said, her sharp gaze fixed on Frida. "That took courage."

Frida nodded. "Someone had to lead our people after King Knut's death. I offered because there was no one better."

"Aye. Your father would be proud of you."

"Perhaps. He never wanted to be king." Both of Frida's parents were gone. Her father had taken his final swim four years earlier, while her mother had perished in a storm only weeks after Frida's fifth birthday.

"You're right," Ursula said. "But every good father wishes for his children to surpass him. And when this is over, perhaps you'll be queen of the world."

Frida hadn't thought that far, and the idea filled her with unease. "Or I might be dead within the week."

"Don't say such things. We'll keep you safe." Ursula paused. "I've spoken to some of the sea witches from the other ships."

"And?"

"King Knut's death struck a hard blow to our men's morale. And while you were fairly chosen as our queen, Anders's men still grumble about him not being king, and some of Sigurd's men resent him for not stepping forward. We need to rally them all behind you."

Frida nodded. "I assume you have a plan."

"I'll ask the sea witches to spread the tales of your accomplishments among our men. We'll tell them of the raids, the battles, the fight with the bear, the chase around Cape Storm, and all the rest."

Frida allowed herself a small smile. She rarely spoke of her adventures, but the bards had already spread the tales far and wide, weaving a few of them into song.

"Many of the northlanders have heard the stories already," Ursula continued. "The people of the southern provinces, less so. I'll visit Sigurd's fleet, and I'll send a few sea witches to Anders's ships."

"A few bards, too," Frida added.

"Aye. The stories will raise the men's spirits."

"Speak to them about plunder and riches, too."

"I will." Ursula took a deep breath. "That takes care of the fighting men. We still need to talk about the leaders."

"Can I trust them?" Frida asked.

"What do you think?"

Frida leaned forward, resting her hands on the table. "Lothar will follow me, as he promised. He's brave and loyal. I believe he'll do his duty."

"As will Sigurd," Ursula said. "Show him respect, ask for his advice when you need it, and allow his men to plunder freely. Do that, and he's yours."

"What about Anders?" Out of them all, Frida knew him the least.

"He's a good strategist. Perhaps the best of us. He's ambitious, too. I don't think Gunnar likes him."

Gunnar, Frida thought. *Where are you, old friend?* She'd asked her fleet's lookouts to send word if they caught sight of the *Floating Castle*. So far, they hadn't.

"If you want to turn Anders into a strong ally," Ursula continued, "you'll have to give him something. Land, gold, or both."

"I've thought about that all morning," Frida said.

"And?"

"He wanted to take Hearthstone. We could do that later in the war, after Queen Marion and Queen Elena weaken each other."

Ursula nodded. "King Knut would have done the same."

"Once Hearthstone is ours," Frida continued, "I'll place the Verdant crown on Anders's head. He and his men will keep fighting by my side until the end of the war. And if we win and Njord remains the last of the gods, I'll let Anders keep the crown, and the kingdom as well. What do you think?"

Ursula grinned. "Aye. And if that's not enough for him, then he'll get a knife between his ribs, or an ice spear through his eye."

Frida frowned. "It has to be enough." The Verdant Kingdom was over four times larger than Hemland, and more fertile, too. She lowered her voice. "Let's not think about killing each other, Ursula. We have plenty of enemies already."

"That we do." A thin smile graced Ursula's face. "Will you speak to Anders, or should I?"

"I'll do it myself after Hearthstone is ours. But only if Njord agrees to it."

"He will."

"What about Lothar and Sigurd? Will they have anything to say about it?"

"They won't." Ursula tilted her head to the side. "Lothar needs no crown; he'll be content with a generous tribute from the Julian Empire. As for Sigurd, I spoke to him in private yesterday, and you were right: he doesn't want to pick a fight with Anders. He'll seek his own treasures, farther south."

She means the desert kingdom, Frida thought.

She smiled. "Look at us, dividing the world's riches among our people. Meanwhile, King Knut's dead, and we haven't even reached the mainland's shores. And most of the enemy armies outnumber us."

"We're the only ones who have cannons," Ursula said. "Besides, all this talk put a smile on your face. I think you needed that."

Frida nodded vigorously. "I did. Thank you, Ursula."

The sea witch placed a hand on Frida's arm, "As Magnus said, you're going to sail us through the greatest storm of our lives. May your hand stay firm on the helm, Frida Gretasdottir, queen of the Islanders and captain of the sea. May you lead us with strength and wisdom. And with some luck, Njord will rule the world for a thousand years."

Frida straightened in her chair. "I'll do my duty, Ursula. For Njord, and for our people. I'll lead us to victory, if it's within my power. And I'm glad to have you by my side."

The Verdant Queen

Queen Marion rode through the forest at the head of her party, taking in the familiar sights.

The path widened as it neared the Lady's temple. The towering beech trees created a tunnel of shadows, with occasional rays of sunlight piercing the dense foliage. The ground was soft underneath the horse's hooves.

Marion's Companions rode behind her in a column three wide and twenty deep. They were all trained knights, and more than half held crossbows, swords, and maces at the ready, though there was no threat anywhere nearby.

The first six were sons of nobles, chosen by Marion herself. They wore their enchanted armor, as did Marion; tight-fitting suits of overlapping steel plates, strong yet light, painted green, and blessed by the Lady herself, hundreds of years earlier.

After two decades of daily weapons training, Marion saw the armor as her second skin, and she wore it often. It could withstand a giant's hammer blow and absorb the shock. Most of it, at least.

How the Lady had convinced Malleon, the god of the giants, to craft these suits of armor for her followers, Marion did not know. How he'd made them adapt to the sizes of their owners, and gift them with inhuman strength and speed, was an even bigger mystery.

We're almost there, she mused, gazing at a stout tree to her right. Two decades earlier, she and Sandra had carved their names into its bark. They were children then, and life was different. Simpler, and full of joy.

Now they were the Verdant queen and the High Priestess of the Lady. Her two foremost champions, fighting a war that would decide the fates of the gods. And that of the world itself, for a thousand years.

She didn't stop at the side of the tree, not this time. Instead, she lifted her visor and nodded at the two men in the archer's nest, farther ahead and to her left. They bowed to her in return, one at a time, while the other scanned for threats.

She smiled. *My sister is well-guarded. As she should be.*

She passed two more archers' nests and smiled as she recognized the man standing in the middle of the path. Alphonse, one of the most skilled wizards in the realm and a disciple of Eugene the Trickster, the Lady's third champion.

The wizard spread out his hands. "Welcome, my queen!" he shouted, and the forest echoed his words. "The High Priestess is expecting you."

"We go on foot from here," Marion said in a level voice. She leaped from the saddle and landed gracefully at her horse's side, her enchanted armor cushioning the impact. In moments, her Companions dismounted as well.

The wizard Alphonse whispered a few words, and the horses trotted onward. "I'll see them fed and watered," he said.

"Thank you, Alphonse," Marion replied. Her followers had already gathered behind her.

She removed her helmet and passed it over her shoulder. One of her Companions — most likely Milton, her favorite, or perhaps Nelson, his twin — took it from her hands. Then she strode onward, the others matching her pace.

Six hundred feet ahead, the path opened into a wide clearing, and in its midst stood the Great Temple of the Lady.

It looked like a simple wooden longhouse, except that it was thirty feet tall. Its windows were small for its size, and shuttered, even now at midday. An ancient oak sprang through the temple's roof; two hundred feet tall and fifteen feet thick, almost a thousand years old, and blessed by the Lady. Its crown stretched far and wide, shading the better part of the building, except for the entrance.

Marion advanced toward the door, and it opened when she was ten feet away. Her twin sister stood in the opening.

She wore a green blouse with long sleeves and a green skirt that reached the ground. In her right hand, she held the Scepter of the High Priestess; over three feet long, its handle made of noble wood, its metallic head painted green and shaped like an ornamented cross with a circle passing through the midpoints of its arms.

Her chestnut hair was straight and cropped just below the ear, unlike Marion's, whose curls reached the middle of her chest and back. A thick curtain of hair covered the right half of Sandra's face, as it always had since the accident.

Marion walked onward as the footsteps of her Companions stopped. They'd bow to her sister, as was customary before a High Priestess.

She hugged her instead, and whispered, "Happy twenty-sixth birthday, big sister." Sandra, the firstborn, was a few minutes older.

"Happy birthday, little sister," Sandra replied. "Though I sense it is anything but."

Marion stepped back. "I need to speak with you alone."

"Then do so," Sandra said. She walked into the temple, leaving the door open.

Marion turned to her Companions and signaled them to wait outside. She followed her sister past the threshold, and the door closed behind her, with the lightest of squeaks.

"I should do something about that," Sandra said. "Then again, it doesn't matter now."

Marion blinked twice as her eyes adjusted to the interior of the temple. Hundreds of candles hung from the slanted ceiling, illuminating the great hall with a cheery glow. They burned night and day, yet they were never entirely consumed, they did not fill the hall with smoke, and no wax dripped down to the ground. Another one of the Lady's tricks.

The ground was bare, and the first half of the hall held no furniture. The ancient oak stood in the temple's midst, the Lady's likeness sculpted into its trunk and painted green.

Marion dipped her head toward it, as was custom. As the Verdant queen, she didn't have to kneel — not even in front of the Lady herself.

Beyond the ancient tree stood two rows of wooden tables with chairs on both sides. Marion knew that silent servants would fill them with food and wine as soon as her sister ordered it.

At the end of the hall stood a single table, raised on a dais. Two identical high chairs waited behind it, facing the hall; the left one for the High Priestess, the right one for the queen, or for the Lady, when either was present.

Various trophies from the Lady's hunts hung from the walls: bearskins, wolf pelts, deer antlers, a vampire's right wing, and even a couple of orc heads, their tusks longer than Marion's fingers. To the right, a large pair of antlers drew her attention.

"That one's new," she said.

"Sixteen months old," Sandra said. "You should visit more often, sister."

"I know. I'm sorry I wasn't here for our last birthday. I was—"

"Trying to procreate," Sandra finished her sentence, as she often did. "Without success. Speaking of which, how's Simon these days?"

"Drinking himself into a stupor, for all I care." It had been a political marriage, as most of the Verdant queens had endured for centuries. The King Consort was in his late forties and was more interested in his feasts and his hunts than in sharing Marion's bed.

Why that was, she did not understand. She'd had plenty of suitors before.

She'd done her duty when the opportunity arose, though without enthusiasm. But three years had passed, and no children were forthcoming.

"If we win this war," she said, "perhaps you should ask the Lady to give him a stroke, and give me another husband. She'll listen to you." She hadn't listened to Marion.

"Even if we do win," Sandra said, "I am not certain that we'll both be alive at the end."

"Your confidence is astonishing," Marion tried to joke, though she'd had the same thought the day before.

"I say things as I see them, sister."

"You should come with me, back to Hearthstone. You'll be well-protected there."

"I am well-protected here," Sandra said. "I'll stay for a while longer and ask the Lady for guidance. As much as she can give us. Besides, you may not stay at Hearthstone for long either. Not if the vampires attack."

"And what if the giants come down from their mountains?" The Enchanted Glade neighbored the Rockfalls province, one of the giants' so-called lowlands. It was a good place for a first strike, if they decided to move against the Verdant Kingdom.

"Then I'll give them my love," Sandra answered, and pointed her scepter toward Marion.

Thick vines erupted from the ground around her and instantly grew six feet tall. They trapped her legs and arms and tightened around her armor, yet only slightly, as Sandra had intended. Then, with a flick of Sandra's wrist, they shattered into a thousand pieces.

Marion nodded in appreciation. "That was faster than the last time."

The scepter amplified the High Priestess's own magical powers. Even so, Sandra wouldn't be able to battle more than a few giants at a time.

Marion sighed. "It *is* quite hopeless, isn't it? We're surrounded by enemies."

It was true, and they both knew it. The vampires and their serfs would invade soon, in great numbers. They'd march into the Broken Lance province, burning towns and villages along the way, and make their way into Godric's Valley — unless Marion's knights managed to stop them. The giants would come down from their mountains, and between the vampires, the Julians, and the Lady's followers, Marion's kingdom was the easiest target. The Islanders would have to land somewhere, and

Marion had a nagging suspicion it would be on her shores, though whether they'd choose Lysennia or Godric's Valley, she did not know. As for the Julians…

"We need to strike a pact—" Sandra said.

"With the Julians," Marion finished her sentence. "The question is, will they agree to it?"

"They will, if you look down upon them," Sandra joked. At five foot five, the twins were taller than most Julian men. Yet what the Julians lacked in size, strength, and enchanted armor, they compensated through discipline and sheer numbers.

"They're led by a child." Lucius Antonius, the Boy Emperor, was barely fifteen. His uncle had murdered his father two years earlier and had declared himself emperor, but his reign had been short-lived. Only three weeks later, the Augustian Guards had crushed the usurper's forces, brought him to justice, and installed young Lucius on the throne.

Apparently, most of the Julian dignitaries loved the boy, despite his lack of experience. Most likely, he was favored by their gods.

"Yet perhaps a child that can be reasoned with," Sandra said.

Marion nodded. "I'll send our most skilled diplomats to negotiate with them. With some luck, they'll be successful." She sighed, and the words tumbled out. "I'm not ready for this, Sandra. I'm not sure I can rise to the challenge. You should have been queen."

"That was taken from me," Sandra said, and Marion understood her meaning. The noble families wouldn't choose her, not after the accident. They wouldn't accept a one-eyed queen.

They'd elected Marion easily, out of five noble candidates, at the age of twenty-three. Some had chosen her for her qualities, others were motivated by their allegiance to her extended family or to that of her husband. As for Sandra, she had become the High Priestess of the Lady, as tradition dictated for the queen's twin.

"Yet I do not miss it," Sandra continued. "The woods are my home now, and the Lady visits often."

"More often than she visits me." Before the previous night's encounter, when the Lady had told her of the coming war, Marion hadn't seen her for over three months. Though she prayed to her, every night.

Sandra's face grew serious. "The Lady's attention was taken by a work of magic of the utmost importance, sister. She has labored on her great task for the past five years, and it was my privilege to assist her, along with a handful of trusted priests and wizards. And now, as her task is nearing completion, the War of the Seven threatens to destroy us all."

"Tell me more about this great task," Marion said, though she did not expect a proper answer.

Sandra shook her head. "Some things are bound to remain secret. Even from you, sister. But I can tell you this: the Lady did not spend more time with you because she found you a capable queen. One who could rule well on her own and did not need her constant guidance and advice. She told me that, and I believe her."

I wish she had told me that herself, Marion thought.

"I am a good queen, yes," she said. "I can walk into a group of squabbling nobles and get them to agree with a few gentle words. I am kind to the commoners, I can hold my own in training bouts against most of my knights, and few uphold the Lady's ideals of honor and chivalry better than I do. But this... This is too much for me. I am not a wartime leader."

"Yet you will do your duty," Sandra said. "When the time comes, you'll cast your doubt aside and rise to the challenge. Our knights are skilled in the art of war, as are many of our nobles — and they will follow you. You have plenty of wizards as well. And you'll have me at your side."

"So, you are coming? Back to Hearthstone?"

"You need me, and you will have me."

Marion smiled inwardly. A first victory already. "Thank you, sister."

"You will have to show strength," Sandra said, and Marion knew she was right. "You cannot show weakness, or it will be the end of us all."

"I must show strength I do not have." She was exaggerating her weakness to draw her sister closer. She hoped Sandra wouldn't notice it.

"I'll help you get it, by the Lady's will," Sandra said. "As will Sir Galahad."

"The Paladin is not with me. Though I wish I had him by my side." The Lady had named him as her fourth champion, and he was more than worthy of the honor.

"You will, and soon," Sandra said. "The Lady told me he'll be coming this way. He should arrive by nightfall. As for Eugene, he and his Rangers are roaming the forests of Godric's Valley."

"I know," Marion said. "I spoke with him two weeks ago, before he left the capital." Back then, she hadn't known that a great war was coming, nor that she, her sister, Eugene, and Sir Galahad would serve as the Lady's champions. "I expect he'll join us in Hearthstone."

"We shall leave tomorrow morning. Or today, if you wish."

"Tomorrow's fine, sister," Marion said. Her knights could use some rest. "For now, shall we have a small feast? My men and I haven't eaten since sunrise."

"We shall," Sandra agreed. She pointed her scepter to the door, and it opened, with the lightest of squeaks.

"Bring me food," Sandra said, and the forest echoed her words. The silent servants would soon arrive, carrying platters filled with food and goblets of wine. "And you, brave knights. Join us inside."

They turned from the door and walked toward the high chairs, hand in hand, as Marion's Companions filled the hall. And for a few brief moments, all was right in the world.

Order and Justice

"Prepare yourself, priest. We're about to land."

Kirill's stomach lurched at the thought. He muttered a prayer to the vampire god and willed his pounding heart to slow down.

Below them lay the town of Ravensflight, with its wooden houses arranged in neat rows and a wide rectangular gap marking the main square. The estates of the local nobles stood proud on the town's western edge; four brick mansions surrounded by ample courtyards, with the count's palace overlooking them all.

The vampire Nikolay swooped downward at great speed and turned his flight into a glide that ended less than a dozen feet above the ground. Then, flapping his wings, he descended slowly and landed in the center of Ravensflight's main square.

Kirill let out a sigh of relief. The descent hadn't affected him as much as he'd feared, and neither had the landing, though the ground did seem to slide under his feet.

"Steady yourself," Nikolay said.

Kirill planted his feet on the ground. He leaned to the right and left, and soon his sense of balance returned. "I'm ready," he said.

"Good." Nikolay released the straps that held Kirill tight to his chest. "Tell me, did you enjoy your flight?"

Kirill turned to him. There was a mischievous glint in the vampire's eye.

"More than I thought I would," he answered truthfully.

"Very well," Nikolay said. "I, for one, have a great thirst I need to quench."

Kirill tilted his head to the right.

The vampire grinned. "Not from you, priest. It would weaken you, and you need to be at your best, to make a strong impression upon these serfs."

A crowd was gathering in the square, their eyes fixed upon the two travelers who'd just dropped into their midst. They were all dressed in gray, their simple garments bearing the symbols of their trades. And none of them looked deathly ill, or destitute, or on the brink of starvation. The vampire nobles treated their serfs well, as long as they knew their place in the world.

"I'll drink from one of them," Nikolay continued. "And you, wipe that blood off your head."

Kirill remembered the goose that Nikolay had hunted, and a shiver ran down his spine. He brushed the top of his head with his fingers and they came up clean. Of course, whatever blood still remained must have dried by now.

"I need water."

One of the serfs rushed to him and handed him a waterskin.

They'd all be quick to obey him. His expensive garments marked him as a priest, and a high one at that; and among the serfs, a priest's word was law. Unless an even higher priest, or a vampire noble, or the kingdom's laws, said otherwise.

Kirill nodded at the man. "Some clean cloth as well."

Moments later, he was scrubbing the last of the bird's blood off his bald head, just as Nikolay sank his fangs into a woman's throat.

She staggered backward when he was done, but Kirill knew she'd felt no pain, and her weakness would pass before nightfall. One of the women nearby steadied her and whispered something in her ear.

Nikolay nodded. It was time for Kirill to begin.

"I have grave and great news to share with you all," he shouted.

The crowd drew closer, though they kept a respectful distance from him and Nikolay.

"Listen to me and spread my words." Kirill continued. "For soon your nobles will call upon you, and together you'll march to war."

Shouts erupted from the crowd.

"Be quiet!" Nikolay roared, and the serfs fell into silence.

"Listen to him," the noble said in a lower voice. "For he is Kirill Skromnik, and Serya Krov has chosen him as a champion in a war that will decide the fate of the world. Tell them, Kirill."

He told them of the great threat of the Vengeful One, and of the gods' meeting, and of their Godly Pact. He told them that the last of the gods would rule the world for a thousand years. The serfs listened intently, their gazes fixed upon him. And through it all, not a single voice spoke up from the crowd, and not a single hand came up, for Nikolay had ordered them to be quiet.

"And so, we will march to war," Kirill said at last, "and bring the Verdant Kingdom to its knees, as Queen Elena has commanded. But Queen Elena doesn't just want her people to obey her. She wants you to know what you're fighting for. A better world, one ruled by order and justice. And for that, she has sent me among you, for I have more to say."

He paused for a moment. "First of all, Kirill Skromnik is not my first name. On the day I came into this world, my mother named me Francis."

"What?" a man in the first row shouted. He'd recognized the foreign nature of the name. Nikolay growled, and the man sank to his knees, his eyes downcast.

Kirill motioned him to stand. "I'll answer questions when I'm done."

Only after glancing at Nikolay did the man rise to his feet.

Kirill sighed. He hadn't told his story in twenty-seven years, yet the memories came to him often. They'd always be a part of him, and the passing of time had not dulled his pain.

"I was born in a small town in Godric's Valley," he said, "and was raised to worship the Lady, the so-called benevolent goddess of the Verdant Kingdom. My father was a renowned scholar, and he trained me to follow in his footsteps. He taught me that the Lady's nobles were men and women of great virtue, who dedicated themselves to the pursuit of honor and chivalry; and he taught me that the vampires were monsters, and that Serya Krov was the divine manifestation of ultimate evil."

He used scholarly words without restraint, and few of the Verdant Kingdom's peasants would have understood those. Yet the Vampire Kingdom's serfs did. They had to, for their nobles used such words often.

"For thirty years, I believed those lies. Then everything changed. And it all started with one fateful day.

"My little sister married young and moved to her husband's village, twenty miles from mine. A village ruled by a so-called chivalrous lord, who took a fancy to her as soon as he set eyes on her.

"She rejected his advances, more than once. Then, after a night of heavy drinking, the lord barged into her house with six of his guards and raped her in front of his men.

"Her husband, who had been sleeping in the next room, rushed to her rescue. The lord's guards seized him and made him watch. She screamed, but no one else came to her aid."

He watched the faces of the serfs. Many of them seemed saddened or enraged by his words, yet none spoke up. Not without his permission and Nikolay's.

"When the drunken lord was done, he had them both hanged in the village square. And the Lady, the so-called goddess of honor and chivalry, let it all happen."

He blinked a few times, trying to erase the image of his dead sister from his mind.

"I learned of it the next day," he continued. "One of my sister's neighbors came to my hometown and told me of her fate. I rode back to her village with him, and saw her body, just before the lord's men took her down.

"I tried to raise a mob, to storm the lord's manor and make him pay for his crime. I went from door to door, but only five of the villagers rallied to my call — and when they saw how few they were, they scattered off, like cowards. Alone, I stood no chance.

"I waited for a while, hiding in the neighbor's cellar, hoping the Lady would avenge my sister's death. Yet she did not strike the wretch down. He feasted in his manor, and his men came to the village tavern night after night and boasted of what they'd witnessed. Of what they'd done.

"I killed one of them, two weeks after my sister's death. I caught him alone and buried a knife in his throat. But I knew they'd be more cautious after that. They'd look for me and hunt me down. So, I renounced the Lady, stole a horse, and fled from Godric's Valley, through the Broken Lance province, and over the border, into the Labor Plains.

"I reached a village on this side of the border just as my food was running out. I told the serfs my story, and they took me to their master, Count Krasimir. He sent me to Dragos Castle with a letter for Queen Elena and a promise that the monster who had defiled and killed my sister would be dealt with. He kept his promise; the murderer was dead within the year.

"Queen Elena welcomed me and gave me a new name. She asked me to become a priest and told me of my duties. Serya Krov himself visited me a week later.

"He spoke to me. And for the first time in my life, I understood how the world truly works. I saw that the Lady's worship was based on lies, as was that of the Julian gods. I understood that only the noble vampires had the answers I was seeking.

"I learned the laws of the kingdom, and I started paying the blood price, as we all must. At first, I did find that… unsettling." He could have used a stronger word, but decided against it. "Then I understood what it was buying, and I accepted it willingly.

"We have order and justice," he continued. "That is what the vampire god and our noble masters are giving us. Just last week, as I stopped to take water, I forgot my month's pay on the edge of a well. When I went back for it half a day later, the money pouch was still there. Hundreds of serfs had passed by, and dozens must have taken water from the well, yet none took the coins. In the Verdant Kingdom, they would have vanished in minutes."

A few serfs nodded.

"But that is not all," Kirill said. "I have a wife now, and two daughters. Our nobles won't rape them." Of course, that would have been beneath them, but he didn't need to say that out loud. "Nor would they kill them without reason. Neither would anyone else. If they did, Queen Elena would learn of it, and she'd bleed the offenders dry. And so would your own nobles, if any of you, or your loved ones, suffered such an injustice."

Many of the serfs nodded at that.

"As a high priest, I have great power. I command and you obey me. Yet I would never abuse that power. If I did, the punishment would be swift and final. Instead, I serve, and do what must be done. As do we all."

He sighed. "As for the Lady's so-called ideals, they'll never work. They *sound* noble, yes. The Verdant Kingdom's priests and scholars tell good stories, and some of those are even true. But men fall prey to their instincts easily, and those in power are the worst. Unless a firm hand keeps them in line.

"So, tell me, friends. Do you want to live in a world that gives you the illusion of freedom, only to bring you pain and sorrow? A world that allows great injustice to befall you and allows it to go unpunished? Or will you fight for Serya Krov, and for Queen Elena, and for their vision of a world of order and justice?"

The serfs remained quiet. A few of them raised their hands.

"You may speak now," Nikolay said.

The crowd erupted with shouts, and Kirill smiled. Some of the serfs were chanting Queen Elena's name, or that of the vampire god; others shouted for order and justice; and perhaps a few tried to ask him questions, but their voices were lost in the noise.

He held up a hand, and the crowd quieted.

"I'll answer your questions one at a time," he said, and a dozen hands went up.

Ancient Memories

Queen Elena focused and her wings sprouted from her back. She flapped them once, twice, then leaped off the edge of her balcony and took to the air.

She soared above Dragos Castle, under the light of the moon, as she'd done countless times over the past five centuries. It was her hour of solace, of ancient memories. Her time of trying to recapture, for a few brief moments, what had been forever taken from her.

I could just dash myself against one of the towers one night. She'd flirted with the thought many times before, yet there was no point to it. Her bones would break, yes; but she'd heal before morning.

Noble blood gave her that power.

She could have dived headfirst into one of the spires from above, at full speed, and that would end it all. But she'd made a promise to Dragos. A promise that she'd broken once already.

#

"Live," he'd told her on that fateful morning, before flying to battle. "Do not risk your life, as I must. Survive, whatever befalls me."

"I will," she said, her eyes brimming with tears.

"Promise me."

She did, and watched him fly away.

She prowled her mansion's courtyard like a caged beast, her mind clouded with dark thoughts, a small part of her hoping against hope that they would not come to pass. A few agonizing hours later, one of the nobles came with the news.

"The battle is lost, Countess Elena. We've been routed, and King Dragos is dead. The Lady's Paladin stabbed him through the heart with his sword."

"No!" she shouted at him. "That's not true! It can't be! Take it back!"

He backed away from her. "I'm sorry. I saw it happen, but there was nothing I could do. I was too far away."

She could have ripped him to pieces. But he was young, and he'd already lost a hand, and his death wouldn't change a thing.

She sank to her knees. She howled with pain and rage, her talons raking deep gashes into her cheeks. Then a shadow appeared in the sky, and moments later, Serya Krov was at her side.

"What would you give," he asked, "to get him back?"

"Everything," she replied. "My life. My heart, if you'll have it." Though she knew there was no way to bring her lover back. The dead stayed dead forever.

"Done," the vampire god said.

She looked at him. "Can you really bring him back?"

"I am a god," Serya Krov said. "I'm the one who brought your kind into the light. I can do this, yes. But only once. And the price is high."

"Take it," she said, without hesitation.

"I'll take your heart," the god said, "and put it in his chest. I'll bring him back to life, and you'll live as well. But you will feel no joy, not anymore."

"Will he still love me?" she asked. Then she shook her head. "It's not important. All that matters is that he lives again. When do we begin?"

"First, you have a choice to make. I can replace your heart with a wineskin, or with a waterskin. It will keep you alive, by my divine will, though you'll have to feed it with noble blood."

"The blood of our kind?"

"Yes. After I do this, the serfs' blood will be poison to you. It won't kill you outright, but it will make you suffer for days. The noble blood will nourish you."

"And the choice?"

"If you take the wineskin, you'll forget many things, over and over, but you will feel no pain. If you take the waterskin, you'll remember everything."

She chose the waterskin.

Serya Krov spoke a few words in a strange language and she crumpled to the ground, motionless.

The god climbed atop her fallen body, though she did not feel his weight. His claws dug into her chest, and everything went black.

When she woke a week later, back in Dragos Castle, she was the vampire queen, revered by all her nobles for her sacrifice. The right side of her face had darkened, the only visible reminder of what she'd done. And Dragos was still dead. He'd fought another battle, and Sir Godric had put a lance through the heart thumping in his chest. *Her* heart.

#

Perhaps I should have chosen the wineskin, she thought. *It would have saved me so much pain. Five centuries of pain.*

Then again, it's a good thing I didn't. The Lady took Dragos from me, and now it's time to make her pay.

Instinct made her look up. By the light of the moon, she saw the familiar shadow loom above her. She descended into the courtyard, and moments later, Serya Krov joined her.

He shrank to her size and looked her in the eye. "Thinking of that day again?"

She nodded.

"Still no regrets?"

She nodded again.

"I have good news, my daughter," the vampire god said. "Katrina has made her first kill. King Knut Haraldsson is dead, and Njord is down to three champions. Now tell me about your army."

Two Bandits

Deep within the verdant forest that covered the northern part of Godric's Valley, Squinty Jack whistled and pulled his long knife from its sheath.

He stepped from behind the tree and into the middle of the path, holding his weapon at waist height.

"Well met, traveler," his companion said as he emerged from the other side of the path. Pete the Bruiser carried a rusty sword with a dull edge, unlike that of Jack's knife. Then again, Pete was scary even without a weapon. Six feet tall, built like a barrel, and with a permanent scowl etched upon his face, the mere sight of him was enough to make most men wish they'd had pressing business somewhere else that day.

Yet the old traveler facing him did not seem impressed.

Jack looked the man up and down. He was as tall as Pete, but much, much thinner. *'Built like a stick'* were the words that came to Jack's mind. His coat and his pointy hat were verdant green, the Lady's favorite color. His bushy beard sported various shades of gray and reached past his chest. He carried a walking stick, though he seemed to have no need for it.

"Well met, strangers," the man said. "What's with the blades, though? Are you… expecting bandits, perhaps?"

"We *are* the bandits," Squinty Jack replied, as his friend seemed at a loss for words. "Give us your money and we'll let you go free."

"I'd wallop him once or twice, Jack," Pete said matter-of-factly.

Jack glared at him. "Don't. Remember what happened with the last one. Do you want to spend the next two hours digging a hole?" He turned back to the traveler. "Toss me your money pouch. Now."

The old man smirked. "I gather you don't know rule thirteen of banditry, do you, lads?"

"What's rule thirteen?" asked Pete.

"You don't, under any circumstances, stop a thin old man with a fox. If you do, you suffer the consequences."

Jack knew what he was talking about. It was said that the great wizard Eugene the Trickster often roamed the Verdant Kingdom's forests, with his pet fox at his side. One of the Lady's favorites, he was. People said he could make wolves and bears drop dead with a gaze, and turn men into toads, and worse, though Jack did not believe those stories. Or at least he tried not to.

"You don't have a fox, old man," he observed.

"Jack?" Pete said.

"What? He doesn't."

"Ja-ack? Look over there!"

Jack looked to where Pete was pointing. A snout peeked out from behind a tree. It edged forward, and a reddish-brown fox stepped onto the path.

Jack's heart pounded in his chest. What if the stories were true?

"Run!" he yelped.

He whipped around and broke into a run, but something tripped his legs and he fell to the ground, face down. The knife flew from his hand and into a bush. A moment later, the old man's walking stick was pressing into his cheek.

"I'll let you go this time," the traveler said. "But only because you told your big friend not to wallop me. Not him, though. He stays. Don't be anywhere near this place when my Rangers get here, and don't ever come back."

"I… I won't," Jack managed to croak. Then the stick lifted. The patter of small feet told Jack that the fox was passing by on his other side.

He lay on the ground for another minute. When he rose to his feet, the old man was gone — and Pete the Bruiser was hanging upside down from a tree, twenty feet in the air, suspended by thick vines wrapped around his legs.

Squinty Jack squinted at Pete's face. He didn't look toad-like, at least not more than before. Or… did he?

"Cut me down!" Pete shouted, but Jack was already running away.

The Sea Witch

Ursula Gudrunsdottir yawned as she looked into the flames.

It was a quiet evening in the Islanders' camp; and here, on the shore of the Verdant Kingdom, the weather was mild. Ursula's fire was one among thousands. Six men sat with her, three of her own sailors and three from Frida's ship. They drank, laughed, and rejoiced in telling old stories to new friends. They'd been doing so for hours, under the moonlit sky.

Two days earlier, their fleet had anchored here, in Sapphire Bay. It was a natural harbor, with an entrance a quarter of a mile wide. A rocky limb of land extended from the north-east and protected the ships from storms, and the lighthouse that had been built on its tip was now garrisoned by Frida's men. A small river that spilled out into the bay provided them with enough water to quench their thirst and refill the barrels they'd emptied on the sea voyage.

They'd found the fishing villages deserted and had taken them over, covering the beach and the nearby fields in a sea of tents. And now they were resting, waiting for their leaders to decide their next moves.

Their ships rested at anchor, watching over the camp like enormous floating guardians. Frida's fleet had advanced the farthest into the bay, with Lothar's ships and Sigurd's ships following. Anders's fleet guarded the mouth of the bay, with half a dozen of his ships patrolling the deep waters beyond.

They'd easily snuff out any threat coming from inland. The ground was flat, and the forest started half a mile away, well within cannon range.

It was a peaceful place, and for a moment Ursula wished they could make it their home. But sitting and waiting would not win the War of the Seven, and sooner or later either Queen Marion, or Queen Elena of the vampires, would bring their whole might against them. Besides, the Islanders were quick to anger and slow to forgive past transgressions. Without enemies to fight, they'd soon fight each other. And that, Ursula could not allow.

She rose from her seat at the campfire, bade her shipmates goodnight, and headed toward her tent. Her hair smelled of smoke and ash, but that didn't matter now. She'd wash it in the morning.

She stepped carefully over a sailor who'd fallen asleep in the middle of the path, with an empty wineskin at his side. Her resting place awaited less than twenty paces away.

It was a simple sleeping tent; narrow, six feet long, and barely reaching her chest. The sea witches of Ursula's order forswore comfort early in their training and thought of the elements as their friends. Yet once in a while she did enjoy the warm embrace of a thick wool blanket on a cold night.

One of her young disciples guarded the tent. She nodded as Ursula approached her.

"Any news, Ingrid?" Ursula asked her.

"All quiet here. Except for a drunk southerner who tried to claim your tent for himself, maybe half an hour ago."

"And?"

"I told him I'd freeze his balls off if he took another step."

Ursula chuckled. "Good. That must have sobered him up."

"I wouldn't go that far," Ingrid said. "*He* did, though. With his tail between his legs."

"He'll go farther tomorrow," Ursula said. "As will we all. We've lingered here for too long."

Ingrid shot her a hopeful look, which Ursula could barely see in the light of a nearby fire. "So, Queen Frida has made a decision?"

Ursula shook her head. "We're still fractured. Anders would march to Hearthstone and take the Verdant capital itself, or die trying. Sigurd says we should remain on the coastline, as King Knut would have done. And Lothar thinks we should leave the Lady's followers alone and strike at the Julians instead. He says we'll do better there. As he's done from the beginning."

"And Queen Frida?"

"She prefers Sigurd's way. After all, we can't march our ships to Hearthstone, and we only have enough wagons for a third of our cannons, if that. But she hasn't decided yet."

"Whatever path she chooses, some of our captains will resent her for it."

"She knows that, Ingrid. She also knows that a clash with Queen Marion's knights would weaken us. She'd rather face them after they'd fought the vampires, if she had the choice. And so would I."

A temporary alliance with Queen Marion would have been even better. But Sigurd's raiders had plundered the Verdant Kingdom's shores too many times, and had claimed the life of the queen's uncle in one of the raids, thirteen years earlier. There'd be scores to settle.

"And yet you say we march tomorrow," Ingrid said.

"I'll make them go with Sigurd's plan. I'll say that Njord came to me in a dream, and that this is his will. Unless Njord himself tells me otherwise. Besides, the others will resent Frida less if I take this upon myself."

Ingrid gave her an appreciative nod.

Ursula tilted her head and gazed at the sky. Two distant stars shone brightly in the north. Njord himself had named them Hrothgar's Eyes, after Hrothgar Longbeard, the first Islander pirate to reach the shores of Ethasar's mainland.

"Do you think he's watching over us?" Ingrid asked.

"Hrothgar? No." The old adventurer had taken his final swim over seven centuries earlier. Now, his bones rested on the bottom of the sea. "He did his part, and now we must do ours. And in this war, we're the only ones without a home." Hemland had been forbidden to them for the next seven years, with Njord's enchanted mist already barring the way. "We're invaders wherever we go, fighting on foreign ground."

"As we always did," Ingrid said. Barely eighteen, she'd joined Ursula on half a dozen raids already.

"This is different, Ingrid. We'll be facing armies. Wizards, too. And they'll be ready for us."

"But we'll still win, yes?"

"By Njord's will," Ursula answered with a confidence she did not feel. She yawned again. "I guess I'll go and have that dream now. You should rest as well. I'll see you in the morning."

She lifted the flap of her tent, crouching as she entered. Her candle was still burning, though it wouldn't last much longer. Her pack lay at the head of her sleeping mat, where she'd left it.

She sat down next to it, pulled out her flask, and took a sip of seawater, as she did every evening. It tasted salty, and faintly of fish, with a tinge of seaweed.

"Make us strong, Njord," she whispered. "Bind us together under Queen Frida. Help us win, for your fate and ours, and for those of the ones we've left behind."

Advise me, she thought. *Give me your wisdom, if you can.*

Outside her tent, the fierce men and women of the sea god sat around campfires and shared stories with their friends. They'd sleep in their own tents, or simply wrapped in blankets under the night sky. The few longhouses of the fishing village couldn't fit them all, though at least Queen Frida had taken one, as had some of the captains. The camp itself was well protected; they had guards who would abstain from drinking, and scouting patrols, and both Anders and Lothar had small crews aboard their ships, ready to fire their cannons if they were attacked.

Ursula stretched out on her sleeping mat. She was about to blow out the candle when something caught her eye.

A shadow, outside. A small creature that passed by the nearest campfire and trotted away. A cat, or perhaps... a fox?

Yes. It had to be a fox. Cats did not have tails like that.

She rushed outside, but the creature was nowhere in sight.

A fox wouldn't venture into our camp, not by itself. A wizard with a fox might. And that had to be Eugene the Trickster, the Lady's third champion.

No. It can't be. He's an outsider. Our guards would have spotted him. Then again, if he dyed his hair blue, and his beard, too…

"Ingrid," she said.

The young woman turned to her. "Yes?"

"Keep this quiet," Ursula whispered. Her eyes darted left and right, scanning the shadows. "We might have intruders in the camp."

"Really?" Ingrid whispered back. "Did Njord tell you this?"

Ursula shook her head. "He couldn't if he wanted to. The Godly Pact forbids it. But never mind that. I saw a fox, and I know of only one wizard who uses those. Eugene the Trickster, one of the Lady's champions."

"He's come to kill Queen Frida," Ingrid whispered. "Or you." Her eyes were scanning the night as well. "What would you have me do?"

"Spread the word among our men, but do it quietly. I don't want him to run. If you spot any intruders, kill them on sight. I'll go and warn Frida."

Ingrid nodded and left. Then Ursula focused and muttered a quick spell, readying her magic. If she laid eyes on the wizard, she'd send an ice spear through his heart before he could react.

She strode to the campfire on her left, where Astrid, the most skilled of her sea witches, shared stories with half a dozen sailors.

"We're going to see the queen, Astrid," she said. "Now. You too, men. Come with me."

Astrid stood, and Ursula whispered in her ear. "Keep your eyes open. One of the Verdant wizards might be among us. Old man, tall and thin, has a fox for his companion. Kill him on sight. Don't tell your men, not yet."

They walked side by side at the head of their men and headed toward the village leader's house, where Queen Frida had chosen to reside. It was close, and they reached it without incident.

Frida had been sleeping, yet her guards woke her at Ursula's request. She sat on the edge of her bed, with two men standing at her sides, both armed to the teeth: Arne Olafsson, her bodyguard for the past ten years, and Torsten Eriksson, King Knut's former bodyguard.

"Are you sure of what you saw?" she asked after Ursula told her the news.

"I am," Ursula said. "Then again, maybe he's toying with us. Maybe he's not even here, and he just sent his creature to rob us of a good night's sleep."

"Even so," Frida said, "I'll have our people looking for him. Torsten?"

"Yes, my queen?"

"Sound the alarm. Send word to the ships, too, to Lothar and Anders both. We need to be ready for anything."

"Wait," Ursula intervened. "If he's here, we want him dead, yes?"

"Yes. And?"

"We know he might be among us, but he doesn't know we know. If he did, he'd flee and set up a diversion to cover his tracks."

Frida leaned forward. "So, what do you propose?"

"Throw a net around him. Spread the word, but do it quietly, as I did. Tell your guards, and send word to the edge of the camp, and then let it trickle inward. By the time he knows we're on to him, he'll have nowhere to run."

"I like it," Frida said. "I'll do as you say, Ursula."

"Very well. As for me, I think I'll head back to my tent and slip under my blanket."

Torsten shook his head. "No. You should stay here, sea witch. We'll keep you safe."

"I'll be safe enough among my crew," she countered. "They'll be on alert, as will Astrid and Ingrid; and they're fierce, these two. Besides, I'll only pretend to sleep. If the Lady's wizard comes to pay me a visit in the night, and manages to sneak past my guards, I'll have a nasty surprise ready for him."

77

Eugene the Trickster

Half a mile from the Islanders' camp, just beyond the edge of the forest, Eugene the Trickster turned to his right as an owl's call pierced the quiet night. Robert, the leader of his Rangers, stood at his side, an arrow already nocked to his bow.

Ahead, four tall, burly men advanced among the trees. They couldn't spot Robert, hidden as he was behind a thick oak. As for Eugene, he'd already cast a concealing spell upon himself. It wasn't perfect, but darkness was his friend.

With a practiced move, Robert drew the bowstring and let his arrow fly. It whistled as it cut through the air, and one of the burly men fell.

More arrows struck the other three. Then a few of Robert's Rangers leaped down from the trees and descended upon their foes, their blades rising and falling. Eugene held his breath, but no screams came from the fallen men. In moments, the quiet struggle was over.

"That was too close, Master," the Head Ranger whispered. "We can't linger here."

He's right, Eugene thought. They had ambushed another patrol less than three hundred heartbeats earlier. Soon, the Islanders would notice their men's absence and sound the alarm.

Even so, he wouldn't abandon his mission.

He placed a hand on his man's arm. "Patience, Robert. Vixen will return."

The patter of small feet on the ground confirmed the truth of his words. In moments, his fox was at his side.

Eugene crouched down and patted her head. *Did you find her, Vixen?* he thought at her.

Not the captain, Vixen replied. *But I found the old witch.*

Eugene nodded and ran his fingers through his beard. *Good. You've made me proud.*

He could speak to her with his thoughts. A rare skill, even among the Lady's most talented wizards. Then again, he and Vixen had had decades of practice.

An old fox, she was. Under his careful ministrations, she'd reached thrice her normal lifespan. He'd lose her soon, and there was no time to train another. Yet on this night, she'd served him well.

Where is she? he asked.

Small tent among many tents.

Eugene frowned. *That's not very helpful. Give me more.*

Big brick house nearby. Wide door. One window shuttered.

Oh. Good. He knew the house. *How close is it?*

At his side, Robert grunted. "We must strike soon, Master," he whispered. "That, or we must fall back."

"Quiet, Robert," Eugene whispered back.

He asked Vixen for more details, until he was certain of the sea witch's location.

I hope she'll stay in her tent. It would be a waste of a good spell if she didn't. A spell that had taken him half a day to prepare. It would leave him weak as a kitten when it was done, but that was a small price to pay.

He turned to Robert. "Gather your men. I have a target for you."

The Ranger let out a low whistle. Somewhere to the left, another whistle answered it. Then, one by one, his men appeared from behind the trees.

In less than two hundred heartbeats, all two dozen of them had assembled.

"Remember to use the green-tipped arrows," Eugene told them.

"As if we'd ever forget, Master," replied Jonah, the newest of the men.

Robert tilted his head toward him. "He always says that, Jonah. You'll get used to it." He turned to Eugene. "The target, Master."

"You know the village head's house, yes?" Eugene asked him.

"I do. He's married to my cousin."

"Good. It's a small tent, fifty-three paces closer to us and twenty-seven to the right." From this distance, all he could see were the dots of the Islanders' fires. But not seeing the target didn't matter, not when Robert knew where it was.

"From the south-eastern corner of the house?" Robert asked.

Eugene nodded. "Yes. If it was from the center, I'd tell you. Oh, and it's facing east."

The Head Ranger spoke to his men, a complicated thing about angles and wind speed that Eugene thought best to ignore. Their aim would be true, and the spell would do its work. It always did.

Robert lined up his men in four rows of six. He nocked an arrow and raised his bow at a high angle, and the others followed him in unison.

They drew as one, and let their arrows fly.

They'd fly for half a mile. Eugene's spell would give them the speed they needed. And they'd land right where he wanted them to.

Ingrid

We'll get him soon, Ingrid thought.

She faced Ursula's tent, with her friend Astrid standing behind her, both ready to hurl their ice spears at their enemy as soon as he revealed himself.

Around them, sailors sat at their campfires. They laughed and boasted about great feats of bravery and cunning, as they'd done for hours; but their hands never strayed far from their weapons, and they didn't raise their wineskins to their lips. Not since they'd been warned.

The trap was set. Now all the old wizard had to do was fall into it.

He'd be forced to reveal himself. Soon, Ursula's message would reach the camp guards. It would spread to the sides, and then inward. After that, the entire camp would be looking for the intruder. He'd have no chance of escaping.

Perhaps he'll make his move then. And we'll be ready for him.

Inside Ursula's tent, a dim light died. She'd blown out her candle. She'd pretend to sleep, and make herself an easier target, though she was anything but.

Ingrid admired Ursula. She was an accomplished sea witch, and unlike herself, she had mastered the heat as well as the cold. And her skill with magic was only one of her many strengths.

As a teacher, she was unequaled. She inspired her disciples and did not punish them for their failures with magic, nor for their other occasional mistakes. *Do better tomorrow*, she'd say instead. And, *tell me what you've learned from this.*

They all loved her for it. But there was more to her. Much more.

She was one of Queen Frida's trusted advisors. She'd advised King Knut Haraldsson before her, and King Harald as well, and they'd both placed great trust in her judgment. She had joined them on their raids countless times. She'd saved King Knut's life once, and his father's life thrice. But there was more to her. Much more.

She was *kind*. A rare trait among the Islanders.

Ten years earlier, she had grabbed a young street urchin's hand as it was reaching inside her purse. But instead of giving Ingrid a good thrashing, as was well within her right, Ursula had taken an interest in her. She'd brought her to her ship, she'd given her a grown man's rations and a cabin of her own, and she'd spoken to her about magic.

For Ingrid, it had been the chance of a lifetime — and she'd grabbed it with both hands. And now, here she was. A skilled sea witch in her own right, both trusted and feared.

Ursula had no children of her own and was long past childbearing age. Perhaps that was why she'd chosen Ingrid.

With some luck, Ingrid thought, *she'll let me call myself Ingrid Ursulasdottir once this war is over.* She'd never known her own parents.

She looked left, then right, for the hundredth time, but nothing seemed out of place. "All is well," she whispered.

"Same here," Astrid said.

Ingrid smiled and took a deep breath of salty sea air mixed with campfire smoke. She squeezed her right hand into a fist and felt the power course through her veins. She opened her hand and—

A hail of arrows punched into the side of Ursula's tent.

"No!" Ingrid screamed, and darted forward.

She burst into the tent and found her teacher lying still. Life was gone from her already.

Five of the arrows had struck her. She could have survived the two in her leg and the one in her shoulder, but a fourth arrow had pierced her lung, and another had opened her throat. At least a dozen more had landed around her, in a neat rectangular pattern.

She'd been crouching, like a serpent ready to strike, and her face was frozen in concentration. Death had taken her by surprise.

Ingrid roared like a wounded animal as she took it all in. But there was nothing she, or anyone else, could do.

Anders Svensson

On the deck of his flagship, in the dim light of a torch, Anders Svensson faced the two dozen captains who had answered his call. This would be the most important gathering of their lives.

"As many of you have heard," he said, "we just lost Ursula Gudrunsdottir, our second champion. We're down to Frida," he did not call her queen, "and to that raving lunatic, Gunnar."

"How did this happen?" shouted one of his captains.

"She was struck by arrows. Where they came from, we do not know. But you're asking how, when you should be asking why."

He let them ponder his words for a few moments. Then he continued. "There can be only one reason for it. It is Njord. The sea god has deserted us."

"He can't!" Ingmar, one of the younger captains, stepped forward. He hadn't yet learned when to let his betters do the talking.

"He has," Anders said, in a tone that did not admit contradiction. "Our god, whom we have bled for, and shed rivers of mainlander blood for, has abandoned us!"

"Aye!" three of the captains roared; his most trusted men. They knew what was coming. He'd told them before gathering the others.

"Njord has made mistake after mistake," Anders continued. "He let our king waste himself in the arms of a vampire spy, even before this contest began, and it cost him his life. He chose Gunnar as his fourth champion, though he would have done better with any of you. He chose Frida as his second, instead of me. I can't fault him for choosing Ursula, she was worthy. But letting her die like this? It is shameful, aye?"

"Aye!" roared the three loyal captains, and this time, the others roared with them.

"Njord is finished," Anders said. "Of this I have no doubt. Perhaps the girl Frida dies next, or perhaps Gunnar. But when one of them does, so does Njord. And I won't just sit around and wait for it to happen. No. He's betrayed us, and it's time to pay him back in kind. I would have us leave his sinking ship and side with the strongest of the gods."

"You speak of treason!" shouted Sigvard, a captain in his early forties; a peerless navigator, who knew the star charts better than Njord himself.

"I speak of doing what's right for my men!" Anders shouted back. He'd have to watch this one. "And for my women, too! And if Njord is so powerful, if he's a god worth following, then let him strike me down now!"

He raised his fists to the sky. Nothing would happen, and he knew it. The Godly Pact would not allow it.

A loud *Boom!* echoed in the distance, but it wasn't Njord's doing. It had to be a cannon fired in Ursula's honor.

He waited for a dozen heartbeats, and Njord did not touch him, nor did he speak to him. Then Anders grinned. "I have a plan, my brothers. A plan that will ensure our survival, and that of our families, and that of all those we've left behind in Hemland."

Magnus

In his cabin, Captain Magnus gritted his teeth and picked at the dirt under his fingernails with the tip of his knife.

He had volunteered to scour the forest for Ursula's killers, but Queen Frida hadn't allowed it. "Go to your ship, Magnus," she'd told him. "I can't lose you, too." And now, here he was, with fourteen seasoned warriors standing on the deck above, while Frida remained ashore, surrounded by hundreds of loyal guards.

To the west, a cannon roared. The noise jolted Magnus, and he winced as his blade split his skin open. A drop of crimson blood welled into the cut.

"You're going to chop off your finger, if you're not careful," Karl, his second-in-command, told him.

Magnus growled and set his knife on the table. "What was that, Karl?" A few ships had fired their cannons in Ursula's honor, but that had ceased over an hour earlier.

Karl shrugged. "Let's go and find out."

Magnus rose from his seat, sheathed his knife, and followed his friend onto the deck. Sailors darted to and fro, including a few men Magnus did not recognize. In the distance, more cannons fired.

"There you were, Captain," a voice came from the side.

Magnus turned. Anders Svensson strode toward him, holding a torch in his left hand. "What's going on, Anders?" he asked.

"We're under attack," Anders said as he approached.

"Is it the Verdant fleet?" Karl cut in.

Anders shook his head.

"Then who?" Magnus asked.

"Me." In an instant, a knife appeared in Anders's hand. He lunged toward Karl and stabbed it into his belly.

Magnus roared and drew his own knife, but strong arms seized him from behind. His weapon was wrenched from his grasp, and someone thrust a gag into his mouth. He tried to struggle, but the two men behind him forced him to his knees. Anders dashed away, blade in hand, seeking another target.

Magnus tried to escape his captors' grasp, but they overpowered him easily. At his side, Karl's body twitched, then grew still.

More foes darted among Magnus's men, cutting them down with brutal efficiency. A few of his warriors formed a shield wall near the ship's mainmast, but they were outnumbered three to one. Axes thudded against shields, arrows whooshed through the air, and men screamed as they fell. In moments, it was all over.

The two men holding Magnus bound his hands behind his back, and then Anders was facing him again. He tilted Magnus's head back, forced his mouth open, and removed the gag. More cannons fired into the night, and a few screams came from a nearby ship.

"Why?" Magnus growled.

Anders grinned. "You chose Frida as your queen. Now, I'm making myself king."

"You traitorous bastard!" Magnus shouted.

Anders backhanded him across the face. "I'll have you go down with your ship, as any good captain should. You don't have to be alive for it, though."

"Queen Frida will take your head for this."

"I'd like to see her try." The knife was in Anders's hand again, and he drew it across Magnus's throat. Warm blood spilled from the cut. Marcus slumped to the deck, and everything went black.

The Aftermath

"He's doomed us all," Frida muttered.

Ahead of her, ships were burning on the surface of the water. Other ships were sinking, taking water faster than her men could repair them. And to the north-west, long gaps in the lines marked the places where many of her vessels had already sunk beneath the waves.

Farther to the left, Anders's fleet sailed away into the night.

Seven of her own sixteen warships were lost, her flagship among them. Two had been sunk by cannonballs shot from close range, the others set on fire by Anders's men. One more was engulfed in flames, and her men were bravely trying to put out the fire. Her nine fishing ships were untouched, but that was small consolation. They only carried two cannons each.

First my king, then my fleet, she thought. *And it all happened on my watch.*

She'd only left small crews aboard her ships, while most of her sailors camped on the beach. They'd been taken by surprise when the first fires started.

Anders's fleet had anchored at the mouth of the bay. Whether he'd planned it or not, she did not know, but he'd made good use of it. He'd pulled his crews back to their ships without her noticing, and had struck quickly and decisively. Some of his men had set the other captains' ships ablaze; others had detonated barrels of powder against the ships' hulls;

and yet others had boarded five ships, overcome their crews, and were sailing them out of the bay.

And, of course, he'd fired his cannons into the ships closest to his own. Sigurd's, Lothar's, and two of Frida's. And cannon fire from such close range was devastating.

How fiercely loyal Anders's men must have been, to do a thing like this.

If only they'd been loyal to me instead. But only two days ago he called himself king, and me his queen, and I rejected him. She'd suspected his men would hold that against her, but she hadn't expected anything like this.

A loud explosion came from the burning galley to her right, and a tongue of flame shot up into the air. The blaze had reached the ship's gunpowder stores. There was nothing to be done after that.

"You still have eight of your warships," Lothar said at her side. His guards and Frida's surrounded them in a loose circle, ready to protect them with their lives. "I'm down to six. And ten fishing ships. And Sigurd has fared the worst of us all."

"How bad?"

"Only a dozen of his ships remain." He had set sail with thirty. "And only four of those are heavily armed."

To make matters worse, Anders had also stolen Sigurd's flagship and King Knut's former flagship. And though Sigurd roared and raged as the betrayer fled into the distance, he wasn't about to give chase.

Frida turned to Lothar. "We're broken, my friend. I don't think we can recover from this."

"We still have most of our men," he replied. Anders and his fellow traitors hadn't fired their cannons upon the beach. Then again, perhaps his men would have disobeyed him if he gave *that* order, and put an end to his betrayal.

"We must have lost hundreds. If not more." Some had perished in the fighting, others trying to put out the fires. "Not counting the cowards who did this."

"That leaves us with over sixteen thousand. And three hundred cannons, give or take a few. I wouldn't count us out yet."

"We can't even beat Anders." He had more warships and more cannons now, though only half the men.

Lothar looked into the distance, where the traitor's fleet sailed away with the tide. "You have to admit that it was a very effective strike."

"Is that *admiration* I hear in your voice?"

"It was swift and sudden, with minimal losses. Pretty much like the best of our raids. It would have made Njord proud."

"Except that this one was against him."

"There's that, aye."

"And to think the traitor wanted me to marry him!"

"If you did, he would have killed you in your sleep and blamed it on some foreign assassin. Njord would have died with you. And then we'd be godless, with Anders as our king."

She looked him in the eye. "We are Njord's last hope, Lothar. Us and Gunnar, and we still don't know where Gunnar is. And this blow has weakened us greatly."

Lothar ran his fingers through his beard. "That bloody Anders. I wonder who he's fighting for."

"It can't be the Lady," Frida answered, "though it must have been her archers who killed Ursula." How they'd gotten past her patrols and close enough to make their shots, she did not know. "She stands for honor and chivalry, and this was a dishonorable act. Queen Marion would string him up before she thanked him, though his actions helped her. No. It must be Serya Krov, the god of the vampires."

"And now Anders is taking his cannons to those monsters. They'll use them to tear Queen Marion's castles down."

Frida nodded. "And when the knights sally out, the bloodsuckers will overwhelm them with their strength and with their servants' numbers." She grinned as the thought hit her. "Unless Queen Marion had cannons of her own."

Lothar eyed her as if she'd grown a pair of horns. "Did you just say that out loud?"

She nodded again. "I need to think it through. But we'll sail through this storm together, my friend, and we'll find ourselves stronger on the other side. I am certain of it."

The Reward

Anders Svensson entered his cabin and found Katrina, the fourth of Serya Krov's champions, sitting on the edge of his bed.

Naked.

Desire stirred within him, as if he'd been fifteen years younger. His heart beat faster as he looked her up and down.

She'd changed her looks, though only slightly. King Knut's former lover used to paint her lips blue, yet now they were an intense red. Her muscles had hardened, just the way Anders liked them. Her neck was longer now, her chin smoother, her eyes wider. There was more red in her hair, and she still wore that hairpin, which she could turn into a deadly weapon in a heartbeat. She'd pressed it against his neck the first time they'd spoken, before showing him her fangs.

Perhaps some of his men might recognize her, if they paid attention. But very few of Anders's sailors had met King Knut's lover. Besides, they were fiercely loyal to him. They'd believe anything he'd tell them.

She smiled at him, her fangs showing. "You were magnificent."

"So, you won't kill me tonight?" He'd asked her the same question the night before.

"Why would I? You're fighting for my god. Now get naked."

He pulled his shirt over his head. "So, it's true. Once we win, I am to be made king over my people."

She nodded. "With me as your queen."

He stepped out of his boots. "I couldn't think of a better one."

Katrina raised an eyebrow. "Only two days ago, you were pining for Big Frida, the bear slayer."

"You're better than her. Much better. And I only wanted her for her men." And for her breasts, too, though he wouldn't say that out loud, not to a woman who could rip his head from his shoulders. "It's a shame they all have to die."

"Not by your hand. Once we win, you'll be a hero to your people."

He unlaced his trousers. "As I deserve to be."

"I knew you had potential," she said, "from the first time I laid my eyes upon you. And tonight, you fulfilled it. You showed me what you're capable of."

He advanced toward her, as naked as she was.

"You'll get your reward," she said. "But first, you'll pay the blood price. As all men must."

She had warned him of it. He exposed his neck without hesitation, and her fangs sank into his flesh. There was no pain, though his knees weakened as she took a deep draught.

She pulled back and licked her lips. Then she took his hand and guided him to his bed.

"I used to think your kind didn't mate with ours," he said as she climbed on top of him.

She smiled. "You'll give me pleasure, as King Knut did. *More* than he did. Besides," she said as her sharp talons traveled across his chest, "you're the king of your people now. And Serya Krov will see your devotion rewarded."

I can do this, Anders thought as she caressed his face. Her talons swept from left to right, mere inches away from his eyes.

He was playing a dangerous game. If she decided to kill him, now or later, he couldn't stop her. His only chance was to prove himself valuable. Luckily for him, he had something that her god wanted: his people's loyalty.

They'll accept me as their king. No one was better suited for it;

certainly not Queen Frida, nor any of the others. He'd demand that they paid the blood price, and they would obey him. In return, they'd be elevated as one of Serya Krov's favored people, second only to the vampires themselves. They'd keep ruling the seas, as the vampires ruled the sky.

Without Anders, the vampire god would face centuries of resistance from a hardened people. That, or having to purge Hemland of every living soul. He didn't want either, and had said so explicitly.

Katrina's talons flashed over Anders's chest, and one of them broke his skin. He gasped, forcing himself to smile as she licked her lips. "I thought I'd paid the blood price already."

She winked. "Don't spoil my fun, my king. You won't miss another drop or two."

He chose his words carefully. "I'll give you that and more, my queen. I'll give you rivers of blood. We'll spill it together, you and I."

He had three tasks, and none of them were easy. He had to keep himself in Katrina's good graces, and she was a bit too fond of killing, so he had to be careful. He had to help the vampire god win the War of the Seven; and for that, he had forty ships, four hundred and sixty-eight cannons, eight thousand loyal men, and the help of the noble vampires and their countless serfs. And, finally, he had to convince the Islanders of the righteousness of his actions, once he returned to Hemland as their king.

All in all, it was a hard challenge. But Anders was a hard man, and he was cunning. And since that night when he'd killed his three older cousins as they tried to kill him, days before his ninth birthday, he'd been a survivor. He would survive this as well, and his people would benefit from it for centuries to follow.

He thought of this and grinned. Then Katrina lowered herself onto him, and all thoughts of the future slipped from his mind.

It was time to enjoy the present, with its glorious reward.

The Gods and their Champions

The Lady: Queen Marion, High Priestess Sandra, Eugene the Trickster, Sir Galahad

Njord: ~~King Knut~~, Queen Frida, ~~Ursula~~, Gunnar

Serya Krov: Queen Elena, Duke Zoltan Barko, Kirill Skromnik, Katrina

Aljin: to be revealed

Augustus: to be revealed

Grok the All-Father: to be revealed

Malleon: to be revealed

Bonus Content

Congratulations! You've finished Part Two.

To explore the bonus content, including the evolving campaign map, a small image gallery, and the song *King Knut's Final Swim*, visit https://bradtowers.com/wots-bonus-2/ or scan this QR code:

Part 3: The Trickster God

Champions of the Gods

Seven days earlier, on the gods' divine island.

Augustus, the trickster god of the Julian Empire, watched the other six gods in turn.

Only moments earlier, they'd sealed the Godly Pact with their essence. All that remained was for them to choose their champions and share their names with the others.

At Augustus's side, Njord frowned, perhaps uncertain of his choices. Serya Krov seemed relaxed, as did Aljin, the desert men's god; no doubt they'd chosen their champions already. Grok's enormous muscles bulged, as if he was readying himself for a fight, though others would have to fight for him.

As for Malleon, the god of the giants, he was staring at the Lady.

Augustus followed his gaze.

He looked the Lady up and down, a pleasant experience overall. She was green from head to toe; as green as Njord was blue, if not more. Her green hair, a few shades darker than her skin, reached her waist and fluttered gently in the breeze. Her wavy dress was dark green and reached down slightly below the knee, showing off her delicate ankles. Everything about her was green, save for the whites of her eyes, her deliciously red lips, and the golden pendant hanging from her neck.

He took a deep breath. She even *smelled* green, like the dewy grass in the morning.

As for her face… No words could do justice to her beauty. Countless mortals would give their lives just to see her face and spend a few moments in her company. Such was her power, and her followers weren't the only ones who were seduced by it.

Perhaps—

She's using her glamor, he realized, and suddenly he was an observer again. Unlike Malleon, who kept on staring.

Augustus grinned. *She's trying to charm him. To gain an advantage over him.*

The Lady flashed Malleon her most enchanting smile, and Augustus knew the power of those smiles. It was time to put a stop to this.

"Malleon!" he shouted.

Malleon flinched, before slowly turning to him. "Yes?"

"Have you chosen your champions yet?"

"I… have," Malleon rumbled.

"Good. I thought you'd fallen asleep there for a moment."

"I was just… contemplating," Malleon replied. "And chose the wrong moment for it." He nodded. "Thank you, Augustus."

Augustus nodded back. "You're welcome, friend." *I've snapped him out of his trance.*

He flashed the Lady a triumphant smile, and she looked away.

Malleon cleared his throat. "And now it's time to reveal our champions' names."

"It is," the Lady said. "We'll speak to them tonight, and tell them of the great struggle, and of the parts they have to play. Tomorrow, the War of the Seven will begin." Her gaze darted from one god to the other. "The names, then. Grok, would you go first?"

The orc god's chest puffed with pride, as if he'd been chosen for a far more meaningful task. "King Ghark Bloodaxe. For the priest, Hagor the Sniffer. The witch Rorra Fireborn. And, of course, Krakkar the Fist, my fourth and final champion." He turned to Malleon. "Let's see your warriors beat that one, my friend."

Augustus knew the name, and the story. Alone on a bear hunt three years earlier, Krakkar had wandered onto the wrong side of the mountain and had stumbled into one of the giants' slumber caves. They'd rushed him, and he had no choice but to draw steel. It was said he killed ten of them in honest battle, before escaping and returning to his camp.

"I'll go next," Augustus said. "Lucius Antonius, the Boy Emperor. Marcus Severus, the High Priest of Ares. And my next two choices will surprise you."

"Leticia and...?" the Lady asked.

Of course, she'd had to guess right on the first try. He repressed a biting retort and continued. "Leticia Alba, the Bringer of the Harvest. And Selenius Gracchus."

"I don't know that one," Njord said.

"A skilled bureaucrat," Augustus said. "He can squeeze gold out of stone, even better than your pirates — and he does it with words instead of blades."

"You're thinking of the long game," said Aljin, who liked to call himself the sun god. A convenient lie that his followers believed. "But you may not get one. My names. King Ammon bin Zuybar, though I wish Zuybar himself were still alive for this. Nasir bin Fatih, the king's confidant, whose arrows fly true as if the Lady guided them herself. The wizard Achmad bin Fayzal. And Al-Khanjar, the Black Blade, my people's most skilled assassin."

"Ah," Augustus said. "So that's why you agreed so quickly that the fourth champion is not to be exposed."

Aljin nodded. "You can't reveal him to your followers, for we're bound to it through our Godly Pact. What do you say now, old friend?"

"I say my Julians have the best guards," Augustus answered, more confidently than he felt. "I say, send Al-Khanjar against us and you'll lose him."

"Perhaps I won't," Aljin replied noncommittally. "How about your champions, Njord?"

The sea god shook his head. "Lady first."

"You'd have guessed them all, I'm sure," the Lady said. "Queen

Marion. High Priestess Sandra, her twin sister. The wizard Eugene the Trickster."

Augustus nodded at that, being a trickster himself.

"And for my fourth champion," the Lady continued, "Sir Galahad, my Paladin."

Serya Krov laughed. "That old man will piss his breeches and fall off his horse when my nobles come swooping at him."

The Lady answered his challenge. "If I recall correctly, Sir Godric was even older when he put that lance through your pet Dragos's heart."

"Not *his* heart," the vampire god said, and left it at that.

Njord spoke next. "King Knut Haraldsson. Captain Frida Gretasdottir for my priest. Ursula Gudrunsdottir, the sea witch. And Old Gunnar Sigurdsson."

"Old Gunnar?" asked Grok, the All-Father of the orcs. "I thought that one defies you. He doesn't even dye his hair blue."

"He dyes his beard," Njord replied, "and he braids it, too. It will have to do."

"Fewer men than women," Serya Krov said.

The sea god frowned. "Two and two. Wait. Who are you calling a woman, Gunnar or King Knut?"

"He's calling one of them dead," Malleon said, and Augustus understood. Aljin was not the only god with an assassin in play. "And you can't stop it, Njord. You're bound by our Godly Pact."

The sea god huffed, and the ensuing gust of wind bent half of the palm trees in the grove, almost to the point of breaking. Not beyond it, though, as that would have angered the Lady. And Augustus judged that a god with only three champions soon to be left in play wouldn't want to make fresh enemies.

"Which one?" Njord asked as the wind died down.

"You'll find out soon enough," Serya Krov replied. "Malleon, you go first."

Malleon rattled off the names. "King Tassadar. Paeren the priest. The wizard Neressia. And Eldris the Duelist." He turned to Grok. "Let's see your Krakkar the Fist beat that one, my friend."

"He will," Grok answered the challenge. "But perhaps not right away. Maybe I'll have him start with humans, or vampires, and work his way up."

"I pity the fool who has to rouse Eldris from his slumber," Augustus said. "I'd love to see that for myself," he added on an impulse.

"Be my guest if you like," Malleon answered. "Just watch yourself, so that he doesn't step on you."

Augustus could have taken the bait. He could have drawn himself up to a height where his head reached the clouds, with one of his feet alone covering the whole beach — but now was not the time for that. Instead, he chuckled. "Good one, old friend. I'll be sad to see you go, when the time comes."

"And I you," answered Malleon.

"Which one?" Njord asked again, his eyes fixed upon Serya Krov.

"First, my names," Serya Krov answered. "Elena Kylareva, the heartless queen. The priest Kirill Skromnik, her loyal servant. Formerly one of yours, Lady, if I am not mistaken?"

The Lady glared at him.

"For my wizard, Duke Zoltan Barko," the vampire god continued, "who's more than a match for any of your champions. Even for yours, Malleon. And the fourth, the name you've been waiting for, Njord. Unlike your men, you would know her as Katrina."

The sea god paled a little at that, his face turning to a lighter shade of blue. Then, just like that, the pallor was gone.

"So, you see, friend," Serya Krov said. "Fewer men than women for you. Deny it if you can."

Njord shook his head.

"We're done here, then," said Grok. "I'll go and rouse my warriors."

Malleon placed a hand on his shoulder. "Not until tonight. You know the rules."

Grok gave him a light shove that would have uprooted a tree. "Of course I know the bloody rules, Malleon! I'll go prepare my words. That's what I meant and you know it. All of you."

"We do," the Lady said. "Go swiftly now, Grok the All-Father, and may we meet again. In a thousand years, if not before."

"May we meet again," Grok answered, and disappeared in a puff of smoke.

"May we meet again," Njord said, and leaped into the sea.

"May we meet again," Augustus said, and soared into the sky. After all, he had his own rousing words to prepare.

The Desert Priest

The day after the gods' meeting

Nasir bin Fatih, high priest of Aljin and the second of his champions, wiped the sweat off his brow and pulled an arrow from his quiver.

His king, Ammon bin Zuybar, stood at his side, silent as a statue. Ahead, the rolling dunes, sculpted by the winds, lined the horizon. Here and there, hardy shrubs emerged from the golden sands. The distant oasis seemed like a dream, a promise of relief in the vast expanse of the desert. All was quiet, save for the soft breathing of Nasir and Ammon's horses, which stood obediently a few steps behind.

"You're sweating more than usual, Nasir," King Ammon's voice broke the silence.

"Aljin is blessing us with his gaze," Nasir replied.

"He's overdoing it a bit. Perhaps without meaning to. You should speak to him about it."

Nasir shook his head. "The sun god makes no mistakes, my king. Everything he does is according to his divine will." Of course, his king was only taunting him.

He nocked the arrow, his movement as natural as breathing. After all, he'd done it a thousand thousand times. Eighty paces ahead, a desert hare advanced cautiously toward the nearest shrub, unaware of the swift death that was about to descend upon it.

"That one's a bit far," Ammon said. "You might miss, my friend."

"You know me better than that, my king," Nasir answered the challenge. A slight wind blew from the right, but that didn't matter either. He'd made harder shots than this one in the heat of battle.

He drew, adjusted his aim, and loosed. The arrow flew true and took the hare through the neck, just as he had intended.

"We'll take the next one at a gallop," Ammon said. "A race, if you agree to it."

"I do," Nasir said.

They mounted their horses and spurred them into a gallop across the sands at Ammon's signal. The next hare was over three hundred paces away. They closed the distance swiftly, side by side, and though the creature tried to flee, there was no place for it to hide.

It was a race that Nasir could win, if he wanted to. But he meant to build up his king's confidence. So, he took too long to aim, and Ammon's arrow left his bow an instant before his own.

They both struck the hare in the back, one after the other, and Nasir knew each shot would have been fatal.

"You've won this one, my king," he said as they pulled up. He dismounted, retrieved the arrows, and handed Ammon his prize.

"By less than half a heartbeat." Ammon stuffed the hare into one of his saddlebags. "Next time we'll hunt with hawks."

They rode back, and Nasir retrieved the other hare along the way.

"A good shot, that one," Ammon said. "Soon we'll be hunting two-legged creatures, my friend."

"The question is which ones," Nasir replied as he climbed back into the saddle.

He knew what Ammon's father would have chosen. But King Zuybar was gone from this world, taken by a fever three months earlier. Ammon held the power now.

He would have made a great king, given more time, Nasir mused. At thirty-two, Ammon had the strength and vigor of youth, was tested in battle more than a dozen times, and had been educated by the foremost scholars of the desert men, including Nasir himself. But he had yet to acquire the quiet wisdom that came from decades of experience.

Zuybar died before his time. I hope this challenge will not prove too much for his son.

Ammon pondered his question. "We do not have to decide that just yet."

There were at least two possible meanings to his words. So, Nasir remained silent and waited for Ammon to speak again.

"I'll take most of our mounted forces to the eastern border," Ammon said. "Fifteen thousand riders in all. As for the infantry, I'll leave ten thousand warriors in the capital, and five thousand more to defend the floodgates."

"And the rest?" Nasir asked.

"A sixth of our warriors will guard our western border and punish the vampires if they choose to come our way. You could lead that force if you wanted to."

Nasir longed for vengeance against the vampires. Back in his mid-thirties, during his three-year captivity in the Bloodriver province, his skin had turned gray from the repeated bloodlettings. After King Zuybar had led a daring raid to rescue him and had brought him back to good health, he'd implored the sun god to restore his olive tan, but his prayers were met with silence. Then again, Aljin had a reason for everything he did, or chose not to.

Yet vengeance was not the most important thing, not when the fate of the sun god himself hung in the balance. Nasir shook his head. "My place is by your side, my prince."

"King." There was steel in Ammon's voice. "I know you miss my father, Nasir. But he's not with us anymore."

Nasir bowed his head. "Apologies, my king. I was lost in a memory for a moment."

"You're forgiven, my friend," Ammon spoke in a gentler tone. "I miss him too."

It was time for Nasir to bring their focus back to the upcoming war. "So, we shall ride to the eastern border. Do you mean the Bane, or the

Road of Bones?"

"The Bane," Ammon said. It was an inland province, bordering both the Julian Empire and the Howling Rocks, one of the lands of the orcs. Many battles had been fought in the Bane over the centuries, and the ruthless sands had devoured the corpses of the vanquished.

"I expect the orcs to march against the Julians in great numbers," Ammon continued. "They'll tear each other apart. And after the first clashes are done, we'll ride out from the desert and move against the survivors."

"It is a good plan," Nasir agreed.

"Our enemies may have the advantage of numbers. But we will strike quickly, like the desert snakes. We'll vanish and make them come after us. And if we draw them into the desert, we'll have the upper hand. Even against the orcs."

Nasir nodded. "They'll have no chance against us among the sands. Then, when these enemies are spent, perhaps we should move against the vampires?"

"If the Lady's followers don't crush them first. Or the orcs, if they decide to split their forces."

"And when all is done, the sun god will rule over the world for a thousand years."

Ammon sat taller in the saddle. "I am not my father, Nasir. But I am well-trained, and I have Aljin's favor, just as he did. I'll let the other gods' followers destroy each other, and choose the right moment to strike, time after time. I will choose wisely. And in the end, we will prevail."

"We will," Nasir agreed. "Your father will be watching you from his place in the night sky, my king. I am certain you'll make him proud."

A Giant Awakens

In the deepest of the giants' slumber caves, Eldris the Duelist roared as his eyes snapped open.

Another giant leaned over him; a priest, chanting the final words of the awakening spell. He was older than Eldris, and bald, except for a single braid of white hair sticking up from the top of his head. His arms and chest were bare. He wore a bearskin as his loincloth, and a long brown cape that hung from a thick furry neckpiece. A rusty iron belt completed his outfit.

In one swift move, Eldris sat up and shoved the old priest with both hands, sending him sprawling into the nearest wall. "Why?" he growled as he stood from his resting place. "Why me? Why now?"

The priest groaned as he staggered to his feet, and rubbed his back where he'd hit the wall. "You didn't have to do that."

"Paeren," Eldris said, remembering the priest from his last awakening. Back then, Paeren had far fewer wrinkles and didn't smell like an old mountain goat. "Tell me why."

"Our god needs you," Paeren said.

"Of course he does. Couldn't he have waited a little longer? I was in the midst of a magnificent dream."

He closed his eyes for a long moment, savoring the memory. His sword, *that* sword, singing as it cut through the air.

He opened his eyes again and wrinkled his nose as Paeren drew near.

"I was fighting a three-way battle. Against Elena the Heartless, the young vampire queen, and some Paladin. And I was winning."

"It wasn't just a dream," Paeren said in a solemn voice. "It was a portent of what is to come."

"So, Elena's still the vampire queen?" Eldris growled. "How soon did you wake me?"

"You've been asleep for four hundred and fifty-seven years."

But vampires don't live that long, Eldris thought. *Or, at least, they didn't use to.* Then again, many things could have changed in four centuries and a half.

He wiped his eyes, shaking away the last remains of his slumber, and noticed the five giants gathered behind the priest. Three were younglings, less than two hundred years old, the tallest of them carrying a torch. The fourth had to be the wizard Neressia, his former lover, though she looked at least three centuries older. And the fifth… Could this be?

"Tassadar?" he asked. "Is that you?"

The giant he'd spoken to stood under one of the six torches that were set high on the walls. His face hadn't changed much over the years, save for a deepening of lines in his skin, a vivid purple hue with no sign of blue, and the length of his white beard, which now reached his belt. And the cape draped around his shoulders… was it really…?

"It's King Tassadar now," his friend replied.

"I'm sorry," Eldris said. "About your father." In his dream, he'd been wearing the royal cape himself, but he wasn't going to tell his friend *that*. Besides, he'd never held such ambitions. "How did he die?"

"He died well," Tassadar answered. "In battle, fighting the orcs. Over three centuries ago."

"And you didn't wake me for it."

"It was Father's choice not to. He said he would respect your wish." Like many of his kind, Eldris wanted to see what the far future would bring. And the only way to do that, without expiring of old age, was to retreat into the deep sleep as the centuries passed him by, and to be woken only when his kin, or his god, needed him.

Apparently, he was needed now.

"I will mourn his passing," Eldris said. He turned to the priest. "You said my dream was a portent. So, we're marching to war against the vampires. And against the Lady's people, too?"

"It's more than that," Neressia interjected. "We're fighting everyone. And if we don't win, we'll lose our god for a thousand years. And perhaps this world as well."

"I'll tell him myself, Neressia," King Tassadar said.

He did, and Eldris could not believe his ears. A great war was about to begin, and at least two of Malleon's champions had to survive until the end. If they succeeded, their god would battle a powerful deity for the fate of the world.

Tassadar had learned it all from Malleon himself. After that, it had taken eight days for Paeren to rouse Eldris from his slumber, for the awakening from the long sleep could not be rushed.

They were all gathered in this room, the four champions. King Tassadar; the wizard Neressia; Paeren the priest, the earliest-born of them all; and Eldris himself.

"How many warriors do we have?" Eldris asked.

"Ten thousand roaming the mountain's side," Tassadar said. "A third of them are already here, near the caves. I sent runners to gather the others."

"Another ten thousand taking the long sleep," Neressia added. "And a hundred priests working hard on waking them. It will take them a year to wake them all."

"A bit longer than that," Paeren the priest said. "But once we finish, we can beat anyone."

"But not everyone," Neressia added.

"I see," Eldris said. "So, we must choose our battles, and wait for the other kingdoms to weaken each other while we get stronger, yes?"

Tassadar nodded. "As you say, friend."

"You are Malleon's secret weapon, Eldris," Paeren said. "His fourth champion, the one that the other gods cannot reveal to their followers.

Our people's greatest warrior. And you, Eldris, you'll have a weapon of your own."

He strode to the wall on his right and set his palm against it at eye level, and the wall opened. A shallow vertical gap revealed itself, stretching from floor to ceiling. Inside it stood a two-handed greatsword, longer than Eldris was tall, with its grip painted purple.

He recognized it instantly. He'd been wielding it in his dream.

"I can't believe it!" His heart beat faster. "This is—"

"The Reaping Blade." Paeren pulled the sword from its hiding spot. "Forged by Malleon himself from the heart of a dying star. The only weapon that can kill a god."

He handed it over to Eldris, who tested its balance. He grinned. "It's perfect. I never thought I'd get to wield it myself."

Two of the younger giants leaned forward, eager to get a better look at the sword. The third took a step back. Then another, and another.

There was something strange in his eyes. Fear, perhaps?

Eldris pointed the Reaping Blade toward him. "Where are you going, friend?"

The retreating giant whirled around and broke into a run.

"Stop him!" Eldris roared, and gave chase, sword in hand.

He ran as fast as he could, as did the others after him, but the fleeing giant was unnaturally fast. Eldris followed him all the way to the entrance of the cave, where the giant took a mighty leap and soared into the air.

The Julian God

Augustus, the god of the Julians, broke into laughter as he rose into the sky.

"He meant to ambush me!" he shouted. "Me, the trickster god! The nerve of that Sleepy One!"

He shed his giant disguise and shifted into Ares, the Julian god of war, complete with his orange armor and his lightning-tipped spear. The giants below would see the transformation and notice his new color and his smaller size, but that didn't bother him.

He thought of the last meeting of the gods, when they'd discussed the upcoming war. Back then, Malleon had allowed him to witness Eldris the Duelist's awakening. Only to have his champions meet him with the Reaping Blade; the only god-killing weapon in existence, thought to have been hidden by the Supreme One himself, in a secret place outside space and time. At least that's what Malleon had told him centuries earlier.

He must have lied, Augustus thought. *Or maybe the Supreme One brought it back and returned it to him.*

Either way, it doesn't matter. I escaped.

If things were different, I would have fought them. I would have destroyed them all without breaking a sweat. But he was bound by Godly Pact. He couldn't hurt Malleon's champions, and they had no such restrictions placed upon them.

He enjoyed shifting into Ares. He'd modeled him after Grok the All-

Father, when he'd created the Julian pantheon — except for choosing a human appearance. Back then, impersonating other gods had been his favorite pastime.

The six gods had been amused by his deception, and Augustus had quickly bound them in Godly Pact to keep it secret from all mortals. And so, for ten centuries, the Julian people had worshiped his creations. They'd prayed to them, received their wisdom, and built great temples in their honor.

They would never learn that their whole pantheon was a great lie, and that all the Julian gods were simply Augustus's disguises, which he wore as he saw fit. Ares had been the first, and many more had followed.

It's not Ares I need right now, Augustus thought.

He turned to his right, heading toward the Julian Empire, and shifted into Athina, the goddess of wisdom. On other worlds, she'd been a war goddess as well. On this one, having Ares was enough.

He was high enough that the giants below wouldn't notice the change. They'd only see a dot in the sky, if they were still looking.

Using Athina's keen mind, Augustus saw the encounter with Malleon's champions in a new light.

If Malleon wanted me dead, he could have had one of his followers take me by surprise. He could have told his priest to take the sword from its hiding place and give it to another of his kin. A lesser giant, one who I wouldn't be expecting at the event, so that I wouldn't be surprised to find him missing.

That giant could have come later, keeping the blade hidden. He could have struck me from behind as I watched the four champions, and that would have been the end of it. And Malleon is certainly clever enough to think of such things.

Perhaps he didn't want me dead after all. Perhaps he wants us to be allies, at least for a while, and he chose to show me his secret to gain my trust. He wants me to remember this as I watch his champions make their next moves.

And perhaps he wanted to intimidate me as well.

There was something else. *He told me to watch myself, so that Eldris doesn't step on me. Was that some kind of warning?*

Augustus grinned, still wearing Athina's disguise. *Well played, my friend. I'll miss you when you're gone.*

He wasn't going to share this with any of the other gods. They were his rivals now. And, no matter what else came to pass, he was going to stay far, far away from that blade.

Al-Khanjar, the Assassin

Two hours after sunset, atop the roof of a three-story Julian villa, Al-Khanjar crouched low and watched the gates of Athina's temple. Lucius Antonius, the Boy Emperor, had entered it a hundred and thirty heartbeats earlier, along with a dozen of his guards.

"Nothing is forbidden to us," Al-Khanjar whispered. It was the first part of the Assassin's Tenet.

"And everything is as we make it," the hooded man at his side whispered back. He had no name; Al-Khanjar only knew him as Arrow.

"We work in the darkness," Al-Khanjar said, "to do the sun god's will. We are assassins."

They were six in all, the other four scattered on the rooftops of neighboring villas. Each of them was worth ten Julian soldiers. They all wore black, and had painted their skin in the dark gray color of their trade. And tonight, the sky was filled with clouds. They'd be little more than shadows.

The blade of Al-Khanjar's sword was black, as was that of his dagger. His weapons had earned him the moniker Black Blade. In minutes, one of them would taste the blood of an emperor.

Nine days, he'd taken. Two, to gather his men and tell them of the great war, and of the part they had to play. Four more to learn the target's movements, using coin, torture, and deception to further his goal. Three more to plan their mission. And now he was ready to strike.

His hawk, Vengeance, was at his side. A gift from Zuybar, King Ammon's father, granted days before he'd passed away. Black as the night was the bird, except for its dark brown chest. But nobody would see it now.

Al-Khanjar released it. *Fly, Vengeance. Watch us from the sky.*

The bird soared into the air, and moments later, he lost sight of it. It would find him the next day. It always did, after a mission.

It was time. He looked left, then right—

—the hawk Vengeance let out a hoarse screech—

—and a new procession rounded a corner and marched toward the temple at a quick pace. Seven men, six of them wearing armor and plumed helmets, carrying spears and large rectangular shields. Augustian Guards, the elite soldiers of the empire.

The man leading them was one of Al-Khanjar's targets. Marcus Severus, High Priest of Ares, Commander of the Augustian Guards, Stout Defender of the Empire, and the second champion of the Julian gods. Al-Khanjar had seen him twice before, years earlier, when the desert men and the Julians were at peace.

He was powerfully built and taller than most Julians, though four inches shorter than Al-Khanjar. He wore a sleeveless vest and a cape that reached his ankles, and carried a scepter in his right hand and a slow-burning torch in his left. He'd grown heavier than Al-Khanjar remembered him, but that was no reason to underestimate him.

On another night, Al-Khanjar would have called off the attack. There were too many unknowns. But on this night, he'd take out two champions at once.

He waited until Marcus Severus and his men reached the temple gates. Marcus spoke briefly with the two soldiers standing guard. Then he and his group disappeared inside.

Al-Khanjar let five dozen heartbeats pass. Enough so that the attack would take his targets by surprise.

He nodded to Arrow, who readied his bow, pulled two arrows from his quiver, and nocked one. Two guards, two arrows. And Arrow never missed.

It was time. Al-Khanjar rose to his feet and leaped forward from the rooftop.

Before nightfall, he'd left a cart on the street below. It was loaded with bales of hay. It would cushion his fall — and the guards hadn't thought to move it.

As he fell, he heard the familiar whoosh, and knew that Arrow had let his arrow fly.

The Stout Defender

Athina's temple consisted of a series of rooms and corridors, spiraling toward the altar room. They were decorated with ancient sculptures and more recent drawings, and lit by the sun's gaze during the day and by slow-burning torches between dusk and dawn. Thousands of Julians visited the temple daily. At night it was closed to all, except for the empire's ruling class and their trusted men.

Two hidden passages offered faster access to the altar room. They were known only to the senior members of the Augustian Guards, and used in times of great urgency. They'd served their purpose twice, two centuries earlier. Maintenance was done in secrecy, by the senior guard members themselves, on a rigorous monthly schedule.

Marcus Severus did not use the passages, not yet. There seemed to be no need for it.

He took the long way instead, his footsteps echoing onto the marble floor, his men following him. In the next room, he found an empty torch stand and left his torch there.

He passed the Boy Emperor's guards; first two, then four, then four again. He found the last two at the entrance of the altar chamber. They uncrossed their spears and pushed the heavy doors open, and Marcus and his guards strode into the room.

Inside, Lucius Antonius, the Boy Emperor, knelt on a soft cushion in front of Athina's altar. The statue of the goddess, twice as tall as he was, watched him silently.

The Boy Emperor leaped to his feet, whirled around, and met Marcus with a smile. "Ah. It is you, my friend."

He was fifteen, and truly his father's son. Average in height at five foot three, he surpassed most of his subjects in intelligence. He had this curiosity about him, and at times his questions and his ideas bewildered the empire's foremost scholars. In the past year, he'd designed a more powerful ballista and a new way to lift heavy loads across a mountain's side. He had also started thinking about the inner workings of the human body, and about how one could stave off aging. He'd taken to speaking with Athina about his ideas and visited her temple every other day.

"She's not here, Marcus," he said. "She told me she'd be here tonight, waiting for me at the appointed hour. And she's never late."

Marcus snapped his fingers and his men turned, facing the doors, their weapons at the ready. His fears had been right.

"There can only be one reason for it, Your Majesty," he said. "She can't be here because she's bound by Godly Pact. She can't interfere when the fates of our champions are at stake."

"That means I'm in danger," Lucius said as he advanced toward Marcus. He frowned. "Not from you, I think."

"We must have enemies in our midst," Marcus said. He'd had a premonition, less than ten minutes earlier. Not one given by the gods; it was his decades of experience that had aroused his instincts. He'd grabbed the first squad of guards he'd found and rushed to the temple, leaving word for others to follow.

"Do we wait for them here?" Lucius asked. "Or will you take me back to the palace?"

"We'll head back. But not yet. I have more men coming. Close the doors," Marcus said over his shoulder.

The guards outside pulled the doors closed. A moment later, a light thud came from the hallway.

"Bar them!" Marcus shouted.

Before his men could act, the doors burst open.

Four men stood on the doorstep, all taller than Marcus and dressed in black, their faces painted gray. Two of them wielded swords, a third carried a heavy axe, and the fourth was hooded and had an arrow nocked to his bow.

He released it and one of Marcus's men fell. Adris, who'd just transferred into the squad. The other five closed ranks and raised their shields, hiding Marcus and his emperor from their enemies. The tips of their spears peeked above their shields.

It was the Augustian Wall, a battle formation that few men could break. But these attackers were no ordinary men.

"Pull back!" Marcus shouted. Then three of the four black-clad men rushed forward.

They struck first, the Julians blocking their blows with their shields. Actius stabbed his spear forward, and the enemy swordsman facing him howled in pain. But one of his companions hooked the guard's shield with the head of his axe and yanked it away from him, and a moment later, an arrow pierced Actius's throat.

Silas threw his spear. It flew true, but at the last moment, the archer twisted to the right. The spear struck his left shoulder, yet it did not kill him, and the man did not scream.

He dropped his bow, pulled out the spear, threw it to the ground, and darted toward Silas. As he ran, twin daggers dropped from his sleeves into his hands.

He was fast. Too fast. Silas parried his first two strikes with his shield and pulled out his short sword. But the man knelt, quick as a snake, and Silas screamed.

That assassin stabbed him in the foot, Marcus thought.

Silas swung his shield downward, perhaps hoping to break his opponent's arm — and the man with the axe seized his chance. He slashed at just the right moment and struck Silas's head clean off his shoulders.

They've practiced this before, Marcus realized as his man's head landed at his feet.

The last three guards held their own for now, deflecting their enemies' swords with their spears and shields. Young Olivian muttered under his breath as he fought, and Marcus knew what would come. But they were already outnumbered, and though two of the black-clad men were wounded, their attacks were relentless.

It was time for Marcus to join the fray.

"Get behind the altar!" he shouted. He had no doubt the Boy Emperor would listen.

He darted forward and to the right, just as Olivian finished his spell. Three flashes of heat and light sprang from the tip of his spear, blasting three of the assassins in their faces.

It wouldn't burn them; only the strongest of the Julian wizards could do that. But the man with the daggers raised his hands to protect his face, and half a heartbeat later, Titus's spear found his heart.

The swordsman facing Marcus flinched as well, and Marcus struck with his scepter, which made for as good a battle mace as any. At the last moment, his opponent deflected his blow with the dagger in his left hand.

"Well met, second champion," the man said.

He slashed at Marcus twice with his black-bladed sword. Marcus parried the first blow with his scepter and took the second on his unarmored left forearm. His training helped him ignore the pain. The healers could patch him up later, if he survived.

The swordsman raised his left arm above his shoulder and hurled his dagger forward.

"No!" Marcus shouted.

At his side, the other swordsman stabbed Olivian through his right eye.

The wizard fell, and a moment later, so did Gaius, the youngest of them all. Titus lasted five heartbeats longer, though he took the axeman down with him, and threw his shield to Marcus as he fell. And now Marcus was alone against the two remaining swordsmen.

He could beat both of them if he had his armor, though not without difficulty. But his armor was back in his room at the Imperial Palace.

He fought with all his might, but they evaded his blows and rushed him from opposing sides.

As the man on his left battered his shield, the other stabbed his sword toward his face, and Marcus knew too late that it had been a feint. The swordsman slashed at his hand, and fingers flew through the air as his scepter fell to the floor. The man on his left kicked at his shield and sent him tumbling to the ground.

As he fell, he twisted toward the altar. The assassin's thrown dagger hung in the air, held by the protective spell that Athina's wizards had placed around the area. There was no sign of the Boy Emperor; he must have hidden behind the altar, as instructed. And a panel in the wall to the right burst into pieces; the entrance to the secret tunnel. It spat out Augustian Guards, two at a time, armed and armored, rushing to his aid.

They'd be too late, and Marcus knew it. One of the black-clad men had stepped on his shield. The other kicked him in the face, and his mouth filled with blood.

"Goodbye," was the last word he heard before the assassin's blade entered his throat.

A Betrayal Like This

Eldris the Duelist, the fourth champion of the giants, yanked his sword upward and deflected yet another brutal strike from King Tassadar's hammer. He grinned. "You almost got me with that one."

His arm shook from the impact. Of course, the Reaping Blade would not be harmed.

They sparred on an ancient plateau, flattened by Malleon himself with a great thump of his hammer, more than a thousand years earlier. It was holy ground, warded by Malleon's will and forbidden to all other gods. No one would spy on them here, though the orcs had invaded it once — and had been swiftly punished for it.

They'd started with strength exercises, picking up boulders and lifting them over their heads, then throwing them as far as they could. After that, they'd moved on to wrestling, and finally, to weapons play.

Tassadar panted from the exertion. "Time for a break?" he asked in between breaths.

"Aye," Eldris said, squinting against the descending sun. "We can train again tomorrow. What's for dinner, roots and leaves again?"

"And branches. Don't forget branches."

"As if I could," Eldris grumbled.

Tassadar grinned. "And on top of that, a mountain goat for me, and a whole wolf for you. Slightly burned, just the way you like it."

"That's better," Eldris said. This high up on the great mountain, hunting had been poor for centuries.

They would sleep under the night sky, after the evening's meal. It was that or the caves.

The giants didn't build and had no reason to. Rain and snow didn't bother them much, and neither did the cold. They had few needs for material things, except for their treasured tools and weapons, which they carried with them wherever they roamed. And despite their size, they could withstand thirst and hunger better than most mortal creatures. In a great war such as this one, those traits would serve them well.

Tassadar set his hammer down. "I gave you a good fight, didn't I?"

Eldris nodded. "Better than I expected." His armor was dented in three places and his left shoulder hurt from Tassadar's repeated blows. The smiths would repair the former, and Neressia would heal the latter.

The king had sparred without armor. It was the ultimate gesture of trust; an errant cut with the Reaping Blade could have easily removed an arm. But Eldris was the most skilled warrior of the giants since the beginning of time, and Tassadar trusted him to hold his blows.

"I missed our sparring sessions," Tassadar said. "Too few of my warriors can give me a proper contest these days."

"Anyone I remember?"

"Borthos. But only when he's properly rested."

Eldris nodded. "He showed promise, even before I took the long sleep."

"You're still as good as I remembered, though," Tassadar said. "You could have killed me twenty-seven times today. And I, what? Five, perhaps?"

"Six, if you count the time when I slipped on that root."

"Six, then." Tassadar paused. "Have you spoken to her about…?"

He didn't finish the question, but he didn't need to.

Eldris shook his head. "I haven't. Nor will I. There's no need to reopen the old wounds."

"She hasn't taken another mate after you. Not while I was awake, and not while I took the long sleep, either."

"It's too late for us now, Tassadar. We can be friends. Companions, of a sort. But nothing more."

"Besides, she's older now," Tassadar teased him.

"She is." One didn't age during the long sleep, and Eldris's sleep had been long indeed. The priests had awakened Neressia three centuries earlier.

"Do you still resent her for her decision?"

"I made peace with it a long time ago." Over five centuries earlier, after their son's death in a great battle against the orcs, Neressia had chosen to take the long sleep. Though Eldris had begged her not to.

"She talked to me about it, after we woke her," Tassadar said. "She had no choice but to leave the world behind. Valthorin's death broke her."

"It broke me, too," Eldris said. "Yet I had to stay and fight for our people. She left me when I needed her the most. But enough about that. Tell me, what did I miss?"

"While you rested?" Tassadar gazed into the distance. "History, my friend. The passing of my father. My election as king. The Midnight War, when we fought the orcs half a dozen times under dark skies, with only torches and fireballs lighting up the night. A few other wars and border skirmishes. The great famine. The advances of the Julian Empire. Most of Queen Elena's peace." He sighed. "And all of Ortheon's life."

"Ortheon?"

"My son." Tassadar's features grew harder. "I missed too much of his life myself. Even after I became king, I went into slumber for years at a time, while the realm was at peace. I wanted to hold on to my own youth. And then he was gone, taken from me too soon."

"How did he die?"

"Two hundred and fifty years ago, he went on a hunt on the edge of the Western Lowlands with a dozen of his friends. It was night, and they crossed into the vampire realm. The vampires warned them back, and most of Ortheon's friends returned to our lands, but he did not. He told the vampires that he was my son, and that they wouldn't dare to harm him." Tassadar ran a hand through his beard. "He was a boy, Eldris. Only a hundred and fifty years old. But it didn't matter to them. At least they allowed his friends to take his body back to our lands."

"You sought vengeance." Eldris tilted his head. "You should have woken me for it."

"I brought my army to the border, and Queen Elena herself came to meet me. She told me that she had judged her nobles herself, and found that they'd acted in accordance with their law. She urged me not to break the peace."

"And?"

"I only had three thousand warriors with me. Not enough for a proper invasion."

"So, you took them back."

"I did. Five years later, Ortheon's killers were slain by the desert men's assassins. I might have had something to do with that. But vengeance didn't bring my son back."

"You could have other sons."

Tassadar shook his head. "Erendra's gone, and I won't take another mate after her." He slapped Eldris on the shoulder. "But enough about the past. Now, we have to win this great war, and make Malleon the last of the gods."

"We do." Eldris frowned. "Something troubles me, friend."

"What is it?"

"This." Eldris raised the Reaping Blade. "I wish I knew why I got it."

"To kill a god. That's what it's for."

"But none of them will face us in battle. Their Godly Pact forbids it."

Tassadar ran his fingers through his beard. "Hmm. I hadn't thought of that. But Malleon must have. And if he wanted us to kill that Julian god when he came to see your awakening, he would have given us warning, yes?"

They both pondered the issue. Then Eldris groaned as the thought hit him.

"We're not going to kill a god *in battle*, Tassadar. Instead, we'll betray a god who thinks we're his friends. We're going to propose an alliance to our neighbors, and call upon our gods to witness it, and that's when I'll do it."

Tassadar frowned at that. "No. This can't be what Malleon wants. A betrayal like this... They'll hate us for a thousand years. *Ten* thousand."

"I know. And perhaps you're right. We'll ask Malleon when we see him. But I can't think of anything else I'm supposed to do with this sword."

They both turned toward the mountain's peak. On its southern side, the orcs would be gathering their Great Horde. Not knowing that, soon, King Tassadar would call for an alliance — only for Eldris to betray it at the moment of its forging, and strike down Grok the All-Father with the Reaping Blade.

A Godly Pact

Deep in the verdant forest that surrounded her Great Temple, the Lady summoned her bow and arrow and they appeared in her hands. Two hundred paces away, a young deer sipped water from a stream.

"A fine target, that one," said the goddess at her side.

It was Augustus, though he'd arrived as a different aspect: Artemisia, the forest goddess. The Julian goddess of nature, of plants and wild beasts, and also the goddess of the hunt, of chastity and childbirth. How he'd made the last two fit together, the Lady could not fathom. Then again, she hadn't put much thought into it over the years.

The Julians had bought Augustus's lie, as they had all the others. They'd been worshiping Artemisia for ten centuries.

The nerve of him! the Lady thought. Artemisia mirrored her perfectly. Side by side, the two goddesses looked like twins, except for their colors. Where the Lady was green, Artemisia was orange.

They had the same angular face; the same piercing eyes and elegant nose; the same lips that invited a kiss, though few had been granted the pleasure. Their garments were identical, except for their colors. They had the same long, wavy hair that reached the small of their backs. The Lady had styled it differently in preparation for their meeting, parting it slightly to the right and adding a few light-green highlights, and Artemisia had mirrored the changes within moments of her arrival.

She — or he — couldn't mirror her powers, nor her enchanted bow and arrow. The Julian goddess wore a quiver at her hip, and though it refilled as soon as it emptied, her archery skills were no match for the Lady's. They'd staged a contest once, with Malleon as their witness, and the Lady had emerged the clear winner.

As she would now. Though this contest was different.

She smiled. "I'll make it a challenge. Between those two branches." She pointed. "And straight through the deer's heart."

"Not a chance," Artemisia said. "The angle's all wrong."

The Lady nocked her enchanted arrow. "Watch me." She drew and released.

The arrow passed between the two branches. Artemisia snapped her fingers, and a few feet from the deer, another branch snapped.

The noise startled the deer, and it darted away, but the arrow was already back in the Lady's hand. She shot again and pierced the deer's heart. The arrow returned to her hand, as it always did.

"Hey!" Augustus said in his deep voice, and as the Lady turned to him, she saw he'd shifted into his favorite aspect. "That was cheating!"

"You're the one to talk, trickster god! And I never said *one* shot, did I?" She let her bow and arrow fade away and held up her empty hands in a gesture of innocence.

"Fine. You win." Augustus took a deep breath. "The air is fresh here. I like it."

"Of course you do," the Lady said. She didn't tell him about the delicate balance that she was maintaining, nor about the toll it had taken on her over the past five years.

She'd fought the magical blight that had threatened the forests of Ethasar once more. Her efforts would keep it at bay for another decade or two, though the struggle was getting harder every time. If she did not reinforce the wards, and simply let the blight run its course, many of the forests would wither and die — and that, the Lady could not allow.

Out of the other gods, only Aljin knew about her work — and Aljin had his own great task to contend with. He protected the world from the sun's terrible gaze, and the Lady thought his burden was as heavy as her own.

She sighed inwardly. *The last of the gods will have to carry on Aljin's work as well as mine. I'll ask Aljin to teach me what needs to be done.*

Augustus interrupted her thoughts. "Now let us talk about why you summoned me here."

"You know why."

"It surely wasn't just so I could admire your archery skills. Again."

She focused, though her face remained impassive. She ran her fingers through her hair, in *that* way. A gesture no mortal could resist. They'd dash their heads against rocks after seeing *that*, if she asked them to.

Of course, Augustus was no mortal. So she flashed him the Smile as well.

He smiled back. "You're using your glamor, aren't you?"

"Should I stop?"

He shook his head. "Don't. I like it."

"Fine." It would still serve her, though he'd seen through it faster than she'd expected. She gave him another Smile.

"It's stronger than I remember," he said. "You were about to charm old Malleon, back when we all met on Aljin's beach. Before I snapped him out of it. And he's not even our kind."

The fact that he thought of their kind as human-like creatures amused the Lady, but she did not speak of it. Instead, she raised an eyebrow. "Are you jealous of Malleon, the gentle giant?"

"He's anything but gentle when provoked."

"He would have been gentle with me, if you hadn't interfered."

Augustus nodded. "Fair enough. I couldn't let him become your ally, and you know why. Only one of us can survive this contest."

"And yet you still came when I called you."

"I'd rather be friends with you than have my Julians fight against you and Old Sleepy when we're the last ones standing."

"So, we're of one mind," the Lady said. "An alliance."

"A pact of non-aggression," Augustus replied. "Our followers won't fight each other, not until we're the last of the gods. But don't ask my legions to fight and die for the Verdant Kingdom."

She nodded, since there was no better choice. "They'll be busy enough, with the orcs and the desert men marching against them."

"And you'll have to contend with the vampires coming from the west. And with the Islanders, who have already landed on your shores."

"I can deal with Njord's followers. It's Serya Krov that worries me."

"Serya Krov is a funny little lizard that Malleon's giants will stomp out of existence."

The Lady sighed. "Your Julians are lucky to be so far from his lands, Augustus. They've seen the vampire god in their dreams, and they fear him, as all mortals do. But they haven't felt the wrath of his followers. They haven't seen the burned villages, the mountains of skulls, the thousands of dismembered bodies on the blood-soaked battlefields. My people had to bear the brunt of it all."

"That is true," Augustus said. "It's also why my Julians haven't conquered your lands yet. Your kingdom provides a useful obstacle to the horrors of the west."

She huffed and flicked her hair over her shoulder. "You haven't conquered us because we have stronger warriors, better wizards, and fortresses you could not even dream of taking. Not to mention my nobles' enchanted armor, forged by Malleon himself." She licked her lips. "And... because you *like* me, Augustus. Say it."

He answered her with a smile. "I didn't come here to argue with you, Lady. I accept your proposal. A pact of non-aggression it is."

It was *his* proposal, not hers. She would have preferred an alliance, with her knights and the Julian legions facing their common enemies together. Yet this was as much as she would get from him.

For now.

"Fine," she said. "And if one of us dies?"

"Then your followers can do as they please."

He'd just called her the first to die between the two of them. But she wouldn't show how much that stung her. Instead, she shrugged. "And so can yours."

He placed a hand over his heart. "Well played, Lady. I'm sure one of us will miss the other when this is over."

"Me too." The truth of her words took her by surprise. Now that she thought about it, out of all the gods, she did find that she liked him the most. *Ah, unless—*

"Do you have a glamor as well, Augustus?"

He laughed at that, and the Lady knew his reaction was genuine. "I can affect the mortals, yes. But something powerful enough to work on you? I could only wish."

"Then I truly like you more than any of the others," she said. There was no harm in admitting it.

He smoothed an eyebrow with his finger. "Of course you do. I am very likable." He stepped toward her. "I do have a question, now that we've agreed. And a proposal. And some other thoughts." His face shifted from teasing to sober to mischievous, and she found herself resisting the urge to laugh.

"Yes?"

"First, the question. Aljin's second champion. Is he—"

"Yes, he is. Aljin and I struck a pact four centuries ago. Since then, I've been blessing one of his chosen followers and greatly enhanced his archery skills. I have made him exceptional; better than my Rangers, even. And when he dies, I always bless another."

"He, or she."

"It's always a *he*." She rolled her eyes. "You know Aljin."

"I still think our own pact was better," Augustus said.

"It was," the Lady agreed. Decades earlier, she'd given a young Julian wizard the power to channel a part of her magic and use it to bless the empire's harvests. Leticia Alba was her name, and now, in her later age, Augustus had chosen her as one of his champions. In return, if famine ever struck the Verdant Kingdom, the Lady's followers would buy grain and smoked meat from the Julians, at reasonable prices.

The pact was more valuable for the Julians, and the Lady knew it. But it had made Augustus think of her even more fondly than before, and that had great value in its own right.

Of course, Leticia thought her power came from Demetra, the Julian goddess of the harvest. But Demetra was merely one of Augustus's aspects, and Augustus did not have the power to grant such a boon.

He ran his fingers through his beard. "So, what you're saying is, I wouldn't want my Boy Emperor to get anywhere near Nasir. Not as long as Nasir can use his bow, at least."

The Lady nodded. "Nor any of your other champions. Speaking of which, I know you lost Marcus Severus already. He was a good man."

"A great man. A true hero of the empire. I'll go to his funeral, or at least Ares will. Once we're finished here."

"Which will be as soon as we forge our Godly Pact." There wasn't much more she could get from him now.

He shook his head. "There's more, Lady. I would visit your Great Temple."

"You've come to worship me?" she jested, though she understood his meaning. It was a sacred place, hidden from all the other gods. They couldn't be spied upon.

Augustus nodded. "In a way, perhaps."

That took her by surprise. "Fine. We'll have the temple for ourselves. Queen Marion left, and Sandra went with her. They took their retinues as well."

"I knew that," Augustus said.

She took him by the hand and lifted the wards, dropping her glamor as she did. A moment later, they were inside the temple, facing her likeness carved into the ancient oak.

Augustus turned away from it, as she had expected, and his gaze panned across the trophies on the wall to his left. "You forgot to bring the deer."

She released his hand and shrugged. "Food for the wolves. Now tell me, my friend. What is it?"

Augustus turned to her. "First, promise me that whatever happens here remains our secret."

"I promise." Secrets were a currency that the gods used often, and they did not break each other's trust. Besides, soon they'd be bound by Godly Pact.

"If you win, Lady," Augustus said, "you'll rule the world for a thousand years. Do you realize how long that is?"

"Longer than you and I have lived so far. Though not by much." On their thousandth birthday, the Vengeful One would arrive. The Supreme One had told them that.

"That is, if you defeat the Vengeful One," Augustus said, as if he was reading her thoughts.

"Of course I will." She couldn't afford to doubt it. Doubt was the silent killer.

"But what you haven't thought about is how lonely you will feel."

"I'll have my followers. And not just the people of the Verdant Lands. They'll all follow my guidance. Even the orcs and the giants. I'll *make* them, if I have to."

"And yet it won't be the same. Think of Elena, the heartless queen."

"Why should I think of that monster?"

"For her, there's nothing that can replace King Dragos. Nothing. And you took him away from her."

"He was butchering my men, so I asked Sir Godric to rid me of him." She'd used her glamor then. "And he did. Twice. You expect me to feel sorry for her?"

"I expect you to understand her. If you win, then for a thousand years, you'll feel the same way she does. Worse, even. For you are a goddess, and you will truly know what you have lost. All of your peers. Me, Malleon, Njord, Aljin, and even Grok and Serya Krov."

She scoffed. "Serya Krov, I can do without."

"But you'd miss *me* greatly, and many of the others, too. You know this as well as I do."

"Well played," she mirrored his earlier words. "What you say does ring true, in a way."

"I've been feeling lonely ever since the Supreme One brought me into this world," Augustus said. "There's no one like me, though all six of you are exceptional, each one in your own way. And so, I had to create my own peers."

"You've mirrored us," the Lady said. "Ares is Grok, though more refined. Nepthus is Njord, but aged and with a proper nose, and without those silly braids of his. Artemisia is me, and she's your best imitation of them all. Apollon is Aljin, but orange, and so much prettier." It was not that Aljin was ugly; the best word she could use to describe his face was *otherworldly*. "Volcanus, the craftsman god, is Malleon, though smaller and more human-like, and with a lame leg. And he seems older, though Malleon is the oldest of us all. As for Serya Krov, it's a good thing you didn't mirror him. One of those is more than enough."

"And what of the others? Demetra? Afrodisia? Mercantius? Athina? Bellator?"

"I'll never know, will I? Is that what you're going to tell me?"

"I haven't just mirrored the five of you," Augustus said, a hint of pride in his voice. "I also took inspiration from the gods of another world, though I've changed them slightly and added a few creations of my own." He ran his fingers through his orange hair. "In that world, they were a family. They squabbled, and they fought each other — wife against husband, sister against brother. Yet, through it all, they were never alone."

She considered what he'd said. "Are you afraid of *winning*, Augustus?"

"I'll do my best to win. For myself, and for my people, too. They'll keep worshiping their gods, all of them. All of *me*. But yes, I'll be lonely. Lonelier than you can ever imagine. For a thousand years."

She couldn't recall seeing him like this before. "You've been spending too much time in Athina's skin. It makes you gloomy."

"It's not just Athina, Lady. It's *me*."

She'd never imagined the world without the other gods. Then again, until now, she'd had no reason to. And perhaps Augustus was right. A thousand years was a long time to be alone.

She decided to cheer him up. "If Malleon felt that, he'd just go to sleep and let the world rule itself, until the Supreme One brought us back."

"But Malleon is not me, and I am not Malleon."

"So, what you're saying is that whichever of us wins will feel lonely for a thousand years. As long as it's not Malleon, who has his escape. Or Aljin, who would rejoice as he turns the whole world into a desert, according to his liking." She couldn't think of Serya Krov winning; she would not allow it. "I am starting to see the truth of your words."

"Forget Malleon," Augustus said. "Forget Aljin. Forget all the others. This moment is about you and me." He stepped closer, brushed a strand of hair off her face, and looked deeply into her eyes. "I want you, Lady. Here and now."

Of course you would, the Lady thought. *My glamor is strong.*

With a jolt, she remembered she'd dropped her glamor when they'd appeared inside the temple.

She didn't know how to answer him. Was this one of his games? He was the trickster god, after all. And yet today he seemed so... different.

She had to find out. "Is that a condition for our pact, Augustus? In which case, the answer is no."

He raised a hand in a conciliatory gesture. "You misread me. Our pact stands, whatever your answer."

"Why do you ask for this? It's not like you don't have thousands of followers who crave a fleeting moment of your affection." The stories of the Julian gods' dalliances had been known for centuries.

"My followers are not enough," Augustus replied. "Not anymore. I want what those other gods had. Those from a different world. I want to feel... something different. *With you.* Like we are both part of something bigger. A *family*, of sorts. Even if it's only for a short time, and even though one of us must die soon."

"Is that all?" she asked, and wished she could take it back. He'd said *with you*, and *we*, and *both*. This was not just about himself. And here she was, making light of it.

He shook his head with a rueful grin. "There's also the pleasure. The exquisite sensations you'd expect from sharing yourself with another one of your kind. I'm sure you've thought about it too, more than once."

She had. She'd acted upon it as well, with Njord. But that had been a long time ago, and it would remain their secret. She'd used her glamor then, before he'd learned of its power.

She remained silent, waiting for Augustus to speak.

He looked into her eyes again. "You're not saying no."

"Let us strike our Godly Pact first. Let us not have fighting between our followers, not until we're the last two standing. And then we'll see," she said, though she'd already decided.

He ran his fingers over the back of her neck, his touch arousing sensations she hadn't felt for centuries. "And then we'll see."

"Or maybe we don't have to wait that long."

She closed her eyes and inched forward, and their lips touched. After that, there was no need for words.

The Boy Emperor

The Imperial Stadium of Lux Aeterna was a circular amphitheater, six hundred feet wide and four stories tall. It could hold fifty thousand guests and had twenty-six entrances, though all but two were barred now.

Lucius Antonius, the Boy Emperor of the Julians, paced the sands of the arena. Six squads of Augustian Guards watched him from a respectful distance. Four hundred archers stood in the highest row of seats, ready to unleash death upon anyone who dared disturb the peace. The two entrances were guarded by fifty men each, and another two hundred soldiers patrolled the nearby streets.

Lucius sighed. Hundreds of brave men surrounded him, each willing to die for him. Yet in this moment, he felt alone. A boy of fifteen, carrying the weight of the world upon his shoulders.

He wore his armor now. The last of the black-clad assassins had escaped, and though General Mercurius's legions scoured the city, they hadn't found him yet. And one could never be too careful.

Only two days earlier, he'd faced Marcus Severus on the sands, armed with his spear and his heavy shield. They trained together twice a week, and Marcus had been impressed with Lucius's progress, though he could still beat him easily. And now the former Commander of the Augustian Guards was dead, slain by the desert men's assassins. An early casualty in the War of the Seven.

He died protecting me, Lucius thought. *I won't let his sacrifice be in vain.*

A trumpet sounded to his right, making him turn. Two hundred feet away, one of the gates was opening.

"Princeps Farus, Your Majesty," one of the guards announced.

Lucius smiled. *He's come faster than I expected.*

The gate opened fully, and two riders advanced at a trot. They dismounted at the edge of the arena, handed their horses' reins to the nearest guards, and strode forward, their clothes dusty from their ride. They'd come all the way from Farus's estate.

They were a good-looking pair. Farus, the younger of the two, ruled the Twin Rivers province, which bordered the realms of the giants, the orcs, and the desert men. Tall and muscular, he already resembled his father, a great statesman and warrior who'd defended his province for twenty-two years, until his untimely death.

He'd perished in Aquila's insurrection, fighting side by side with Lucius's own father, Emperor Vesperus. Three weeks later, after several days of fierce fighting on Lux Aeterna's streets, Marcus Severus and his Augustian Guards had vanquished the usurper's forces and had placed Lucius and Farus on their fathers' seats of power.

That had been two years ago, and Lucius had been thirteen at the time. Farus was three years and sixteen days older.

At his side walked Naereus, his lover. The twenty-year-old son of a diplomat, he'd met Farus in the capital six months earlier, and the two had quickly taken a liking to each other. Naereus hailed from the Orchard of the Gods, the northernmost province of the empire. Lucius valued him for his keen mind and for his knowledge of the Verdant Kingdom.

They both bowed to Lucius as they drew near, though he didn't need them to. It was only for the benefit of his guards.

He embraced Farus warmly, ignoring his dirty clothing. "I'm so glad to have you here, my friend."

"We came as fast as we could," Farus said. "Augustus himself urged us on." He looked away, far into the distance. "He told us of Marcus Severus's death. He was a great man."

"He saved my life," Lucius said. "Ares came to his funeral and spoke at great length about his deeds."

"Are the assassins dead?"

"All but one. We're still looking. They were only six, and the death count on our side was high. Twenty-three men in all." Marcus Severus, the six Augustian Guards in his squad, two more of those who had come to Lucius's rescue, the twelve palace guards he'd brought to Athina's temple, and two temple guards.

"He won't strike again," Farus said. "Not here. He must have left by now."

"He might have," Lucius said. "Or he might be holed up somewhere nearby, biding his time and planning his next attack."

"I'm sure we'll catch him, if he's still around," Naereus intervened. "On our way here, we saw the soldiers searching the houses, and they were thorough."

"That they were," Farus agreed. "So, the War of the Seven has begun in earnest. What will you do, Lucius?"

"I'll tell you as soon as Silvanus arrives," Lucius said. "Otherwise, I'll have to tell you twice."

Farus smiled. "We just rode past him. He'll be here in a moment."

Just then, one of the guards shouted, "Princeps Silvanus, Your Majesty."

The young prince passed through the same gate Farus and Naereus had used. He was on foot, and joined by six guards, though they stopped outside the gate as he walked on. Only five feet tall and slightly plump, he ruled over Augustus's Table, a province bordering the Lady's lands and two of the giants' provinces. He usually had one of the daughters of senior officers and high nobles by his side, though never the same one for too long. It was partly his wealth and position, and partly his boyish charm, that drew so many hopeful suitresses to him.

Lucius strode toward him, and they embraced. Then Silvanus and Farus clasped arms.

"Finally," Silvanus said. "The Terrible Three are reunited."

They'd earned the moniker from their teachers, and for good reason. They were all smart and cunning, as evidenced by their progress with their studies and their various elaborate pranks. But after Aquila's rebellion, many things had changed. They'd all become orphans, and had assumed their fathers' leadership roles years before they were fully trained.

"The Terrible Four." Farus placed a hand on Naereus's shoulder.

Silvanus laughed. "Never. He's not terrible enough. No offense, Naereus."

"None taken, my friend," the diplomat's son replied.

Farus turned to Lucius. "Since we're all here, I'll ask again. What will you do?"

Naereus raised a hand. "I can leave if you want me to, Your Majesty."

Lucius shook his head. "Stay, Naereus. You need to hear this as well. Besides, I have a mission for you."

Farus raised an eyebrow, but he remained silent.

"The goddess Athina visited me last night," Lucius continued. "We spoke at length, and I place great trust in her advice. This morning, I met with our generals and gave them their orders. Tomorrow, I'll speak to the Senate, with all of you at my side."

"I heard of your meeting with the generals." Silvanus wiped a few beads of sweat from his brow. "You should have invited me."

Lucius nodded. "Perhaps. Then again, it wouldn't have changed a thing. Athina's advice was sound, and you would have agreed with it. Besides, General Patricius doesn't like you."

"Only because I wouldn't marry his daughter," Silvanus said. "But you can't fault me for that. She's not as clever as she thinks she is, nor as pretty. And she doesn't like cats." Which, for Silvanus, was worse than worshiping the vampire god.

"And yet if I asked you—"

"I'd do it, of course. But you won't. Will you?"

"Of course not," Lucius answered. He had no reason to torture his friend. Besides, he'd heard that young Polonia had a thirst for adventure — and she wouldn't find much of that with Silvanus.

"Our generals, then," he continued. "Justinian is raising the five legions of the Twin Rivers province, and I asked Patricius to ride to his aid. His officers will raise three legions from the capital province to follow him within the week."

"That gives them eighty thousand men," Silvanus said. "Plus the twenty-four thousand men guarding the border forts. Those are impressive numbers."

"But not large enough to stop the orcs," Farus said. "Not if they march with their full strength."

"I'll send more men to their aid as quickly as we can muster them," Lucius said. "In the meantime, the generals will do whatever it takes to keep our enemies back."

"Meaning?" Silvanus asked.

"Defense in depth," Farus said gravely, and Lucius knew he'd understand. It was what his father would have done. "Our generals will deprive the orcs from enjoying the fruit of our land."

Silvanus's eyes grew wider. "You call it defense in depth, but what you really mean is scorched earth. Burn the villages, burn the crops we can't gather in time, drive the herds toward the capital, slaughter the animals that fall behind, and have Farus's people leave their homes and seek refuge in the fortified cities, or closer to the capital. Those who aren't taking up arms. I didn't think it would come to that, not in my lifetime."

"It won't," Lucius said, "if we're lucky. The orcs may decide to strike at the giants first, though they've been at peace for a while. Or they might move against the vampires."

"But you don't think they will," Silvanus said.

"Neither do I," said Farus. "I'll return home swiftly and help the generals organize the war effort."

Lucius shook his head. "You won't. I need you here. Besides, if our armies are overrun, I'll need people I can trust to lead the counterattack. And that would include you."

"Fine," Farus said, though he didn't seem happy with the decision. "What of the other generals?"

"Albus will return to the Farmlands. He'll raise more troops and send them to the frontline. And Mercurius will continue to guard the capital, until I decide otherwise. He'll fortify the city, raise three more legions, and make sure all the soldiers passing through our province are well-armed and properly supplied."

"And if the giants move against us as well?" Silvanus intervened.

"We'll wait for them here," Lucius answered, "though I didn't tell my generals that. I said I'd decide later."

Farus swatted a fly that had landed on his shoulder. "They'll pass through my province." He wiped his hand on his tunic. "Or through his." He pointed to Silvanus.

"Athina doesn't think they'll trouble us, at least not yet. Perhaps they'll march against the Verdant Kingdom, or against the orcs. Or fall upon the vampires. We simply do not know."

"I can find out," Naereus volunteered.

Lucius raised a hand. "No. I have another task for you, my friend. You will secure a pact of non-aggression with the Verdant Kingdom. Augustus says they'll be open to it. You'll travel to Lysennia and make it official."

"I would at least join him in that," Farus said.

"You won't," Lucius replied. "As I said, I need you and Silvanus by my side. If we are to win this, the Terrible Three must stick together, and be of one mind. Besides, Naereus's mission carries no risk. You'll see him again, and soon. Be certain of it."

"Fine," Farus said. "What would you have me and Silvanus do?"

"He'll have us melt in the midday sun," said Silvanus, who was sweating profusely. "You should have put up a tent, Lucius."

"You're right," Farus said. "A nice shady tent in the middle of the arena, and perhaps a pretty young woman with a fan to keep you cool, and another one to serve us refreshments."

Lucius smiled. He knew where this was going.

"That would have been nice, yes," Silvanus said.

Farus thumped him on the shoulder. "This is a war council!" he shouted. "You don't need to be comfortable; you need to be thinking about winning."

Silvanus smiled. "There's no reason I can't do it with a nice drink in my hand."

"He's chosen the Stadium for a reason," Farus said. "It's the place of the war games, and has been so for centuries. And now, we're playing the biggest war game of all."

You don't know the half of it, Lucius thought. "Before I give you your tasks, my friends, I'll tell you about our champions."

"Leticia has to bless the harvest," Silvanus said. "But only in the east."

"Exactly," Lucius said. When the enemies invaded from the west, hundreds of thousands of Julians would flee from their advance. The eastern lands would have to feed them all, and supply the army as well.

Farus nodded. "You must give her a heavy guard. Half a legion, at least."

"She'll do it from here," Lucius said.

He respected the gifts that Leticia Alba brought to the empire, now in his wiser age. Only five years earlier, two weeks after his tenth birthday, he'd made fun of her plump constitution and her waddling gait in front of his friends, within her earshot. His father, Emperor Vesperus, had taken him to his room, and there he'd beaten him hard, with his leather belt, for the first and last time.

You don't make fun of the hand that feeds you, he'd told Lucius. *And Leticia feeds the whole empire.* He knew it to be true now.

Farus grunted. "I thought she needed to walk the fields. Some of them, at least."

"She'll do it from here," Lucius said again. "She'll pray to Demetra for help. Athina told me the Goddess of the Harvest will be amenable."

"And what of Selenius?"

"I'm sending him to the Orchard of the Gods. He'll get the noble families to open their purses and draft young men into our legions. In this, he'll speak with my voice."

"He'll make himself a target," Silvanus intervened.

"He's one of our champions, yes. But no one has to know that." The gods knew, but they were bound to keep the names of the fourth champions secret.

"Yet if he speaks with your voice," Silvanus said, "perhaps our enemies will come for him anyway. They'd do so just to destabilize us."

Lucius nodded. "I've thought of this. He'll speak with my voice, but he'll do it *quietly*. He'll meet with the nobles in secrecy. Even better, I could have someone else do the talking, and have Selenius advise him beforehand."

Farus huffed. "So, we're all just pieces in your game, and Athina's. Or Augustus's, I forget who's playing for the gods. You tell us where to go, and what to do, and you hope for the best. But we're fighting against six other factions, and they're all strong, and we've already lost a champion. And though our gods outnumber the others, there's not much that they can do for us. The Godly Pact has hobbled them."

Lucius smiled at that. "Calm down, my impulsive friend. Silvanus, what do you think?"

"I've pondered Augustus's choice of champions," Silvanus said. "I think he has some tricks up his sleeves, and so do you. For one thing, you plan to keep Leticia here, though she'll bless the harvest all over the eastern lands. But I suspect that's only the beginning."

"You're right," Lucius said. "Our gods can't help us in battle, but there are other ways. Augustus considered them when he negotiated the Godly Pact, and he and Athina promised me a special gift. One that will help us win this war without breaking the gods' rules."

"And that is?" Farus inquired.

"The best trainers in military strategy that one could have."

"Those would be General Patricius and our old teacher, Captain Apulius. Unless you count one of Queen Marion's generals." Farus scoffed at the notion.

Silvanus raised a hand. "Books. You mean books, Lucius."

"Of course you'd say *books*, Silvanus," Farus said. He'd always preferred the spoken word, much to the desperation of his teachers.

"We'll read books, yes," Lucius replied. "Ours, and those of the

Lady's followers, and those of the vampires as well, which my father acquired at great cost in his final years. We'll play war games and learn how to lead our armies to victory. And our gods will show me visions from other worlds. Visions of military commanders who won battles against impossible odds. I'll learn from their successes, and from their mistakes as well. And I'll use what I learn to win this war."

He placed his hands on Farus and Silvanus's shoulders. "And you, my friends, you'll be by my side. Every step of the way."

The Gods and their Champions

Aljin: King Ammon, Nasir bin Fatih, Achmad bin Fayzal, Al-Khanjar

Augustus: Emperor Lucius, ~~Marcus Severus~~, Leticia Alba, Selenius Gracchus

Grok the All-Father: King Ghark, Hagor the shaman, Rorra Fireborn, Krakkar the Fist

The Lady: Queen Marion, High Priestess Sandra, Eugene the Trickster, Sir Galahad

Malleon: King Tassadar, Paeren, Neressia, Eldris the Duelist

Njord: ~~King Knut~~, Queen Frida, ~~Ursula~~, Gunnar

Serya Krov: Queen Elena, Duke Zoltan Barko, Kirill Skromnik, Katrina

Bonus Content

Congratulations! You've finished Part Three. The bonus content for this part includes the evolving campaign map, a few images of Ethasar's heroes, the song *Defender of the Empire*, and some fun surprises.

To explore the bonus content, visit https://bradtowers.com/wots-bonus-3/ or scan this QR code:

Part 4: The Three Queens

Queen Frida's Proposal

The Throne Garden of the Verdant Kingdom was placed on a gentle slope, less than five hundred feet from the royal apartments. A leisurely walk, which Marion had made hundreds of times. She much preferred the Garden to the throne room back at the palace, though she'd gladly use the latter on rainy days.

She smiled at the members of her court, noting that they were all in attendance, and sat herself upon her throne. *This should be interesting.*

The throne stood on the Garden's lowest point. In that, the Garden resembled a Julian amphitheater, though there wasn't much else they had in common. The Garden was much smaller, and surrounded by rose bushes and apple trees, all kept in bloom for nine months of the year by the Lady's magic; the benches were straight instead of curved; and they were made of wood instead of stone.

There were twelve of them, arrayed in three rows of four, facing the throne. One for each of the noble houses, though the bench of the Verdant queen's family was always left unoccupied, in accordance with the law. Each of the other benches seated three: the Head of the House, always a woman; her Knight Protector, always a man; and her foremost advisor, who could be either.

Twelve noble families, the ruling class of the Verdant Kingdom. Two from the Broken Lance province; a land of chivalry, knightly tournaments, great feats of arms, and border skirmishes with the vampires. Three from Godric's Valley, including Godric's own descendants, whose ancestor had passed into legend after slaying Dragos, the vampire king. Two from the Hunting Grounds, the capital province. Two from the Enchanted Glade, which hosted the Great Temple of the Lady. And three from Lysennia, the province named after the ancient Queen Lysenna, who had unified the five realms into the Verdant Kingdom after twenty years of diplomacy and conquest.

Only two of Lysennia's benches were occupied.

Marion could imagine her mother sitting on the third bench, as she'd done for two and a half decades. Once an unsuccessful candidate for queenhood, she'd become an important member of the Council, advising Queen Catherine first and Queen Beatrice after that. And though the letters she sent Marion from their ancestral home were full of joy, Marion had no doubt she still missed the court life.

Then again, Mother's greatest desire, after not being elected herself, had been to see one of her daughters as queen. In that, she had succeeded. After Queen Beatrice had announced her decision to retire at the age of sixty-three, Marion's election had swiftly followed.

With that, one of Queen Lysenna's descendants sat on the throne once more.

On Marion's right, on a throne identical to hers, sat her twin sister Sandra, the High Priestess of the Lady. On her left, on a much simpler wooden chair, sat her husband Simon, the King Consort. On Sandra's right, on a chair similar to Simon's, sat Sir Galahad, the Lady's Paladin and her fourth champion in the War of the Seven. And to Simon and Galahad's sides stood two of Marion's foremost Companions, the twins Milton and Nelson, descendants of Sir Godric. They were both armed and wore their enchanted armor, as did Sir Galahad.

A square wooden platform separated the thrones from the benches. Ambassadors, messengers, and various other petitioners would stand there, addressing the queen.

Today, a single man was granted an audience. Marion had caught a glimpse of him as she walked toward the throne, though she hadn't spoken to him.

"Let us begin," she said. "Let Queen Frida's messenger step forward."

Her voice carried, amplified by magic. Moments later, the Islander envoy walked onto the platform.

He bowed at just the right angle and she looked him up and down. Over six feet tall, he had the constitution of a bear and the elaborate dress and mannerisms of a Julian diplomat, though he was neither. His blue hair was cropped short, and his blue beard was braided in a single strand, perhaps one foot long. The sheath at his belt was empty; he'd surrendered his sword to the Queen's Companions before entering her presence.

"You may speak," Marion said.

"Queen Marion. My name is Haavard Haavardsson, as was that of my father, and that of his father before him. I bring a letter from Queen Frida of the Islanders. A message of friendship."

He took a scroll from his pack and lifted it to his eyes. Marion arched her eyebrows as the scroll unrolled to his hip and the messenger struggled to hold it straight in the light breeze.

She cleared her throat. "Do you know its contents?"

"I do, Your Majesty."

"Then tell me the important parts. I'll read the details myself after that."

"Queen Frida offers you an alliance and the use of her cannons until Njord and the Lady are the last of the gods. If either of them dies, our people will remain allies, and fight for the one who remains. We'll ask Njord and the Lady to strengthen our alliance with a Godly Pact of their own."

Marion was quick to grasp the benefits of the proposal. The Islanders' cannons would serve her well against the vampires, and against other foes as well. Not to mention they would no longer be a danger to her own people.

"Interesting," she said. "And what does she ask for in return?"

"She asks for our destinies to be joined, and for the fates of our gods to be decided in a manner that will surely be to your liking. If the Lady and Njord both survive until the end, Queen Frida will face one of the Lady's champions in a combat to the death, without the use of spells. You can choose your champion, of course. The outcome will determine the fates of our gods."

"I see," Marion said. The terms were as reasonable as they could be, though the Islander queen stood to gain more than she did.

She wasn't worried about the final condition. In her enchanted armor, she'd beat Queen Frida easily in a one-to-one contest, if it came to that. She'd beat almost anyone.

She stretched out her hand. "The letter, please."

The Islander advanced. Marion knew that, at her sides, Milton and Nelson readied to spring into action at the first sign of treachery, as did Sir Galahad. As for Sandra, she'd lash out with magic. But Marion wasn't worried. She wore her armor, and her Companions had searched the messenger for hidden weapons, and found none.

He handed her the scroll and took three quick steps back, with his hands held loosely at his sides, no doubt aware of the attention his closeness to the Verdant queen had gotten him.

She smiled at him. "I'll need a minute, Haavard Haavardsson."

She skimmed through the text. The first few paragraphs matched the messenger's words. She read on — and frowned. "What's with this part about my sister?"

The Islander's face remained impassive. "As you have surely heard by now, Queen Marion, we've been betrayed twice already since this war began. Those betrayals have cost us the life of our king and a large part of our fleet. I am sure you understand Queen Frida's need for a strong guarantee."

He did not call Sandra a hostage out loud, and Marion understood why. He was letting her decide how much she wanted to share with her nobles, and when.

She nodded. "I do understand, Haavard. Perhaps I'd feel the same way, if I were in her place."

She did not say, *I have a thousand times more honor than a two-faced pirate*. In diplomacy, insults revealed much and gained nothing.

She rose from her throne. The ladies of the Verdant Council rose with her, as did their advisors and their Knights Protectors.

"Tell your queen that I will need time to consider this," she said. "She'll have my answer within fifteen days, and I'll deliver it myself. In the meantime, she is to wait on the beach she's taken, and not plunder my lands — and there will be no further aggression against her. You will relay this to her, Haavard Haavardsson, the third of your name. But first, Sir Milton will hold a feast in your honor and show you to your quarters for the night."

The blue-haired Islander shook his head. "I would leave at once. With your permission, Your Majesty."

"Granted," she said. "Go now then, Haavard. Sir Milton, please escort Queen Frida's messenger to the royal stables. Give him one of our fastest horses and a token of safe passage. Do the same for his men."

The messenger left, with Milton at his side, and Marion addressed her ladies. "We are done here, councilors. I'll see you at dinner and tell you of my decision. Now I need to speak with my sister. Alone."

They filed out in orderly fashion, as they always did. Simon, the King Consort, was the last to leave, walking at a leisurely pace. He did not hurry to join his mother, the Head of his former House. Not this time.

He'd be waiting for Marion in bed tonight, and he'd be sober; she'd made him promise. It was not a pleasant duty, but it was duty, nonetheless. They'd have twins one day, if the Lady willed it. And perhaps one of them, or one of their descendants, would be queen again.

But first, she'd speak to Sandra about Queen Frida's proposal, and about the decision she'd just made.

Fleeing Peasants

The long column of peasants advanced eastward at a desperate pace, along one of the few paved roads that connected the border of the Broken Lance province with its interior.

Queen Elena watched them from the sky, and snarled.

They moved as fast as they could. Sons supported their aging parents; mothers carried their babies in their arms; and here and there, ox-drawn carts carried the peasants' meager possessions and food for the journey.

All fleeing from my advance, Elena thought as she looked into the distance.

She'd taken the better part of a month to gather her army at the Verdant Kingdom's border. More serfs would arrive in the weeks to come, but Elena would not wait. She'd start her invasion, and when the stragglers finally joined her, they'd hear the tales of her early victories.

She looked down again. Only a few of the peasants were young, able-bodied men. The local lord must have pressed those into service as soon as the news of the war had reached him.

Most of the travelers walked with their heads down, while some looked forward — but they weren't looking up. They hadn't noticed her yet.

At her side flew Vladimir, her young guard. He was in high spirits; she'd taken blood from him in the morning, and he'd taken blood from Igor the High Priest before that.

Four more vampire nobles followed them closely. Together, they'd tear through five hundred peasants like a hot knife through butter, if it came to that.

Of course, if Queen Marion and her lords were smarter, they'd have hidden a handful of knights among the fleeing party, wearing rags over their armor. Perhaps a wizard as well. They'd try to take Elena by surprise, and she'd lose a noble or two, before she could adjust her tactics. But Marion wasn't that crafty. She was a peacetime queen, and the War of the Seven would break her, sooner or later.

Elena hoped it would be sooner.

She swooped downward, twisted in the air, and landed in front of the column, her double-headed axe raised to the sky. An instant later, Vladimir landed at her side. The other nobles joined them, two on either side, arrayed in a loose semicircle.

The peasants screamed in terror, as she knew they would. They cowered and pressed against each other, as if that would offer them safety.

She scanned the faces she could see and spotted a single brave soul among them. A young man who carried a pitchfork and stood tall while the others pulled back. His gaze screamed defiance, which was just what she wanted.

"Men and women of the Verdant Kingdom!" she shouted. "I am Elena Kylareva, the vampire queen. You're in my power now."

"Never!" the young man shouted, brandishing his pitchfork.

She raised a hand, signaling her nobles to wait, and strode toward him. She threw her axe to Vladimir as she advanced, and faced the man with empty hands.

He swung at her with his pitchfork. She deflected it easily with a flick of her wrist and struck him with an open hand, her talons scoring four deep gashes across his cheek. He fell back, screaming and clutching his face, though he did not drop his weapon.

"I could have ripped his head off!" she shouted. "But today, I give him mercy. Today, I give mercy to all of you."

She moved toward him as he shrank back among the other peasants, who dashed away from him as if he carried a deadly disease. Vladimir walked at her side.

She'd take to the skies, if they rushed her. But they weren't going to.

"I don't want your deaths!" she shouted. "Only your submission."

"Kneel!" Vladimir roared. "Kneel before the vampire queen!"

He darted forward, snatched the young man's pitchfork from his hand, and shoved him to the ground. No one dared intervene. Many men and women were already falling to their knees.

Cowards, Dragos would have called them. But five hundred years of ruling had taught Elena better. There was no cowardice in seeking to preserve your own life when faced with a power greater than your own. And no power in the seven realms was greater than the vampire queen. None but the gods themselves.

She watched the crowd, and no one dared defy her. A few of the younglings darted away from the column, seeking to hide in the forest. Elena's nobles could track them easily, if she wished.

"Kneel!" Vladimir roared again, at the top of his lungs.

More and more peasants, young and old, followed his command. Mothers and fathers pushed their children to their knees, hoping to save their lives.

"Where are your brave Verdant knights now?" Elena shouted. "Are they here, fighting for you? Or are they hiding in their castles, like cowards?"

She knew the answer. Sir Roland had closed his castle's gates and had sent these peasants away, and they weren't the only ones. She'd intercepted two other columns already.

"They've abandoned us," a middle-aged woman answered. She was already on her knees. "Please have mercy on us, Your Majesty. We've done your kind no harm."

"Your name," Elena said.

"Sara, Your Majesty."

"Call me your queen from now on, Sara. Say it."

The woman lowered her head. "My queen. What will you have of us?"

"You'll turn around," Elena said, "and travel to my lands. You'll follow Count Boris." She pointed to the count, who flapped his wings and rose twenty feet into the air. "Once you cross the border, a score of my nobles will meet you, and every man and woman above the age of fourteen will pay the blood price. Then you'll be taken to our villages. You'll be split up, though each family will stay together. I'll give you safety and justice, as long as you obey the Vampire Kingdom's laws and keep paying the blood price. As all humans must."

She didn't need to kill them. Her fight was with the Lady, and with her champions. And as new sources of blood, the peasants she was taking from the Lady's lands would make her nobles stronger.

She continued. "If you try to flee, and stray from the path Count Boris guides you on, he'll fly back to me. He'll tell me of your disobedience. And then nothing will save you from my wrath. I'll tear you all to pieces."

Of course, it wouldn't come to that. Not if they obeyed her.

Sara bowed her head. "I'll keep them on the path you want us to take, my queen. My father was the village elder. They'll listen to me."

"See that they do, Sara," Elena said, and soared into the sky.

Vladimir joined her, as did three of her other nobles. Only Count Boris remained.

"We should have killed a few," one of the nobles said. Baron Sergey, the oldest of them, one hundred and twenty-seven years of age. "A dozen, at least. I was ready to get my talons wet."

Flying closer to him, Elena looked him in the eye. "And what would that have accomplished, Sergey?"

"It would have been a blood offering to honor King Dragos's memory. He would have welcomed it. At least that's what the legends say."

She growled. "Don't talk to me about Dragos." She continued, softer. "Would you kill your own serfs without reason, Sergey? Knowing what I'd do to you if you did?"

He paled a little and shook his head. "No, my queen. I would not." His voice was barely audible over the flapping of their wings.

"These men and women are mine," Elena told him. "As are all the men and women of this world, once we win the War of the Seven. The orcs and the giants, too. They'll all pay the blood price, and they'll do it often. And some of them, I'll give to you, Sergey. More than you deserve, if I feel like it. But I won't waste their lives without reason."

She grinned, though she felt no joy, and couldn't. "Some will fight me, though. And when they do, you'll do more than get your talons wet. You'll bathe in their blood, if you wish."

Sir Roland

Thud.

In his room on the second floor of his keep, Sir Roland clutched the bars of his window and howled with impotent rage as another peasant crashed onto the stones of the courtyard below.

Unlike the ten before him, this one hadn't screamed.

The invaders had reached Blackstone Castle an hour earlier. Their forces were massed in front of the castle walls, out of arrow range. They didn't seem to have siege weapons, and though the four vampires that hovered above the army gave them an edge, it wasn't strong enough to storm a well-defended castle without taking heavy losses. Instead, they'd resorted to terror.

They'd taken prisoners. And now they flew them high above the castle, one by one, and dropped them onto the ground. Or onto the castle's buildings, at times. The seventh victim had left a man-shaped hole in the ceiling of the Lady's chapel.

They were careful, the monsters. They flew high enough that Sir Roland's archers wouldn't reach them with their arrows, though a few of them still tried. And the only wizard he had at hand was a healer, not a warrior.

The vampires had sent an envoy to the gates upon their arrival; a serf woman carrying a white flag, her skin darkened from the repeated bleedings. She'd made their demands known. They asked for the surrender of the castle, of all weapons and armor, and of Sir Roland's life. The guards' captain had declined, and minutes later, the executions had begun.

The sound of footsteps made Roland turn from the window, just as Patrick, one of his attendants, entered his room.

"I heard you scream, my lord," he said. "Are you all right?"

"All right?" Roland growled. "How can I be all right, Pat?" He ran a hand through his hair. "You've seen what's happening outside."

Patrick nodded. "I have, my lord."

"This is the world that the vampire queen would bring about," Roland said. "A world of blood and savagery. Our Lady's ideals of honor and chivalry would be shattered, and we'd all end up like those spineless serfs who grovel in front of their masters. We'd have to give our *blood* to them." He growled again. "No. I can't let this go on, Pat. Not for another minute."

"There's nothing we can do," Patrick said. "Not until they attack."

There *was* one thing. "Fetch me my armor. Send the captain of the archers to me and tell Sir Robin to ready his lancers. I intend to sally forth."

"But my lord, they outnumber us vastly!"

"I know. Yet honor compels me to fight. Besides, if we hit them hard enough, perhaps they'll pull back."

"I would counsel against it, if I may."

"I hear you, Pat. But I will not stray from this path. Now go and do my bidding. And before I forget, fetch me a bottle of that sweet Julian wine for tonight's dinner. I plan to celebrate my victory."

"As you wish, my lord," Patrick said, and rushed to do his duty.

Roland slumped into a nearby chair and touched the symbol of the Verdant Cross etched into his sleeve. The wine bottle would remain unopened. Most likely, this was to be his final battle.

In his late forties, he was in excellent shape. He could easily best soldiers half his age, even without his enchanted armor, which he'd gifted to his oldest son. But he had only forty knights, and they would sally out against thousands of serfs.

Minutes passed, and two more men screamed as they fell from the sky. Peter, the captain of the archers, was the first to arrive, and Roland gave him his orders.

The captain left, and Patrick returned, carrying Roland's helmet and a bottle of wine. Three more attendants followed, bringing Roland's armor, along with his sword and crossbow.

He donned his armor, with the attendants' help, and strode down the spiral staircase, perhaps for the last time in his life. Sir Robin waited on the landing, his face grim.

Roland forced himself to smile. "What is it, Robin? Will you try to dissuade me from my path, too?"

The young man shook his head. "It's been an honor serving under your command, Sir Roland. I would ride at your side, if you'll have me."

Roland nodded. "For the Lady."

"For the Lady," Robin echoed his words.

The rest of the knights waited in the courtyard, arrayed in a neat formation. Squires and stable boys rushed toward them, handing them their lances. Roland's gaze panned upon his knights, and his chest swelled with pride, for these were some of the finest warriors in this border province.

Perhaps this is a mistake, he thought. *Perhaps we should flee east instead, and join Queen Marion's force.* But his mind was already made up, and abandoning his post would brand him a coward.

He climbed into the saddle, took a lance from his squire, and raised it toward the sky. "Follow me," he shouted.

He led his men through the castle's gate, and Sir Robin took his place at his side. The other knights spread out to the left and right, a thin line of forty-one men, strong and well-trained, their armor painted green.

A mass of enemies dressed in gray outfits stretched out ahead, their tents rising behind them. Half a dozen vampires flew above their serfs now, and Sir Robin knew they'd swoop down and strike at his men when the fight began.

"We're ready," Robin told him.

Roland's fist clenched around the reins. There was no need for a rallying speech, not with these men. "For the Lady!" he shouted.

"For the Lady!" forty powerful voices replied.

They lowered their visors and rode forward. When Roland judged the distance was right, he lowered his lance and spurred his horse into a gallop.

Arrows flew to meet him, and two slammed into his armor, but they did not punch through. To the right, one of his knights fell. A vampire swooped down, and Sir Robin fired his crossbow. Roland leaned forward in his saddle, his gaze fixed on the foes who stood against him.

His lance punched through a man's chest, sprang out of his back, and spilled the guts of the man behind him. The impact wrenched the weapon from Roland's grasp, and he drew his sword. His armor deflected a spear thrust, and Roland chopped off the spearman's arm, just above the elbow. The man howled in pain, and one of Roland's knights buried his axe in his face.

Roland roared, found another foe, and struck with all his might, but the man deflected his sword with his shield. Roland's second blow opened a deep gash in his cheek.

The man screamed and fell back, dropping his weapon and clutching at his ruined face. More of his companions advanced into the fray, and Roland and Robin cut them down. The tip of a spear scraped ineffectively against Roland's armor.

All around them, men screamed and died. A knight was pulled from the saddle. A horse reared up, his hooves crashing into the men facing him, but a lucky spear thrust opened its belly. The beast fell, leaving a small gap on Roland's right.

"Fall back!" Roland shouted.

He wheeled his horse around and galloped toward the castle. Other knights followed, less than two dozen in all. Arrows flew past him.

To his left, a knight screamed. Roland glanced over his shoulder and saw that a vampire had dragged him from the saddle. Two more vampires descended upon the knight, and Roland fought the urge to turn back. *He'll be dead before I reach him.*

As he neared the castle gate, he raised his visor and slowed his horse to a trot. A line of squires waited in the courtyard, each man holding a fresh lance. Roland rode to the end of the line, grabbed a lance, and turned his horse around.

"Again?" Robin asked him.

"Again." Roland spurred his horse onward and was the first to ride out through the gates. His knights followed him and spread out again, ten men on each side.

Roland's stomach lurched. *We lost half of our number already.* He'd trained them for years, and called them friends, and now they were gone, their lives snuffed out in a single heroic charge. *Not that the rest of us will live much longer, either.*

He closed his eyes, and memories flooded him.

His sons, playing in the castle's courtyard, ten years earlier.

His wife, carrying their newborn daughter in her arms. The smile on her face as she handed him her precious burden. The smell of her hair, and the warm touch of her hands. He'd sent them both away on the eve of his daughter's sixth birthday, as the news of the war had reached him.

The Lady's face, a vision of beauty like no other. She'd visited his castle three years earlier.

His oldest son, standing tall in his enchanted armor. *"I'll make you proud, Father,"* he'd told him ten months earlier, before riding away to join Queen Marion's Companions.

You've already made me proud, son. A father's words, forever left unsaid.

He opened his eyes. "For the Lady!" he shouted.

"For the Lady!" twenty powerful voices replied.

They lowered their visors and rode forward.

Queen Marion's Reply

Queen Frida Gretasdottir walked forward to meet the last of her scouting patrols, the sand of the beach crunching underneath her boots. The three young men were panting and sweating under the morning sun.

"They're here, my queen," said Bjarke, the leader. "The Verdant knights and their foot soldiers. They'll come out of the trees in minutes."

"How many?" Frida asked, though she'd asked the earlier patrols as well.

"Hard to say, but I'd wager at least thirty thousand. They're spread out, and at least a few thousand are mounted. Lots of archers, too. They're ready for battle."

She gave him what she hoped was a reassuring smile. "Merely a show of strength. Now go to your ship, Bjarke. Your captain has his orders."

The young man nodded and hurried onward, along with his companions, and Frida watched him go. Out at sea, less than a mile from the opening of the bay, Njord's enchanted mist lined the horizon.

Her ships could not sail into it. It would make the air hard to breathe, and if a ship went on, its sailors' deaths would soon follow. The open sea was closed to them.

She turned to Lothar Bjornsson, who stood at her side. She'd made him her second-in-command. "Well?"

"We've done all we could," Lothar said. "Now we wait."

They did, as did the ten thousand men she'd kept on the beach, a show of her own strength. The rest had boarded their ships an hour earlier, as the news of the Verdant army's advance had reached the camp. The cannon teams were ready, and Sigurd Larsson himself would fire the first shot, if it came to that.

Five dozen rowboats lined the shore, with twenty oars each. If Queen Marion decided to give battle, Frida and a part of her forces would escape to their ships, under the cover of cannon fire. Many lives would be lost, but Marion's losses would be higher.

"What of their archers?" asked Torsten Eriksson, King Knut's former guard. "What if they try to kill you from a distance, as they did Ursula?"

"They won't," Frida answered for what felt like the hundredth time, though it was only the fourth. "Not before we speak. Queen Marion has promised it, and Njord believes her." He'd spoken to her two nights earlier. "Besides, Ursula's disciples will protect me." Ingrid, Astrid, and Helga stood a few steps behind her.

"We're ready, my queen," Astrid said.

The first of Queen Marion's knights appeared from between the trees. They were too small to see clearly from half a mile away, so Frida raised her spyglass to her eyes.

The knights were splendid in their green suits of armor and carried long lances. Many of the horses were armored as well. They proceeded in a battle line three deep, and behind them came thousands of archers and men-at-arms. Frida shuddered as she took in the size of Queen Marion's force.

She hoped against hope that they came as allies. But they didn't need their lances for that.

The Verdant Kingdom's infantry halted at the edge of the forest. If Frida fired her cannons, she expected that they'd retreat between the trees to minimize their losses.

The knights advanced, and soon they were no more than six hundred paces away. They stopped, and two riders darted forward. They were both clad in green armor, as were their horses, and their helmets and visors kept their faces hidden.

"This must be her," Frida said. "Keep our men steady, Lothar."

The two riders reined in their horses halfway, perhaps three hundred paces away. Then a voice boomed, "Let Queen Frida Gretasdottir step forward." Coming from that distance, it had to have been amplified by magic.

A moment later, one of the riders turned away and headed back to his line.

"I have to go," Frida said.

"At least let me come with you," Torsten replied.

"Or me," said Arne, her bodyguard for the past ten years.

She shook her head. "Wait here, both of you. I'll be back soon."

She strode forward, hands itching to rest upon the twin trident daggers at her belt. Behind her, four hundred archers stood ready to let their arrows fly, if Lothar gave the signal. Farther back awaited forty-five ships, the remains of the Islanders' fleet, with their two hundred and ninety-four cannons.

Slightly more than half of those were trained inland, ready to rain death upon Queen Marion's army. The rest were facing the wrong way. Even so, having her fleet at her back gave Frida strength.

She kept her chin up and her eyes fixed upon the lone rider who waited for her. When she was ten feet away, the rider removed her helmet.

"This is far enough, Queen Frida," she said.

Frida stopped. The woman facing her was at least half a foot shorter than she was, and did not seem particularly strong, by Islander standards. Yet she had the bearing of a queen.

She sat straight in the saddle. Her horse was as dark as night and taller than most horses Frida had seen before. Her green eyes pierced Frida's with an unsettling intensity. Her angular face resembled that of the Lady, at least according to the few portraits of the goddess that Frida had seen, most of them plundered from the Verdant Kingdom. Her chestnut hair, freed from the confines of her helmet, fell to the middle of her chest.

She had to be Queen Marion. She matched the envoy's description and the drawings Frida had seen of her.

She was well-armed. The sheathed sword at her belt was four feet long, its tip reaching past her left ankle. A medium-sized shield, painted green and emblazoned with the Verdant Cross, hung from a hook on her saddle. A bow and a quiver full of arrows were strapped across her back. Her most impressive asset was her armor; green, made from interlocking steel plates, crafted by Malleon, and blessed by the Lady.

Frida had wanted one of those ever since she'd heard of their existence. But now was not the time to dwell on that.

"Well met, Queen Marion," she said. "I see you've brought your army along. You didn't have to."

The Verdant queen smiled. "A small part of my army. Merely a welcome party." She took a deep breath. "I've come for my cannons."

"*Our* cannons," Frida replied. "Those were the terms of our proposal."

"I reject your proposal, Queen Frida."

Frida's heart sank. With only forty-five ships, more than half of them lightly armed, and no allies, she was fighting a hopeless war. Yet she had prepared for this.

"So, we fight," she said. "You'll live to regret this, if you're lucky."

"Perhaps we don't have to fight," Queen Marion said. "I have a proposal of my own."

"I'm all ears," Frida said.

The Verdant queen looked her up and down, her eyes resting on the scars that marked the top of her chest. "So, it is true. You did fight a bear, and won. On my lands, yes?"

Frida nodded. "Your terms, Queen Marion. We can exchange pleasantries later."

"You won't like them, Queen Frida. Yet, in time, you will understand. You would do the same if you were in my position."

Frida remained silent, waiting for Marion to speak again.

"Your proposal came from a place of strength," the Verdant queen said. "A strength that you do not possess. You asked me to place my sister's life in your hands, and to give you a chance at making Njord the last of the gods. But Njord has already lost."

"We still have two champions," Frida countered. "And most of our warriors. And cannons. Hundreds of them."

"Fewer than you had when you landed on my shores."

Frida wasn't about to discuss her weakness. "What are your terms, Queen Marion?"

"Your pirates have raided our lands countless times throughout the centuries. It would be my duty to bring them to justice, and I have the strength to do it. Yet while the Lady is strong and just, she can also be merciful. So here are my terms, Queen Frida.

"Your men are mine now. My officers will break them into small groups and spread them among my troops. They will remain free men, and their past transgressions will be forgiven. Of this, you have my word, and that of the Lady herself. Of course, should they break our laws in the future, they will answer to the Lady's justice.

"You and your captains will stay on my mother's estate as my family's guests until the War of the Seven is over. You will be guarded, and you will be treated well. After that, you can return to Hemland, or remain on our lands, or do what you please. As long as you obey our laws.

"We won't harm any of you, and your men will fight alongside ours, as you had intended. Except for one man, or woman, which you will surrender to me. Njord's fourth champion."

"He's not here." The words escaped Frida before she could stop herself.

Queen Marion sighed. "Then I will need one more thing from you, Queen Frida. Your life. For the Lady has decreed that Njord is to die, and I am here to enforce her will."

"I'd give my life willingly to protect my people," Frida said, and knew it was true. "But I won't let the sea god die because of me."

"You don't have a choice. If you reject my offer, we will fight, and you will die."

"My men will hold the shield wall and I'll escape to my ship, while my cannons decimate your forces. You'll win nothing but pain and sorrow on this beach today."

Queen Marion looked her in the eye. "Your cannons have one shot, Queen Frida. One. Then my knights will be upon your shield wall."

"*Some* of your knights. Less than half, I'd wager."

"I'll send them in waves, a few hundred paces apart. Your cannons will kill some, but not as many as you think."

"We outnumber your knights at least three to one."

"It won't matter. They are well-trained, and some of them wear enchanted armor. Besides, my foot soldiers will rush to join them. I'll send them in waves as well, so that your cannonballs don't kill so many. It's only half a mile from the forest to the shore. The first of the waves will join the knights in four minutes, maybe five. I am confident my knights can keep your men busy for that long. We'll take some losses, yes; and I'll mourn them when this is over. But I've come to terms with it already."

Frida sighed inwardly. The Verdant queen had planned this well.

"After that," Queen Marion continued, "your cannon teams will have to fire upon your own men, and many will hesitate. We'll drive your forces into the sea. Then my men will take your boats, and your ships after that. I am willing to grant your men mercy, but that stops as soon as the first shot is fired. Those who surrender after that will be chained and sent to the mines, and those who don't will dine with the fishes."

"Even if you take our boats, your men won't reach our ships." The closest of the vessels were more than two hundred paces from the beach. "We'll sink the boats before they do."

"Boats make for difficult targets. Besides, I'll have plenty of archers on the beach within minutes, and they'll fire upon your cannon teams. Our wizards will join them and play their part. You have no idea how many wizards I've brought. Some of the boats will reach your ships, and we've brought our own boats as well, though you can't see them yet. We won't take all your ships; some will escape us. But we'll take enough."

"You speak as if you've thought of everything."

Queen Marion nodded. "Would I tell you so much about my battle tactics, Queen Frida, if I thought you had any hope of countering them?"

It was time for Frida to play her last card. She turned and pointed. "See those two galleons to the west? That one's my ship, and that's my second's ship. They're too far away for you to reach them. If some of our ships are overwhelmed, my men have orders to blow up the powder stores; and if they don't, Lothar and I will fire upon them. I'll do what Anders the betrayer did. I'll sink my own fleet, and you won't get my cannons. Then my ship and Lothar's will sail away."

The Verdant queen was silent for a moment. Then she spoke again. "You expect your men to follow your orders."

"And you hope they won't. We'll see which of us is right."

Queen Marion frowned. "You are still thinking of ways to deny me your cannons, Queen Frida. When you should be thinking about the fates of your men."

"I can't let Njord die. Not without a fight."

"Njord has already lost. You haven't thought this through to the bitter end, have you? Let's say for a moment that you escape with your ships; maybe just the two, or perhaps a handful more. I assembled the fleet from Lysennia within days of your arrival and told them where to come. They'll be here before nightfall. You can't beat them, not with your diminished strength. You can't sail into Njord's enchanted mist. And if you run from my fleet and sail west, you'll fall right into Anders's lap."

She paused. Frida could not find fault with her words.

Queen Marion continued. "For the sea god, this is the end. And for you as well, since you don't have a fourth champion to offer me. Whether it happens today or a week from today doesn't matter much. But if you accept my terms, your warriors will survive. They'll become my own, and I'll treat them fairly, regardless of their past crimes. Their lives are worth your sacrifice, yes?"

This is it, Frida thought. *The moment of decision.*

And it is mine, and mine alone. Njord couldn't help her. The Godly Pact forbade it.

She couldn't ask Lothar and Sigurd for advice, either. She was the Islander queen, and this was her burden to bear.

"Queen Marion," she said, "answer me this. What would you do if you were in my place?"

The Verdant queen nodded. "So we fight. I was hoping you'd choose differently."

"Is there no hope for peace?"

"None but the one I offer."

"I have two requests. First, you will wait until I rejoin my troops."

Queen Marion nodded. "I will, unless your side attacks first."

"Secondly," Frida said. "If all my warriors die today, or a few weeks from today, along with our god, I would have your bards tell our story. I would have the people of Hemland learn of what we did today on this beach."

The Verdant queen nodded again. "It will be done. It is only fair. In another life, Queen Frida, we would have been friends."

"There is no other life," Frida replied. "Not for us. For our gods, perhaps."

She could pull out her daggers and charge the Verdant queen. She'd kill her horse first, and then her, though with Queen Marion's enchanted armor, the odds were against her. But that would accomplish nothing. The Verdant knights would charge, and she couldn't outrun them. They'd ride her down, and Njord would die.

It was better to take her chances in battle. And though she was not bound by the constraints of honor and chivalry, as Queen Marion was, Frida looked upon her opponent with respect.

"I'd say I'll be looking for you in the shield wall," the Verdant queen said.

"But you know I'll be running to my ship," Frida finished the thought for her.

"I do. Die well, Queen Frida. Today, or another day. Your story will live on."

They regarded each other silently for a few long moments. Then Frida turned and walked away. The time for words had passed.

It was time for blades and cannonballs to do the talking.

The Charge

Marion turned her horse around and rode back to her knights.

This is it, she thought. *The time to truly earn the Lady's favor.*

The goddess had rarely visited her during her years as queen, but the War of the Seven had changed that. They'd talked for hours the evening before; Marion, Sandra, and the Lady, clustered around a small campfire, with the Queen's Companions watching them from a respectful distance.

The Lady had promised her a better life once the war was won. A new husband, perhaps one of her choosing. Children, too.

It was a future worth fighting for. Today, she'd strike the first blow. If all went well, Queen Frida and her god would meet their end upon this beach. Then Marion would take her army west, to face Queen Elena and her monsters.

She reined in her horse and fell into line between two of her Companions: Milton and Nelson, proud descendants of Sir Godric, both wearing their enchanted armor. They stood straight in their saddles, their lances at the ready.

"So, we fight, my queen?" Milton asked.

She nodded. "Her fourth champion is not here. She wouldn't have given him up if he was, nor will she give her own life. I made her see that she's outmatched, and that we're going to win the day. Yet she's determined to fight us to the bitter end."

"Then let us crush her," Milton said. "I'll lead the first charge myself."

"Only after she rejoins her men." The Islander queen was walking slowly, as if trying to postpone the inevitable. Soon, arrows and cannonballs would fly, and the ground would tremble underneath the horses' hooves.

"She'll make a run for it," Marion said. "Eugene."

"Yes, my queen?" the wizard replied. He'd advanced with the cavalry, as had his men. The head of his fox peered from his saddlebag.

"I expect Queen Frida to flee to her ship. As soon as she gets on a boat, have your Rangers take her out."

"They'll try," Eugene said. "But I make no promises. She has guards and sea witches, and they'll protect her. Besides, we may lose sight of her after she joins her men."

"Do what you can," Marion said. "Milton. Prepare to charge."

BOOM!

The noise startled Marion. She'd heard cannons before, but not like this. It was as if her wizards had amplified the sound. She pulled on her reins to keep her horse from bolting.

Around her, horses whinnied and men raised their hands to their ears.

A second *boom* sounded high above her head. It was loud, though not as loud as the first one.

What is this sorcery? Marion thought. Cannonballs did not explode in mid-air. Yet this one had.

She raised her spyglass and looked behind, toward her footmen, who stood at the edge of the forest. They hadn't been hit by the blast, and neither had her knights.

A warning shot. Or perhaps the gunner had misjudged the range.

She looked forward and to the left, where the shot had come from — and her heart skipped a beat. *What is that?*

A new ship had arrived at the entrance of the harbor; an enormous one, easily three times as long as the flagship of her own fleet. And *tall*. Really tall. Its deck stood high above the water, and its masts were two hundred feet tall, if not more. A plume of smoke rose from somewhere close to its prow, and Marion knew it came from the cannon that had fired the shot.

She took a deep breath and steadied herself. Yes, the newcomers had taken her by surprise, but none of her men seemed hurt. And how much of a difference could one ship make?

"Do we charge, my queen?" Milton asked. He did not seem unsettled by the cannon fire.

Marion nodded. "Give them death, Milton." Queen Frida had already rejoined her forces.

The young knight raised his lance. "We ride!" he shouted. "For the Lady!"

He spurred his horse onward, and five hundred knights rode with him.

The Shield Wall

Frida was less than twenty feet away from her shield wall when she heard the deafening sound. She recognized it instantly.

It had to be *The Sailor's Thunder*, Gunnar's favorite cannon. She'd heard it fire thrice before, the last time at her father's funeral. Finally, Njord's fourth champion had come to her aid.

To her left, the enormous masts of the *Floating Castle* had appeared at the entrance of the bay. A cloud of smoke rose from the ship's prow, as it always did from a cannon's mouth.

She turned toward the enemy forces. A second *boom* came as the shell exploded in mid-air, high above Queen Marion's knights.

He's done it! she thought. *He's perfected his special shells.* Why Njord hadn't told her of it, she did not know.

The fragments didn't harm Queen Marion's knights, but that did not surprise Frida. Njord must have told Gunnar of her message to Queen Marion. Most likely, Gunnar thought of the Verdant knights as potential allies.

Which he would greet with cannon fire. Because Gunnar was… well, Gunnar.

A sliver of hope surged inside her. Perhaps the battle was not lost after all.

She stepped backward, keeping her eyes on the knights, and the shield wall opened to receive her. In moments she was in the third rank, at

Lothar's side, with the guards Torsten and Arne and the sea witches Astrid, Ingrid, and Helga surrounding them.

"You don't seem happy," Lothar said.

"We fight," she said. "Raise the yellow flag."

The first line of Queen Marion's knights darted onward.

"We should be going," Torsten said. "To your ship," he added when she did not reply.

She shook her head. "Not yet. Stay by my side."

She held out her hands, and one of her men handed her his axe and shield. Her twin daggers weren't meant for fighting in the shield wall.

Another great cannon fired from Gunnar's ship. *A Woman Scorned*, he called it. Frida recognized it by its high-pitched sound. This time, the shell exploded ahead of the charging knights — and its contents tore a wide gap in the line, felling horses and men alike.

Frida knew what it had released, though they were too far away for her to see. Hundreds of small lead balls, scattering forward after the shell's explosion. At their speed, they'd punch through armor, and *had*.

Two more of Gunnar's big cannons fired: *The Mad Seahorse* and *The Oarsman's Glare*. Then Frida's own cannons joined in, and the battlefield was filled with the sounds of cannon fire and the screams of the dying.

More cannons fired from Gunnar's ship. Firing at an angle from the knights' line, and with their scattering shot, they inflicted more damage than her own.

The first charge was in disarray. Many of the knights had fallen; others struggled with their horses, spooked by cannon fire; and perhaps less than a hundred were still on their way. But Marion's second wave of knights was coming, and though Frida's cannons had opened more than a dozen gaps in that line, the riders weren't stopping.

"Green flag!" she shouted, hoping Lothar would hear her above the din of battle. Just then, her archers let their arrows fly.

They smashed into Marion's first wave of riders, now less than a hundred paces away, and many of the knights fell. Then the first rank of Frida's men raised the nine-foot-long spears they'd left lying on the ground. The second rank advanced, covering them with their shields. In the third rank, Frida raised her shield and braced herself, as did Torsten on her left and Lothar on her right.

The knights crashed into Frida's line, and many men fell on both sides. One of the riders aimed his lance at Frida as he charged, but Astrid the sea witch sent an ice spear through his visor with such speed, it yanked the knight back in his saddle. His head lolled and his hands fell to his sides as Lothar stabbed a short spear through his horse's neck.

The man on his right rode for Torsten, and his aim was true. An instant before his horse impaled itself on an Islander's spear, his lance struck Torsten's shield — and shattered it. Yet King Knut's former bodyguard kept his feet, and swung his axe with such ferocity that it took the man's leg off at the knee. He howled in pain, and Frida's guards dispatched him before she could land a blow of her own.

Then her cannons fired again.

With the yellow flag, she'd ordered a half-salvo. On each ship, only half of the cannons had fired. The green flag had fired the rest.

They had to shoot blindly now, as the smoke from the first salvo hid the battlefield from sight. But Frida trusted her cannon teams.

They fired round shot and canister shot, and the projectiles smashed into the second wave of Queen Marion's knights. More of Gunnar's cannons fired as well, taking out more than a dozen knights at a time.

The second charge hit Frida's line moments later and had no more impact than the first. Too many of the knights had been brought down by cannon fire. The shield wall held, and to her left and right, Frida saw her men dispatching the riders with spears and axes.

The battle had gone well so far. There was just one problem.

If they keep coming, we are doomed.

Marion's next wave of riders would reach them before Frida's cannons could reload. The bulk of her knights were only six hundred paces away. And though the cannonballs had cut through their ranks, too many of them were still standing.

If they charged now, they'd reach the shield wall unchallenged, unless

Gunnar had kept some of his cannons in reserve. Then Queen Marion's footmen would join them, wave after wave, and they'd overwhelm Frida's forces.

A trumpet call sounded, amplified by magic. The few knights who were still battering the shields of Frida's men turned about and rode back toward their lines.

"Your plan worked," Lothar said at Frida's side. "We scared them off."

"Only because Gunnar came in time," she said.

"Black flag?" Lothar asked. It would tell the cannon teams to fire as soon as they reloaded.

Frida shook her head. "Not yet. Wait. Perhaps they'll charge us again."

She raised her spyglass to her eye and watched the retreating knights. When they reached Queen Marion's line, one of them spoke briefly to the queen.

"They're pulling back," Frida said as she lowered her spyglass. Many of the knights were cantering toward the forest. How Queen Marion had signaled them all, Frida did not know. She turned to Lothar and—

"Look out!" Torsten shouted — and shoved her in the chest, sweeping her legs from under her.

She yelped as she crashed to the ground, and Torsten landed on top of her. A moment later, three arrows thudded into the sand, less than a foot away from her face.

Torsten leaped to his feet and held out his hand. "Apologies, my queen. This was the fastest way to keep you safe."

She nodded as she understood. His shield had been destroyed in the first charge.

She took his hand and stood. The men around her kept their shields high. Two of the shields sported a few arrows jutting from them, though they hadn't reached their bearers. Lothar's left hand clasped his right shoulder, and she could see blood underneath.

"Just a scratch," he answered her unspoken question.

"Arrows," Torsten said. "From six hundred paces. Helped by magic, I'm sure." There was no way an arrow could fly that far on its own, and definitely not on target. "That must be how they took out Ursula."

He groaned and turned to the side, and Frida winced as she saw the arrow jutting from his back. "You've been hit, Torsten."

"Nothing that our healers can't fix," he replied, before collapsing to the ground.

The sea witch Helga dropped to her knees next to him. She placed her hands on his back and started chanting.

Frida shot her a look, and Helga nodded. *I'll get him through this*, she was saying.

I hope so, Frida thought. *He saved my life.*

She looked ahead. Marion's knights were galloping toward the forest.

"Black flag?" Lothar asked again.

She shook her head. "No. Let them go, Lothar. We've won the day. Get the men back to their ships and join me on Gunnar's *Floating Castle*."

The Mad Champion

At the prow of the *Floating Castle*, Gunnar, the fourth of Njord's champions, whooped as the long line of Verdant knights retreated toward the forest.

"Run!" he shouted. "Run with your tails between your legs!"

His second, Oskar Gustavsson, grinned. "Shall we bid them farewell?"

Gunnar nodded. "Black flag, Oskar. Give them all we've got."

Oskar raised the flag, and the symphony of gunfire began anew. There wasn't much time for the cannon teams to aim before the knights passed the tree line, and some ammo would be wasted, but Gunnar didn't care.

"They should have accepted her terms," he whispered. Far in the distance, scores of horses and men died, torn to pieces by his shrapnel shells.

A heavy hand lay on his shoulder, making him turn. The sea god himself stood at his side; blue, naked to the waist, with his hair and his beard fashioned into fine braids, and with a wild look in his eyes. His trident rested against the ship's deck.

Gunnar raised an eyebrow. "What's with you, big guy? I thought you couldn't interfere."

"I'm not," Njord replied. "I was watching the battle with the Lady, and she conceded." Around them, dozens of sailors cheered, knelt, and looked at Njord with awe and pride in their eyes.

"Awaaay!" Gunnar roared. "Away, all of ye! The grownups need to speak!"

The sailors rushed away, quick to obey his orders. He turned to Njord and grinned. "See? I'm the true god here, big guy. Not you."

"Only because if I strike you down, I die as well."

"Keep telling yourself that," Gunnar said. "Hmm. I wonder what Loki would have said if he saw me laughing in the sea god's face."

Njord raised an eyebrow. "Loki?"

"A strange god from a vision I had last night. Funny lad. I think we'd get along." He picked out a morsel from between his teeth. "Not one of the visions *you* would show me, of course. You only come to me to speak of war and death." It must have been the Supreme One himself who'd gifted him the vision.

Njord frowned and looked into the distance for a moment. "Ah. I see. He's from another world. A trickster god, and a shapeshifter, too. Augustus would have liked him."

Gunnar hadn't seen Loki change his shape, but Njord's words did not surprise him. After all, Njord himself often shifted into his sea serpent form. "You still haven't told me why you're here," he said.

"To celebrate today's victory with my champions. Why else?"

"You didn't come to me when I carved a path through Queen Marion's fleet, did you? Maybe you were huddled up with Anders and a cask of ale to celebrate *his* victory." Njord himself had told him of the betrayal.

The sea god shook his head. "Frida will be with us soon, Gunnar. This is a momentous day for her. The day of her first victory as queen, fighting for her god. Don't spoil it with your ramblings."

"You know I didn't want to fight for you," Gunnar said. "Prophecies be damned."

Njord sighed. "Yes, Gunnar, I do know it. You've told me a dozen times. But you fight for Little Frida. And that is enough."

Reunion

It's taller than I remember, Frida thought as she looked up at Gunnar's ship.

She and Lothar stood at the prow of a longboat as the oarsmen pulled it closer to the ship. A climbing net had already been tossed over the *Floating Castle*'s starboard railing. It reached the water, rising and falling with the ship's swaying motion.

"We go," Frida said, and jumped overboard. A splash to her left told her Lothar had done the same.

They climbed the net, hand over hand. Frida climbed faster and stopped twice to wait for Lothar to catch up. Finally, she vaulted over the railing and landed on the forecastle deck with a thud.

Gunnar was waiting for her, and he was not alone. Njord, the sea god, stood at his side. Four inches taller than Frida, supple yet muscular, with his intricate braids and his trident in his hand, he was a vision of perfection. Frida had met him in his other aspect as well: the magnificent sea serpent, growing thrice as long as Gunnar's ship when he wished it, who could easily wrap himself around a galleon and pull it to the bottom of the sea, or simply crush it with his might.

None of Gunnar's sailors were near, though many had gathered on the lower deck in celebration. They clasped arms, raised jugs of ale, and toasted to Njord, to Gunnar, to Queen Frida, and to each other. Most likely, Gunnar had sent them away, so that he and his guests could speak in private.

Njord turned toward Frida, his blue eyes giving away nothing. She lowered her gaze and dropped to one knee.

He advanced, bringing forth a wave of power that crested and washed over her. When he placed a hand upon her head, raw power coursed through her veins, and her spirits lifted like a ship at high tide. She tensed her muscles, feeling stronger than ever before.

"Rise, Queen Frida," Njord said. "You've won a great battle today. You've made me proud."

"I did my best," she said as she stood.

The sea god smiled at that. "Never one for many words, are you?"

She dipped her head. "I only did my duty. Besides, I couldn't have won without Gunnar's help."

At that moment, Lothar caught up with her, breathing heavily. Focused on Njord as she was, she hadn't heard him climb over the railing.

"I've already thanked Gunnar," said the sea god.

"You ha—" Gunnar started, and paused, open-mouthed. "Your thanks were well received, my Njord. Now, may I approach?"

Njord moved to the side, and Frida gave Gunnar a once-over as he advanced. Tall and lean, only two inches shorter than she was, he still possessed the wiry strength of experienced swimmers, even now in his early fifties. His long hair had turned gray, and he kept it that way, though he did dye his beard blue. He had the same familiar glint in his eyes, which Frida's father had described to her as half-madness, half-genius.

He caught her gaze. "Welcome to my *Floating Castle*, Little Frida."

"It's *Queen* Frida," Lothar said sharply.

"I was there when she was born, Lothar," Gunnar said, "and when she took her first sip of mother's milk from Big Greta's breast. I was there when she got her first ship, and we took her second ship together. And unlike you, I was there when her father died, and I fired my cannons to honor him. I get to call her whatever I like."

"That he does," Frida agreed, and placed her hand on Lothar's arm.

Lothar stepped back and Gunnar embraced her, pulling her close. She hugged him tightly, though she was the first to let go.

He pulled away and looked her over. "You've gained weight, Little Frida."

"Gained it *back*," she replied. Last time they'd met, her father was dying of a strange fever that not even the best of his healers had been able to cure. She'd spent days and nights at his side, holding his hand and speaking to him even when he could no longer answer — and she hadn't eaten well in weeks.

Gunnar nodded. "No offense meant. It looks good on you. Show me those big arms of yours."

She flexed her biceps, and her two tattoos, the dolphin and the trident dagger, danced as she did. "I'm getting stronger every year."

Gunnar smiled. "You could snap me like a twig." He gave Njord a quick glance and set his eyes upon Frida again. "If only Big Greta could see you now."

"If only," she whispered. Her mother, a skilled captain in her own right, had perished a few weeks after Frida's fifth birthday, her ship caught in a bad storm out on the open sea. And though her face was now a distant memory, Frida would always remember her love, and the stories she'd told her, and the way she used to hold her close during cold winter nights.

"You've grown truly fierce, Little Frida," Gunnar spoke again. "Beautiful, too, but you were always thus." He ran his fingers through his beard. "If Njord were to take a wife, he couldn't do better than you."

"You overstep, Gunnar!" Lothar snapped.

Njord simply raised an eyebrow, his eyes studying Frida's face.

She lowered her eyes. "I'm not worthy of the thought." Unlike the Julian gods, Njord did not dally with mortals. Besides, she already had Ulrika waiting for her back in Hemland — though if she returned as the sea god's wife, she expected Ulrika would rejoice.

Gunnar chuckled. "I did say *if*. Though if you ask for it, I don't think Njord would refuse. You're one of his last champions, after all."

A loud grunt came from Njord. "Enough with that, Gunnar. Today, the two of you have defeated Queen Marion, and I am grateful for it. The Lady herself conceded the battle to me after you destroyed her knights. But the War of the Seven is far from over. Today, we sail out of this bay and celebrate our victory. Tomorrow, we'll hold a war council and plan our next move. Anders Svensson is still at large, and I am not allowed to punish him for his betrayal. We must decide whether you are to face him or head east instead. But you can't sail into the open sea, not with my mist barring the way."

"We'll find a way to win, my god," Frida said, "though it will take us some time to recover our losses. For now, we must focus on staying alive. Gunnar and I will protect each other, and there are no traitors among my men. Not anymore. I am certain of it." After Anders's betrayal, she'd asked the sea witches to sniff out any other signs of treachery. They'd found none.

"Nor among mine, my Njord," Gunnar said.

Njord advanced toward Lothar, whose bandaged shoulder seeped blood from the arrow wound. *That's why he took so long with the climb*, Frida realized, though Lothar hadn't complained.

The sea god placed a hand on his shoulder. Lothar winced and gritted his teeth, but a moment later he let out a sigh of relief.

He ripped off his bandage. There was no sign of the wound.

"Thank you, my god," Lothar said, and fell to his knees.

Njord grinned. "The Godly Pact has imposed many restrictions upon me, but there are still things I can do. Now rise, Lothar Bjornsson." He turned to Frida. "How fares Sigurd?"

"Worse than the last time you saw him. He can't come to terms with the loss of his ships."

"Yet he did help you win this battle. He commanded your cannons, yes?"

"He fired the first shot," Frida said. She'd given her captains their orders before Queen Marion's arrival, with Lothar and Sigurd standing at her side.

"I'll go and bring him here," Njord said, "and then we'll celebrate. It will give you and Gunnar time to speak." He turned to Gunnar. "Remember what we discussed, my friend."

Gunnar raised an eyebrow at that, but Frida did not ask why. If they'd discussed anything she needed to know, Gunnar would tell her.

The sea god took two measured steps forward and leaped overboard. In mid-air, he shifted into his sea serpent form, growing longer and thicker as he fell. He sank into the sea with barely a splash, and the water closed above him.

"He's given us time to speak," Gunnar said, making Frida turn toward him. "I'd make good use of it. Lothar can stay, of course."

A grunt came from Lothar, but he did not protest.

She nodded. "You've fulfilled the prophecy today." It had been told for a long time that a descendant of Gunnar's grandfather would save Njord from destruction, though no one knew where the prophecy had come from. Perhaps not even Njord himself.

"I didn't fight for Njord today," Gunnar said. "I fought for the babe I held in my arms twenty-nine years and four months ago. I fought for the last soul that ties me to your father, and to Big Greta, and to all my childhood friends who now sleep beneath the waves. I fought for you, Little Frida."

"Thank you, my friend." Frida sighed. "We're the last of Njord's champions, Gunnar. If I die, he dies. If *you* die, he dies. And then our people will suffer for a thousand years under a foreign god."

"We can't worry about a thousand years, Little Frida. We only have today, and if we play our cards well, we get to have tomorrow."

"Then let us take each day at a time," she said.

"Aye," Lothar added, as if to remind them of his presence.

Frida nodded at him. "Your rain of steel, Gunnar," she said, steering the conversation to lighter topics. "You've finally perfected it."

Gunnar stroked his beard and grinned. "Rain of steel. I like it. Though I call them shrapnel shells."

"What's a shrapnel?"

"Not what. Who. Henry Shrapnel, a man with a funny haircut. I saw him in my dreams. An officer of the British Army, whatever that is. A man from another world."

"Oh." Strange visions had troubled Gunnar's bloodline for generations, and they were more madness than genius. Though Frida had to admit that these shrapnel shells had won the day.

"The man's experiments saved me years of trial and error," Gunnar said. "And I had three years to perfect his inventions before bringing them to battle today. I'd like to think I have surpassed him. Unless a new vision shows him the better of us two." He paused. "Sadly, my foundries are back in Hemland, and the shells on my ship are all that we have. Until we capture some foundries, at least."

"Perhaps we will," Frida said. "How big is your fleet, Gunnar?"

"Just the *Floating Castle*, with a hundred cannons, and four fishing ships with two cannons each. Those are waiting just outside the bay. We cut through the Verdant fleet like a hot knife through butter."

"We'll do so again if we sail east. Unless they flee from us."

"We must go east, yes," Lothar said. "Let us leave the Verdant Kingdom behind and sail to the shores of the Julians instead."

"This is not about raiding the Julians, lad," Gunnar said, though he and Lothar were roughly the same age. He continued, paying no heed to Lothar's frown. "This is about our survival, beyond that of the other realms' champions. A hard task, if you ask me."

Lothar frowned. "I didn't say anything about raiding, *Captain Gunnar*. Queen Frida was right. We must seek an alliance if we are to survive. And Queen Marion has rejected us. So, it must be the Julians that we join our fates with."

"And just how do you see that working, lad?"

"We'll help them fight off the orcs, the desert men, and whoever else decides to attack them. Our warriors and our cannons will turn difficult battles into great victories and save tens of thousands of Julian lives. In return, we'll get them to commit to fight for Njord, if their gods fall, and we promise them that Njord will treat them well. They wouldn't want to be ruled by Grok, or Aljin, or the vampire god. And if Njord falls first, we'll ask the Julian gods to take good care of Hemland, and to refrain from taking revenge for past injuries."

"And if they refuse, like Queen Marion did?" Gunnar asked.

"Then we'll take one of their coastal cities," Frida intervened, "and make it our own. We'll strike from the sea and unleash your rain of steel upon them. The shrapnel shells, as you call them. Once the city is ours, we'll strengthen the walls, place our cannons upon them, and make it impossible to conquer. We'll defend the city against all attacks and wait for the other factions to tear each other apart. We'll recruit more men to replenish our forces. And after most of the other gods are dead, we'll fight whoever is left for the ultimate victory."

"If we survive that long," Gunnar said.

"I know it's a long shot, Gunnar," Frida said. "Tell me if you have a better idea."

He frowned and was quiet for a few moments. "Not yet," he said at last. "But perhaps the Julians will accept an alliance. And then we'll have their legions fighting for us, as we fight for them."

"No hostages this time," Lothar said.

"No hostages," Frida agreed. "We'll ask Njord and Augustus to match our pact with one of their own, and that will have to be enough."

"Then it is settled," Gunnar said.

"It is," Lothar said, and Frida nodded.

Lothar raised an eyebrow. "We just held tomorrow's war council today. Without Njord. And the path forward is clear."

Gunnar chuckled. "Aye, lad. We even decided what the sea god must do for us."

"We'll hold council tomorrow as well," Frida said. "With Njord and Sigurd. And if they have better ideas, we'll go with those." Though she couldn't imagine what better ideas they could come up with.

"Speaking of Njord," Gunnar said, and pointed.

Frida turned, just in time to see the great serpent leap out of the sea, with a man upon his back. It shifted in mid-air, and Njord landed on the deck. His right hand held his trident, while his left clasped Sigurd's arm.

"We're all here now," Njord said. "It's time to celebrate our victory."

"Fetch me a barrel of ale, men!" Gunnar roared. On the deck below, two burly sailors hurried to obey his command. He turned to Sigurd. "Welcome to my ship, lad."

Sigurd pulled him in a tight embrace, lifting him off the ground. "You came just in time, you mad bastard! Your cannons sent our enemies scurrying back into the forest."

Frida smiled as she watched them. They were together now, Njord's last two champions and his loyal captains, and their god was with them. They'd already won a battle and had a plan for what to do next. And even after King Knut and Ursula's deaths and Anders's betrayal, her fierce Islanders were still in the contest.

The Envoy

Queen Elena hovered above her army's camp, three hundred feet in the air, with the guard Vladimir at her side.

Below her, the tents of her subjects were arrayed in neat rows, leaving plenty of distance from one another. The serfs' tents were painted gray, while the nobles' lodgings were the color of fresh blood.

Elena's command tent towered above all others. Twelve feet tall and twice as wide, it stood less than two hundred paces from the edge of the forest. Six men-at-arms guarded the entrance, and Serya Krov's banner fluttered in the wind, raised atop a thirty-foot pole.

"A splendid sunset, my queen," Vladimir said.

I wish I could enjoy such things, Elena thought. She'd lost the ability five centuries earlier, along with her heart and the love of her life.

She circled one more time, surveying the edge of the forest to the north and the riverbank to the south. Everything was calm, just as she had expected. She'd set up patrols on both sides, and a few of the serfs bowed as they noticed her glancing their way.

The camp was at ease. The men were taking their evening meal, sharpening their blades, or darting to and fro as they ran errands for their officers. As for her nobles, she'd given them the evening off, until midnight's war council.

She glanced toward the Blackstone Castle, just in time to see the gates open.

A single rider came through, clad in armor and carrying a white flag high atop a tall pole. He headed straight toward her forces. The gates closed behind him.

Elena turned to Vladimir. "A messenger. Have him brought to my command tent. He's not to be harmed."

"As you wish, my queen," Vladimir answered, and flew toward the front of the camp.

Elena swooped down, landed in front of her tent, and pushed aside the flap. Two of Serya Krov's champions waited inside: Duke Zoltan Barko, her strongest wizard, and Kirill Skromnik, Elevated Priest and former follower of the Lady.

"They're sending a messenger," Elena told them. "I'll see him here with you, Duke Zoltan. Kirill, you go back to your tent. I'll send for you if I need you."

The priest bowed and retreated without a word.

"Why did you send him away?" Zoltan asked.

"They might be sending an assassin, or a wizard. And Kirill is too... vulnerable." The first word that had come to her was *squishy*, but that did not seem appropriate. "You and I can take whatever comes our way."

"That we can," Zoltan said. "He's a good man, Kirill."

He was indeed, and useful as well. From dawn to dusk, he spoke to the human officers in Elena's army and made sure that their men were properly drilled, and that their morale was high. He'd talk to the soldiers as well, stoking the flames in their hearts with his stories. As for Igor, her head priest, he was in charge of the supply train and keeping the army properly fed. The noble vampires themselves spent less time worrying about such things.

"So you don't doubt him anymore?" Elena asked.

Zoltan shook his head. "Not for now. I'd still keep an eye on him. We haven't shed that much Verdant blood yet." He grunted. "About the messenger. Do you want me to strike first, just in case?"

She nodded. "Be subtle, Zoltan. Just a bit of fear. Not too much."

"As you say. Until then, a quick drink, perhaps?"

He was offering her his blood, but she did not need it now. She didn't want to refuse him either, so she chose to misread his words. "Go ahead. Come back quickly, though."

He grunted and strode out of the tent. She imagined him sinking his teeth into one of the guards and taking a long, deep draught from the man's throat.

He returned less than a minute later, licking the last few drops from his lips. "I needed that more than I'd thought."

"I hope you didn't take too much," Elena said.

"He'll be fine by morning. I told him to go lie down and asked for a replacement."

Elena nodded. "Very well. And now we wait."

They did not have to wait long. Soon Vladimir lifted the tent flap and strode inside, with Sir Roland's messenger following him. Vladimir stood to the side and motioned for the man to advance.

He was in his mid-twenties, tall and fit, with long brown hair and boyish good looks. He carried no weapons and was clad in armor, with the Verdant Cross drawn upon his breastplate.

He had to be a nobleman. His armor was well made and fit him well.

He bowed. "Queen Elena. I bring a message from our officers."

Not from Sir Roland, Elena realized. She clenched her left fist, knowing that Zoltan was watching.

"Your name, boy," the wizard growled.

"I am called Robin," the young man answered. If Zoltan's magic had touched him already, he did not show it.

More like Sir Robin, Elena thought. "I expect you've come to offer your surrender."

"First," Robin said, "I have orders to thank you for stopping the executions."

She nodded. A few of her nobles had made a sport of throwing peasants to their deaths from high above, trying to get them to fall upon the castle's various buildings. She'd put a stop to it upon her arrival, and none of the nobles had dared protest her decision.

Of course, they hadn't sacrificed any of those whom she'd promised safety. They knew better than to defy her wishes.

The killings had been Zoltan's idea, and she had to admit his method had been effective. He'd gotten the knights to charge. After three charges, only two had survived, with one of them gravely wounded. And while they'd slaughtered over two hundred serfs in those charges, Elena's nobles were unscathed.

"How fares Sir Roland?" she asked.

"He hovers on the brink of death," the envoy replied.

So he was the wounded one. "I heard he took an arrow through the throat. I wasn't here to witness it."

"That is true, Queen Elena."

Soon you'll call me 'my queen,' she thought. "Your surrender, then."

"Our officers are discussing it. They'll give their answer at dawn. I'll deliver it myself, if you'll allow it." Apparently Sir Robin had the good sense to admit that his life had been forfeit the moment he'd entered her camp, white flag notwithstanding.

"I'll allow it," she said. "But I trust you remember our conditions. We require the castle, all your weapons and armor, and Sir Roland's life. In return, you will all cross the border, pay the blood price, and live on as my subjects. You'll be under my protection, as long as you obey my laws."

"My officers won't murder our lord," Robin said. "Nor would they surrender him to you. Doing either would go against everything we stand for. Then again, they won't have to. Our healer did what he could, but he doesn't think Sir Roland will survive the night."

"And if he does?"

He met her gaze. "Then honor compels us to defend ourselves."

She snarled, baring her fangs. "And the War of the Seven compels me to destroy you." Her fight was with the Lady's champions, not with the men who defended this border fortress; but she couldn't afford to have them at her back, striking at her supply lines. "That, or to have your surrender."

"I understand," Robin said. "As do our officers."

He's the one leading them now, Elena realized, though he wouldn't admit it. He'd said, "*my* officers" before. A slip of the tongue, but she'd caught it.

His gaze did not waver under hers. There was something in his eyes, and it wasn't fear. Even here and now, he thought he had an edge.

Elena pretended not to notice.

"So, they sent you to beg me to wait till morning," she said. "What else?"

"We hope that there will be no more executions until I speak to you again. Would you agree to it?"

It was a trap, of course. He could always send another envoy, or no one at all. Which would either forestall the executions forever or make her break her word.

"There will be no more executions until noon tomorrow," she said, "and my forces won't break the peace before then either. I'll give you that and nothing else. After that, you'll give me your surrender, or I'll give you death."

Sir Robin nodded. "I will relay your message to our officers."

"Very well," she said. "Now go. Vladimir, escort our guest to the edge of the camp. Then come back here. I will have need of you tonight."

Vladimir raised an eyebrow, and since he stood behind the envoy, the man could not see it. "As you wish, my queen."

She waited until Sir Robin and Vladimir left the tent, and another few moments after that. Then she turned to Zoltan. "So. Did you?"

"I gave him just a bit of fear, as you asked me to."

"Then he's a braver man than most."

Sir Robin

The night was dark as Sir Robin advanced quietly through the forest, with three hundred men at his back.

They'd left Blackstone Castle through its escape tunnel, and soon they'd reach the northern edge of the enemy camp. His archers had taken out two of the serfs' patrols already, before they could raise the alarm.

He had no chance to overwhelm Queen Elena's forces. Judging by the size of her camp, the bulk of her army was yet to arrive; or perhaps other groups, led by lesser vampire nobles, were striking at other fortresses along the province's border. Even so, they outnumbered his men two dozen to one, if not more. But he wasn't seeking a total victory tonight.

"Lady, give me strength," he whispered.

He raised his hand. Through the trees, he could already see Queen Elena's red command tent; lit by torches, towering above the other tents, and with the vampire god's banner standing at its entrance.

He glanced over his shoulder. His men had halted, and Peter, the captain of the archers, walked to his side. "So, it is time," he whispered.

Sir Robin nodded. "Give me three minutes, Peter. Then we strike."

They clasped arms, most likely for the last time. The chance of both of them living through the night was too small to consider. But if their mission was a success, their sacrifice would be worth it, and Queen Elena would finally join her long-lost lover.

The Blood Rage

It was just after midnight when the serfs' screams started at the northern edge of Elena's camp, followed by the clang of steel on steel. A few heartbeats later, dozens of flaming arrows whooshed through the air, and then Elena's command tent caught fire.

Elena watched it burn, from the entrance of another tent, a safe distance away. Vladimir and Zoltan stood at her sides.

"Now, my queen?" Vladimir asked.

"Not yet," she said as the sounds of fighting drew closer. A column of serfs darted toward her command tent, carrying buckets of water. Others rushed onward, holding spears and heavy shields.

She waited another dozen heartbeats. Then she spread out her wings and said, "Now."

With a shriek that pierced the night, she took to the air, her battle axe in hand. She angled left, then right, but no arrows came toward her. More shrieks followed as her nobles rose from their waiting places.

The enemy soldiers had advanced into the camp, their battle line having passed the first three rows of tents. At least two hundred men, most of them wearing armor, and all of them on foot. They battered the shields of Elena's men with swords, axes, and the occasional battle mace, and they were gaining ground. They'd already left scores of dead bodies in their wake.

With a roar, Zoltan swooped downward and crashed into their midst.

Elena left him behind. With Vladimir at her side, she flew on toward the edge of the forest, where the archers had to be waiting. They had no burning flames now, but she spotted two of them easily among the trees. No doubt there'd be more.

She folded her wings and dropped toward the ground at an angle, and several arrows passed overhead. She darted between two long branches, narrowly avoided a tree, and landed among the men. Half a dozen surrounded her, and more were coming.

Three of her enemies had arrows nocked. She threw two knives with her left hand and two of the men fell, while Vladimir barreled into the last one. Then she was dancing among the remaining foes, her battle axe cleaving limbs from torsos and heads from necks with every blow. The edge of the forest filled with screams as warm blood seeped into the ground.

The archers were not armored and didn't put up much of a fight. When another three of her nobles joined the fray, Elena took to the air again and returned to the camp, with Vladimir following her.

The enemy forces were in disarray. Zoltan had torn a wide gap into the line, as had Boris and Sergey to his left. More of Elena's serfs had joined the fighting, many of them armed with long spears. Half of the attackers were dead. The others had clustered in small groups, fighting back-to-back, hoping to sell their skins dearly.

Elena wouldn't have that. "Burn them!" she shouted.

One of her serfs smashed a pot of tar onto the ground, just ahead of a pack of enemies. Another man threw a burning torch, and the liquid quickly caught fire.

The soldiers turned away from the flames and charged, but they were met by a forest of spears. When Sergey swooped above them and struck two helmets with his twin maces, Elena knew the fighting would be over soon.

She soared into the sky and turned toward the castle. A lone figure rushed toward the gate, already out of arrow range. Fleeing from the fight.

"I want that man, Vladimir," she said, without looking back.

Her guard darted forward, flapping his wings quickly to gain speed.

He's getting too close to the walls, Elena thought, and almost called him back. But no arrows came to meet him. Then Vladimir angled downward and crashed into the running figure.

He took to the air again a few moments later, his hands clutching his prey's belt. His victim hung without moving; unconscious, or perhaps dead.

Elena flew to meet him and landed at the edge of her camp. Behind her, the sounds of fighting were replaced by cheers of victory.

Vladimir landed and deposited his captive in front of her. It was the young man who'd visited her tent a few hours earlier. He slumped to the ground, his breathing shallow.

"Wake him," she said.

Vladimir yanked his arms behind his back and sank his talons into his flesh, and the man screamed as his eyes snapped open.

"I knew you were coming, Sir Robin," Elena told him as Vladimir raised Robin to his feet. He tried to fight, to bring his arms forward, but Vladimir overpowered him easily and brought him to his knees.

Sir Robin ceased struggling and lowered his head. "How?"

"I've ruled the vampires for five hundred years. I am the oldest mortal alive, except for some of the giants. The most powerful creature, save for the gods. Did you really think I'd fall prey to your little tricks?"

"I had to try," he said, his voice thick with defeat. So he was indeed the leader.

"How did you leave the castle without us seeing you?" Elena asked, just as Zoltan Barko landed at her side.

"A secret tunnel," Sir Robin said. The fight was gone from him. "It comes out into the forest."

"We can use it to take the castle, my queen," Vladimir suggested. "Where is it?" he shouted, and Sir Robin flinched from him.

Elena shook her head. "Why would I use a tunnel, Vladimir, when I have the sky? We've just taken out most of their soldiers. The officers, too, I expect. If we strike now, the castle will fall easily." She looked Sir

Robin in the eye. "Tell me I'm wrong."

His shoulders slumped. "I surrender Blackstone Castle to you, my queen. I bid you to accept it without further loss of life."

"Too late for that," Zoltan said, and pointed to the castle.

Elena watched as eight of her nobles flew toward it.

"We questioned some of the men we spared," Zoltan continued. "You're right, my queen. The castle is defenseless. Our nobles will take it and kill everyone inside."

"They're just servants!" cried Sir Robin. "Spare them, I beg you!"

Elena thought for a moment. He wouldn't beg for servants' lives, would he? There had to be more to it, and she could easily find out what it was. Besides, whoever was still in the castle would be in her power soon enough.

"Fine," she said. "I'll call them back."

"Don't," Zoltan said as she unfurled her wings. He placed a heavy hand on her shoulder.

She whirled toward him and bared her fangs. "You dare?" she shouted.

He stepped back and fell to one knee. "The blood rage is within them, my queen. You can't control them, not now. They'll turn against you if you try. They'll tear you apart and put me in your place. And that would be a disaster."

The blood rage. She knew it well, though she'd never felt it herself. A state of intense hunger mixed with joy and boundless power, where the vampires' vision turned red and they fell prey to their instincts, tearing their enemies apart and leaving death and destruction in their wake.

It had never taken her while Dragos was alive. After she'd given her heart, it couldn't.

"It doesn't seem to affect *you*, Duke Zoltan," she said. "Or you, Vladimir."

Zoltan nodded. "A wizard of my skill has more control than most."

"And I barely fought," Vladimir said. "I was always at your side, and I only killed three men."

In the distance, behind the castle walls, men and women were screaming.

"Please," Sir Robin begged. "My mother's in there!"

"Then pray to your Lady she dies quickly," Zoltan replied.

Hatred burned in Sir Robin's eyes, but only for a moment. He sagged, and Vladimir released his arms and shoved him to the ground.

"Take my life as well," Robin said softly.

Elena nodded. "Do it, Vladimir. Make it quick." It was the right choice. If she let him live, he'd be a mortal enemy.

Vladimir knelt and drew his talons across the man's throat. In the distance, the screams grew louder.

"Do you wish to see it, my queen?" Zoltan asked.

She shook her head. "I'll visit the castle when it's over."

It would be a massacre. A needless waste of life. But Zoltan was right. She couldn't have stopped it if she tried.

She looked down at the young man's body. "He was a worthy adversary, this brave Sir Robin. A true knight, as his people would say. Though he did flee from battle."

"That was my doing," Zoltan said. "He was leading the attack and putting up a good fight. So I lashed out with my magic and gave him weakness and fear enough for ten men. Then some of his soldiers charged me and I lost sight of him."

"I see." Elena turned her thoughts away from the man. "Did we lose anyone in the fighting?"

"Countess Vera took a spear through her chest," Zoltan said. "She'll recover, though. The others were unharmed, as far as I can tell."

He wasn't talking about the serfs. *Those must have died in their hundreds,* Elena thought. *Three or four, at least.*

"And Kirill?"

"Nikolay kept him away from the fight. I expect he's still at his side. I passed them when I flew here, and they were fine."

"Look, my queen," Vladimir said.

High in the sky, an enormous shadow dropped through a cloud: Serya

Krov, the vampire god. He hovered over the castle, no doubt watching the carnage below.

He couldn't interfere in the battle. The Godly Pact forbade it. But the fighting was over now, though the dying was not.

"Feast, my children!" his voice boomed, high in the sky. Below, the screams intensified.

He could have put a stop to this, Elena realized. But that was not his way.

Maybe this is what we need, she thought. *I could set free some of the peasants I captured and have them spread the story of what happened here to nearby towns and castles. It will strike fear into the hearts of the Lady's followers. They'll surrender, rather than suffer the same fate.*

It would bring me closer to defeating the Lady and getting my revenge for Dragos's death.

Or maybe this would rally our enemies against us and make them fight harder. Just as I used Kirill's story to rally our serfs to our banners.

She sighed and looked to the side. Was this the queen she wanted to be? She stood for order and justice, not for needless killing. She'd done so for centuries, and her rule was firm. Yet the vampires' blood rage was strong, and what had happened on this night would happen again and again, before the War of the Seven was won.

Perhaps we truly are the monsters everyone else says we are. But she couldn't dwell on that now. It was time to face her god and celebrate her victory.

She spread her wings and took to the sky, and Zoltan and Vladimir followed.

The Gods and their Champions

Aljin: King Ammon, Nasir bin Fatih, Achmad bin Fayzal, Al-Khanjar

Augustus: Emperor Lucius, ~~Marcus Severus~~, Leticia Alba, Selenius Gracchus

Grok the All-Father: King Ghark, Hagor the shaman, Rorra Fireborn, Krakkar the Fist

The Lady: Queen Marion, High Priestess Sandra, Eugene the Trickster, Sir Galahad

Malleon: King Tassadar, Paeren, Neressia, Eldris the Duelist

Njord: ~~King Knut~~, Queen Frida, ~~Ursula~~, Gunnar

Serya Krov: Queen Elena, Duke Zoltan Barko, Kirill Skromnik, Katrina

Bonus Content

Congratulations! You've finished Part Four.

To explore the bonus content, visit https://bradtowers.com/wots-bonus-4/ or scan this QR code:

Part 5: Invasion

Upon the Mountaintop

Four days after Eldris's awakening

The sun shone brightly in the sky as Eldris the Duelist climbed the steep path to the mountaintop, leaning on the walking staff he'd fashioned for the journey.

Gravel crunched underneath his boots. It was barely mid-spring, but the snow on the World's Peak had already melted. The sun god's doing, perhaps.

The Reaping Blade hung in its harness on Eldris's back. It was a heavy burden, though it was not the weight of the sword that troubled him. It was what he needed it for.

Malleon's instructions had been clear. Ask the orcs for an alliance; request that the gods themselves be present at its forging, to bind themselves in Godly Pact; and strike down Grok the All-Father with the Reaping Blade. The only weapon that could kill a god.

They'd been friends, Grok and Malleon. The closest friends among all the gods, some said, though their followers had fought each other many times over the centuries. But the War of the Seven was about to change that.

Eldris gritted his teeth. *They woke me up for this. All the things I've done for my kind, all the battles I've fought and won, and this is how I'll be remembered. Eldris the Treacherous. Eldris the God-Killer.* But his duty was to obey his god, whether he liked it or not.

He rounded a bend and, for the first time after his four hundred and fifty-seven-year slumber, he admired the tip of the World's Peak up close.

The mountain's summit was a rocky, inhospitable place. No plants grew there, not even a blade of grass, and no birds dared fly above it. A sacred ground for giants and orcs alike, it had been the site of countless battles over the centuries, passing from one race to the other as their strength and ambition had waxed and waned. And now, there was no garrison upon it. No warband, no coven of wizards, not even a lookout post. And not a living thing.

Just two enormous flags, blowing in the wind.

On the purple flag, Malleon's image stood tall, with his long white hair reaching past his shoulders. He wore his necklace of great lizard's teeth and his favorite cape, made from the hides of a dozen bears. His great hammer was slung across his back. The red flag showed Grok the All-Father in a heroic pose; bare-chested, red of skin, hair, and eyes, wielding a massive sword in his right hand and a flaming torch in his left.

A short climb later, Eldris walked between the flagpoles.

He took a strip of white cloth from his pack and tied it to his walking staff, and a third flag stood upon the mountaintop, though his was much smaller than the others. He advanced and gazed south, upon the orcs' realm below.

The orcs' kingdom was almost as large as that of the giants, and two of its five provinces met at the mountain's top. To Eldris's right began the province known as Grok's Lair, where the orcs' capital stood proud and strong, a few days' walk from the summit. To his left lay the colossal valley called Mother's Cauldron, too vast for the eye to see in its entirety, and shaped as if a mighty fist the size of a country had left its print upon the landscape.

A steep ravine separated the two provinces. It plunged at least five hundred feet, its walls smooth, as if cut into the rock by an enormous sword. It stretched for over eighty miles, with a few hanging bridges spanning it in places. Eldris had seen its far end once, more than seven centuries earlier, at the end of a glorious war against the orcs. He still recalled the clash of arms as lightning flashed in the sky, and the roars of victory as the defeated orc army fled the field of battle.

He wasn't going that far now.

He crossed into the orc lands, carrying his white flag, and had barely advanced five dozen paces when a voice from farther ahead shouted, "Who goes there?"

"It is I, Eldris the Duelist," Eldris said. "I speak for King Tassadar. Show yourself!"

An orc warrior appeared from behind an outcropping in the rock, twenty paces ahead of him and lower down the slope. He was clad in full armor and had a great axe slung across his back and an arrow nocked in his bow. His beastly nose was crooked, and two long tusks jutted upward from the corners of his wide mouth.

"You're on the wrong side of the mountain, Elvis the Duelist," he said.

"Eldris," Eldris said evenly, though he knew the orc had mangled his name on purpose. "I have a message for your king."

"You'll give it to me. And to my friends here."

The orc whistled and six other orcs appeared from behind various rocks. Two carried bows, while the others held long spears and heavy wooden shields. Knowing their tactics, Eldris had no doubt that more warriors lay hidden.

He towered over them, and it wasn't just the slope of the mountainside. Yet these warriors were well-built. On flat ground, the tallest three of them would reach almost to his chest.

"And you are?" he asked.

"Great Chief Horgo Surehand," the first of the orcs replied.

It was a high rank. Eldris nodded in respect.

The great chief lowered his bow. "Your message, Eldris."

"King Tassadar asks the great king Ghark Bloodaxe to drink from the cup of friendship." The words tasted sour on Eldris's tongue. "He wishes for our kind and yours to be joined in an alliance. To fight together side by side, as brothers in arms, until all gods but ours are vanquished."

"And then?"

Eldris recited the words Malleon had taught him. "A year of respite, if there is time. A month, if there is not. After that, we'll fight a single battle, here at the top of the world, with all our surviving champions present, and let that battle decide our fates."

He took a deep breath. "To seal our bond, our king and yours will feast together here, on the World's Peak, a week from today. Each will bring a small honor guard along. And Malleon and Grok the All-Father will join us at the feast, and forge a Godly Pact of their own. They'll promise that they'll keep our alliance true, and that the final winner will favor both of our kinds equally, for a thousand years to come."

The great chief shook his head. "I don't think so."

Eldris frowned. "*You* don't think so? This is a decision for your king. And for your god."

"King Ghark's not here. He's already marched to war."

"Which way?"

Horgo grinned. "You'll trust my word for it, giant?"

It was a good question. Before Eldris could ponder it fully, Horgo spoke again.

"He went east, with the warriors from the capital. He sent messages to the clans and summoned the Great Horde to his banner. When it finally gathers, he'll lead our warriors against the Julians. If you don't believe me, ask Malleon to take a look. That won't be against the rules, I reckon."

"You'll get my message to your king, Horgo," Eldris said.

"Aye. I'll send my fastest runners, but it'll take them at least two weeks to catch up with the king. By then, I expect King Ghark will be busy smashing the Julians and plundering their lands."

Eldris thought quickly. "Our offer for an alliance still stands. Have your messengers tell King Ghark that King Tassadar expects his reply."

Horgo nodded. "I'll give you his reply myself, when it arrives. Until then, don't let me see any of your kind trample over the mountaintop."

"We don't want to fight you. Not yet, at least."

"You'd take Grok's Lair easily if you wanted to, now that our warriors are gone. Me and my lads can't stop you, and most of the passes are undefended. But walls are just walls, and we can always rebuild."

"Walls are just walls, aye," Eldris agreed. "I reckon King Tassadar will keep the peace."

"Very well." Horgo raised his bow again. "Now hurry back to your land, friend, before I put an arrow in your eye."

Eldris shrugged, turned around, and walked calmly up the mountain. He was not in danger; he carried the white flag, and besides, the great chief had called him "friend."

He sighed. *If he only knew.*

He had no doubt that Malleon would still want him to slay the orc god. Though it seemed he'd need to wait a little longer to do it.

The Red Tide

Forty days after the gods' meeting

And so it begins, thought Ghark Bloodaxe, the king of the orcs.

Less than half a mile ahead, past the edge of the forest, the Julian fort stood defiant, an ugly construction of earth, wood, and stone. It had a ditch, and a rampart, and a wooden palisade, and four gatehouses, one on each side. And four stone watchtowers at its corners, thirty feet tall at least, and no doubt brimming with archers and crossbowmen who'd sell their lives dearly when the attack began.

Forts like this one lined the border every five miles or so, and the orcs didn't like them much. When one of their raiding parties crossed into the Julian lands and the locals got wind of it, these forts would spew forth hundreds and hundreds of little soldiers, and dozens of horses as well. They'd cut off the raiding party's retreat and overwhelm it with their numbers, allowing a single warrior to escape. On such a night, the mourning songs would howl through the hills, and angry chieftains would pound their chests and vow to avenge the raiders' deaths, in the name of Grok the All-Father.

They'd go on the warpath at times, and burn a fort or two, and sing the mourning songs again for those fallen in battle. But the little men came back, in larger numbers, and the orcs returned to the hills, and the Julians rebuilt their forts, again and again.

Well, not anymore. Ghark would put an end to it. On this day, he'd brought the might of the Great Horde against them.

From Grok's Lair they'd come, and from the Hills of Spite, and from Mother's Cauldron as well, except for those he'd left behind. All the way here into the Howling Rocks, the orc province that bordered the Julians.

He'd split them into seven warbands, six of them led by great war chiefs who carried the All-Father's banners with pride. The seventh, he led himself.

They'd all strike tonight, under the cover of darkness. Each war chief would take a different fort, at least thirty miles apart; and after they burned their first target, they'd take their warbands to the next fort in the line, and to the next one after that. They'd burn them all, and quickly, before joining forces at the appointed place and readying for the great clash with the bulk of the Julian forces in the Twin Rivers province. After that, they'd march into the heart of the empire, burning and pillaging along the way.

But first, tonight.

He turned around. Five thousand brave warriors faced him, standing among the trees. His elite forces: strong and proud, red of skin and hair, armed to the teeth, and bloodied in brawls and battles. With them at his side, he'd conquer the world.

Another three thousand would arrive by morning. But Ghark would not wait. Summer had already begun, and his warriors were becoming restless.

"My brothers!" he shouted. His voice was amplified by magic, though not so loud that it would reach the little men's ears. "Tonight is the beginning of the end. Tonight, the red tide sweeps across the Julian border. Tonight, we burn their forts; and tomorrow, too, and the day after that. We'll burn their villages next, and their crops, and their walled cities. This we shall do, my brothers, in the name of Grok the All-Father, until the Boy Emperor himself lays his sword at my feet and surrenders his champions to me. And then I'll strike them down, and banish their gods from this world, for a thousand years!"

"Bloodaxe! Bloodaxe! Bloodaxe!" his warriors roared, raising their fists in the air.

"So, sharpen your blades, and string your bows, and ready your spells, and sing your songs of battle. Look to your chiefs and obey them; they know the battle plan. And fight hard, as if Grok the All-Father himself was fighting at your side. For he'll be watching us tonight!"

"All-Faaa-ther! All-Faaa-ther! All-Faaa-ther!" the warriors shouted. Some pounded their chests, others clanged their swords and spears against their shields.

He silenced them with a gesture. "Rorra. Hagor. Krakkar."

In moments, the three champions gathered around him. Behind them, the warriors were clustering around their chiefs. Soon, they'd all know the battle plan.

"This will be a night to remember," Hagor the shaman said. He thumped Krakkar on his shoulder. "One more great victory to add to your legend, my friend."

"And in the end," Rorra said, "we'll make a pile of the men's skulls, and feast on their horses."

Ghark regarded his companions in turn. The witch Rorra Fireborn hailed from Mother's Cauldron, and like all the great witches of that province, she was a mother too, and had a cauldron of her own. Her leathery skin was covered in ritual scars, one for each spell she'd cast. Her white hair, which had lost its fiery red hue a decade earlier, fell down her shoulders and toward the small of her back. A sturdy breastplate protected her torso and her ample bosom.

A head-turner she'd been once, despite her less-than-average height; and now, at fifty-seven, she still walked with a spring in her step, though her arms had lost some of their strength and her left tusk was chipped and turning gray. Three of her sons fought in Ghark's warband, and five of her grandsons, too.

The shaman Hagor the Sniffer was taller, though not as tall as his spear was long. A dozen kinds of leaves and herbs hung from the collar he wore over his sleeveless tunic, marking him as a great healer. Besides his skill with herbs, he was a keeper of legends; a bard who knew a thousand stories, sang them around the campfires, and could whip the troops into a frenzy before battle. Though he was only thirty-five, his hair, which was a tangled mess, was turning gray.

The most impressive of them all was Krakkar the Fist, the Giant-Slayer. Even now, in his early forties, he was known as the greatest orc warrior alive, and perhaps among the greatest of all time. Clad in armor and wearing spiked vambraces on both forearms, he held a battle mace in his left hand and a long double-bladed axe in his right. Two long, curved swords were slung across his back. On a night like this, all his weapons would taste blood. As would his fists, and perhaps his tusks as well.

His long red hair was tied in a topknot at the back of his head. His sunken eyes and his prominent jaw made him look older than he was, but nobody would dare say that to his face, not if they wanted to keep all their teeth.

He'd brought a son to battle. The lad hadn't inherited his father's strength or his skill with weapons, yet he'd make himself useful. He was a competent tracker and hunter, and could put an arrow through a squirrel's heart at fifty paces. And that was no small feat.

King Ghark himself thought he looked younger than Krakkar, though he'd just passed his fiftieth birthday. His hair had turned gray the year before, but his mind was as sharp as ever, and he kept his body strong. He wrestled boys half his age in training, and often won. And while he'd never been the biggest or the strongest of his kin, his rousing words and his feats of arms had earned their respect over and over again.

No children of his own would be fighting tonight. His daughter was pregnant for the third time, and his young boy was only eight. As for his firstborn, he'd died in battle against the desert men six years earlier, slain by an arrow through the eye.

If only he were here, at my side, Ghark thought. But no one could bring back the dead, not even Grok the All-Father.

Hagor grunted, snapping Ghark from his thoughts. "You wished to speak with us alone."

Ghark nodded. "My friends," he said. "Tonight we go forth with strength, and with great numbers. We'll pound our enemies into the ground."

"And burn them," Rorra added. A small fireball appeared in her right hand, though she didn't need it. She didn't seem to mind the ritual scar she'd cut into her skin within the hour. At least a dozen more would join it after the battle.

"And burn them, yes. I said it in my speech. But that's not what I wanted to say to you. I wanted to tell you, be careful."

Krakkar scoffed at that. "You mean, smash 'em and bash 'em and slice 'em to bits, yes?"

"That, too. But also, don't die. The All-Father needs us all, and he needs us alive. Until we've won the War of the Seven for him."

"Actually," Hagor said, "the All-Father only needs two of us. It's *you* who wants all of us to live on. Yes?"

Ghark nodded. "We don't have to take just one fort, my friends. We have to take the world. And maybe some of us will die before the end. But not today."

"Not today," Rorra said.

"Not today and not tomorrow," Hagor added.

"The man who'd cut me down hasn't been born yet," said Krakkar.

"So, that means you need to watch out for a woman," Rorra said. "Or a newborn baby."

Krakkar grunted. "I meant maybe a giant could try to take me, or one of the vampire nobles. Not that I'd let them. But I see none of those here tonight." He didn't see the men in the fort either, not from this distance, but Ghark knew it was only a figure of speech.

"Krakkar," Ghark said.

The warrior shrugged. "Fine, Ghark. I'm not dying today. And not tomorrow, and not the day after. Happy now?"

"Happier than before," Ghark said. Of course, he'd assigned a dozen of his trusted guards to watch over the three, and to come to their aid at the first sign of trouble. But they didn't need to know that, not yet.

"And you?" Rorra asked.

"I'm not dying either."

"Then it is settled," Hagor said. "We meet at Rorra's fire when we're done."

They didn't have to ask Rorra where she'd light her fire. They'd see it all right. She liked her fires tall, and bright, and smoky, too. They'd spot it from miles away.

"They're waiting for us there." Rorra pointed at the fort. "They have to know we're coming. And they must have a plan."

Krakkar laughed. "Everyone has a plan, dear Rorra, until they get a mouthful of this." He raised his battle mace high. "Or an arrow through the throat. Or maybe the sight of one of your fireballs, just before it melts their eyes off, and their brain, too. Save me a seat at your fire, and one of those honey cakes of yours, and we'll share stories as we drink to our victory." He thumped Hagor on his shoulder. "And you, friend, you'll put our stories into song."

Krakkar the Fist

From the shadows of the forest, Krakkar the Fist stared at the Julian fort.

Two thousand orcs stood with him, the All-Father's other three champions among them. The rest would charge the enemy fort from the sides. With the advantage of numbers, and striking from three directions, they planned to overwhelm the defenders quickly.

Two hundred paces past the treeline, the fort squatted in the moonlight like an old bear too stubborn to die. Dark silhouettes of Julian soldiers patrolled the battlements, their spears and shields glinting faintly in the light of their torches.

Krakkar grunted. *If they know we're coming, they must be shaking with fear. Good.*

To his right, King Ghark Bloodaxe stood silent as a stone. Behind Ghark, Hagor the Sniffer crouched over a small bowl of smoldering herbs, muttering words of power. Wisps of smoke drifted up into the night, carrying the sharp scent of burning roots.

Rorra Fireborn made her way to Ghark's left, her scarred hands moving in practiced gestures as she muttered a spell. A small flame flickered in her palm, no brighter than a candle's glow. Her white hair tumbled around her shoulders, and her tusks gleamed in the firelight. "Soon," she whispered, her voice hungry.

Krakkar raised his battle axe above his head, gripping his mace tighter with his left hand. Both weapons would taste Julian blood tonight, cracking skulls and shattering bones. He glanced back at the mass of orc warriors, all eager for blood and glory, their weapons sharp, their eyes wild.

"We've waited long enough," Krakkar growled, his voice low and rough.

Ghark turned his head slowly, his face impassive. "Hold, Krakkar."

Hold. Hold while the fort taunted him with its walls and towers. Hold while his blood boiled and his muscles ached to swing and crush and slice. Hold while the Julians pranced about with their spears, tricks, and traps.

Krakkar squeezed the handle of his axe. *Tonight, we shall send them to their deaths.*

From the wall, a trumpet sounded, a long, wailing note.

"They sound their own doom," Rorra said quietly, her flame growing brighter.

Krakkar glanced at her. "What do you think they'll do when we're on the walls?"

She smiled, her tusks framing the grin like gleaming daggers. "They'll scream."

Ghark's deep voice rose above theirs. "Signal the attack, Rorra."

Rorra raised her arms. Her flame flared and swelled into a roaring ball of fire as large as a man's head, painting the nearby orcs in its orange glow.

A hush fell over the forest. Even the wind seemed to pause, and Krakkar's muscles tensed. This was the first heartbeat of a battle, where time held its breath before the slaughter began.

Somewhere, Grok the All-Father would be watching.

Rorra hurled the fireball skyward. It rose through the air, leaving a fiery trail in its wake. With a roar, the orcs sprinted forward, and Krakkar ran with them. Weapons clanged, shields rattled, and the ground trembled under thousands of pounding feet.

He dashed out past the treeline, the grass flattening beneath his boots as he and his battle brothers surged onto open ground. A Julian horn sounded again, sharp and frantic now.

Then came the groaning of war machines.

A ballista fired, the cords snapping like thunder. A long iron spear hurtled through the air and struck the orc to Krakkar's left with a sickening crunch, punching through his chest, impaling him all the way through. The warrior fell, and those behind him rushed onward.

Krakkar growled and kept running.

More ballistae launched their deadly projectiles. Iron spears tore through the charging ranks, hurling red-skinned warriors back in crimson sprays. Warm blood splattered across Krakkar's face. Without breaking stride, he wiped it off with the back of his hand, his mace glancing off his armor with a clang.

Arrows rained down next. Krakkar snarled as the shafts clattered against his armor, bouncing off his pauldrons and vambraces. One glanced off his thigh, but his steel turned it aside.

He grinned. *The weaklings might as well throw pebbles.*

Ahead, the ground opened into a wide, spike-filled ditch. The fort loomed larger now, its walls lined with defenders. One screamed and fell backward, struck in the chest by an orc witch's fireball.

"Ladders! Shields! Move!" Krakkar bellowed to the orcs nearby, his voice carrying above the din.

The first ranks reached the ditch. A warrior tripped and fell forward, impaling himself on a long wooden spike. Those coming after him slowed their pace, rather than share the same fate. A volley of arrows struck from above, and more orcs fell, the merciless spikes waiting to receive them as they crashed to the ground. Screams of pain and rage rose into the night, and Krakkar answered them with a growl.

With a few quick blows of his axe, he chopped down a two-foot-long spike, then two more. Other orcs followed his example, shields raised above their heads, and within moments, they'd cleared a safe path to the base of the wall. To the right, the battering ram pounded against the gates.

"Ladders!" Krakkar shouted. He hung his axe and his mace to his belt, grabbed a shield from a fallen warrior, and raised it above his head. "Get the ladders!"

Orcs rushed forward, carrying long ladders through the storm of arrows. A warrior shrieked as a torrent of boiling water thrown from above splashed onto his face. Others pushed past him, dragging the ladders upward.

A ladder slammed against the wall to Krakkar's right, its hooks biting into the wood. A broad-shouldered warrior roared and began climbing. Krakkar followed, keeping his shield high.

Above, a Julian soldier shouted something. His spear thrust downward, smashing into the lead orc's shield. The blow rattled the warrior, but he growled and kept climbing.

"Faster!" Krakkar roared.

The ladder swayed under their weight. Hot oil poured down from above, hissing and steaming as it splattered against Krakkar's shield and armor. Krakkar gritted his teeth as the scalding liquid seared his skin, but he didn't falter. The fire witches would heal his burns after the battle.

The orc ahead of him reached the top and hurled himself over the battlements with a savage roar. Steel clashed against steel.

Krakkar sprinted up the final rungs. With a growl, he hauled himself onto the wall. The Julians were there, waiting — rows of men armed with spears and heavy shields. Krakkar dropped his shield, reaching for the weapons that hung from his belt.

The closest Julian lunged at him with a spear. Krakkar batted the weapon aside with his axe and swung the mace into the man's face. The blow landed with a dull, wet crunch, and the soldier crumpled backward, blood spraying across the wooden planks.

Another soldier charged at him, thrusting wildly. Krakkar sidestepped, shoved the man in the shoulder, and pushed him off the wall. The Julian's scream cut short when he struck the ground below.

More orcs hurried up the ladder, roaring their fury as they slammed into the defenders. Krakkar turned to his left and advanced, his weapons a blur of motion. His axe cleaved through a Julian's shield, splitting the wood and chopping through the man's arm. His mace smashed into another soldier's helmet, the blow driving the man to the floor.

Another Julian rushed him, spear ready, but Krakkar caught the man with a backhand swing of his axe that sent him sprawling. An orc warrior stomped on the man's head, and Krakkar grinned. This was battle. This was life.

The orcs were swarming the walls now, pushing the Julians back. Hagor's voice rose in a guttural chant, and warriors screamed with renewed frenzy. Further down the battlements, two young fire witches hurled fireballs into the enemy ranks.

Then Krakkar saw Ghark.

The king stood atop a wide fighting platform, a dozen paces away. Six red-skin warriors stood with him, but they were surrounded by a sea of Julian soldiers. Ghark fought fiercely, his axe rising and falling, but he did not have long. One of his guards went down, a spear piercing his gut. Another stumbled back, an arrow lodged in his throat.

"With me!" Krakkar bellowed, motioning to the orcs nearby. He threw his mace and axe forward, striking two Julian soldiers, and drew his twin swords from their sheaths across his back.

He charged, Left Fang and Right Fang gleaming in his hands. Orcs followed him, roaring their war cries. The Julians closest to him turned to face the new threat, raising their shields to defend themselves.

Krakkar struck the first one with a downward slash from Left Fang, the blade cutting into the man's neck. He thrust Right Fang toward another soldier's face, but the man parried it with the edge of his shield.

"Push through! To the king!" Krakkar shouted.

His warriors surged forward, a red tide that smashed into the defenders with shields and steel. An orc fell, clutching his face. Another hurled a Julian soldier off the wall.

A Julian spearman thrust at Krakkar's chest. Krakkar swatted the weapon aside with Left Fang and drove Right Fang into the man's shoulder, twisting the blade before yanking it free. He pushed further into the fray, not bothering to finish off the man. His battle brothers would do it for him.

The orcs cut and hacked their way toward their king, their advance relentless. The wooden planks underfoot were slick with blood. Warriors screamed and died on both sides.

Krakkar glanced at Ghark. The king fought atop the platform, his axe rising and falling in savage arcs. Around him, his last four guards stood their ground. They were bloodied and outnumbered, and one had an arrow buried deep in his arm, but still they fought, roaring their defiance as they defended their king.

"Forward!" Krakkar shouted.

He cut his way through his foes, and his battle brothers came with him. A Julian officer scrambled away from him, panic in his eyes. Krakkar rushed forward and kicked the man's shield, unbalancing him, and slashed Right Fang across his face. He stabbed another soldier through the eye, stepped over his fallen body, and reached Ghark's side.

The remaining Julian soldiers on the platform fled, rather than face Krakkar and his warriors. Perhaps their officer would have called it a strategic retreat, were he still breathing.

Ghark turned to Krakkar, his axe dripping blood. "Took you long enough," he said with a grin.

Krakkar grinned back. "Go back to the forest. I'll finish this."

Ghark nodded. He reached out, and Krakkar clasped his forearm in a warrior's grip. Then Ghark headed toward the nearest ladder and climbed down, his four remaining guards covering his retreat.

Below, the fort's wooden gates splintered with a thunderous crash. The battering ram had done its work. With a roar of triumph, orcs spilled into the courtyard, their weapons flashing as they clashed with the Julian defenders.

Victory was near.

Krakkar turned his gaze to the nearest watchtower, its stone walls rising above the chaos. A cluster of Julian soldiers defended its base, their shields locked together. Higher up, archers loosed arrows into the swarm of orcs flooding the courtyard below.

"With me! To the tower!" Krakkar roared.

He led the way. His battle brothers followed him, and together they carved a bloody path through the defenders. A Julian swung his sword at Krakkar's face. Krakkar ducked and lashed out with Left Fang, slashing across the man's thigh and leaving him howling on the wall. Another orc silenced him with a blow of his mace.

More Julians fell, but not without cost. To Krakkar's right, an orc screamed and dropped to his knees, an arrow buried in his throat. Another collapsed as a spear pierced his chest, his war cry cut short.

Krakkar snarled and fought on, his twin swords a blur of silver and red. Left Fang bit into a soldier's cheek, splattering the planks with blood and teeth. Right Fang caught another man in the gut, spilling his blood onto the stones.

The orcs reached the watchtower. The door had been barred, but an orc with a hammer smashed it open with two great swings. Krakkar stepped into the narrow stairwell beyond.

"Up! Go!" he roared, his voice echoing off the walls.

The stairwell spiraled tightly, the stone walls closing around him. The Julians tried to stop him—shields blocking the stairs, spears thrusting downward, archers loosing their arrows at close range—but Krakkar pushed on. He hacked a shield apart, drove Left Fang into a Julian's chest, and kicked the man's body out of the way. Another soldier lunged, but Krakkar caught the spear mid-thrust, yanked it from the man's hands, and slammed Right Fang's hilt into his face.

More orcs climbed behind him. A Julian above hurled a clay pot of flaming oil down the stairwell. It smashed against the stones, fire erupting in a blinding flash. An orc screamed as the flames consumed him. Krakkar ignored the heat and smoke, pressing upward. Two young orc warriors dashed past him, screaming for blood.

Krakkar followed them at a slower pace, taking the time to catch his breath. He stepped past three dead Julian soldiers, and in a few moments, he reached the top of the stairs.

The stairwell opened into a square chamber lit by flickering torches. The two young orcs lay sprawled across the floor in pools of blood. A

Julian officer stood alone in the center of the room, his sword held high.

He was taller than the others and wore a polished breastplate. His eyes were calm, his stance practiced. Blood streaked his sword, and his breathing was steady.

Krakkar's warriors dashed into the room, but Krakkar raised a hand, holding them back. "This one's mine."

The orcs hesitated, then fell back to the doorway. "Krakkar! Krakkar! Krakkar!" they shouted, their voices echoing through the tower.

The Julian officer shifted his grip on his sword. "Come then, brute," he said.

Krakkar grinned. "As you wish, dead man."

He lunged forward, both blades swinging. The officer met Left Fang with his own sword, the clash ringing through the chamber. Krakkar twisted his wrist, driving Right Fang in a low arc toward the man's side, but the officer sidestepped, quick and graceful.

This one has some fight in him, Krakkar thought.

They circled each other, blades flashing. The other orcs kept their distance, as Krakkar had commanded them.

The officer struck high, his blade slicing toward Krakkar's neck. Krakkar ducked, whipping Left Fang upward in a counterstrike. The man parried again, but the force of the blow drove him back a step. Krakkar feinted a quick cut with Left Fang and slashed Right Fang across the man's thigh, drawing blood.

The officer staggered back, his breathing heavier now. Desperation flickered in his eyes. He lunged, sword thrusting forward in a final effort.

Krakkar deflected the blow and slammed his forehead into the officer's face. The Julian reeled back, blood pouring from his broken nose.

With a roar, Krakkar swung with Left Fang, the blade biting deep into the man's side. The officer gasped, stumbling, and Krakkar drove Right Fang through his left eye. The man fell to the floor, unmoving.

"For the All-Father," Krakkar growled.

The orcs erupted into cheers, pounding their weapons against their shields. "Krakkar! Krakkar! Krakkar!"

Krakkar turned to them, raised his bloody blades high in the air, and roared his triumph.

He stepped to the nearest window and gazed into the courtyard below. Orcs swarmed through the gates, and less than a handful of Julians still stood. Krakkar watched the red-skinned warriors cut them down.

He grinned, his heart pounding with savage joy. "We've smashed 'em and bashed 'em and sliced 'em to bits!" he shouted.

But the fight wasn't over. Not yet.

Three more watchtowers still stood, and their defenders loosed their arrows into the orcs below. A warrior fell, clutching his throat.

Krakkar raised Left Fang high. "With me! To the next tower!"

He dashed down the stairs, and his battle brothers followed him.

Negotiations

The *Floating Castle* lay at anchor half a mile from the northern Julian coastline, surrounded by the rest of the Islander fleet. On its deck, Augustus swayed slightly on his feet, as if the ship's gentle rolling with the waves affected him.

Such trivial things never had. Then again, he hadn't come as himself.

On this day, he was Appius, a young Julian diplomat. Five feet tall, with a slender frame and an elaborate haircut, he wore an orange tunic that fell past his knees and a thin leather belt decorated with orange gemstones. His skin was barely tanned, as that of an aristocrat who spent most of his time indoors and traveled in a palanquin.

At his side stood Naereus, who officially led the Julian delegation. The twenty-year-old came from an ancient noble family and was the lover of Princeps Farus, who ruled the Twin Rivers province. Of course, Naereus was aware of his companion's true identity. Augustus had revealed himself to him the night before.

Facing them were the three leaders of the Islanders, along with their guards.

Queen Frida Gretasdottir stood in the center, the marks of the bear's claws visible across the upper side of her chest. At six foot three, she towered over the Julians. As did most of the Islanders.

On her left, Gunnar, the ship's captain and Njord's fourth champion, leaned against the starboard railing. A dangerous man, gifted with visions of other worlds by the Supreme One himself, he had built the largest ship in existence, armed it with a hundred cannons, and brought shrapnel shells into this world before it was ready for them — and he'd perfected those as well. He did not dye his hair blue, and that was an offense in Njord's eyes, yet the sea god favored him; a consequence of an old prophecy that had finally come to pass.

On Frida's right stood Lothar Bjornsson, her second-in-command. A man of far less importance, though a capable sea commander and a raider who'd visited much pain upon Augustus's followers over the years.

Flanking them were Frida's guards, Arne Olafsson and Torsten Eriksson. They were big and sturdy, even for Islanders, and looked like men who could wrestle with orc warriors and win.

Three times out of ten, perhaps. If they were lucky. And only if biting was forbidden.

I wish I could use my powers, Augustus mused. A single swipe with his lightning bolt would have cut all five Islanders in half and removed their faction from the War of the Seven. Of course, without the pact that forbade the gods to destroy each other's champions, the whole contest would have been very different indeed.

He grunted, and Naereus spoke.

"Queen Frida Gretasdottir. I am Magistrate Naereus, son of Magistrate Flavius. I speak with the emperor's voice."

"The Boy Emperor's voice," Gunnar added.

Lothar Bjornsson frowned.

Queen Frida raised her hand. "Apologies, Magistrate Naereus. My friend Gunnar is known for speaking his mind."

Naereus smiled. "No need to apologize, Queen Frida. Emperor Lucius does not take offense when truth is being spoken. And neither do I."

The Islander queen seemed to relax at that. "Enough with titles. Call me Frida, Naereus."

"As you wish." The young diplomat pointed at Augustus. "This is Magistrate Appius, my trusted friend and advisor. The gods have blessed him with an excellent memory, and he will dictate the words of our meeting to our clerks once we are done, so that they reach the Boy Emperor's eyes."

"So he'll know I called him that," Gunnar said.

"Yet he wouldn't fault you for it," Naereus replied.

He's good, Augustus mused. He'd already watched Naereus negotiate the pact of non-aggression with the Verdant Kingdom, though he and the Lady had agreed to that one in advance. And now, facing these fierce Islanders who'd raided the Julian shores dozens of times, including those of his own province, the young diplomat showed no sign of disquiet. Though perhaps having his god at his side gave him a boost of confidence.

"Let us speak as friends, Frida," Naereus continued. "You want our friendship, and we want the use of your cannons against the orcs, the giants, and anyone else who comes our way. I think we can find some common ground here. At least for a while."

"We will, if the terms are right," Frida said.

She was very different from the Lady, and somewhat sturdy for his taste. Still, Augustus found her appealing in both body and spirit.

He wouldn't do anything about it, not now. Once he won the War of the Seven, perhaps. But he'd have to do it as Afrodisia, or maybe Venera.

He had no doubt he'd succeed, if he set his mind to it. After all, seven years away from Hemland was a long time for a mortal. And though Frida had been loyal to her Islander lover so far, nobody could be *that* loyal. Especially when faced with the charms of one of Augustus's aspects.

"Our terms are these," Naereus said, snapping Augustus from his thoughts. "We will form a strong alliance, sealed by a pact among our gods. We'll fight together, side by side, for Njord and for the Julian gods alike, until they are the last. If the Julian gods prevail, you and your Islanders will become Julian citizens, all past transgressions forgiven. And if Njord wins the contest, we ask for the integrity of our empire to be preserved, and for equal rights for our citizens and those of Hemland."

"This all sounds fair," Frida said. "And now, on to the difficult details. What if our gods are the last? How do we decide the winner?"

Naereus nodded slowly. "A fair question. What do you have in mind?"

"We had proposed to Queen Marion to settle this through a contest of champions. A fair fight, without the use of magic."

Naereus looked Frida up and down. "We'd be fools to accept that. You'd destroy Emperor Lucius easily. Even if he were allowed seven years to train, and to grow into his full strength, he'd be no match for you." He paused. "I think a different contest is in order. A great game of *Battle Armies* between Njord and Augustus, played with the imperial set of pieces, with the winner enjoying the ultimate reward."

"Ha!" Gunnar laughed. "As if we'd ever go for that!"

Augustus suppressed a smile. *Battle Armies* was a game of strategy. And at least this Islander knew that the sea god was no match for Augustus in a feat of great intellect.

Most of the gods weren't, except maybe for Aljin and Serya Krov. Not counting Athina, which was one of Augustus's own aspects.

"I'll have a game of *Battle Armies*, yes," Frida said. "But let it be played with real warriors instead of pieces. Our Islander shield wall against your Augustian Wall, twenty against twenty, and no magic. I'll lead our people myself."

"Your warriors are bigger and stronger," Naereus said. "Twenty against fifty, to make it fair for our side." With those numbers, the Julians would win easily.

"Fifty is too much," Lothar protested. "We'll give you thirty-five."

Augustus spoke for the first time. "We could haggle over this, and maybe we'll get to some numbers that will make each side think they've won. Only for either Njord or Augustus to reject the agreement. Let us not forget that their intelligence is vastly superior to ours." Again, he suppressed a smile.

"My friend Appius is right," Naereus said. "There is a better way to settle this. A game of chance." It was what Augustus had told him to suggest.

"A flip of a coin," Gunnar said. He took a coin from his pocket, tossed it in the air, and caught it without looking, only to let it disappear in his sleeve. "I like it."

"A roll of a die," Naereus countered. "A fair die, tested by our gods beforehand. And none of them will interfere."

"What's the difference?" Gunnar asked. "One chance out of two, or three out of six. Same thing."

"Three out of five for us," Naereus said, "and two out of five for you. If the roll is a six, we roll again. We have three champions and you have two; it is only fair."

"I'll go with those odds, aye," Gunnar said, and for a moment Augustus was worried. What if the man was favored by the Supreme One himself?

Then again, as far as he knew, he didn't like Njord much. Perhaps he hoped for the Julians to win.

"It's not your decision, you madman!" Lothar snapped. "It's Queen Frida's. And Njord's." He spoke the sea god's name with reverence.

"Queen Frida," Augustus said. "Forging this alliance gives your side and Njord a good chance to win the War of the Seven. Yet if you choose to fight alone, you are lost. All the other factions outnumber you, and after Anders Svensson's betrayal, the vampires have more cannons than you do. Even with the *Floating Castle*'s cannons on your side."

"Mine are better than theirs," Gunnar grumbled.

Augustus nodded. "Even so, you know I speak the truth. You will not prevail on your own. What will you take, two out of five for a real chance to win, or a hundred percent of defeat?"

Frida touched the claw marks on her chest. She looked at Gunnar, then at Lothar, then at Gunnar again. She looked far into the distance.

Finally, she spoke. "Aye. I agree to this, if Njord does as well. Though I still think my way was better. But we have more issues to discuss."

"If you are thinking about who will lead our forces," Naereus said, "the choice is clear. Our emperor will command. You will act as one of his trusted generals, second only to him."

"What does a fifteen-year-old boy know about fighting wars?" Lothar asked.

"No offense meant," Frida added. "It is a good question."

"Emperor Lucius has the best advisors," Naereus said, "and seasoned generals who love him and respect him. The Julian armies have fought many wars against the orcs, the desert men, and the giants over the centuries, while your men are used to raiding and looting. Your warriors are formidable, yet you have less than twenty thousand. It is clear who should lead."

"How do I know he's not just going to send me into battle against impossible odds when the war is about to be over? If I die, Njord dies. And then there's no more roll of the die, and your gods get our help for free."

"That won't happen. Our gods will be bound in Godly Pact."

"Yet it is the betrayal of men that worries me."

"The last time you worried about that, you asked Queen Marion for her sister as a hostage. That did not go so well."

Frida raised an eyebrow. "How did you know that?"

"We pay our spies well," Augustus intervened. "And we have many of them. Some among the Islanders as well." Those had sailed off with Anders, but Frida didn't need to know that.

"I'll need their names," Frida snapped.

"They were Anders's men," Augustus said. He'd keep the names secret, if she didn't insist. "I expect they left with him."

"Fine," Frida said. "Back to my concerns. I am not going to be a sacrificial pawn in the Boy Emperor's war game."

Naereus took the lead again. "We'll look for the safety of your champions as well as our own. You have the emperor's word for that. Yet you seek further reassurance."

"I do." Frida paused. "No hostages this time. We are friends after all, are we not, Naereus?"

"We are."

"Then let us join our realms in marriage."

The look of surprise on Naereus's face seemed almost genuine. "You wish to *marry* me, *Queen* Frida? We just met, and I am only a magistrate.

Besides, I am Princeps Farus's man."

"Leave the theatrics, friend," Frida said. "You know what I speak of. A marriage between me and Emperor Lucius. A true joining of our people."

She seeks to control him, Augustus realized. She'd fail, of course; she did not know Lucius's mind, nor that the Julian gods visited him on most nights of the week. There were many things about Lucius that Frida did not know. Either way, she was not the right match for him.

Naereus shot Augustus a look. Augustus shook his head, almost imperceptibly.

"Emperor Lucius will not agree to this," Naereus said.

"Yet perhaps there is another option here," Augustus intervened. "But first, a very important question. Do you like cats, Queen Frida?"

Naereus gave him a hint of a smile, along with the tiniest of nods.

Frida touched the marks on her chest. "I do, as long as their claws are shorter than this."

"Then it is settled," Naereus said. "We offer you the hand of Princeps Silvanus, the ruler of Augustus's Table. You'll rule his province together when the war is over. Along with Hemland, of course."

"It's the smallest province of the empire," Lothar said. "Far from the sea, too."

"Yet it is the best marriage offer we can make." In fact, it was the only one. With Lucius off the table, Princeps Farus having taken Naereus as his lover, and the rulers of the Farmlands and the Orchard of the Gods both old and married, there was no other choice.

"This Princeps Silvanus," Frida asked. "Is he a great warrior?"

"I… wouldn't quite say so," Naereus replied.

Augustus came to his aid. "Five feet tall, a bit plump, likes books. And cats, and pretty women, though he'll be loyal to you. Great sense of humor. More importantly, he's been one of the emperor's trusted friends since childhood. And when he talks, people listen."

"Ah, another child," Lothar grumbled.

"Princeps Silvanus is eighteen," Naereus said. "I realize he's not your physical match, Frida. Still, I think the two of you could get along."

"I'll have him by my side as I lead my men to war," Frida said. "Not as a hostage, of course," she added after an awkward pause. "But if he's to be my husband, we must get to know each other."

"That is true. But it doesn't mean he must go to war with you. I propose that you and Princeps Silvanus discuss and decide this together once you are married."

"Fine. I do have another request. The emperor has no heirs, yes?"

"None so far," Naereus said.

"Then, until he produces one, I'll have him name my husband first in line to the Julian throne."

She's crafty, Augustus thought. "An ambitious request, Queen Frida. A lone dagger in the night would make you empress."

"If it comes," Frida said, "it won't be wielded by my hand, nor by one who follows my orders. I'll give my word on that, with Njord as my witness. But this is war, and Marcus Severus is dead, and so are King Knut and Ursula the sea witch, and they've all been killed in surprise attacks. If the Boy Emperor loses his life as well, I would carry the burden of winning the war myself, with my husband's help. And for that, we would need to rule."

"There's always Princeps Farus," Augustus said. "I heard he has ambitions of his own, and our emperor may choose to name him instead."

"Princeps Farus will step aside if commanded," Naereus said. "I speak for him in this."

Augustus nodded. After Al-Khanjar's attack, Lucius was well-guarded. He'd survive the war, and he'd find a suitable wife and produce his own heir, in time. And if he died without a child of his own, Silvanus would be a wise emperor, and a better choice than hot-blooded Farus.

Naereus spoke again. "Thank you, Appius, for raising your concerns." He was reasserting himself as the leader of the Julian delegation. "Queen Frida," he continued, "I agree to your terms, in the name of my emperor."

"Then let us hope this will be the start of a successful alliance," Frida said.

"There's just one more thing," Naereus said, and Augustus knew what was coming. He was going to disclose the Julians' pact of non-aggression with the Verdant Kingdom.

For Frida's faction, it had serious consequences.

The Julians and the Islanders would fight everyone else together, as allies. They'd stand united against the orcs, the giants, the desert men, and Serya Krov's followers, who were now joined by Anders Svensson and his fleet. And with some luck, they'd win. And then, before rolling the dice for the ultimate victory, Njord's followers would have to defeat the Lady's champions, unless they were already out of the contest. Without the Julians' help.

Yet they'd still accept the path he was offering. They had no better choice.

The Lady will be furious when she hears about this, Augustus thought. He'd only offered her a pact of non-aggression, and she couldn't break it if she wanted to. He'd offered the Islanders an alliance, which included his protection against the other factions.

He thought of the Lady fondly, and often visited the memory of their last time together. Her enchanting smile, her touch, the taste of her lips. The exquisite sensations of their lovemaking.

Out of all the gods, he'd miss her the most. Yet only one could win the War of the Seven, and Augustus played to win. And now, if all went well, he'd have cannons, and Islander ships, and the fierce fighting men and women who sailed them, and a secure border with the Verdant Kingdom. And somewhere out there, Malleon's fourth champion carried a god-killing weapon, which Augustus knew about. Most likely, the other gods didn't.

As for that die roll, he thought, *the Islanders won't get that far. Either Frida or Gunnar will die, perhaps fighting the Lady's followers.*

He'd lost one of his champions to an assassin's blade, and the orcs' Great Horde had burned seven of his border forts the day before. Yet a few early losses hardly mattered. Out of all the gods, he had the best chance of winning the war.

The Fire Witch

Rorra Fireborn, the third champion of Grok the All-Father, took a deep breath as she looked up at the blood moon.

A portent of victory, the red moon was. And victory was near.

She stood behind the four guards that Ghark Bloodaxe had assigned to her. They were tall and sturdy, and carried heavy shields. Though they hadn't yet bloodied their blades in the battle, they hadn't complained. Half a dozen archers stood with her as well, all young boys between fourteen and twenty.

Forty paces ahead, the wall of the Julian fort loomed. Unlike the fort Ghark's warband had taken the night before, this one was made of solid stone; and it was taller, too. Not that it had mattered.

First, Ghark's warriors had dashed forward from the forest, braving the distance under arrow and catapult fire. The bridge teams had placed long wooden planks across the ditch, and the warriors had rushed onward, with their shields raised above their heads. They'd placed the scaling ladders against the wall, and climbed them, and then the massacre had begun in earnest.

The Julians had put up a good fight. They'd thrown their javelins first, and when thrown with full strength from the top of the wall, those could punch through shields, and *had*. Then they'd fought with their big shields and their nimble spears, which seemed to find the smallest gaps in the orcs' armor. All the while, the little men in the watchtowers peppered

Ghark's warriors with arrows, crossbow bolts, thrown stones, and the occasional spell. But the orcs were fierce, and they were many, and the wall was bare now, save for the red flag that fluttered in the wind.

The ground below the wall was littered with the bodies of the dead and dying. Some were red-skinned orcs, brave warriors who had lost their lives taking the wall. More were little men, thrown off by the warriors who'd made the climb. The four that Rorra's fireballs had killed had fallen backward into the inner courtyard.

The bulk of the fighting was inside the walls now, and it was loud. Warriors roared, swords clashed, axes and maces pounded against shields, and the screams of the dying rose above it all. And though Rorra wouldn't scale the wall, at least not until the battle was done, she was going to help. In her own way.

The northern watchtower was still in Julian hands. The little men peered from its narrow windows from time to time, shooting their crossbows into the inner courtyard and throwing Grok-knows-what at the besiegers, who were no doubt pounding on the door.

"Watch," she told the guard next to her. Brakko was as big as he was ugly, which was very big indeed; and while he spoke with a stutter, he wasn't a dullard, at least not when compared to his brothers. She'd taken a liking to him.

Brakko grunted. "Wh-what?"

"This." She raised her hands in front of her chest, focused, and whispered the words of the fire chant. A fireball the size of her head appeared in the air, floating in between her hands.

"I've... I've s-seen that," Brakko said.

Rorra began to count. "Five. Four. Three. Two. One."

A man appeared in one of the watchtower's windows. He hoisted a cauldron onto the windowsill. Whether it was filled with oil or boiling water, Rorra didn't know.

She hurled her fireball forward, straight at the man's face. He fell back with a scream, his hands pressed over his cheeks.

Eight spells so far, Rorra thought. She'd add eight more cuts to her skin once the battle was done, each in a different place, and each cut deep enough to give a single drop of blood. That was Grok's price for the magic he'd granted her.

She was proud of her kill, though battle magic was not her most impressive skill. Her metalworking was better, and so was her cooking; her horse stew was second to none. Too bad there'd be no horse stew tonight.

They hadn't found any horses at the first fort they'd taken, and Rorra didn't expect to find any at this one either. Most likely, the little men had sent their cavalry away from the empire's border. They'd keep their horses for a charge or two, once the red tide advanced farther into their realm. Many warriors would die in a clash like that, on both sides.

"A g-good shot," Brakko said, interrupting her thoughts.

Rorra grinned. "My best one tonight." Her previous fireball had narrowly missed its target. "It's all in the timing."

"T-timing," Brakko said. "I like th-that."

His eyebrows were bushy, like those of Rorra's grandson Dorkon. But unlike Brakko, Dorkon was going back to the hills with two members of his clan, who took turns carrying him on their backs. He'd taken an arrow to the knee in the previous battle.

He'd been lucky; his clansmates had pulled him to safety, and one of Ghark's best healers had worked him over with her magic. Even so, he'd need a month or two to recover.

Dorkon's misfortune had taken those two warriors from the Horde, at least until they got him to safety — and he'd hated that. Still, it was a better outcome than having Rorra chop off his leg at the knee, or worse, sing the mourning songs for him.

When he's ready to fight again, Rorra thought, *he'll come back to me.*

She raised her hands in front of her chest. "One more fireball." She focused — and a flash of light came at her from the tower.

She yelped, averted her eyes, and shielded her face with her elbow. A roar came from her left. She blinked twice and looked around. Three of her guards were safe, huddled behind their shields. But when she looked at Brakko, she sighed.

His eyebrows were gone, singed by the lightning spell. And his eyes...

"I c-can't s-see," he whimpered.

She placed a hand on his shoulder. "Lie down, brave Brakko. Keep your shield above your face. I'll send a healer to look at you when the battle is done."

It would be useless, and she knew it. And a blind warrior wasn't worth much. Though he could at least hold a spear against a cavalry charge — and Ghark's warband would face one of those within weeks, if not days.

"I'll have Hagor the Sniffer think up a song for you," she told him as he lay down on the ground.

"An ho-honor," Brakko said.

"I'll cook the wizard's liver for you, too," she told him, though it was an empty promise. Whoever had thrown that spell would die that night; of that, there was no doubt. But she couldn't recognize him. She hadn't seen his face.

I'll just take a liver from one of the dead, she thought.

It wouldn't help much. But it would give Brakko some measure of vengeance, and that was all she could do for him now.

#

"I'll give you another guard in the morning," Ghark Bloodaxe told her later that night.

They were huddled around Rorra's fire, the four of them: Ghark, Hagor the Sniffer, Krakkar the Fist, and Rorra herself. As always, it was the tallest and the brightest fire in the camp. Their guards surrounded them, sitting at nearby fires and eating smoked and salted meat from their packs — and poor Brakko the Blind was attacking the liver she'd given him with such purpose, that one would think it was the last meal he'd have for a month.

"And I'll think up a song for him, like you promised him," Hagor said. His forehead and his cheeks were bloody, but it was not *his* blood.

"I'll teach him to fight in the dark," Krakkar added. "For darkness is all he has now." From a great warrior like him, that was no small favor.

Rorra sighed and nodded, but it was time to speak of happier things. "How many did you kill today, Krakkar the Fist?"

"Twenty-two," he answered proudly. "Three with this." He raised his mace high. "Six with this." He pointed to his axe, which lay on the ground at his side. "Five each with Left Fang and Right Fang." He'd named his swords thusly. Orcs had tusks and vampires had fangs, but Krakkar the Fist had both.

"That makes only nineteen," said Hagor, who had a talent for numbers.

"I shoved two off the wall," Krakkar said.

"And the last one?" Hagor asked.

"Got him off the wall, too. I roared at him, and he took a step back, and fell off. Hit his head on a rock, he did. Burst apart like a melon. You should have seen it, my friends."

"Not bad," Hagor said. "I only got three. But it's Ghark's fault."

Ghark raised an eyebrow. "Mine?"

"Your guards. Those you have watching over me. They kept killing my enemies before I got to them."

"You should do what I did," Krakkar said. He'd asked his own guards to keep their distance, and he'd told them that if they got in his way, he might *accidentally* bash their heads in with his mace. They had listened, mostly.

"You'll do no such thing, Hagor," Ghark said, his voice hard as steel. "The All-Father needs you alive."

He hadn't fought at all. The Julians knew his face, and during the assault on the first fort, they'd attacked him and his companions with everything they had. After that, Ghark had decided it was best to lead from behind. No one had dared complain, for the name Bloodaxe was well-earned, and besides, he was one of the All-Father's champions.

"Fine, fine," Hagor grumbled. "I'll let your guards do what they do best."

"You'd better," Ghark grunted.

He hasn't smiled since he sat down, Rorra thought. "Something's bothering you, Bloodaxe. It's not my cooking, is it?"

Ghark shook his head. "Your cooking's perfect, as always."

"Then what is it?"

"I'm waiting for the report on our losses. I fear we've lost too many warriors today. Yesterday, too."

"King Ghark," a voice came from the side. It was one of the lesser chieftains.

"Speak," Ghark said.

"I counted the bodies. Four hundred Julians dead, and two hundred and sixty-eight of our own warriors."

"Fewer than yesterday," Krakkar said.

"But still too many," Ghark said. "And that's for one warband out of seven. If we keep attacking these bloody forts, we'll lose a third of the Horde before we're done."

"Hmm." Krakkar frowned. "I haven't thought of it this way."

Ghark placed a hand on his chest. "I've made my decision. From now on, we must fight the Julians in the open field, far from their walls and their towers. We'll do better that way. Tomorrow, we'll leave the forts behind and march deeper into the empire."

"And the other warbands?" Hagor asked.

"I'll send runners to them tonight. I'll ask the war chiefs to cease the attacks, and to meet us at the appointed place."

"It will take the runners a few days to reach them all," Rorra said. The seven warbands had spread out along the Julian border.

"Three days, for the farthest ones," Ghark said. "Maybe four. Which means more attacks and more dead warriors." He huffed. "I thought we'd take the forts with far fewer losses. I should have known better."

Hagor placed a hand on his shoulder. "What's done is done. We must move forward."

"The soldiers from the remaining forts will come after us," Rorra cautioned. "At night, perhaps."

Krakkar the Fist grinned. "Good. Our night patrols will sniff them out, and we'll hack them to pieces."

"It is settled, then," Ghark said. "We'll march into the empire, and wait for the other warbands, and together we'll burn and pillage the Julian lands. If they send their armies against us, we'll meet them in the field, and crush them. We won't stop, not until the Boy Emperor concedes defeat and surrenders the rest of their champions to me; and when he does, I'll take their lives. And then the Julian gods will be vanquished, and gone from the world for a thousand years."

Divide et Impera

The main hall of Augustus's temple was a true wonder of architecture, with eight massive stone columns supporting a high dome that weighed as much as a small hill and had been built by the hand of man alone. On a good day, the Lady would have stopped to admire such a great feat of engineering. But this was not a good day.

She strode forward, her bare footsteps echoing on the marble floor. The orange and white tiles were cold to the touch, but that did not bother her. Not as much as the self-satisfied grin on Augustus's face.

He waited at the feet of his likeness. The monstrous statue was forty feet tall, and carved from a single block of marble, which Augustus himself had transported to Lux Aeterna for the purpose five centuries earlier.

Oh, how she longed to slap him. And the Lady slapped *hard*, even for a goddess. But she couldn't lay her hand on him in anger. An ancient Godly Pact made it impossible.

Instead, she gave him her most vicious glare as she advanced. "Well?"

His smile turned warmer. "It's good to see you again, Lady. You look radiant."

She did not dignify that with a reply.

"Your glamor," he said. "It's stronger than ever."

Of course he'd noticed. And she couldn't drop it, not anymore. Worse, he probably thought she was using it for *his* benefit.

"Why did you betray me, Augustus?" Her voice echoed off the walls. It was unladylike to shout in his temple, but they were alone, and the hall was warded. No human ear would hear their words.

He raised an eyebrow in that way she'd always detested. "I've got a better question, my dear. *How* did I betray you?"

"You offer me a pact of non-aggression. Nothing more. And then you turn around and ally yourself with Njord and his thieving ilk. And that, right after you've seen them blast my knights apart with those murderous cannons!"

He raised his hand in a pacifying gesture. "It's *because* I saw those cannons in action that I offered him an alliance. I couldn't have them rip my own people to shreds, nor tear down my city walls. Better yet, they'll do wonders against the orcs."

"You could have just taken the blasted things."

"Queen Marion tried that. It didn't go so well for her."

As if she needed a reminder. "Marion met them in an honest battle, as is our way. And she only failed because of that madman Gunnar and his inventions. But you're the trickster god. You could have found a different way."

Augustus's countenance was serious when he replied. "Don't think for one second that the thought didn't cross my mind. Yet this was the best way. I get the cannons, and the men to use them, and the knowledge to make more powder if they run out. Besides, my people get the goodwill of the sea god, if he happens to be the winner of this contest. Though I wouldn't wager much on his chances, not with the way I expect Queen Frida to expose herself in battle." He frowned. "I do have a question, though. How did you find out about our pact so quickly?"

"How else? Njord himself came to me and boasted about it."

Augustus snorted. "Of course he would. That's old Blue Beard for you."

"*I've already beaten you thrice, Lady,*" the Lady said, imitating Njord's voice perfectly. "*First, I carved a path through your fleet with Gunnar's ships, then I smashed your knights on that beach, and now*

Augustus values my friendship over yours." She switched back to her own voice. "The nerve of him! As if any of those successes were his own doing."

"Those minor upsets have done nothing to damage your chances. Meanwhile, your trickster wizard brought Njord to the brink of defeat when he killed Ursula, the sea witch."

"The brink of defeat, you say. And yet you chose him as your ally."

"Last time we met, I told you I'll do my best to win. That's exactly what I've been doing."

"Why not ally with me instead?"

"I already have your friendship. You're protecting my lands from the vampires, and our people will fight each other only if we're the last of the gods. I have no allies guarding my other border, which has already been overrun by orcs and desert men. A temporary setback, of course. Besides, as I told you, I expect Queen Frida to throw away her life in some bloody battle. Which would take Njord out of the contest and leave me with his men and their cannons."

"And if she doesn't?"

"Then perhaps you, me, and Njord will be the last ones standing. In which case, Queen Frida will have to fight your people without my help. And this time I don't fancy her chances."

"*Divide et Impera*, Augustus. Divide and conquer. That was your saying, yes? And we're all just pieces in your game."

Augustus shook his head. "Maybe we're all pieces in the Supreme One's game. I'm only doing what it takes to win. Besides, I've been fighting this war ever since I came into being."

He'd never said such a thing before. "What do you mean?"

"You all have strong races. Malleon has his giants, Grok has his orcs, and Serya Krov has his vampires. You have your knights and your woodsmen, and Njord has his pirates, and they are fierce indeed. Aljin's people are strong and harsh, and true survivors. And what did the Supreme One give me?"

He waved his hand, and a large map appeared in the space between them, floating in mid-air. It showed the shape of the Julian Empire, yet it was painted gray, except for a single orange dot, representing Lux Aeterna.

"He asked me to create the weakest of the human races in all of Ethasar," Augustus continued. "And when I was done, He told me to make my people strong, even though they're a head shorter than your men and two-thirds their weight." He was speaking in averages, and he was right.

"You've succeeded," the Lady said.

"I created the first tribe right here, where we stand, and called it the Julians, after their leader. I created three dozen more after that, and spread them throughout the eastern lands."

The Lady nodded. "The Marians, the Sabinians, the Flavians, and all the others."

"Indeed." Augustus smiled. "And, though my people were small and weak, I loved them, Lady, from the very first moment. For how could I not?"

He snapped his fingers, and the orange dot pulsed and grew slightly.

"So, I gave them the orange color, and the orange fruit, and their shields and spears. I gave them Ares, who taught them discipline in training and combat. I gave them Demetra and taught them how to make their lands fertile. I gave them Afrodisia and made them breed like rabbits, back in those early years, though I could never breed them stronger than they were. I gave them Athina, and she gave them knowledge and wisdom. In time, my people's tribes grew stronger, with the Julians leading the way."

He took a deep breath, though gods had no need for that. On the map, the orange dot expanded outward, as the borders of the Julian tribe had done over their first century.

"Back in those early days," Augustus continued, "my people stood on the brink of extinction half a dozen times, and yet they endured. Over the years, the stronger tribes assimilated the weaker ones through diplomacy and conquest. The Julians prevailed over their rivals and forged a vast empire. And yes, at times they used Divide et Impera, for that was the only way to succeed."

The orange color spread over a wider portion of the map, though at times it contracted.

"My people prospered under my benevolent guidance. They built roads, and great cities, and temples, and places of learning. They fought off the orcs' invasions and those of the desert men. They kept the giants at bay and survived the Islanders' relentless raids. They gathered knowledge, pursued the arts, and strengthened the rule of law. Until they forged the greatest empire our world has ever seen. Only for it to be threatened with oblivion."

"As is my kingdom," the Lady said. The vampires and their subjects were already ravaging her western province, and Queen Marion was still gathering her armies. "As is the whole world, Augustus."

"Sooner or later," Augustus said, "all creatures must fight for their survival. One only has to think of the great lizards to know the truth of this."

The Lady nodded. Many centuries earlier, before her time, the orcs had hunted the great lizards to their last.

"I'll fight to protect our world," Augustus continued. "But first, I must win the War of the Seven. And to do that, I must use every weapon and every skill I have at my disposal. Within the limits of the Godly Pact the seven of us made at the war's beginning, and those of all the other pacts that came before and after."

"As I must," the Lady said. Somehow, she wasn't angry with him, not anymore.

No one else could have such an effect on her.

"I can't predict how this contest will turn out," Augustus said. "Maybe your champions will perish in the fight with the vampires. Or maybe I'll be the first to die between the two of us, though my champions are well-guarded. Or perhaps you and I will be the last of the gods."

"Perhaps."

"If that happens, know that I'll do my best to win."

If you do, you'll be killing the thing you want the most, she wanted to tell him. But she couldn't. The ancient Godly Pact was far-reaching, and was imbued with the Supreme One's will.

They couldn't hurt each other. Not directly.

"As will I," she said instead. "In fact, I could start now, and follow in your footsteps."

"What do you mean?"

"I can forge my own alliance. You have Njord on your side. I'll have Malleon on mine."

A dark shadow passed over Augustus's face. "Stay away from Malleon and his kind. I'm warning you as a friend."

She glared at him. "You're doing your Divide et Impera thing again. You just told me you'll do whatever it takes to win."

"No," he said. "No tricks this time, my dear. Believe me, this is genuine. I've already said too much, and saying more would weaken my own chances. But getting too close to Malleon will destroy yours. Besides," he smiled, "he's already making himself useful."

"He is?"

Augustus waved his hand again, and suddenly the map in front of him showed the whole of Ethasar, each realm painted in the color of its god. A thick purple arrow appeared over Malleon's realm.

"His giants are marching against the Vampire Kingdom," Augustus said. "Most of those who've awakened. I thought you would have seen it, too."

She hadn't, not yet. Hope surged inside her. "He aims to take Dragos Castle and cut off the head of the snake."

It was one of the rules they'd agreed to before the war's beginning. If any of the other factions took Dragos Castle and held it for a month, the vampire god would perish. Without such a rule, he could have simply commanded his champions to fly away from battle every single time, and they'd have survived until the end. No mortal could catch them.

Augustus nodded. "Something like that, I'd expect. Though Malleon and I haven't spoken since that meeting on Aljin's beach. Nor will we, at least for a while."

There was something more to this thing with Malleon, but he wouldn't tell her yet. *Perhaps I'll get it out of him the next time we meet*, she thought.

"Fine," she said. "Since he's doing what I want him to do, I'll follow your advice and stay away from him. For now."

"Good," Augustus said. "You should focus on the defense of your lands and take down as many vampire nobles as you can. That would help you and Malleon both."

"And you, yes? As everyone else is getting weaker, you're getting stronger."

"You've read my mind."

She smiled. "If we're the last of the gods, Augustus, I'll give you a good fight. Until then, I expect we'll meet again someday." She needed time to think, away from his presence.

"We will," he agreed. "Goodbye, my dear."

She focused, and suddenly she was standing in the middle of an olive grove, on a nearby hill overlooking the city. Fresh flowers sprang up from the grass at her feet.

Augustus is right, she thought. *I must deal with the vampires, and quickly. I'll defeat them, with Malleon's help.*

Dragos Castle is one of the keys. The other is Queen Elena. Destroy her and her followers will crumble.

I'll ask Eugene to target her. I'll ask Sir Galahad as well.

She still remembered the kiss she'd granted to Sir Godric, on that day five centuries earlier, when she'd asked him to rid her of King Dragos. She'd used her glamor then, and it had been worth it; the Paladin had slain the vampire king. Twice. And the second time, he'd stayed dead.

She wouldn't need to kiss Sir Galahad. She knew his secret, and that gave her all the leverage she needed.

He'd been in love with High Priestess Sandra for more than a decade, though he was eighteen years older and had known her since she was a child. His only failing since he'd become Paladin, yet the Lady could forgive him that. After all, Sandra was special indeed. More so than her sister.

His devotion to her will spur him onward. Especially if I give him hope.

A High Priestess never married, and that was law. Then again, laws could be changed.

He'll kill the vampire queen, or maybe Eugene will. Malleon will take Dragos Castle. And once the vampire god dies, his creatures will flee from my lands. Once that happens, I'll plan my next move.

And, despite everything, I'll come and visit Augustus again.

The Vision

"Close your eyes."

Lucius Antonius, the young emperor of the Julians, did as Augustus asked.

His heartbeat quickened. He didn't know what was coming this time, but it would be intense — and he'd learn from it.

"Today," Augustus said, "I'm going to show you one of the finest fighting forces I've ever seen. Get ready."

It was like a dream, but not exactly.

#

He was seeing through the eyes of a man-at-arms. A soldier in an army of twenty thousand, standing in the first rank, his spear peeking above his shield.

He was taller, and did not wear the Julian uniform, not that he'd expected it. This was a vision from another world.

A wave of mounted archers galloped toward his battle line.

They wore what looked like leather armor and rode short, stocky horses. Their bows were short, but deadly. When they got to less than a hundred paces away from his line, they let their arrows fly.

An arrow punched into his shield, and his left arm trembled as it took the impact. On his right, one of his comrades fell.

He braced himself, though his knees were shaking. *Perhaps they'll charge us this time.*

They didn't. At less than sixty paces, the attackers circled to the left, in perfect order, the riders twisting in the saddle and shooting their arrows at the defending army.

More men fell, screaming in agony, and he felt his bowels turn to water.

The mounted archers reformed their lines and rode away. Farther in the distance, the next wave of riders surged forward.

It was beautiful. The two formations passed through each other at speed, and the gaps in the lines were narrow, yet not a single pair of riders clashed. The discipline and the skill of the maneuver was unlike anything he'd ever seen.

Then another volley of arrows punched into the defenders' line and he fell, clutching his throat, his hands slick with his own blood.

#

Now he was seeing through the eyes of an eagle, soaring above the battlefield.

Everywhere, the defenders' ranks were thinning. And there was nowhere to flee. The horse archers had surrounded them.

Farther to the south, bodies of horses and men lay strewn across the ground. The Mongols had lured the Christian cavalry away from the main force early in the battle, and had surrounded the mounted force and destroyed it utterly. The Christians' leader, a nobleman named Sulislaw of Krakow, had died without landing a single blow.

#

Now he was a Mongol bodyguard, standing inside his commander's tent.

At sixty-six, General Subutai was the foremost general of the Mongols, and his feats had already passed into legend. Coming from humble beginnings, he'd joined the Great Khan's army at the age of fourteen. Within a decade, he'd risen to the rank of general, commanding one of Genghis's vanguard tumens, a fighting force of ten thousand warriors. Since then, he'd led more than a dozen campaigns and had won dozens of pitched battles, bringing many of the great armies of Asia and

Europe to their knees.

He sat, surrounded by the other leaders of the Mongol army as they planned the next day's battle. The prize was great. The King of Hungary himself waited across the river.

"I sent my vanguard to take the bridge and hold it," said Batu Khan. "They won't expect us to march upon it during the night."

"And what if your men fail?" Subutai asked.

"They won't. I'll cross at dawn with my main force, and I'll bring my siege engines as well. We'll destroy them easily."

"Even so," the general said, "I'd like to have options. Sejban?"

"Yes?" the officer said.

"Take your force to the north and ford the river. You know the place. If our enemies hold the bridge, strike at their backs as Batu Khan charges from the front."

"As you wish," Sejban said.

"As for me," Subutai continued, "I'll take my men south."

"Why south?" Batu Khan asked. "There's nothing there. No way to cross."

"Exactly. They won't expect an attack coming from there."

"But the river is too deep, and too wide. You've heard the scouts' reports."

"My men will build a bridge."

"We already have a bridge. It will be mine by midnight."

Subutai looked the younger man in the eye. "Are you questioning my judgment, Batu Khan?"

Batu Khan was a grandson of Genghis and a capable commander in his own right. Even so, he seemed to falter under Subutai's gaze. "No. Build your bridge, general, if you wish. But do it quickly."

#

"It was another great victory for the Mongols," Augustus said.

Lucius's eyes snapped open, the vision over. The leader of the Julian gods stood in front of him, shadowed by the enormous statue of his likeness at his back.

They were alone inside the great temple. Six hundred soldiers stood guard outside, a dozen wizards among them.

"The Hungarians sent an advance party that took Batu Khan's vanguard by surprise," Augustus continued, "and beat it back. They held the bridge for the first hours of the morning, despite Batu Khan's efforts to retake it. But when Sejban and his men arrived, the Hungarians retreated to their camp, rather than have them at their backs.

"When they finally sallied forth with their whole army, Batu Khan's forces had already finished the crossing. The fighting was fierce, with great losses on both sides, until Subutai arrived and struck the Hungarians from the flank. They fell back again, and they were easy pickings after that."

Augustus waved his hand and a paper map appeared between him and Lucius, hovering in mid-air. The lands drawn on the map were not familiar to Lucius.

"This is where the Mongols started." Augustus pointed to a small area on the eastern side of the map. It was painted black. "And this is how their empire grew in less than a century."

The black blotch grew and grew, like an unstoppable plague, until it had taken over a large portion of the map.

"Why not farther north?" Lucius asked. "Or south?"

"Too cold," Augustus said, pointing at the northern region. "And here, can you guess?"

"Too hot."

"That and fierce resistance."

Augustus waved his hand again, and the map dissolved into nothingness.

Lucius sighed. "You've shown me Caesar and Alexander, and I think I could have beaten those." They were great commanders and inspired discipline and loyalty among their troops. But the Julians were disciplined as well, and had greater numbers, and their cavalry had stirrups. "But these Mongols… It's a good thing they're not of this world. I couldn't defeat them in a thousand years."

"You'd be surprised about what a thousand years can bring," Augustus said. "But yes, we're lucky that you don't have to face them. Now tell me what you've learned."

"From today's vision?"

"Today's and yesterday's." The day before, he'd shown him Genghis. The Great Khan himself.

"They were better riders than the desert men," Lucius replied, "and their bows were stronger. They were disciplined, and they mastered both tactics and strategy. They promoted their officers based on merit, not blood. They were ruthless and made their enemies tremble. It's as if they were bred for war."

"They learned to ride as children, and they practiced the bow as well."

"With men like these, I could conquer the world."

"My thoughts exactly," Augustus said. "But since you don't have men like these, what will you do?"

"I'll train my own mounted archers. I'll take General Mercurius's cavalrymen, put bows in their hands, and drill them hard."

"Very well. It won't make up for a lifetime of practice, but it's a start. What else?"

"I'll take his archers and put them on horses. I'll have both groups train together and learn from each other. After a few weeks, I'll split them according to their skill."

"Some will become capable horse archers. Yet many will not."

"I'll split them into several units. The regular archers, the light and heavy cavalry, the soldiers who have some decent skill with both horse and bow, and the elite force. Mounted archers that may not rival the Mongols, but could at least hold their own against the desert men. And though I won't have many of those, the lesser mounted archers will be useful as well."

Augustus nodded. "They'll be fearsome in a charge, and their volleys will do enough damage against massed troops. You can also mix them with your lancer units for an added element of surprise. Besides, it will take some time for their enemies to notice their lower skill, if you use them correctly. What else?"

"Bows," Lucius said. "They will need shorter bows that they can fire from horseback." Then the thought hit him. "Crossbows, too. Easier to master than bows, though harder to reload."

"So far, so good. Have Princeps Farus organize all this."

Lucius smiled. "He'll take it as a challenge and ask to lead these men himself."

"Then you shall grant his request. The men love him, and he's an excellent warrior. He can master any weapon. The soldiers will strive to follow his example."

"In the meantime," Lucius said, "I need to learn how to use these new units. Will you show me more visions?"

"I will," Augustus said. "And you'll talk to General Mercurius about his clashes with the desert men and read the accounts of past battles."

"Many of them for the second time."

"But with a fresh eye."

"With a fresh eye, yes," Lucius acknowledged. "What do you think of our other project?"

"Athina says she's happy with it. You're learning fast. Soon, you'll be ready to challenge your own generals. Or perhaps Ares himself."

Lucius smiled. Indeed, his skill at playing the mock battles was growing quickly. He could beat both Farus and Silvanus seven times out of ten, if their forces were equally matched.

"What of Silvanus?" Augustus asked. "Have you told him about his bride yet?"

"I'd give him a few more days before I do, if you agree. I can't say how he'll react to this betrothal, but he'll do his duty."

"Very well. And our other champions?"

"I just received another letter from Selenius, and it brings good news. Another two thousand men are on the way. As for Leticia, she spends most of her waking hours blessing the harvest, one village after the next." The fact that she could do it from the gardens of the Imperial Palace saved her a lot of effort and placed her out of harm's way. The goddess Demetra was aiding her, more than she'd done over the past years.

"Then all is well," Augustus said. "I'll visit you again tomorrow and show you one of the Mongols' most successful maneuvers."

"Wait," Lucius said as the god turned to walk away. "Any news from the frontline?"

"Justinian's forces are still harassing the orcs, and getting pummeled when they don't retreat fast enough. But I sense our fortune is about to change. And that is all for today."

"Thank you, Augustus," Lucius said, and knelt.

When he raised his eyes from the orange marble floor, Augustus had disappeared. Only his statue remained.

Lucius smiled. Truly, the leader of the Julian gods was a being of supreme intelligence. Among all the gods of Ethasar, only Athina could match him.

He'd gained the upper hand against his rivals. As they'd forged the Godly Pact that had started the War of the Seven, he had ensured that the rules were stacked in his favor.

The Julians would not get his advice and support in the heat of battle, nor that of any of their other gods. But Lucius could benefit from his wisdom, and from his visions, and the rules did not forbid it. He could watch great warriors and generals from another world as they led their armies to victory, and learn from them.

Sooner or later, he'd lead his own army to war and put his knowledge to good use.

A Starry Night

"Have some more," Rorra Fireborn said, and handed Ghark Bloodaxe another bowl of her favorite dish.

Of course, it was horse stew. They'd passed a Julian village two hours before making camp; and though it was deserted, like all the others before, they'd found a horse with a broken leg, freshly killed. Rorra's guards had butchered it and carried the best pieces, and she'd cooked them herself, and Ghark's taster had found the stew free of poison.

Ghark let out a loud belch. "Best food I've eaten this year." He handed her a jug of ale, sweetened with honey, as she liked it. "And you, have another drink."

They sat together at Rorra's fire, the tallest and the brightest in the camp. Hagor the Sniffer was with them, and their guards feasted at nearby fires. As for Krakkar the Fist, he'd left their feast early with one of his many admirers, a fresh-bloodied shieldmaid half his age.

If only I were three decades younger, Rorra thought, *he would have been mine.*

She was fifty-seven now, and such thoughts were better kept to herself. Besides, she'd had a happy union. Her mate Kurth had died of a fever three years earlier, and she would not take another. Not unless King Ghark asked her, or Grok the All-Father himself.

She snorted. *That's the ale doing the thinking for me. I like it.*

She took a big gulp and set her jug down with great care, so she wouldn't spill it. "Last one for tonight." She'd drunk half a dozen already.

She gazed at the clear night sky, dotted with stars. To the north, Hrothgar's Eyes shone brightly, as they always did. To the north-east, another point of light drew her attention: one of the other seven worlds that traveled around Ethasar's sun.

Arcadion, Rorra thought. *Or perhaps Valtaria.*

There were orcs living on Arcadion, along with humans and some pointy-eared creatures called elves. Grok the All-Father himself had told Rorra that. She didn't know much about Valtaria, only that its name meant "Land of the Four" in some otherworldly language.

She tilted her head back as much as she could. The Eagle's constellation loomed straight above her head. It *winked* at her, and she winked back.

Shouts came from the edge of the camp, along with the clanging of weapons.

"Another brawl," Hagor said. "You should send your guards to bash some sense into them, Ghark."

"Maybe not a brawl," Rorra said. The sounds were loud and came from three places along the southern edge of the camp. No. Four.

She made to stand, thought better of it, and signaled one of her guards to help her to her feet. Then a fireball shot up straight toward the sky, and then another, and that could only mean one thing.

"We're under attack," she said.

"You're drunk," Hagor said. "The little men know better than to ride at night."

"It's not the Julians," Rorra said, just as she caught her first glimpse of the creature that galloped toward her fire. It was taller than a horse and had two humps on its back, and a rider, too.

"Help!" she yelped.

Three of her guards dashed in front of her, protecting her with their shields. But their effort was for naught. Ghark Bloodaxe's axe whirled through the air, and his aim was true. The flying weapon opened the camel's throat, and it crashed to the ground, burying its rider under its bulk.

"Take her to safety!" Ghark shouted.

Two of the guards grabbed Rorra under the armpits and dragged her away.

Where's safety? she thought. She focused and whispered the words of the fire chant, and though she was drunk and the guards dragged her eastward, a fireball appeared between her hands. Such was the gift Grok the All-Father had given her.

Now all she needed was a target.

And a target appeared. Another camel, galloping toward her. No, two. Three. Six. Was her vision blurring?

She roared, and threw her fireball, and six galloping camels became five, and she knew that farther ahead, the world smelled of burned camel hair, though the scent hadn't reached her yet.

Brave red-skinned warriors darted into the creatures' paths, ready to die for the All-Father's champions. Some threw themselves at the camels' legs, at the risk of being trampled. Others hurled spears or rocks or whatever they could get their hands on. And five galloping camels became four, then three. Then one, heading straight for Rorra and her guards.

It dashed past, and the rider leaned out of his saddle, and took off Kyrro's head with his curved sword.

"Heeeelp!" Rorra shrieked, and more warriors dashed toward her.

Then she saw them.

They weren't camels, not these ones. They were smaller, and black as night, though she could see them in the light of the campfires.

Desert horses. The most beautiful horses in all the lands, and the fastest, too.

As they crossed the endless sand dunes, they were fed dates and camel's milk, and that gave their meat its sweeter taste. Here on the plains, they'd feast on the Julians' pastures. And what they carried was death from afar.

The horse archers of the desert men.

They were coming, and there was nothing she could do to stop them. The guard on her left fell, an arrow sticking out of his eye, leaving her exposed.

She roared in frustration as the first arrow thudded into her chest. She felt the second one, and the third. Then there was nothing.

Common Enemies

Rain fell in heavy sheets as King Ammon of the desert men rode toward the orc king's tent, soaked to the bone and holding the white flag high.

Two orc girls waited at the tent's entrance, as per the agreement that Ammon's messengers had reached with the orcs. They were young, perhaps eight and ten. The older one raised her hand and Ammon slowed his horse to a walk.

He stopped and dismounted as he reached the girl, and handed her the horse's reins. The other girl searched him for weapons and found none. When that was done, she waved him onward.

The tent was made of rough linen and painted red. It would offer some respite from the rain, but perhaps not much. The tent flap was open, and King Ghark Bloodaxe waited inside, seated on a simple wooden chair, with a small fire at his back.

He was alone and had no weapons with him, at least none that Ammon could see. A second chair faced him, and it was empty.

Ammon advanced, stabbed the pole of his white flag into the ground, and sat down. The chair was dry, and as Ammon looked up, he noticed the animal skins sewn into the tent's roof.

A pleasant surprise, he thought. It explained the burning fire, too, and the fact that no streams of water dripped down into the tent. Maybe the orcs' magic helped as well. But Ammon hadn't come here to admire a tent.

He focused his attention on the orc king.

Even though he wasn't among the strongest of his kind, Ghark Bloodaxe was impressive. His eyes sparkled with intelligence, his bare arms were thicker than Ammon's legs, and his fists were bigger than his head. In an unarmed fight, he would have crushed Ammon easily. Yet Ammon did not fear him.

He'd come bearing the white flag. And though the orcs could be cruel and savage when they chose to, they had honor, perhaps even more than the Lady's followers.

"King Ghark," he said, and dipped his head in respect. He knew Ghark would appreciate the gesture.

"King Ammon," the orc king said. "You asked for this meeting."

"I did. I have a proposal for you."

Ghark growled. "Before you speak of it, I'd ask you about last night's attack."

"We are at war. All the kingdoms are. Fighting for the fates of our gods. You won't tell me that attacking your camp at night wasn't fair, will you?"

Ghark shook his head. "I won't. It was fair, and well done, too. It's just — we had scouts all around the camp. How did you get past them?"

"We rode fast, with arrows nocked. I had my best archers leading the charge, and they killed your scouts as soon as they saw them. My men told me that one of your scouts got to blow his horn before they shot him down, yet I did not hear it. Perhaps neither did you, nor your warriors. After that, it was a matter of speed and swift action."

"It did cost you a few men, I've heard."

"Two hundred and twelve." He'd lost more than half the men he'd committed to the attack, and many of those, he knew well. Then again, it was but a small fraction of his entire force. And in a war for the fate of the world, where only the lives of the gods' champions mattered, it was a price that Ammon was willing to pay.

Ghark grunted. "It won't work a second time."

"I won't need it to." Ammon left it at that. He sensed that Ghark had more to say.

He did. "Your warriors rode straight for my fire."

"The tallest and the brightest in your camp."

"How did you know I'd be there?"

"We captured a few warriors from your southern warband, and questioned them. When five orcs said the same thing, I knew it to be true. We rode for Rorra Fireborn's fire, and I understand she's dead, just as we intended. We didn't know you'd be there as well."

"So, you caught five of my warriors, and they all betrayed me."

Ammon shook his head. "We questioned three dozen. And my men are not beyond using torture to get what they need."

Ghark snarled. "They enjoy it, I've heard."

"Some do, yes. But let us not dwell on the past, King Ghark. Let us speak about the future."

"The future, aye. The future is when I smash your riders, and the Great Horde eats horse stew for a week, if not more. And camel stew. And your men's livers, too."

"Perhaps not yet," Ammon replied. "As I said, I have a proposal."

"Speak it."

"We have common enemies, you and I."

"Aye. All the others. The Julians, the Verdant Kingdom, the vampires, the giants, and the Islanders."

"Yes. But the Julians come first."

Ghark did not reply, yet he seemed to regard Ammon with interest, so Ammon continued.

"We desert men are few in number, and our warriors are fewer still. Your Great Horde outnumbers my riders three to one, if not more. The Julians are weaker than your warriors, but they could drown you with their numbers. So, instead of you losing thousands of brave warriors seeking to avenge Rorra Fireborn's death, let us both fight the Julians. Let us crush them and send their gods from this world. And then, and only then, let us settle our differences. That is, if you still wish it."

Ghark frowned. "You're proposing an alliance. A joining of our forces."

"Not exactly. You will lead your army and I'll lead mine. You'll fight your battles and I'll fight mine. Just not against each other. Not until the Julian gods are destroyed."

"You ask for this after you kill one of my champions."

"My best assassin killed one of the Julians' champions, too. This is war, King Ghark. It is total war, until most of the gods are vanquished, and we cannot pretend otherwise. I am only asking for a temporary respite as we focus on our common enemies."

"And if I say no?"

"Then I'll have no choice but to pull my warriors back into the desert. And you'll fight the Julians alone."

"Or perhaps I'll come after you."

"You'll lose thousands of warriors chasing us through the desert. No. Tens of thousands. In the meantime, the Julians will conscript more men and train them. Even if you defeat us, they'll crush you after that, what with your diminished strength."

"So instead, I should waste my forces against them."

"The War of the Seven is a grindstone," Ammon said, "and our lives are feeding it." He'd practiced these words with Nasir, his confidant and the second of Aljin's champions. "It will grind all of our armies down, in time, yet our choices will determine how it happens. It is best to choose your battles wisely, King Ghark. Do you have a map here with you?"

"I don't."

"We'll do without one, then. As you may know by now, the vampires are ravaging the Verdant Kingdom. Queen Marion is gathering her forces to march against Queen Elena, and they'll whittle each other down. Meanwhile, she won't be fighting the Julians, so we must. If we don't, they'll grow stronger, until they become unstoppable. As for the giants—"

King Ghark grinned. "I'm not too worried about the giants."

"That's because their god thinks of your race in friendly terms. Even if he wins, your kind will be safe."

"That, and another thing. Not that I'd share it with you, of course."

"Of course," Ammon agreed. "Even so. Do you see the truth of my words?"

The orc king frowned, and remained silent, and Ammon knew he was thinking deeply. So he did not break the silence either.

Finally, Ghark Bloodaxe grunted. "Fine. We won't attack you, not until the Julian gods are defeated. And you won't attack us either."

"Very well," Ammon said.

"Will your god bind himself to this?"

"He will. Let us ask him and Grok the All-Father to seal a Godly Pact tomorrow. Perhaps here, in this tent?"

Ghark nodded. "Here. With you and I as their only witnesses."

"Then my task here is done."

"And there's no reason for you to stay a moment longer."

Ammon nodded, rose from his chair, and turned to walk away.

"Wait," Ghark growled, and Ammon stopped.

He turned around slowly, his senses alert. This could be a decisive moment.

"You were brave," the orc king said, "to come and face me unarmed. Except that you didn't. What did my girls miss?"

"The poisoned dagger in my boot," Ammon replied. "I can draw it in a flash. If I died here, you would have died as well. But I was hoping it wouldn't come to that." He smiled. "Are those two your daughters?"

"Nieces," Ghark said. He seemed to be telling the truth.

"My men won't harm them in the battles to come. Not on purpose, at least. You have my word."

The orc king nodded. "Go in peace, King Ammon. Make the Julians bleed."

"And you as well, King Ghark. And you as well."

With that, Ammon strode out of the tent, leaving his white flag behind. Rain pelted him again, but its strength had weakened. The orc girl handed him his horse's reins, and in a flash he was up in the saddle and galloping away.

He'd achieved his goal. And he hadn't given much.

The orcs would not attack his men. They'd focus on the Julians. As for him, he'd attack the Julians as well — but he'd stay away from the bulk of their legions, and only fight those battles that he could win easily.

The War of the Seven was a grindstone, yes. A war of attrition. And the best way to win was to protect your champions, and to avoid losing too much of your army's strength.

Ammon would do both. And in the end, he'd retreat into the desert — and while Aljin couldn't protect him directly, the sands and the harsh weather would. No army could hope to defeat the desert men in their own lands.

Of course, all that would come later.

In the meantime, the other realms' champions were dropping like flies. Aljin himself would tell Ammon of their deaths, as long as it did not break the Godly Pact.

King Knut of the Islanders had been the first to die, slain by a vampire spy hidden among his ranks. The sea witch Ursula Gudrunsdottir had died next, killed from a distance by the wizard Eugene the Trickster and his Rangers. Then Al-Khanjar had slain Marcus Severus, the Commander of the Augustian Guards, though he'd failed to kill the Boy Emperor. And now Rorra Fireborn, the orc witch, had perished as well.

Nasir bin Fatih had fired an arrow into her, though he couldn't claim the kill. At least half a dozen arrows had found her before she'd stopped twitching.

Other champions would perish soon as well. Al-Khanjar, the most skilled assassin of the desert men, would play his part, and slay a few more before the war was over.

Eighteen champions had to die, three for each of the six other realms. Four had died already, and that left fourteen. And if Ammon protected his champions, and Al-Khanjar protected himself, Aljin the sun god would emerge victorious, and rule the world for a thousand years.

War Games

Seated behind his enormous desk in the Imperial Study, Lucius Antonius, the Boy Emperor, furrowed his brows at the thick tome that lay open before him. The day's task proved more difficult than he had expected.

He was studying the accounts of a great battle that his grandfather's grandfather had fought and lost against the orcs, in the valley of the Golden River, and was thinking of ways he could have turned the tide.

He played both sides, putting himself in the mind of the Julian emperor and that of the orc war chief, one after the other, and considering the actions they could take. But whatever his ancestor had tried, or whatever Lucius himself would have tried in his place, the orc side had a counter for it.

If only I had a thousand of those Mongol riders, I could have turned this into a rout. Or some of Frida's cannons. Those would have helped as well.

A knock at the door jolted him. He stood, grateful for the interruption. "Yes?"

A squad leader from the Augustian Guards entered the Imperial Study. He held a letter in his left hand.

He bowed slightly. "Your Majesty. This came by bird, and it is for your eyes only."

"Thank you," Lucius said as he took the letter. He broke the seal as soon as the guard departed.

The letter was encrypted, and the cipher was known to only a dozen trusted people in the whole empire. As for the writing itself, Lucius recognized it instantly. It belonged to Selenius Gracchus, the fourth champion of the Julian gods.

He closed the book he was studying, set it aside, and took out a blank piece of paper from one of the desk's drawers. Then he started reversing the cipher, writing the decoded letters on a blank sheet of paper, and reading the text as he worked.

Your Majesty, the letter started.

I hope this message reaches you well. I am sending two copies, as always; one by bird and one by rider. Please let me know if one of them gets lost along the way.

First of all, I wanted to thank you again for entrusting me with this mission. I've served the empire as an administrator for forty years, since your grandfather's time. Yet this latest posting, here in the Orchard of the Gods, could be my life's masterpiece.

Lucius smiled at that. The fourth champion's mission had been his idea. He'd consulted with the gods, and Augustus had readily agreed, as had Athina later.

The aging bureaucrat posed as an officer's aide and accompanied Captain Cornelius as he rode through the northernmost province of the empire, trying to marshal the local noblemen's support for the war effort.

They rode with a strong escort; four wizards and a hundred and twenty cataphracts, the heaviest cavalry of the Julian Empire, armored from head to toe and carrying ten-foot-long lances. So far, according to Selenius's earlier letters, no enemy force had come to challenge them.

Many of the nobles do not give their support easily, the letter continued. *They are reluctant to send so many of their young men to fight and die in distant lands, and they know that our pact of non-aggression with the Lady's followers cannot last forever. Besides, if the vampires defeat the Verdant Kingdom, they may well decide to march into the Orchard next.*

Even so, we usually manage to convince them.

The word "we" was well chosen. It was Captain Cornelius who did the talking, though Selenius prepared him in advance. The old administrator knew how the nobles thought, even those he hadn't met in person. He knew their families, and the rumors that surrounded them, and their relationships with other nobles in the province, and whether they were behind on their taxes. He knew which of the gods they prayed to, and how often they visited their temples. He'd tell Cornelius what objections they were likely to bring, and how to counter them.

According to his past letters and to those sent by Cornelius himself, his advice had been critical to the mission's success.

We tell them that Your Imperial Majesty will protect them when the time comes, he'd written. *But first, we must vanquish our immediate foes: the orcs and the desert men. Which is why we need their support, and their men-at-arms.*

We tell them to trust in our gods as well. Cornelius speaks to them about Demetra's efforts to give the farmers a bountiful harvest, and about Volcanus giving strength and skill to the smiths that forge the empire's blades, and about Athina and Augustus advising Your Majesty. He tells them how Ares lights the fire in the soldiers' hearts as they train, though he cannot guide them in battle, and how Afrodisia helps young lovers see each other in their dreams, across hundreds of miles, even as one of them marches to war.

At times, with my guidance, Cornelius has to use bribes, or to employ subtle threats. Yet I can't let him go too far with the latter. If he did, the nobles would use one delaying tactic after another, or throw their lawyers at us, or perhaps instigate an uprising — and out of all these, I'm not sure which one is worse.

Lucius smiled again. Selenius's disdain for lawyers was well-known, though he'd been one himself decades earlier, and a good one at that.

This week, I am happy to report that four thousand men are marching south to join the war effort. They're well-equipped and supplied, and their masters have borne the costs themselves. More will come soon.

Another four thousand. It was a good number, and Lucius hoped many of them would still be alive at the war's end.

Of course, the more soldiers he had at his disposal, the better. It was easier to win battles if his generals could bring forth overwhelming numbers, and they'd win them with fewer casualties.

Count Cyrus is proving harder to convince, the letter continued. *He says he'll pay the imperial levy in both goods and men, as is the law, but nothing more. A visit from the gods would bring him to heel, if Your Majesty could arrange it.*

Lucius knew Count Cyrus and didn't like him much. Even so, he had to admit the nobleman was an effective administrator of his lands. He owned a tenth of the arable land in the province, and his crops were abundant; and besides, he had a talent for commerce, and had enriched himself greatly over the past two decades. As Lucius's father had told him once, Cyrus seemed to value his own interests above those of the empire, and this refusal was another proof of that.

Yet Lucius couldn't simply arrest him, or send him into exile, or have him killed, as some of his ancestors would have done. That would lead to unrest in the province, at a time when he couldn't afford it.

I'll ask Athina to speak to him, and compel him, he thought. *In her wisdom, she will accept. Or perhaps she'll choose to send Ares, or*

Tenebris. Any of those would easily achieve what mortals like Cornelius and Selenius could not.

That is all for now, Your Majesty, the letter's final paragraph began. *Expect more news in a week. Until then, I remain your humble servant, Selenius Gracchus.*

The message was simple enough and could have been conveyed in far fewer words. Four thousand new soldiers were marching south, and Selenius needed help from the gods to convince Count Cyrus to provide his support. But Selenius liked writing long letters, and Lucius wasn't going to hold it against him.

Besides, decoding them provided him with an intellectual challenge. Though the evidence of his work would not last long.

He lit a candle and burned the decoded letter, and the original as well. Only a few trusted men knew of the fourth champion's mission, and they kept it secret from all others.

He took a great fan from the shelf behind him and started fanning the smoke away. Then he heard another knock on the door. "Enter," he said.

"As Your Imperial Majesty commands," replied a familiar voice, and Lucius knew his friend Silvanus had said it for the benefit of the guards in the hallway. He entered the room, followed by Farus.

Lucius stepped from behind his desk to meet them. They clasped arms, and he said, "No need for *'Imperial'*. I think 'Your Majesty' is enough."

Silvanus bowed. "As you say, Your Majesty."

Lucius punched him in the shoulder. "No need for that here, either."

"Ow!" shouted Silvanus, though the few moments' delay told Lucius he was feigning the pain. "You're getting stronger. Or at least hitting harder than before."

"It's all the sword and spear drills that my guards put me through," Lucius said. He trained each morning for two hours, and was getting stronger, and more skilled with the weapons as well.

Farus flared his nostrils. "I smell smoke. A message from Selenius?"

Lucius nodded. "Another four thousand men. And he needs divine intervention to convince one of the stubborn nobles to help."

"Let me guess," Silvanus said. "Xyphos, or Cyrus. I hate those two with a passion."

"It's Cyrus. No news of Xyphos, yet."

"And the intervention?"

"I'm speaking with Athina tonight. At her temple. I hope she'll agree to it."

He shuddered at the memory of the night when the desert men's assassins had attacked the temple. He'd been in mortal danger that night, and Marcus Severus, the former Commander of the Augustian Guards, had lost his life defending him. But unlike then, Athina's temple was safe now. Three hundred Julian soldiers guarded it day and night, not to mention his own escort when he visited it.

"Perhaps she could ask Ares to visit Cyrus," Silvanus said, "and bully him into submission."

"Athina will decide, in her infinite wisdom," Lucius said. He turned to Farus. "How's the training going?"

"They're clumsy, most of them. But I do see sparks of talent here and there."

He was training three thousand cavalrymen to use bows and crossbows from the saddle, and putting four thousand foot archers on horses as well. It wouldn't give Lucius the Mongol army he would have desired, but it would help him counter the archers of the desert men.

"And what about you?" Lucius asked.

Farus's chest swelled with pride. "What would you expect?"

"I expect you'll show off for me tomorrow when we meet at the Stadium."

"I will. I'll bring fifty of my men as well. I'm not the best horse archer of them all yet, but I am among the best five."

"Leave the other four back at their barracks tomorrow," Silvanus said, "and bring the rest. That will impress His Imperial Majesty even more."

That earned him two shoulder punches, one from Lucius and Farus each.

"Ow!" he shouted again, and this time it seemed genuine.

Before Lucius could apologize, Silvanus grinned. "Don't think so highly of yourself, Lucius. You're not *that* strong."

Lucius grinned back. "Punch him again, Farus. But this time, do it like you mean it."

Farus bowed deeply. "As you command, Your Imperial Majesty." He brought his arm back and leaned to the side in an exaggerated pose, as if he was winding up for a mighty punch that would throw Silvanus across the room.

"Enough," Lucius said. "I see that you've both ganged up against me."

Farus relaxed, and his face was serious now. "There's one more thing I'm trying, Lucius. You remember the sarissa, yes?"

"I do." Augustus had shown it to him in one of the early visions. It was the spear that Alexander the Great's infantry used, and it was thirteen to twenty feet long. "But you said it's too unwieldy for our men to use."

"Not if two men wield it together."

"Two?" asked Silvanus. "They'd need to move in unison. Have you actually tried this?"

"I have," Farus said. "I'll show you tomorrow as well. Enough of those will stop an orc charge dead, if packed tightly. Of course, right now I only have ten, and they're rather crude."

"I'll write up an order for ten thousand, if they work," Lucius said. "You bring good news, my friend."

"As do you. Four thousand men, and six thousand last week. Our numbers are swelling."

"Meanwhile, the orcs keep thinning them." The news from General Justinian was less encouraging. The empire's borders had been overrun by orcs and desert men, and many of the forts had been burned. Then again, Justinian practiced defense in depth, and sooner or later the orcs would bleed, much more so than they'd done already. That, or they'd starve. Or both.

"I know it too well," Farus replied. "It's *my* province they're burning. They and Justinian, too."

"At least your people are moving to safety, yes?" Lucius asked.

"They are." The exodus of the peasants hadn't reached Lux Aeterna, but it would at some point. "I hope Queen Frida's cannons will help us turn the tide."

"Cannons?" Silvanus asked. "So, we have forged a pact with the Islanders?"

"So, you don't know," Farus said.

"But *you* do," said Lucius.

Farus frowned. "Naereus sent me a letter. If you wanted him to keep quiet, you should have told him."

Lucius smiled, dispelling his friend's frown. "That's all right. He did write that he renounced your claim as my next-in-line in your name, yes?"

"He did. And it was a good thing, too. Just imagine me, barking orders at our oh-so-clever eastern nobles, and perhaps taking a head or two if they complained too much. And that in a time of peace. That is, if we win, of course."

"Of course," Lucius said. "That leaves you, Silvanus. If I die without an heir, you'll be the next emperor. I'll draft the proclamation later today."

"And Big Boy here will be my loyal subject," Silvanus said, pointing to Farus. He did not seem surprised.

"If I must," Farus said. "Then again, I'd rather see Lucius give birth himself, if that were possible. To twins, in fact, so that his succession is assured."

"Only to have his twins fight each other for the throne before his body has grown cold," Silvanus said. "Sixty years from now, of course. If not more."

"You'll make fewer jokes," Farus said, "when you find out who the Boy Emperor has chosen for your wife."

Silvanus's face fell. "No. Not General Patricius's daughter. I told you she doesn't like cats, and she's a bit dull, too."

"It's not her," Lucius said. "I'll give you a few hints. She's a head-and-a-half taller than you, and strong enough to wrestle Farus to the ground without breaking a sweat." Farus grunted at that. "And some people say she killed a bear with her bare hands when she was sixteen, though I heard she used two daggers."

"You said a head-and-a-half? I didn't think Artemisia was *that* tall."

"It's not our forest goddess, silly," Farus said, though he didn't punch Silvanus in the shoulder this time. "It's Queen Frida of the Islanders."

"I knew that, you big oaf," Silvanus replied.

"And it wasn't me who chose her for your wife," Lucius added. "It was Augustus himself."

"Then I bow to the will of our god," Silvanus said. "I do expect her to be somewhat disappointed with me, what with her being used to those big, strong pirates manning her ships."

"She prefers women, actually," Farus said. "Naereus knows such things. Or his spies do."

"Then why?"

"For the alliance."

"For the alliance," Silvanus said. "Fine. You expect me to put a child in her, and soon?"

"That's between you and her," Lucius said. "But I'd rather she fight. If she dies, Njord dies as well; and if she doesn't, she has to defeat the Lady's champions without our help, unless Queen Elena vanquishes them first. So, you'll be a husband first, and a good one; and then a widower, perhaps."

"So, what you're saying is, do not get too attached to her. Not that we'd have too much in common, anyway."

"I'll trust your judgment in this."

"My judgment says I'm too young to be married off to some foreigner. But that's not up for discussion, is it? So I'll do what I must."

"I expect you'll impress her with your brilliance," Lucius said, and this time he wasn't joking. "That is, if she's smart enough to appreciate it."

"If she's not, it's her loss," Silvanus said. "So, we have four thousand men, the need for a divine intervention to convince Count Cyrus to help us, Farus's horse archers, and the use of the sarissa, with two men wielding it. And cannons, and my marriage, and the fact that I am to be first-in-line to the throne until you produce an heir. What else?"

"I'm having trouble with one of today's battles."

"Ah," Silvanus said. "The one against the orcs, where your great-great-what's-his-name fled halfway through the battle, yes?" They were all reading the same books.

"That one, yes. I don't think I can win it."

"I'll give you three hundred horse archers," Farus said. "Two thousand sarissas as well, for your foot soldiers. No cannons, though."

Lucius smiled at that. "I think I can beat you, then. Couldn't do it without the sarissas, though."

"I'll put up a good fight. I spent two full hours thinking of this."

"As you should have. Still, I like my odds better now."

"I'll go set it up," Silvanus said, and strode out of the room. There was a spring in his step. Perhaps he was happy with his royal match after all, or perhaps with the confirmation of him being next-in-line to the throne.

"Orange juice?" Lucius asked Farus. "To calm our minds before the battle."

Farus nodded, and Lucius took two wide-bottomed glasses from the shelf behind him and poured the drink from the large jug that stood on a corner of his desk.

"If it wasn't you yourself handing me the glass," Farus said, "I'd have my taster take a sip first. As you should. We're at war, and our enemies are devious."

Lucius smiled. "One of my tasters drank a full glass before I did. He seemed to enjoy it."

They drank, and stood in silence for a few minutes, thinking about the battle they'd soon be fighting against each other. Then they left the Imperial Study, passed the Augustian Guards lined along the hallway, and entered the throne room.

High on its dais, the Julian throne dominated the room, as it had done for centuries. Seven large wooden tables stood in front of it, each one sporting a miniature landscape. Plains, hills, mountains, rivers, and the occasional fortification were all built to scale, and each had been painted by an artisan's paintbrush.

Each of the tables depicted a battlefield; a new one every day. And each battlefield hosted two miniature armies.

Lucius would play the Julians, as he usually did when the battle involved them. Farus and Silvanus played his opponents: orcs, desert men, giants, Islanders, and occasionally even the Verdant knights or the vampires. While three of the tables recreated historical battles, the other four sported made-up scenarios, designed by Farus and Silvanus the day before the confrontation.

He'd beat them seven times out of ten, if the odds were fair. Less than that, if they weren't.

"I've added the sarissas to your formation," Silvanus said. He waited in front of the third table. "And your horse archers, though I had to use desert men figurines for that."

"I'll have the artisans paint a few of them orange when we're done," Lucius said.

Farus grunted in an orc-ish manner and cracked his knuckles. "Even so, Great War Chief Kroggo will bash your head in today, Your Imperial Majesty. Shall we begin?"

"We shall." Lucius took his place behind his troops, just as Farus did the same. Before they could begin, the door of the throne room opened with a loud scraping sound. Without turning, Lucius said, "I asked not to be disturbed here."

"Forgive me, Your Majesty," a familiar voice said.

Lucius turned. It was General Patricius.

"I thought I'd sent you to reinforce General Justinian's legions against the orcs, General."

The officer bowed. "My troops are doing just that, Your Majesty. But

I heard concerning news from the capital, and I had to return."

"And what news is that?"

The general bowed again. "May I speak freely?"

"Of course."

"My men are fighting and dying in the War of the Seven, with the fates of our gods at stake. And I hear you are sitting here, reading books and playing games with your friends. No offense, Princeps Farus, Princeps Silvanus."

"You have heard correctly. And?"

"May I ask why, Your Majesty?"

Lucius stood even straighter than before. "General Patricius. Know that everything I am doing is for the good of the empire, and in agreement with our gods. Augustus, Athina, Ares, and the others. I see one of the gods daily, sometimes twice a day. And I follow their advice closely."

"I do not presume to judge the gods," the general said. "Even so."

"Even so. You say I am not doing enough for the war effort."

"I did not say it, Your Majesty."

"Yet you implied it. Then listen to this, general. I have gathered five new legions here, in Lux Aeterna. Princeps Farus is training the men with new weapons and new battle formations, with great success." That was perhaps overstating the truth, but Patricius didn't need to know that. "My envoys are mustering more troops from the other provinces. And we have secured an alliance with Queen Frida of the Islanders. Within weeks, she will arrive in Lux Aeterna and marry Princeps Silvanus, and then she'll bring her men and her cannons to the frontline. Do you still have concerns, General?"

Patricius bowed again, deeper than before. "Only one. I wish I'd been told of this alliance earlier."

"I've just received the news myself," Lucius said, though that was not exactly true. He'd known about the alliance with the Islanders on the day of its forging, from Augustus himself. "But you do know now."

"And I am grateful for it all."

"Then go back and defend Princeps Farus's province. Hold back the orcs and the desert men for as long as you can. And know that more reinforcements will come, and swiftly."

"As you say, Your Majesty," Patricius said. "I apologize for doubting you."

"Apology accepted. Now go, and do your duty to the empire, and to our gods. As I am doing."

The general turned to leave.

"Wait," Lucius said as another thought hit him. "Princeps Farus. How many men can you spare?"

"Two legions without their cavalry units," Farus said. "I'll keep training the rest."

"Good," Lucius said. "You heard him, General Patricius. You'll return to the frontline with another eighteen thousand men. I'll draft the orders tonight. Within five weeks, or perhaps sooner, Princeps Farus will march to your aid with the rest of the troops, and with Queen Frida's forces as well. I expect you can keep our enemies busy until he arrives."

Patricius nodded. "Thank you, Your Majesty."

Lucius turned away slightly, a subtle gesture of dismissal.

The general left the throne room with a spring in his step and closed the door behind him.

Silvanus punched Lucius in the shoulder. "That was well handled, Your Imperial Majesty."

"Ow!" Lucius yelped.

"You're faking it," Silvanus said.

Lucius nodded. "I'd say you punch like a woman, but when I think of your future wife, I shudder. I wouldn't ever want to be punched by *her*."

"Less talking, more fighting," Farus intervened. "I sound the battle horn, as Great War Chief Kroggo did, and move my archers forward." He advanced a handful of his miniatures.

"A small mistake," Lucius said as his eyes scanned the battlefield, "since you've given me three hundred horse archers." He tapped one of his pieces.

"Count my troops again," Farus said, though they both knew the numbers well.

"I don't have to." Lucius advanced his ballistae. It would be a closely fought battle, but he was confident he'd win.

As he believed he'd win the War of the Seven, for Augustus and for the rest of the Julian gods.

It was going better than he'd hoped. Many of his border forts had burned, but that was inevitable, and the men defending them had sold their skins dearly. The desert men had crossed his border as well, and he'd expected that; but he didn't think they'd attack the orcs and kill one of their champions. He had the Lady's followers shielding him from the vampire onslaught, and Queen Frida coming to his aid with her cannons; and though Njord had secured a valuable alliance with the Julian gods, Lucius didn't expect him to last until the end. The giants were moving west, most likely planning to invade Serya Krov's realm. And though he'd lost Marcus Severus to the assassin's blade, he still had three champions fighting for the Julian gods: Selenius Gracchus, Leticia Alba, and himself. And all of them were well-guarded.

We'll win this war, he thought. *With the help of our gods. If I listen to them and play my part well, there's no way for us to lose.*

Selenius Gracchus

Seated at his writing desk, Selenius Gracchus, the fourth champion of the Julian Empire, dipped his quill in the ink again.

He'd finish his report tonight, before his candle ran out, and send it to the emperor in the morning. Two copies, as always; one by bird, one by rider, and both encrypted with a cipher known only to a dozen trusted people in the whole empire.

Another eight thousand men promised, he thought, *and half already on the way. The emperor will rejoice at the news.*

He yawned. The report for the emperor would be the second letter he'd write tonight. The other one, detailing his requests for the armorers' guild in the province capital, had taken him the better part of an hour.

At least he'd get to rest the following day. And the villa he'd rented for this sojourn was the right place for it. With its flower gardens, the masterful paintings that adorned its walls, and the shallow pool in its courtyard, kept warm by some magical underground force, it was as relaxing a home as one could have, so far from the imperial capital.

He'd sent all the servants to their homes as soon as he'd arrived, save for the cooks and one of the chambermaids. The cavalrymen in his escort had many skills, from carpentry to drawing and from poetry to pottery, yet none could cook such a sophisticated meal as the five-course dinner he'd just shared with Cornelius. As for the chambermaid, the captain was young, and unmarried, and he'd taken a liking to the woman as soon as he'd laid eyes on her.

They'd both be in his room now, as his men took turns standing guard. Six on the rooftop, five archers and a wizard; six inside the villa itself; and another six patrolling the courtyard. The rest of the men would be asleep in the barracks that lined the outer walls, except for serving their own two-hour guard shifts when the time came.

Selenius smiled. At least he wouldn't have to wake for one of those.

He yawned again, and his eyes fell on the blank piece of paper ahead. *I'll finish it tomorrow.* He'd written a full page already.

The door creaked open.

Selenius turned toward it. "Cornelius, is that you?"

"Nothing is forbidden to us," came the reply.

A man stepped into the room, but he wasn't Cornelius. He was at least eight inches taller, he wore black instead of orange, and his face was painted gray. Besides, his words had betrayed his trade, and his origin as well.

Selenius sighed and steeled himself for what was to come.

"And everything is as we make it," a voice said at his back.

Selenius looked over his shoulder, toward the open window. Another man leaned against the windowsill. How long he'd been waiting there, Selenius had no idea, but he'd entered without a sound.

"We work in the darkness," the first man said, "to do the sun god's will. We are assassins."

They hadn't whispered. And Selenius realized he hadn't heard any noise inside the villa for some time, nor the footsteps of the men patrolling the courtyard.

He turned to the first man. "I guess it wouldn't matter if I screamed."

The man shook his head. "It would only hasten your end. And they won't catch us. I planned three escape routes before we struck."

"How did you get past the guards?"

"A potent sleeping potion. The head cook put it in their soup. We have his wife and child."

"You'll let them live," Selenius said. It was perhaps the last good thing he could achieve before his end came.

The assassin nodded. "I am a man of honor."

"Then you'll let me go as well. I am nothing to you; a mere bookkeeper. You'll find your target on the upper floor. Last room on the right."

"Captain Cornelius took his last breath sixty heartbeats before I entered your room."

"Then your mission is fulfilled."

"The good captain," said the second assassin, "was not the one leading your expedition. Nor is he the one sitting here and writing ciphered letters to a higher power."

"I am merely a scribe."

"You're not talking your way out of this," said the first assassin.

He was set in his decision, yet he didn't seem to know Selenius was one of the Julian gods' champions. And that gave Selenius one more card to play.

He chose his words carefully. "I have something that your god will want you to know. Something he's forbidden to tell you himself. The name and the location of Augustus's fourth champion. Swear that you'll let me go unharmed, and I'll tell them to you. Threaten me or torture me and you'll get nothing."

"No deal," the first man said. "Your fate is sealed. This is the sun god's will."

"But, Master," said the second assassin, and Selenius felt a glimmer of hope.

The first man hissed, and his companion did not continue.

"Since you haven't screamed," the leader said, "I'll let you choose your end. Blade or poison. Either will be quick."

Selenius groaned. He'd been poisoned once, and though he'd survived, it was not a pleasant memory. "I choose the blade. A swift cut, is it?"

The man nodded and strode toward him. A knife appeared in his hand, its blade painted black.

Selenius raised a hand. "Wait."

The assassin stopped. "Yes?"

"Before you do this, let us speak like civilized men."

"Fine. As long as you don't start begging for your life. And no more than five minutes. We're not waiting for the next shift of the guard."

"Two minutes," Selenius said. "Three at most. If Aljin loses, what then?" With his question, he was admitting he was more than just a scribe, but it didn't matter anymore.

"Aljin doesn't lose."

"Our gods are strong. We have a sun god, too: Apollon. Seek an alliance with us and we increase both our chances." He couldn't say it out loud, but perhaps the assassins would grasp his meaning.

"You'd have us strike down one of Njord's last two champions," the leader said, "and negotiate with Augustus after that?"

"If there is no other way."

The assassin grunted. "*Divide et Impera*. Divide and conquer, that is the Julian saying. We can play that game as well, and we can do it better. Think of this, my soon-to-be-dead friend. The orcs are fighting your people, and the vampires are fighting the Verdant Kingdom, and the Islander mercenaries are lending their cannons to whoever would have them. And the giants are doing Aljin-knows-what. But no one's intent on fighting us, not really. If anyone comes for us, we'll retreat into the desert, and I don't see your legions dragging the Islanders' cannons over there. Nor carrying enough water to survive. Our leaders are both strong and wise, and they'll keep far from harm. And in the meantime, everyone else's champions will be dropping like flies. I'll kill a few more myself. So, you see, we have no need for allies."

A few more, he'd said. "You're the one who killed Marcus Severus and tried to kill my emperor."

The man nodded. "I am. And your time is running short. Anything else?"

"My mother was one of your kind."

"I would have guessed," the leader said. "You're too tall for a pure

Julian."

"She was forced to marry at thirteen. A year later, still childless, she fled from her husband's beatings, braved the desert crossing, and took refuge in Julian lands. The Julians were kind to her, and when she married again, five years later, she married for love. Heed my advice and seek an alliance. Let our gods be kind to your people, if Aljin loses."

"Aljin. Doesn't. Lose."

"Then I guess we're done," Selenius said.

His death would leave the Julian gods with only two champions, and another one's death would seal their fates for a thousand years. Yet he could die at peace, since there was no other choice. And he'd done his duty, to the best of his ability. Until his final moments.

He closed his eyes, tilted his head back, and waited for the killing blow.

The Gods and their Champions

Aljin: King Ammon, Nasir bin Fatih, Achmad bin Fayzal, Al-Khanjar

Augustus: Emperor Lucius, ~~Marcus Severus~~, Leticia Alba, ~~Selenius Gracchus~~

Grok the All-Father: King Ghark, Hagor the shaman, ~~Rorra Fireborn~~, Krakkar the Fist

The Lady: Queen Marion, High Priestess Sandra, Eugene the Trickster, Sir Galahad

Malleon: King Tassadar, Paeren, Neressia, Eldris the Duelist

Njord: ~~King Knut~~, Queen Frida, ~~Ursula~~, Gunnar

Serya Krov: Queen Elena, Duke Zoltan Barko, Kirill Skromnik, Katrina

Bonus Content

Congratulations! You've finished Part Five.

To explore the bonus content, visit https://bradtowers.com/wots-bonus-5/ or scan this QR code:

Part 6: The Strength of Blood

Half Rations

Seated on a tree stump at the eastern edge of his camp, King Ghark Bloodaxe ripped the last bit of meat off the hare's bones and raised it to his mouth.

"My last morsel for today, friend," he said. He chomped on the meat and savored the taste. *Just like Mother used to cook it.*

"Take half of mine," Hagor the Sniffer said, and proffered his own portion: a small pheasant that one of the witches had shot down from the sky and braised in her cauldron afterward.

They were alone, seated thirty feet from the nearest campfire. Ghark faced the camp, and Hagor faced Ghark. And though they'd chosen a spot on the fringe of the camp for their dinner, they were safe. Three lines of patrols stood between them and any enemies who would come their way, and Ghark had his axe, and hundreds of warriors who could reach them in moments if he shouted for help.

He shook his head. "I won't take your food, Hagor. Nor anyone else's." The Horde had been on half rations for a week already. Of course, as the orc king, Ghark could take as much food as he desired; but he wouldn't eat while others starved.

"Fine," Hagor said, and took a big bite out of the bird's chest. His muscles bulged even more than before as he tightened his grip on his meal, and that was no trick of the light. He'd lost much of his fat, as had many of Ghark's warriors.

Soon they'd start losing muscle, and then the infighting would begin. Unless Ghark found a way forward or took his army home.

"I still have this," he said as he cracked the hare's spine. He sucked out the marrow and licked his lips, his tongue passing over his right tusk. "Not the best part, but close."

Hagor sighed. "We've lost already, haven't we? Those bastards tricked us. We have to go back."

"Don't put that in your songs," Ghark warned him. "Not yet." He knew his words betrayed his own despair, but Hagor the Sniffer was one of the All-Father's champions, and over the course of the campaign, he had become a friend. One that Ghark could trust.

"I didn't think it would go this way," the healer-priest-storyteller said.

"Me neither," Ghark said. "My plan was to destroy them and burn their lands. I didn't think they'd do it themselves."

Yet the Julians had done it. Every village that Ghark's warriors had reached was deserted, the granaries emptied or burned down, the animals driven away. They'd found dead cows and sheep here and there, but they'd been poisoned. The crafty Julians had burned their crops as well, and had removed or destroyed anything edible.

They'd thrown animal carcasses down their wells, trying to poison the water; but they couldn't foul the rivers, and they couldn't stop the rain from falling from the sky. So, the Great Horde wouldn't perish from thirst.

Hunger, though, was a serious matter.

Ghark and his great war chiefs had driven their forces forward, and hadn't bothered with setting up supply lines. They'd carried food with them, of course; salted meat, and smoked meat, and goat cheese, and that dense bread that Ghark despised. But they'd eaten too much of their supplies over the past few weeks, and they could hardly replenish them.

They'd sent out foraging parties. Most of the time, they'd come back empty-handed. Any village they'd found was deserted, and the wild animals in the forests fled from the advance of the orcs. Other times, a single warrior would return, and tell of how his party had been ambushed by Julian riders, who had let him escape and had killed everyone else.

We sold our lives dearly, he'd say. But that was small consolation. Dead was still dead.

"Soon, we'll have to eat the bark off the trees," Hagor said. "Or each other."

Ghark growled. "No. Don't say that ever again, friend."

Hagor shrugged. "It wouldn't be the first time."

It was a rare thing in the orcs' glorious history. Yet at times, when the Horde had advanced deep into the lands of the giants, or into the Great Desert, they'd been forced to eat the weakest of their own. Twice, those great sacrifices had led the Horde to great victories.

Five other times, they'd been followed by crushing defeats, and had brought great shame upon the orc kings at the time, and upon their clans as well. Four out of those five times, the kings had not lasted the year after that.

Ghark Bloodaxe would do better.

He shook his head firmly. "Not on my watch, Hagor. I won't let it come to that."

"Then what?" Hagor asked as he ripped another chunk of meat off his bird's bones.

"I'll give us two more days." He was monitoring the provisions carefully and getting reports from his war chiefs twice a day. "Then we go forward if we're lucky, and back if we're not."

Hagor spat out a bone. "By the All-Father, how I hate them! I wish they'd face us in an honest battle for once. I'd feast on their corpses after."

"I'd feast on their horses. And on their *food*, once we found any. Even on those stinky oranges."

"Careful with those. It's said they make men weak."

Ghark thumped Hagor on the shoulder. "But we're not men, friend. And we'll never be weak." He grinned. "Maybe they'll visit us tonight, and then we'll both feast."

The Julian riders harassed the Horde during the day, but that hadn't been much of a problem lately, not since Ghark and his war chiefs had posted archers and witches on the outskirts of their warbands. At least twice a week, the skirmishers bothered them at night as well, but Ghark had figured out their strategy. They came around midnight, and only when the ground was smooth enough for the riders to beat a hasty retreat when outnumbered, without breaking their horses' legs.

Tonight, the ground to the east was flat and smooth. So, Ghark had sent three hundred of his warriors to dig shallow trenches, four hundred paces from the edge of the camp, and bury themselves alive. If the Julians came, his hidden warriors would rise from the dirt as soon as the alarm was raised, and cut off the riders' retreat.

They'd eat their horses after that, and the men as well, though Ghark would refrain from the latter. He hated the taste even more than that of orcish bread, and besides, the little men were godly creatures, like his orcs. They just followed different gods.

Hagor nodded. "They'll come, if we're lucky. And we could do with a bit of luck." His nostrils flared.

Ghark raised an eyebrow. "What do you smell, Sniffer?"

"Foragers. Three of them. Coming with news."

Ghark looked past Hagor and noticed the three young orcs approaching. "By the All-Father, friend. Your nose is the stuff of legend."

Hagor raised his hand, as if to silence him. "Horse blood. They're bringing you an offering."

"I'll share." Indeed, the orcs' packs were bulging, and one of them was caked with blood.

"You'd better," Hagor said. "I offered you my bird when I had nothing else." He took another bite and threw the creature's head over his shoulder. "You did well to refuse. I'll put that in my songs."

"You'd better." Ghark stood and nodded at the approaching warriors. "What do you bring, young ones?"

"Horse meat," said the female in the middle. "Head." She pointed to her own backpack, then to the others' packs in turn. "Chest, and rump."

Hagor chuckled. "As if our king would eat a horse's ass," he said without turning.

"Oh, that one's for you, Sniffer," the lass said.

"Tarkanna," Ghark said as he remembered her name. Barely sixteen, she was a skilled tracker and an even better archer. She was also bold and shameless, even for a youngling with a great war chief for her uncle and a fire witch for her mother.

He frowned at her. "You just disrespected one of the All-Father's champions."

She grinned. "Serves him right. He's been staring at *my* backside for weeks."

"And?"

"And he's too old for me."

Ghark shrugged. Hagor was only thirty-five, and would have been a great match for any youngling, what with his renown and his great healing and storytelling skills. Then again, a girl could choose.

"Then here's my pronouncement," Ghark said solemnly, as if he was deciding the fate of the world. "You, Tarkanna, and you, Hagor, will share that horse's ass, and eat it together." He turned to Hagor. "But lay a hand on her without her permission as you share your meal, and I'll give you a thrashing myself. And then her uncle will do the same."

The girl bowed her head. "As you command, my king." Her face showed a hint of a smirk, but Ghark chose to ignore it.

"Aye," Hagor replied. He stood and turned to face the younglings. "Where'd you get the meat from, lass?"

"Five miles west from here. And there's more. Four hundred horses, at least."

"Four hundred," Ghark said. That was good news. "But how did you beat them? We only sent small groups that way."

"We found them already beaten. By the desert men. A small band of those was still on the field, two dozen riders at least. No doubt there'd been more earlier. They said the dead horses were a gift from King Ammon to you, King Ghark."

"How many Julian dead?" Hagor asked, and passed his tongue over his lips.

Tarkanna shook her head. "None for you, Hagor. It's still horse's ass for both of us. The desert men burned the dead warriors, as is Aljin's custom. Their own dead, too, and their dead horses and camels. Even so, four hundred Julian horses is something."

Ghark ran the numbers in his head. Four hundred horses. Five to eight hundred pounds of good meat per horse; the latter if they were lucky and the horses were of a bigger breed. That was twenty thousand to thirty-two thousand pounds. And he still had over forty-five thousand warriors, though ten thousand were away from the camp, scouting in various directions.

Less than a proper meal for each, then. Still, it was more than nothing. "Send a warband to fetch the meat," he said, "and bring it here."

Tarkanna grinned. "First thing I did when I reached the camp. I went to Uncle Zordo and told him where to go. His braves have left already."

Hagor's stomach growled. "He'll share with the rest of us, your uncle," he said.

"Of course. He promised."

"And you'll still share the horse's ass with her," Ghark said.

Hagor bowed his head. "As you command. But I won't put *that* in my songs."

"You'd do well not to," Ghark said. He smiled at Tarkanna. "Finally, some good news. I could do with more."

Hagor's nostrils flared again. "Oh, they're coming. Look behind you."

Ghark turned. A line of burning torches was coming from the east, hundreds of them; and only one would bring forth fire like that: the Great War Chief Syrkka, the sole female among Ghark's war leaders and a fire witch in her own right. He'd sent her to scout the way ahead, with her six thousand warriors.

He couldn't smell the smoke from the torches yet, and marveled again at Hagor's exceptional nose. But he had more important things to worry about now.

"With me," he said, and strode toward the incoming warband.

Hagor followed him, along with Tarkanna and her two companions

— and more warriors were coming from the camp. Hundreds of them, all whooping and cheering at their warmates' return.

A single orc rushed ahead of the line of burning torches, and judging by her impressive height and her long, wild hair, it had to be Syrkka herself.

Ghark and his party headed toward her, and soon they met.

She bowed her head slightly. "King Ghark."

"Syrkka," he replied. "I hope your braves didn't step on my buried guards."

She shook her head. "A few of them leaped out of their trenches as we neared, and showed us the way past the others. I bring news."

"Tell me."

"I found the way to Praetorium." It was the capital of the Julian province.

"Where?" Ghark asked. He knew the city lay somewhere east, but no roads led that way.

"The little men hid the road with that swamp we ran into a week ago," Syrkka said.

Ghark remembered the swamp. They'd reached a crossroads where the main road turned to the left and right, but there was no way forward. The plain ahead sloped downward, and turned into a mosquito-infested swamp — and out of the fools that had ventured forward, a few had sunk to their deaths. The rest had been pulled out with ropes, and that was no easy thing.

"I thought you sent your scouts around the swamp that day," Ghark said.

"They came back with nothing. But I had a feeling. So I went myself, with the bulk of my warriors."

"And?"

"The little men had destroyed the road for another mile past the swamp, and the rain hid the traces of their work. But I took my warriors farther, and found the road, and followed it. We ran into a thousand Julian soldiers along the way, and killed them; those who didn't flee, at least.

The city itself stands twenty miles east of the swamp."

A rich target, Ghark thought. There had to be food there. Unless the Julians had abandoned it.

"It's teeming with people," Syrkka said, putting his worries to rest. There'd be food as well. "It's well-guarded, too. I saw ballistae, and catapults, and more crossbows than I could count in a lifetime."

She couldn't count too high, and Ghark knew it. Still, the news was good. "They won't flee, then. They'll stay and give us a fight."

Syrkka nodded. "I reckon so. I didn't think I could take the city myself, not with my six thousand braves. With the Great Horde, we'll crush them."

"And then we'll feast," Hagor said.

"And then we'll feast," a new voice repeated his words. It was Krakkar the Fist.

Ghark looked over his shoulder and nodded at him.

"We'll smash 'em and bash 'em and slice 'em to bits," Krakkar continued.

"And burn them," Syrkka said, and for a moment Ghark wished Rorra Fireborn, the third of Grok's champions, was at his side as well. But Rorra was dead, killed by the desert men during that bloody night attack.

"And burn them, aye." Ghark raised his voice, so that more warriors would hear him. "Tonight, we rest. Tomorrow at dawn, we eat the four hundred horses that King Ammon has gifted us. And then, with meat in our bellies and songs in our ears, we march to take this city."

Queen Frida's Arrival

Lucius gasped in wonder as he reached the viewing platform on the top of the hill.

"They look like a conquering army," he said quietly.

Six hundred Julian soldiers surrounded him, yet none of them would catch his words. They kept their distance, as he'd ordered them. Only Farus and Silvanus, who stood at his sides, were close enough to hear him.

"That they do," Silvanus replied.

Their viewing platform overlooked the eastern gate of Lux Aeterna, the capital of the Julian Empire. The eastern road was wide enough to let six Julian carts pass side by side, without touching. And now, a large procession covered it for miles; an enormous serpent made of men and beasts and colored in blue and orange.

Queen Frida of the Islanders had arrived.

She'd brought with her sixteen thousand warriors and two hundred and fifty cannons, according to Naereus's letters. She'd left the rest of her men and cannons with her ships, safely anchored at Verrano, the closest Julian port, under the command of a capable captain named Sigurd Larsson. But it was more than sixteen thousand troops and their cannons that traveled on the eastern road.

There were those, yes. And the carts and the war wagons that carried the cannons, and their powder and shot, all pulled by oxen and covered in blue cloth. But there were also wagons and beasts of burden carrying food, drink, and other supplies. And Julian merchants, and craftsmen, and cooks, and entertainers, who had all traveled with the army, hoping for a quick profit. And young women, thousands of them, who sought the embraces of strong Islander warriors; some looking for love, others simply plying their trade.

Forty thousand people in all, according to Naereus's last report. More, if their numbers had swelled since then.

They'd all have to be housed and fed inside Lux Aeterna for a week, before Queen Frida's warriors advanced further westward and joined the fighting. Lucius doubted that many of the hangers-on would follow. They'd return to their homes to the east, and they'd speak of the Islander army's passage for years to come.

General Mercurius, who was protecting the capital, had taken great care with the preparations for the army's arrival. The Islanders' lodgings would be spread across the city, though each man and woman would be housed fairly close to their captain, or to the captain's second-in-command; and Mercurius's soldiers would patrol the streets day and night, in greater numbers than usual, and keep the peace. For no doubt, many of the empire's new allies would be visiting Lux Aeterna's taverns and its pleasure houses, and would perhaps not be on their best behavior as they did.

They'd pay for their drinks, as had been agreed, and for any other goods and services they sought to enjoy. Of course, some would pay with Julian coins they'd stolen years earlier as they'd raided the empire's shores. And *that* could lead to trouble as well.

Lucius smiled, remembering the general's parting words from their meeting on the previous evening. "*I still believe we should have asked them to pitch their tents outside the city, Your Majesty,*" he'd said. But the Islanders were allies, and Njord had insisted that they'd be treated with the respect they deserved, and Augustus had conveyed Njord's wishes to Lucius. And so, General Mercurius had had no choice but to obey the will of the gods, though it seemed as if the task had aged him half a decade.

"Look, Lucius," Farus said, handing him a spyglass. "At the head of the column."

Lucius took the spyglass and held it to his eye.

Queen Frida herself led her warriors and walked with her head held high. She was tall, even for an Islander, and more muscular than any woman he'd seen before. Her hair was braided and dyed blue, as was the Islanders' way. She wore a sleeveless shirt that emphasized her ample bosom and laid bare the bear's claw marks across her breastbone.

She'd be attractive, Lucius thought, *if only the gods would shrink her to our size. Even so, she'd be a bit too brawny for Silvanus's taste.*

As it was, the best word he could think to describe her was "imposing." A true warrior queen. Which was just what the Julian Empire needed her to be.

Two blue-clad men walked on Queen Frida's right. Both were older than she was, and while one's hair was dyed blue, the other kept it gray. He had to be Gunnar, Njord's fourth champion; and perhaps the man at his side was Lothar Bjornsson, Queen Frida's second-in-command.

Then Lucius looked to Frida's left, and his eyes widened.

It had to be *him*.

He was powerfully built, taller than his men, and blue of skin, hair, and beard. He carried a weapon of legend: a blue trident that seemed to ripple with a strength beyond magic, even from a distance.

"Njord," Lucius whispered. "The sea god himself has come."

Naereus walked at Njord's side, but Lucius did not need to mention him. No doubt Farus had seen him as well.

"He has indeed," Farus said in a low voice. "He's pretty majestic, if you ask me. Doesn't have much of a nose, though. I thought the paintings were mistaken."

"I heard he breathes through gills," Silvanus whispered, though they all knew gods did not need to breathe.

"You're terrible, Silvanus!" Farus blurted out loud. He grunted, seemingly embarrassed by his own outburst. "Your Majesty. Your orders?"

Lucius raised an eyebrow.

Farus lowered his voice. "Say something, Lucius. Before this jester embarrasses us in front of our men."

Lucius barely suppressed his laughter as he handed the spyglass back to Farus.

"I've seen enough," he said, loud enough for the nearby officers to hear. "We go back to the palace. We'll meet our allies there."

The Three Julian Boys

"This way, Queen Frida."

Frida followed General Mercurius down the wide hallway, with Gunnar and Lothar at her sides. Their footsteps pounded on the white and orange marble tiles.

Only the three of them had been invited to the Imperial Palace for the first meeting with the emperor. More of Njord's people would join them later in the day, when Frida's wedding was to take place. Njord himself had promised to come and bless the union.

The general serving as Frida's guide had met them at the city gates, and they'd spoken at length on the way to the palace. One of the foremost military commanders of the Julian Empire, he'd fought a dozen battles against the orcs and the desert men over the years, and had won more than half. He was tall for a Julian, which meant the top of his head would reach Frida's chin if they stood face-to-face. Though he was in his early fifties, he walked briskly, and had sustained the pace since he'd met Frida at the city gate, without stopping to rest.

A warrior like Torsten would easily break him in half, and perhaps Frida could as well. But what the Julians lacked in physical strength, they made up for in numbers, discipline, and strategy. Or at least that was what the old stories said.

She walked behind him, taking two steps for each three he took, until he stopped in front of a large wooden door.

At least this place is properly built, Frida thought. During her journey to Lux Aeterna, she'd been housed in various nobles' villas, and had needed to duck through dozens of doorways, as had her men. The door facing her was nine feet tall, at least.

It opened smoothly as General Mercurius pushed it inward, and Frida got her first glimpse of the great space beyond.

The banquet hall of the Imperial Palace was vast. Its ceiling was twenty feet high, and made up of hundreds of glass domes that sat on a grid of metallic squares, each of them over twenty feet wide. The grid itself was supported by rows of marble columns decorated with floral patterns. Intricate chandeliers hung from various junctions of the metallic structure.

They'll be lit for the wedding, Frida thought.

The hall could host two thousand people, or at least that's what Naereus had told her, though fewer than a hundred would take part in her wedding. Not counting the servants, nor the Augustian Guards assigned to the event, who would outnumber the guests.

A single long table stood on the dais, with six ornate chairs facing the room. Ten round tables of nine seats each, spaced widely apart, would host the wedding guests.

They look small in here, Frida thought as she took in the size of the hall. And so did the three young men facing her.

The one on the right was well-built for a Julian and wore military clothes, which made him Princeps Farus. The one in the middle wore a golden crown on his head, which made him the Boy Emperor. And the last one, slightly plump and only five feet tall to her six foot three, had to be Princeps Silvanus, her soon-to-be husband.

She didn't think much of him, not yet. She'd been told she'd come to respect him for his prodigious intellect. But you couldn't spot *that* from a distance, and respect had to be earned.

Three boys, she thought. At twenty-nine, she had more than a decade on them. *And they got to rule the largest empire the world has ever seen. Only to have the War of the Seven thrust upon them. Upon us all.*

They stood in front of the dais, and did not advance as Frida and her companions entered.

"Queen Frida Gretasdottir of the Islanders," General Mercurius announced.

"Thank you, General," the youngest of the boys — Emperor Lucius — replied. "You may retire."

He did, and Frida and her men stepped toward their hosts.

We could end them in a few heartbeats, if we wanted to, she thought. But she was the Julians' ally now, and she'd sworn it in front of Njord. Besides, they'd never get out of the palace alive once they'd done a thing like that; and then Njord would die as well, along with the Julian gods. And come to think of it, the Julians had to have a few concealed archers and crossbowmen protecting them, though Frida couldn't spot their hiding places.

"Queen Frida," the Boy Emperor said when she was six feet away. "Welcome to my palace." Though she towered over him, he looked her in the eye with confidence, as one who'd been trained in the games of power for his entire life.

She dipped her head. "Emperor Lucius. You could have welcomed us seated on your throne. Instead, you chose to meet us here, on your feet. You receive us as equals. Know that I appreciate the gesture."

Lucius smiled. "We're friends now, Queen Frida. As are our gods. As much as they can be, in these trying times."

"Let's drop the titles, then. Call me Frida and I'll call you Lucius, if you agree." She pointed to her companions in turn. "This is Gunnar, and this is Lothar Bjornsson, though I'm sure you knew that."

He nodded. "This is Farus, and this is Silvanus."

The young boy who was to be Frida's husband smiled and held her gaze.

Gunnar grunted. "So, you're the one to marry our queen, little man. I heard you like your women soft."

"Mind your manners, you madman!" Lothar barked.

Gunnar laughed, and Frida did not intervene. Instead, she watched

Silvanus closely.

He did not waver. "You heard well, old sea wolf. But there's something I like even more than soft women. Do you know what it is?"

"What?"

Silvanus grinned. "Winning this war. We can do that together, you and I, yes?"

Gunnar laughed again. He stepped forward and gave Silvanus a hearty slap on the shoulder — and though Gunnar could have a heavy hand when he wanted to, the Julian noble took it well.

"You're not quite the man I imagined for my Little Frida," Gunnar said. "But I guess you'll do. For the alliance."

"For the alliance," Silvanus said.

There was no instant spark of attraction between Frida and him. That was the stuff of old women's tales, and the men in those tales were as different from the Julian prince as one could be. Besides, Frida's lover waited for her back in Hemland. But this was no union of love or lust. It was a political match, a calculated move in the game of gods and kingdoms. A move that would help her people greatly in the years to come.

She could control him easily, and get him to do her bidding. If they both survived the War of the Seven, the Islanders would have a friend in Princeps Silvanus of the Julian Empire, no matter which of the gods won — and he had the ear of the Boy Emperor. And if she died, then perhaps he'd still see the Islanders treated fairly.

Besides, she'd made Silvanus first in line to the Julian throne. If he had any ambition at all, that had to count for something. And if Lucius became a victim of the great war, she'd be the empress of the Julians, and queen of the Islanders as well.

The true prize, the Boy Emperor himself, stood at Silvanus's side. But marrying him had been denied to her — and she suspected that Magistrate Appius, Naereus's second, had made that decision. She hadn't seen Appius since.

Silvanus stepped toward her. "Now that your friend Gunnar has accepted me, it's time for the two of us to get to know each other. I could show you the rest of the palace, and the temples of our gods as well."

She imagined them walking side by side. The top of his head wouldn't even reach her shoulder; and perhaps her own people, seeing them together, would mutter amongst each other about the unfortunate choice their queen had made. Then again, she'd deal with that when the time came.

She thought for a moment, then shook her head. She was the Islander queen, and a woman among boys. It was better to make him wait.

"Perhaps tomorrow," she said. "Right now I am tired from the journey, and in need of a warm bath." The latter, at least, was true.

She turned to Lucius Antonius, the Boy Emperor. "Before that, is there anything important that you wish to discuss?"

"Nothing that can't wait," Lucius said.

"Then we'll see each other at the wedding."

"I am looking forward to it," Silvanus said.

"Augustus himself will officiate it," the Boy Emperor said. "In the meantime, one of General Mercurius's officers is waiting outside. He'll lead you to your apartments, here at the palace. Each of you will have a dozen servants and two dozen guards. Ask for anything within their power and it will be provided. Tomorrow, your soon-to-be husband will show you our city, and Farus will show you the best of our warriors."

"Show me yours and I'll show you mine," Farus added.

Silvanus strode past the Boy Emperor and punched Farus in the shoulder. "You don't get to say *that* to my future wife, you big oaf!"

"*Small* oaf," said Gunnar, who was taller than Farus.

Silvanus laughed at that. "We'll get along well, you and I," he told Gunnar.

Frida smiled. *Children, all of them. Children playing at princes. Yet Gunnar likes them.* And that mattered, a lot.

"I'll see you all at the wedding, friends," she said. "And before you ask, I brought my own festive garments. And now I'll go and have that bath."

Another Victory

I haven't seen such a blood-red sunset for weeks, Queen Elena thought as she looked into the distance. The color of the western sky matched the bloody scene she'd left behind.

She folded her wings and descended among the Islanders' cannons. A moment later, Vladimir landed at her side.

She handed her axe to him and called to the nearest Islanders. "I wish to see King Anders. Find him for me."

"At once, my queen," one of the men replied.

My queen, he'd said. She nodded at that. *Soon the whole world will bow to me. And in a few decades, once I crush the last of the rebellions that are bound to arise, all this needless killing will be a thing of the past.*

Less than half a mile behind her, the Verdant fortress lay defeated. The Lady's followers had named it the Twin Sentinels, no doubt because of its two towering keeps, built from solid stone. But now one of the twins lay in ruins, destroyed by Anders's cannons.

The castle had been well-defended, and without the Islanders' deadly weapons, Elena might have avoided it. Since she had them, she'd ordered a siege — and after six days of relentless pounding, Anders and his cannon teams had reduced much of the northern keep to rubble, and had breached the walls as well. She'd sent the serfs forward after that, and they'd died in the thousands, but in the end they'd overwhelmed the defenders with their numbers.

She hadn't risked her nobles in the assault, not after Count Boris had fallen from the sky on the first day of the siege. A bolt shot from a great ballista had pierced him through the chest, and that had been the end of him. And now that the resistance had been crushed, her nobles were taking revenge.

She closed her eyes and winced as the sights and the sounds came back to her. The screams of the Verdant men and women as her nobles tore into them with fangs and talons. Bodies dropped from the sky, some of them still alive. Limbs ripped from their sockets. Heads smashed against walls.

It had been too much for her. She'd had to fly away.

She couldn't stop the carnage. The blood rage had taken her nobles, and they wouldn't listen to her, not now. They'd turn against her and rip her apart.

Elena understood the blood rage, though she'd never felt it herself. It was part of her nobles' nature, however distasteful. And even superior beings had to have their flaws.

She hadn't seen them in this state before the War of the Seven's beginning. As queen, she'd spent most of her days at Dragos Castle, away from the ugly business of war. After all, her duty was to rule.

Over the centuries, she'd improved the laws of the Vampire Kingdom, turning it into a realm of order and justice. All her nobles past the age of majority visited her frequently, and bent the knee, and gave her their blood. She'd visited the other provinces at times, though never for long. But she'd left the fighting to others.

Until the War of the Seven had given her the chance to destroy the Lady and avenge her lover's death.

"My queen," Vladimir said, jolting her from her thoughts. "He's here."

She opened her eyes. Anders Svensson was walking toward her, accompanied by two of his men.

They were no longer blue-haired, nor blue-bearded. They'd abandoned Njord, after all. They wore gray garments, as Elena's serfs did, yet their powerful build and their braided beards marked them as Islanders.

As they reached Elena, they knelt in unison, as if on an unseen command.

She let a few moments pass. Then she said, "Rise, King Anders."

He did. The others remained kneeling, until she said, "You two as well."

"My queen," Anders said. "I congratulate you on your victory."

She favored him with a smile. "Your cannons helped. Thank you. I won't forget this."

"They'll help again and again. We'll turn the Lady's castles into ruins."

"You know that's not all I'll ask of you." When Queen Marion's army finally came, over half of Anders's men would stand in the shield wall, bracing against the Verdant knights. Many would die in such a battle.

Anders nodded. "Aye. My men will do their duty."

"And you'll get your reward. As promised."

She didn't *need* the Islanders. She could have her serfs kill them all in one night, and take their cannons, and that would have been the end of it. But she had no reason to do so. They were her subjects now, and she'd give them order and justice, as long as they obeyed her laws and paid the blood price.

Which reminded her. "You." She pointed to the man on Anders's right. "Offer your blood to my guard."

"Aye," said the man. He tilted his head, exposing his neck. A moment later, Vladimir's fangs sank into his flesh.

She wouldn't give him Anders's blood. Only one vampire had a claim to that: Katrina, the fourth of Serya Krov's champions, also now known as Queen Katrina of the Islanders. She took it every night, during their lovemaking, and she made sure everyone knew it.

Vladimir stepped back, as did the Islander facing him. The man rubbed the side of his neck with his hand, but he did not complain.

"Our campaign has gone well so far, Queen Elena," Anders said.

"It has indeed," she answered. It had taken her less than a month to raise her army and start the invasion. She'd advanced into the Broken Lance, the westernmost province of the Verdant Kingdom, taking towns and castles as she went. Less than six weeks later, most of the province was under her control, with only a handful of castles still standing against her.

The conquest had cost her twenty thousand men. Even so, her army still numbered over a hundred and forty thousand serfs, not to mention Anders Svensson's Islanders. He'd brought seven thousand of his men to Elena's army and had left another thousand with his ships, their numbers bolstered by ten thousand serfs from the Labor Plains.

She'd captured tens of thousands of Verdant people and sent them to the Vampire Kingdom, to become serfs to the local nobles and pay the blood price. More of the Lady's people had fled eastward, away from Elena's advance. As for those who dared to fight against her, they did not live long.

Meanwhile, Marion, the Verdant Queen, was still gathering her army.

She'll meet us in the field soon, Elena thought. *We'll have a decisive battle. After that, I'll take my army into Godric's Valley, and then onward, into the Hunting Grounds. I'll conquer the whole Verdant Kingdom if I must. I'll destroy all those who oppose me, until three of the Lady's champions are dead.*

Then, with the Lady gone, I'll focus on other enemies. The Julians, perhaps. Unless the orcs and the desert men destroy them first.

Anders raised his gaze to the sky, and the sound of flapping wings came to Elena's ears.

She turned. It was Katrina, and she was getting ready to land. Elena watched her as she dove toward her husband.

Her glamor is impressive, she thought.

Katrina's wings sank into her back the instant she landed, and her gray skin took on the pale rosy color she liked to wear among the Islanders. Her hair, once dyed blue, was almost as red as Elena's now, though she'd kept her blue outfit. Her bodice was laced up in the front and did not leave much to the imagination. Her midriff was bare, and her skirt was blue, as were her belt and her high-heeled shoes.

Anders and his men had abandoned Njord's color for the gray of Elena's subjects. But Katrina was a queen in her own right, and one of Serya Krov's champions. The rules did not apply to her.

She gave her husband a long, passionate kiss. Then she turned and bowed to Elena. "My queen."

"Queen Katrina," Elena said, for the benefit of Anders and his men. "I thought you'd be feasting with the rest of my nobles."

Katrina smiled. "I've had my fill of Verdant blood," she said, though her face and her garments were immaculately clean. "I'm in the mood for something stronger." She winked at Anders. "But it can wait a little longer."

"I was thanking your husband for his role in our victory."

"I'll thank him as well, soon enough," Katrina said. "I heard we lost Boris. So sad. I liked him." There was no emotion on her face as she said it.

"I did, too," Elena replied.

She felt the losses of her nobles deeply; she'd known most of them since they were children. And every noble's death made a dent in her elite fighting force.

The vampires were the strongest of the mortals, save for some of the giants, and they were the only ones who could fly. But too few of them were warriors. Some were too young to fight, and others were in their final years and could barely take to the air. Of the rest, many were artists, thinkers, engineers, and administrators. Those had stayed behind in their mansions, along with a few dozen war-trained nobles who would guard the Vampire Kingdom from invasion.

"I just saw Duke Zoltan," Katrina said. "He's really given himself to it this time."

She meant the blood rage.

Elena had allowed it. It was good for her nobles to see one of their leaders partake in the celebration of their victory, though she herself could not. The mere thought of it made her sick to her stomach.

"I didn't see Nikolay," Katrina continued.

"He's guarding Kirill Skromnik when he's not at my side." After Sir Robin's night attack, the second of Serya Krov's champions spent his nights in Elena's sleeping quarters. There was no safer place than that. But during the day, she'd only see Kirill when she needed to.

"Of course," Katrina said. "We need all of our champions alive." Njord was down to two, as were the Julian gods, and Grok the All-Father had lost one; but Serya Krov had all his four champions. As did the Lady, Aljin, and Malleon. For now.

Katrina flicked her hair over her shoulder. "We've won a great victory today. You should celebrate."

"I'll drink from three of my nobles tonight: Baron Sergey, Duke Zoltan, and you."

Katrina looked her in the eye. "I don't think so. My queen." She fell to one knee, her posture impeccable. "I am tired from today's fighting. My blood would be too weak for you."

She's defying me, Elena realized.

She weighed her choices. She could easily impose her will upon Katrina, but that would diminish the younger vampire's standing among the Islanders. If she was to be their queen, that would not do. Besides, she was one of Serya Krov's champions, and that mattered.

She nodded. "Not today, then. Get some rest and get stronger. I'll summon you later." This way, neither of them would lose face — though she'd have to bully Katrina into submission soon enough. "I'll have you as my third, Vladimir," she continued, knowing her guard would rejoice.

"Perhaps I should try noble blood as well," Katrina said sweetly.

Elena growled. That was too much. No vampire was allowed to drink another vampire's blood, except for herself.

She bared her fangs at Katrina as her hands turned into fists. "You dare?"

Katrina flinched and bowed lower. "It was only a jest, my queen. I apologize."

I should rip your wings off for this, Elena thought.

"Let this be the first and last time you speak of such things," she said out loud. "Go now, Queen Katrina. I see you are tired indeed. Spend the night with your husband and celebrate our victory."

"As you wish, Queen Elena," Katrina said. She took her husband's hand. "Come, my dear. Our queen orders us to celebrate."

Elena watched them walk away, her talons digging into her palms.

I must speak to Serya Krov about her, she thought. *And if she defies me again, I must punish her.*

She couldn't kill Katrina, not when she was one of the vampire god's champions. Instead, she'd arrest her and place her under guard for the remainder of the war. It would still give Anders and his Islanders a queen, though a much diminished one.

Then again, maybe it didn't need to come to that.

She'd bring Katrina to heel, with Serya Krov's help. And all would be right again.

The Royal Wedding

The banquet hall of the Imperial Palace was splendidly decorated. Hundreds of garlands of citrus flowers climbed up the marble columns; the tables were laden with the most expensive tableware of the empire, crafted by peerless master artisans; the four hundred guards had taken their positions; and all the chandeliers were lit. Just as Lucius had desired.

It was to be the second ceremony in recent times that Augustus himself would officiate. The previous one, Lucius's coronation, had been shadowed by the grief of mourning all those who had died in Uncle Aquila's insurrection, including Lucius's own parents and those of his closest friends.

This one will be happier, he thought as he adjusted the imperial crown upon his head. *Even though it's just a move in the War of the Seven.* And this time, not one, but two gods were attending.

Augustus sat on Lucius's right, his back straight against his chair. The lines on his face were those of a man in his fifties, and Lucius knew he'd chosen that aspect on purpose. Unlike most gods, Augustus could change his appearance to look younger or older, as he desired.

He wore a white toga with orange motifs, and a laurel wreath — a symbol of victory — that rested upon his head. The toga's embroidery, a lighter shade of orange than Augustus's skin, depicted scenes from the history of the empire.

At the far left end of the high table, next to the two empty chairs, sat

Njord, the god of the Islanders. If he'd seemed majestic when Lucius had watched him through Farus's spyglass, he was even more so in person. Every inch of his being emanated power.

He was taller than everyone in the room, including Augustus. He'd chosen to come naked to the waist, with his hair and his beard fashioned into intricate braids. He wore no crown, but he didn't need one; not when his eyes — those deep blue eyes, several shades darker than his blue skin — spoke of the vastness of the sea, and of heaps of sunken treasure, and of sights that no human would ever see.

His nose, though. Whoever had made *that* — and it had to have been the Supreme One himself — had not been at his best at the time. Perhaps he'd had too much of that fermented mare's milk of the desert men, or even more of the orcs' ale. Few other things could explain it.

In comparison, Nepthus, the Julian god of the sea, seemed older and wiser, though less powerful. If Njord were to suddenly age, and his hair and skin turned orange, and he'd unbraid his hair and beard and grow a proper nose, he could be mistaken for Nepthus's twin.

Two gods, one wedding. An alliance that could decide the fate of the world.

To Lucius's left, the soon-to-be-wed Princeps Silvanus drummed his fingers on the edge of the empty plate in front of him.

Lucius placed a hand on his shoulder. "She'll come. Have some patience, my friend."

There was no room for Farus at the high table, but he didn't need it. He sat at one of the round tables, facing the dais, with Naereus at his side — and judging from the way they held hands and whispered in each other's ears, they were taking great pleasure in being reunited. They sat together with seven nobles from Farus's province, who had withdrawn from the orc onslaught, while General Justinian and General Patricius defended their lands.

The ten round tables were fully occupied, seating nine each. Three tables for the Islanders and seven for the Julians. That, Augustus and Njord themselves had agreed on.

The Islander guests had been brought in shortly after the Julians, and they'd all introduced themselves before taking their seats. Mercifully, the introductions had been brief.

Lothar Bjornsson sat proudly at the leftmost table, together with eight of Queen Frida's captains. The table next to his hosted nine of the Islanders' most skilled sea witches. The third Islander table was occupied by Frida's bodyguards, Arne Olafsson and Torsten Eriksson, along with seven other warriors of note: five men and two women.

The Julian tables hosted the most prominent nobles, wizards, and military commanders of the empire that Lucius and his friends had decided to summon. General Mercurius had taken the seat of honor at his table, facing the dais, and next to him sat his wife and son. The rest of the table was occupied by the wives and daughters of the other three generals: Albus, Patricius, and Justinian, who were all away from the capital, raising troops or fighting for the empire. Leticia Alba, the third champion of the Julian gods, sat together with eight powerful wizards, adepts of Demetra, Ares, Athina, Nepthus, and Afrodisia. Lucius knew them well.

They were all waiting. One of Afrodisia's priests had instructed Queen Frida and Gunnar in the rites of the Julian wedding ceremony, and had explicitly asked them to arrive on time. But after meeting Gunnar, however briefly, Lucius was not surprised at the delay.

He'll have to do something to keep this interesting, he thought. *Though he won't show us outright disrespect.*

Gunnar's and Frida's were the only empty seats in the hall. Frida would sit next to Silvanus, her betrothed; and Gunnar, as the man who would give her away in the absence of her father, would sit between her and Njord. A place of honor.

But first, they had to arrive.

"You should send someone to look for them," Silvanus muttered.

Lucius shook his head. "If the gods can be patient, then so can we."

Just then, the doors to the banquet hall opened and Queen Frida strode in, with Gunnar at her side. A collective hush fell over the room.

She knows how to make an entrance, Lucius thought as he looked

Frida up and down.

Her blue sleeveless dress, decorated with sapphires, clung to her curves and left her tattoos fully exposed. It was short for Julian standards and sat tight on her body, highlighting her form, strong yet feminine. It was almost transparent, and underneath it, Lucius — and everyone else — could see the marks of the bear's claws on Frida's breastbone, as well as the shapes of her swimming garments.

A memory from an old book came to Lucius. After an Islander wedding, it was customary for the newly married couple to go for a swim together, and Frida had come prepared. There'd be no swimming tonight, though.

The crown that had once belonged to King Knut sat high on Frida's head, and she wore it well. As for the expression on her face, she was fully aware of the effect she'd had upon the room. Of the pairs of eyes that scanned every inch and curve of her body, and of the audible gasps that came from at least half the tables.

What a woman, Lucius thought. *And what a queen.* For a moment, he was envious of his friend.

He shook himself, let the moment pass, and studied her companion.

Gunnar was — well, Gunnar. He wore a simple mariner's blouse and matching trousers, as he had when Lucius had first seen him earlier in the day. Except that these were clean, and did not sport any holes, or at least none that Lucius could see.

They advanced between the rows of tables, and soon they stood in front of the dais.

A hand fell upon Lucius's shoulder. "It's our turn," Silvanus whispered in his ear.

Lucius nodded and rose from his seat, and together with Silvanus, he walked to meet the Islander queen. Augustus and Njord descended from the dais as well, and joined them.

"You look amazing," Silvanus told Frida. He was dressed in his best Julian finery, but that did not change the fact that Frida stood a head and a half taller. Even so, he looked her in the eye — and if he was intimidated, he did not show it.

"I know," Frida said. "Shall we begin?"

"When the gods will it," Lucius said.

"We have gathered here today," Augustus said, "to witness the marriage of two of the highest nobles of our realms." His booming voice reverberated throughout the banquet hall. "But this wedding is not just about them. It is a union of our peoples, of Julians and Islanders fighting side by side, in a war that decides the fate of the world for a thousand years. Let all those who are here remember this night, and let its memory drive us to victory!"

"Victory! Victory! Victory!" came the shouts from three of the tables, and the others joined them.

"I had prepared a long speech," Augustus continued. "But we're already late, and I sense that some of you are hungry."

That earned him a few laughs.

"So, I'll keep this brief, and move straight to officiating the marriage. But first, Njord, my friend, would you like to say a few words?"

"From the sea we are born," Njord began, "and to the sea we shall return."

"I can't swim," Silvanus whispered. Both Frida and Gunnar chuckled.

"Some of us, at least," Njord continued. "The others are leading figures of the greatest empire the world has ever seen. And together, fighting as one, we shall prevail. I stand with Augustus!"

"And I stand with Njord," Augustus said. "Until the end."

Lucius smiled inwardly. Of course, Augustus wouldn't mention the fact that the Islanders would have to defeat the Lady's champions without the Julians' help. Then again, many of the guests had to know of it.

"Then let us proceed," Njord said.

Augustus nodded. "Princeps Silvanus. Do you take Queen Frida to be your wife, for as long as you both shall live?"

"I do," Silvanus replied loudly. "For the alliance," he whispered, and Frida nodded.

"Queen Frida," Augustus said. "Do you take Princeps Silvanus to be your husband, for as long as you both shall live?"

"I do," Frida answered. "For the alliance," she whispered as well.

"Very well," Augustus said. "If there is one in this room who would speak against this marriage, let them do so now."

Lucius smiled. It was the last step before declaring the marriage completed. Of course, it was unnecessary. Nothing of note happened when such a call was made, not in a thousand weddings.

A hand went up.

A young woman's hand, from General Mercurius's table.

"I do! I wish to speak against this marriage!" the woman said as she stood.

Lucius stifled a groan. It was Polonia, the daughter of General Patricius. The young woman who'd been courting Silvanus as of late, and didn't like cats.

"Speak then!" Augustus thundered.

"Princeps Silvanus can't marry Queen Frida. He was promised to me!"

Lucius turned to Silvanus, who shrugged. "Nonsense," he said.

"By whom?" Augustus asked.

"My father," Polonia said. "General Patricius. He promised! And Princeps Silvanus, he — he touched me improperly!"

At her side, her mother, Livia, turned pale.

"I only kissed her once," Silvanus whispered. "Or twice. I forget."

Queen Frida frowned. "I don't like this, at all. Deal with it."

She was looking at Lucius. And he didn't know what to do.

He could order General Mercurius to lead the girl out of the banquet hall, and Augustus would officiate the marriage after that. But if he made an enemy of General Patricius, that did not bode well for the war effort.

Then again, he had to act fast. And he couldn't think of any other way out of this.

He raised his hand and—

"Foolish girl!" Augustus boomed. "You dare speak against a marriage that I myself have gone to great lengths to secure! And for what? Your father's promises, which he had no right to make? And half a dozen kisses, which you gave willingly, more than three months ago?"

"Fine, half a dozen," Silvanus whispered. "In my defense, she plied me with wine."

Confronted with the anger of her god, the girl was trembling now. "I... Mighty One, I didn't... please..."

"I know you, Polonia," Augustus said. His voice was calmer now. "Since you were little, your mother and father kept filling your head with ideas beyond your station. They've told you you'll be a princess one day. Haven't they?"

The girl did not answer.

At her side, her mother buried her head in her hands. Lucius thought she was about to cry.

"HAVEN'T THEY?"

"They... they have, yes... please..."

"Well, tonight they'll get what they wished for. Tonight, I'll make you a princess. You." He was looking at one of the Islander tables. "Lothar Bjornsson, yes?"

The Islander stood up. "Aye."

"You're Queen Frida's second-in-command. A prince among the Islanders, one could say." Lothar's chest swelled with pride. "And you have no wife."

"Not for two decades, no."

Lucius had read the reports about Lothar. His wife, a young pirate captain, had perished in a raid against the Lady's followers.

"Can you still give a young woman pleasure?"

Lothar grinned. "I've been giving young women pleasure for three and a half decades."

"Then I'll have two weddings here tonight instead of one. I'll marry you and this girl, Polonia, daughter of one of our foremost generals, and strengthen the union of our peoples once more. Unless Njord objects."

A guffaw came from Njord's direction. "Why would I object to such a splendid idea?"

"And you, Polonia," Augustus said. "Are you going to defy the will of your god twice in one night?"

"N... no. No. If Your Divinity wishes for this to happen, then I will obey."

"Will your mother object?"

Slowly, Livia shook her head.

Good, Lucius thought. Livia was a renowned scholar and a priestess of Athina, versed in the intricacies of politics and law. Perhaps she had realized that Augustus's decision was the best way to keep the alliance on track.

"Then, Princeps Silvanus and Queen Frida," Augustus said, "I declare you wedded in the eyes of the Julian gods, and in those of Njord as well. May you enjoy a happy and fruitful marriage."

"Aye," Njord added.

"You may take your seats at the high table," Augustus said, "and witness the second wedding of the night."

They did as Augustus had commanded. Lucius and Gunnar took their seats as well.

There was no kissing of the bride, and Lucius had no doubt that Augustus had skipped it on purpose. Yet as they sat down, Silvanus whispered something in Frida's ear, and she laughed.

They were married now, despite everything — and starting on a good note.

"General Mercurius," Augustus said in a kind tone. "And you, Polonia, sweet girl. Leave your seats and head to Prince Lothar's table."

Gunnar laughed at that. "Prince Lothar," he said, loud enough for Lucius to hear. "I'll never hear the end of it."

"Away, you two!" Lothar said. Two of his captains rose from their seats and moved to exchange seats with Mercurius and Polonia. As for Augustus and Njord, they headed toward the Islanders' table.

"We have gathered here today," Augustus began again. And soon the second marriage was officiated. This time there was a kissing of the bride, and Lucius was happy to see Polonia enjoying it.

She was a princess at last. And if she yearned for adventure, like he'd heard she did, then perhaps a match with this "Prince Lothar" was better than being married to Silvanus. Especially for one who didn't like cats.

The rest of the wedding proceeded without disturbance. There was braised pheasant, and hare in a tomato-and-garlic sauce, and enormous fruit platters, and even some salted fish that the Islanders had brought with them on their journey, along with a few barrels of ale. Wine flowed in abundance as well, some from the Orchard of the Gods and some imported from the Verdant Kingdom; and both kinds were well-appreciated by the guests, though none of the six seated at the high table took a single sip.

Augustus and Njord had no need for wine, and Lucius rarely let more than a few drops pass his lips. Frida had refused both kinds of wine when the servants had proffered them, and Silvanus had followed her lead. As for Gunnar, he said he'd drink and celebrate later, by himself.

The banquet hall was filled with joy and laughter, and singing, and sharing of stories. And not a single fight broke out. Though perhaps the presence of the four hundred Julian soldiers who stood guard inside the hall did help with the latter.

The feast continued until late into the night, when the gods bid the married couples farewell and the guests retired to their rooms.

When the last of the Julian nobles departed, Lucius sighed. Four hundred soldiers still surrounded him, yet he felt alone. A boy of fifteen who carried the weight of the world upon his shoulders and fought for his gods in a deadly contest, where victory was far from certain.

He couldn't go to sleep, not yet. Instead, he headed to the Imperial Study to prepare for the next day's battle games. He was leafing through a large tome of military strategy when he heard a knock on the door.

"Enter," he said.

It was Polonia. She strode in, and bowed as the guard outside closed the door behind her.

"I took leave of my husband for a few moments, Your Majesty," she said. "I needed to speak with you alone."

"You're unhappy with your match, then?" There wasn't much to be done about it. Not when she'd been married off by Augustus, with Njord's approval.

Polonia rolled her eyes. "With *Prince Lothar*? I'll have him eating out of the palm of my hand in a week."

There was something in the way she'd said it. "So... you knew? Did you and Augustus plan this?"

She flashed him an innocent smile. "Do you truly think I am capable of such clever scheming, Your Majesty?"

She wasn't denying it. "Why didn't you tell me in advance?" Lucius asked. "Why didn't Augustus?"

"They were all watching, our people and Njord's. Your reaction had to be genuine. And, before you ask, my mother didn't know, either." She looked him in the eye. "You're not alone in this war, Your Majesty. You never were. Augustus wanted you to know that. He must be busy keeping Njord entertained, or he would have come to tell you himself."

"And your mission?"

"To make sure my husband stays true to our alliance, whatever comes our way. That and nothing more. And now, with your permission, I'll take my leave."

He nodded. As the door closed behind her, a new thought hit him.

If Queen Frida loses her life in the battles to come, Silvanus will have no power over the Islanders. Not according to their customs. They'll choose a new king, and more likely than not, they'll choose Lothar.

And Polonia will be at his side.

He smiled. The evening had gone far better than he'd expected. Even so, he couldn't rest, not yet.

He flipped through the pages of the strategy book until he found what he was looking for: a clever trick that his great-grandfather had employed against the orcs seven decades earlier, with great success. A way to beat Farus in the next day's battle game.

Of course, Farus was reading the same books as he was.

I'll use it, but add my own twist, he thought, and started reading.

Champions at Odds

Seated on the edge of the bed, Anders Svensson watched Katrina pace through their room at the conquered Verdant fortress.

He braced himself for what was about to follow. She'd been all sweetness and smiles at the Islander celebration, but Anders knew it was the calm before the storm.

"This," she spat between clenched teeth. "This is what she gives me. Hardly better than a prison cell."

She wasn't wrong. Placed at the center of the keep, the room had a single door, made of stout oak, and no windows. With its ornate furnishings and its large four-poster bed, it wasn't exactly a dungeon, though it could easily be turned into one.

"You angered her," Anders said. "You didn't have to."

"Don't lecture me!" she snapped.

He shrank back, as she would expect.

Katrina hissed. "Of course, she had to take the upper room in the tower for herself. The tower you didn't knock down, that is. I wish you had."

"It's only one night. Tomorrow we'll be far from here, and soon all this will be forgotten."

She whirled toward him, stopping only inches from his face. Her talons traced his cheek, though she didn't break the skin. Not this time.

"You abandoned Njord, and Frida, too. Because they were weak. Do you think Elena is a queen worth following?"

"It doesn't matter what I think."

She pressed her talons deeper. "Answer the question."

He grabbed her wrist and pulled her hand away. Over the time they'd spent together, he'd learned when to submit to her and when to show strength.

She growled, but did not strike him.

He let go of her wrist. "She's ruled your kingdom for five centuries. From what I've heard, she's done well. She's made it *efficient*."

"She's a good bureaucrat, yes. But a wartime queen? She doesn't even join us when the blood rage takes us. I don't think she has the stomach for it."

Neither did Anders, judging by what he'd seen in the castle courtyard. He was no stranger to violence, and had used it himself many times. But this... this was slaughter.

"I heard she doesn't feel the blood rage like you do," he said.

"She could at least pretend."

"It doesn't matter, Katrina. We're the strongest side in this war. We're going to win, and you and I will rule over my people together."

"With her as the high queen. I'll have to bow to her."

"As you always have."

Katrina raked her talons down the frame of the four-poster bed, leaving deep gashes in the wood. "We're fighting for the fates of the gods, Anders. And I've served mine well. I killed King Knut and brought you to our side, with your men and your cannons. I made myself the queen of your people. And what has she done? Flying around and chasing peasants, that's what she's done!" She lowered her voice. "Of course, if you tell Elena any of this, I'll deny everything."

"Don't even think about that," Anders said. "My fate is tied to yours."

He wished it wasn't. But there wasn't much he could do about it, not without great risk to himself. And Anders was a survivor. Besides, if two of the vampire god's champions were at odds, that was a problem for Serya Krov himself to solve.

I'll try to pacify her, he thought. *That's all I can do for now.*

Katrina smiled at him. "I believe you. You'll be loyal, for your own good and mine."

"Aye."

"When my kind wins this war," she said, "we will need to rule the world with a firm hand. You can't expect all the realms to simply bend to Elena's will. She's not strong enough. Then again, she may die before it's over."

Anders frowned. "If you're saying what I think you're saying, the answer is no."

"I'm not asking you to kill her! It would weaken our god, and I'd never do that. Never. But we'll be fighting Queen Marion, and then the Julians, and the giants, and everyone else who's still standing. And anything could happen."

"Even so. If she's in danger, we shall protect her, yes?"

She sighed. "Yes. Yes, we shall protect her. And Zoltan, and Kirill the priest. But I've had enough of this for tonight. Show me how much you want me."

He leaped off the edge of the bed and pushed her against the wall.

I could have played this differently, if I were still loyal to Njord, he thought as he kissed her neck. *I could have pushed her and Elena against each other. Or I could have taken more direct action, and killed one of them, and perhaps the priest Kirill as well.*

He and five of his best men could have done it, if they picked the right moment. It would be a suicide mission, though one that would earn him a place in history. But he wasn't fighting for Njord, not anymore. He'd seen the sea god for what he was: a true force of nature, but not much else. Proud and vain, but lacking wisdom.

He'd thrown in his lot with Serya Krov. A stronger god, and one worth following. And Queen Elena had promised Anders that his reward would stand, and he'd be king of the Islanders.

Unless she and Katrina rip each other apart before the war is done.

Pillow Talk

Frida advanced down the corridor, holding her husband's hand. The door facing them was wide and massive, and decorated with an intricate pattern of smooth, curved lines cut deep into the wood. The two Julian guards who stood at its sides parted their spears as Frida and Silvanus walked toward them.

"My apartments," Silvanus said.

Frida smiled. "So, this is where I get to meet your cats, yes?"

"No, these are just my lodgings at the palace," he replied. "My cats are at my villa, on the outskirts of the city. You'll like Fluffy best."

He nodded at the guards, and one of them pulled the door open.

They entered a hallway, bare save for the two torches at the far end and the five wooden doors: two on the left, two on the right, and one straight ahead. The main door closed behind them with the lightest of squeaks.

At last, no guards. Frida dropped her smile and let go of Silvanus's hand.

"Thank you," Silvanus said.

She turned to him. "What for?"

"Not embarrassing me out there."

She smiled. "We're friends, you and I. Friends don't embarrass each other. Not in front of underlings, at least."

She liked Silvanus. But she liked him in the way one would like a second cousin who's ten years younger, and clever beyond his years, and wouldn't be of much use in a fight.

"You have quite a few rooms here," she told him.

He pointed to the doors in turn. "Reading room. Salon. The privy. And, of course, the bedroom." It was the room straight ahead.

"And that one?" Frida asked, pointing to the last door on the right.

"I call that my Chamber of Secrets. I'm the only one who has the key."

If he'd meant to arouse her curiosity, she wouldn't rise to the bait. Instead, she walked straight into the bedroom.

It was dimly lit with scented candles; two on the nightstands, the other two placed on tall poles in the opposite corners of the room. The bed itself was at least eight feet long and ten feet wide. It was covered with cushions and heavy blankets, and smelled new, as if the imperial carpenters had built it in a hurry after learning that Frida's marriage with Silvanus had been decided. The wide window was covered with heavy drapes of a dark orange color, though a glimmer of moonlight did sneak in. A large sofa rested against the wall opposite the bed.

The mood would have been romantic had Ulrika been there, waiting for her.

Instead, the Julian boy joined her. He looked up, straight into her eyes.

"So," he said. "Are we going to, you know...?"

She shook her head. "I am marching to war in a week, to fight for your gods and mine. I'm not going to do so with a child in my womb."

Of course, there were herbs that could prevent that, but she hoped he wouldn't bring those up. She'd have to reject him more directly if he did.

"I understand," he said. She sensed relief in his voice, and that was good.

"The women of my bloodline are as fertile as one could be," she said. "My mother had seven brothers, and the first time she lay with Father, she gave him a son. The second time, she gave him me."

Silvanus raised an eyebrow. "I didn't know you had a brother."

"Little Sverre died of a fever before he turned three."

Silvanus sighed. "I'm sorry for your loss."

She sat on the edge of the bed. "It was a long time ago, and I was a babe. I only know him from my father's stories."

"And after that?" He sat next to her, without touching her.

"My birth was hard on my mother's body. She said she'd have no more children after me, and Father understood. Besides, she longed to lead her ships again, and she wouldn't do so with a child in her belly." She paused for a moment. "Five years later, as she led half a dozen ships to raid the Verdant shores, she was caught in a bad storm out on the open sea, and took her final swim. I wish I'd known her better."

"She seems like quite a woman," Silvanus said.

"One in a generation."

"As are you."

Frida nodded at the genuine compliment. "Thank you, Silvanus."

"Thank you, *dear husband*," he said. "It's good to practice in private."

"Thank you, dear husband," she said. There was no harm in it.

He smiled. "You Islanders live exciting lives. You'll find mine quite boring, I'm afraid."

"If we win this war," Frida said, "I could get used to a boring life." Though she'd rather have it back in Hemland, with Ulrika.

If Ulrika waits for me. She'd said she would, but seven years was a long time.

"So, no lovemaking for us tonight," Silvanus said. "Or any other night, at least not before you march to war. What should I tell the emperor and Princeps Farus?"

"Tell them I am the most amazing woman you've ever spent the night with."

He nodded. "I won't even have to lie."

Another good compliment. "Will they ask for details?"

"If they do, I think I can dodge their questions well enough."

"Very well." Frida yawned. "I'll take the bed then. You'll be fine on the sofa, yes?"

"It will be the first time I use it for sleeping. But yes, I'll make it through the night."

"First, can you help me with my dress?" She stood and pointed to two spots on her back. "These two strings, here and here."

"My pleasure," Silvanus said, and pulled them.

"Thank you. Now turn around."

He walked to the sofa and stood there, facing the wall, as Frida swung her dress over her head and dropped it to the floor.

She removed her shoes, shoved a few cushions off the bed, and slid under the cover. "I'm ready." The bed was soft, but not *too* soft; just the way she liked it.

"I'll sleep in my wedding clothes," Silvanus said as he sat down on the sofa. "We should have some pillow talk, at least."

"Pillow talk. I like it." She grabbed one of the pillows and threw it to him, and he caught it easily. "Here's a pillow. Now talk."

He lay down, placing the pillow under his head. "You're going to war. I'm staying here."

"I thought you'd come with me."

"I have an important task, here in Lux Aeterna."

"And what is it?"

"I'm helping Lucius become the most skilled military commander in the history of the world."

"Really. Lucius. A boy of fifteen."

"A boy who has the ear of our gods and sees one of them daily. Sometimes twice a day."

She only wished Njord would grace her with his presence that often. "Still, that doesn't make him a skilled general."

"Not in itself. But we have visions from other worlds, and new weapons, and mock battles, and other things. I'll show you tomorrow."

That all sounded intriguing. "I can't wait," she said, and meant it.

She wouldn't miss Silvanus on the frontlines, not really. Having him around could hurt her image in front of her men. Still, she had to get to know him, and figure out how to make use of him for her people's benefit; and now she'd only have a few days for it.

"While you're gone," he said, "I won't have my suitors, not anymore.

Not as a married man. So, I was thinking I'd take a concubine or two. I don't think you'd mind, and neither would Ulrika."

How does he know of Ulrika? Frida wondered. Not even Gunnar did.

"We have the best spies," Silvanus said, as if guessing her thoughts. "And we pay them well. So. Concubines."

It was a negotiation, then. "As long as you don't mind sharing them with me when I return," Frida said. Though she was lying down and couldn't see him, she imagined him smiling.

She spoke again. "I am your wife now, Silvanus. You're the first in line to the throne, and that is my doing. I might be empress one day. I won't have you disrespect me."

"So, no concubines."

"None."

"And I guess no visits to the pleasure houses, either."

"People would know, and they'd talk. Besides, I don't want to come back from winning this war, only to have to deal with half a dozen of your bastards."

"There are herbs for that. But I hear you. No concubines, and no fun at the pleasure houses. I'll obey your terms, as long as you promise to win this war quickly."

She laughed. "I'll do my best, *dear husband*."

"You know we'll have to produce an heir when this is over. Two, in fact. One for my province and one for Hemland."

"We'll deal with that when the time comes. And yes, if we both survive, I'll do my duty. As long as we live in a world where these things still matter."

"What do you mean?"

"Imagine that the worst comes to pass, and Grok the All-Father wins the War of the Seven. Imagine that he's the last of the gods, with no other to challenge him, and that he decides to purge the leaders of the Julian nobility. Then we're both dead. Or maybe we're on the run first, and *then* we're dead."

"We'll stop Grok and his champions before that happens," Silvanus said. "And you'll play your part in it. With your cannons."

"I'll do my best," she replied. "Speaking of the gods. If Njord loses, and if your gods lose as well, which of the others would you like to see win?"

"The Lady," Silvanus said instantly. "She has her ideals of honor and chivalry, and we've been at peace with her people for centuries. She'd treat us right. She might even allow Lucius to keep his seat as the ruler of the empire, under her benevolent guidance."

"I don't like the Lady. There'll be scores to settle, if she wins. With my people, I mean."

"Then who would you favor?"

"Malleon."

"Why?"

"He's the oldest of the gods, and one of the wisest. At least that's what Njord says. And since his giants live inland, we've never raided their realm. He'd treat us right. Perhaps your Julians too."

"At least you didn't choose the vampire god."

Frida scoffed. "Serya Krov can have Anders Svensson, that double-crossing bastard. Until I shove a dagger down his throat."

"I heard of his betrayal. It must have hurt you a lot."

"Yet it led me to you, *dear husband*," she said in her most honeyed voice.

"Hey! Not fair!" Silvanus said. "Not if you truly want me to stay away from your bed."

Frida smiled. He'd said, *your* bed. She had him right where she wanted him.

"Apologies," she said. "Good night, Silvanus." She blew out the candle to her left.

"Good night, Frida," Silvanus said. She didn't see what he did, but the other three candles winked off in an instant.

She closed her eyes and waited for sleep to come.

Though she was in the Imperial Palace, surrounded by thousands of Julian guards, she felt at ease. She wouldn't be woken in the middle of the night with half a dozen guards holding her down, while Silvanus — or anyone else — prepared to have his way with her, or worse. The last Godly Pact that Njord and Augustus had made earlier that day was unbreakable, and it had been specific.

If any of the Julians tried to harm her or Gunnar, Augustus himself would obliterate them. As Njord would strike down her men, if any of them moved against the Julian champions.

They were all safe from one another, at least for a while. But the War of the Seven would go on. And in this conflict, no one was truly safe.

What It Takes

In the middle of the night, up in the room atop the tower, Queen Elena hopped onto the windowsill.

She leaped off and dropped toward the ground.

Her wings sprouted from her back, and she flapped them with all her strength, arresting her fall. Then she was soaring above the fortress, above the sea of tents outside the walls.

Above the world, with its suffering and death.

The full moon waited far ahead, forever out of reach. She'd tried once, at the age of seventeen, against her parents' warnings — and had found that, high enough, the air was too thin to support her flight. No matter how hard she tried, she couldn't ascend any farther.

Then again, I wasn't drinking noble blood back then, was I?

A shadow passed over the moon, and Elena stopped her climb, hovering over three thousand feet in the air.

He'll come to me, she thought. *As he always does.*

The shadow grew smaller as it descended, until Serya Krov shrank to her size and stood three feet away, facing her.

"You can rest now," he said.

She stopped flapping her wings, and the vampire god held her in the air with his power. She felt weightless in its grasp.

"Something's bothering you tonight," he said. "And it's not the memory of King Dragos."

"It's Katrina, Divine One. She's challenging me."

"I see." He did not seem surprised.

"So you were watching?"

Serya Krov shook his head. "After the battle was won, I flew onward to take a look at Queen Marion's army. Of course, the Godly Pact forbids me from telling you what I saw."

"Of course."

"Tell me what happened with Katrina, my daughter."

"She denied me her blood, with others watching, though she tried to dress it as her being weak after the battle. And then she said that perhaps she should try noble blood as well."

"I see. And did you punish her?"

"I gave her the worst room that's still suitable for her station. I expect she'll get the message."

"I have no doubt she has already." There was a hint of amusement in Serya Krov's voice.

"Were she not one of your champions, I'd have her whipped for her first offense. Worse, for the second."

"As would be well within your right."

"I can't have this happen again, Divine One. What would you have me do?"

"I'd have you worry less about Katrina. I'll deal with her myself."

She nodded. "I would appreciate it."

"Katrina is a weapon," Serya Krov said. "Same as the assassin Al-Khanjar is Aljin's dagger. But it is King Ammon, and not Al-Khanjar, who rules the desert men. And it is you, Elena, who rules the Vampire Kingdom. And soon, the world."

She remained silent, sensing he had more to say.

"I'll do what it takes for your kind to prosper. As I've always done. I struck that ancient pact with Aljin and brought the vampires into the light. I raised the plateau high from the ground, for King Dragos to build his castle above it and make it the strongest fortress in the world, though I had to shift the tectonic plates to accomplish that."

"Tectonic plates?" Elena asked.

"It would take too long to explain. I allowed you to give your heart to save Dragos, and made you queen after his demise, and allowed you to drink noble blood and make use of its power. The first and last of your kind who has this privilege."

That excluded Katrina. Elena answered with a joyless smile.

"I supported you in the third decade of your reign, when the southern nobles questioned your leadership."

"I have not forgotten it, Divine One." He'd used both persuasion and brute force to silence the dissenters, and he had advised her well. Only half a century later, their descendants had become some of Elena's most loyal supporters. She'd had no more trouble from their families over the centuries.

"You have been a great queen for five hundred years. You *are* a great queen now. I have always supported you, and I will always have your back. Have I ever given you reason to doubt me?"

"Never."

"Then do your part, and win this war for our kind. And I'll do mine. I'll speak with Katrina and put an end to this unpleasantness." He chuckled. "Besides, I know what her problem is."

"And what is it?"

"She's an unsheathed weapon without a target. We need to find her a new mission. Something important that will advance our cause, perhaps as much as her killing King Knut and bringing Anders and his cannons to our side already has. And then she'll focus on that. She'll take her place in the rightful order of things, and her thoughts of disobedience will fade away."

If only, Elena thought. Then again, her god had spoken the truth. She had no reason to doubt him.

"Let her do what she does best," Serya Krov said. "Let her be a weapon, and let your hand be the one that wields it. She'll play her part. I'll speak to her and make sure of it."

"Thank you, Divine One." It was what she needed, after all.

"Then let us speak of this no more for now. Just stay here with me."

They hovered in silence, the strongest of the mortals and the strongest of the gods, above the world they would soon rule together.

It was a cruel world, where the great war raged, where armies clashed and men died. Women and children as well; and orcs, and giants, and vampire nobles. But after the war was won, High Queen Elena would set it right.

She'd turn it into a world of order and justice, where vampires ruled supreme. And Serya Krov would be the only god above it all, for a thousand years.

The Morning After

Frida opened her eyes as the rays of the sun caressed her face.

She pushed the soft blanket aside, relinquishing its warm embrace, and sat up. The night's rest had refreshed her, as if she'd slept for a week.

This is how the giants must feel after their decades-long slumber, she mused.

She was alone in Princeps Silvanus's bedroom. His and hers now, as husband and wife. Until she marched to war, at least.

The folded piece of paper on the nightstand caught her eye. She opened it and read the elegant writing.

> *I've gone for my morning walk, dear wife. Your belongings are in the reading room, along with some wedding gifts that I hope you will enjoy. Take your time, and follow the guard at the entrance when you're ready. He'll bring you to me, and food will be provided.*
>
> *Yours,*
> *Silvanus*

She smiled. Always the courteous one, this young Julian. She had to admit that, since the forging of the alliance, she'd been treated like royalty.

Which she was, though not the kind who lived in a palace. Her people lived hard lives, both in their harsh land with its long, snowy winters and out on the open ocean. And that bred hard men and women who rose through their strength and skill, mastered the seas under Njord's benevolent guidance, and took what they wanted.

If only Mother could see me now, she thought.

"*I see greatness in your future, my child,*" Big Greta had told her on her fifth birthday, only weeks before sailing to her death. And now, Frida was the queen of the Islanders, leading her people in a great war for the fates of the gods, and forging a strong alliance that increased their chance of winning.

She blinked, sending the memory of her mother away, and rose from the bed, still wearing her swimming garments. *Time to get moving. But first, a quick look around.*

She opened Silvanus's closet and found lots and lots of fancy Julian clothes, all colored in white and orange, but nothing of note. No jewelry, no weapons, and no other possessions that could tell her more about him.

That done, she crossed the empty hallway and entered the prince's reading room.

It was large and sparsely furnished. A small round table surrounded by three comfortable-looking chairs stood in its center. Frida's twin daggers rested upon it, as did a tall glass of orange juice. Her two small coffers, which she'd brought from her ship in an ox-drawn cart, awaited at the table's side.

The wall to Frida's left was lined with shelves, all filled with books, while a large map of the world covered the opposite wall. Straight ahead, a wide window opened toward the courtyard. Next to it rested a wide leather sofa, and on it lay a festive dress and a suit of armor, both blue with orange streaks and no doubt fashioned for her size.

His wedding gifts, she thought.

They could wait a little longer.

Frida drank the orange juice. She opened her coffers and found everything in its place. Then she studied Silvanus's book collection.

It was vast and neatly organized. Books about each of the seven realms were clustered together, with the Julian collection being the largest, its books grouped into more than ten categories. The section on the Islanders was the smallest, yet it still had two dozen items, at least.

He's organized, Frida thought.

She scanned a few titles. *Rising From the Depths. The Three Great Sagas — A Julian Interpretation. Sigvard's Revenge. Sea Battles of Note. The Shield Wall and How to Break It. All That We Know About Njord, and Some Things We Speculate. The Last Word on Shipbuilding. Deep Sea Fishing Techniques.*

He must have read a few of these before I arrived, she thought.

It was a good collection and covered many areas, from legends and history to various crafts. Then again, a treatise on shipbuilding had nothing on a skilled shipwright with two or three decades of experience. Frida had plenty of those among her ranks, and had left most of them with Sigurd and the fleet.

She gave a cursory glance to the books on the orcs, but curiosity got the better of her and she strode toward the leather sofa.

The festive dress was sleeveless, and longer than the one she'd worn the night before. Its dark blue color matched Frida's hair perfectly. Its plunging neckline was contoured with small sapphires and would reveal the bear's claw marks, but nothing more. A few swirling patterns sewn with orange thread added a dash of the Julian color. After marrying Silvanus, she could hardly object.

Frida tried on the dress and found it fit her perfectly, as did the pair of sandals that had been hiding underneath it. Even better, the slit on the right side of the dress allowed her great freedom of movement.

The seamstresses must have worked through the night, she thought. *Or maybe some Julian servants took my measurements somewhere along the journey to the capital, as they were washing my clothes, and sent them onward.*

The battle outfit was far more interesting.

It was made of interlocking steel plates, dyed blue except for a few dashes of orange. Two symbols decorated its pauldrons: Njord's trident on the left and Augustus's lightning bolt on the right. The breastplate bore no marks and would accommodate her large build. She inspected the greaves and the gauntlets and found them flawless.

The armor she'd seen Queen Marion wear was better. It had been crafted by Malleon, blessed by the Lady, and would confer its wearer unnatural strength and speed. Still, Frida's new armor appeared to be of the highest quality that the imperial craftsmen, or any other human craftsmen, could provide.

The helmet rested on the sofa's backrest. Next to it, Frida found a note, written in the same elegant script as before.

I hope you like your presents. You should wear the dress for now. There'll be plenty of time for the armor later.

Yours,
Silvanus

She considered it. It was the second time he was telling her what to do that day, and she hadn't even seen him. She could wear the armor, just to spite him, or perhaps some of her other clothes. Then again, they were allies, and he'd been a gracious host so far.

She'd keep the dress on, for now.

She visited the other rooms briefly, though the one Silvanus had called his Chamber of Secrets remained locked. Then she opened the main door of the apartment. A stone-faced guard waited outside.

"Take me to my husband," she said.

The guard nodded. "Of course, Queen Frida. He's waiting for you in the throne room. Follow me."

They arrived less than a minute later, and that was good. It meant the Boy Emperor wanted to keep her husband close.

They both waited inside, as did Gunnar and the other Julian boy, Princeps Farus. No one else was in the throne room, not even a small team of guards. Frida's guide retreated promptly, closing the door behind him.

The throne room was vast. That, Frida had expected. But the way it was furnished took her by surprise.

Seven large tables stood in front of the dais. Each table sported a miniature landscape, though they were different; one was mostly forested, another held a model of a Julian fort, and yet another held the towering shape of Dragos Castle, which Frida recognized from a painting she'd plundered from the vampires a year earlier. But it was not just terrain and buildings that the tables held.

Two miniature armies faced each other across each setting.

Each army was composed of various figurines; little soldiers, only two or three inches in height, wielding tiny bows, swords, axes, and spears. Some were mounted. They were painted in the colors of their realms: gray versus green, orange versus red, blue versus green, purple versus gray. And so on.

An eighth table stood to the side, and this one was laden with food.

Frida advanced, and Princeps Farus spoke first. "You're here. Good. We can begin."

Silvanus placed a hand on his shoulder. "You forget your manners, my friend." He smiled at Frida. "Good morning, dear wife. I trust you slept well?"

She smiled back. "Our bed was comfortable, yes." She glanced at Gunnar, and he nodded. All was well.

"Did you enjoy your wedding gifts?" Silvanus asked.

"Enough to wear this one."

He looked her up and down. "You look ravishing. Would you like some refreshments?"

She nodded and joined him at the food table. It was laden with over a dozen platters, which contained oranges, olives, grapes, seven kinds of cheese, three types of bread, lamb sausages, and a generous selection of salted fish. On one end, five decorated cups stood in a line, facing several carafes filled with water and orange juice.

"Try these," Silvanus said as he offered her a fruit-and-cheese platter.

She bit into the first slice of cheese and found it delicious.

She licked her lips. "So, dear husband. You're trying to tame me with your nice gifts and your fancy food. You'll find that I'm not that easily tamed."

"We don't want to tame you, dear wife," Silvanus said. "We need you to be fierce. We need you to destroy the orcs, together with these two." He pointed to Farus and Gunnar. "But there's no reason to deny ourselves some comfort between now and then."

"Go ahead and eat, Little Frida," Gunnar said. "I've had a full plate myself."

She took another bite, but something nagged at her. "What about Lothar? Why is he not with us?"

"He wasn't invited," Lucius, the Boy Emperor, replied.

"And why not?"

"You'll find out soon enough. Besides, he must still be resting after his wedding."

Frida nodded at that. Lothar could drink with the best of the Islanders, even now in his early fifties; and he *had,* with his new wife at his side. He'd need time to recover after that.

"Unless he's engaged in more... pleasant activities," Lucius continued.

You're a boy who speaks like a man, Frida thought.

She took a bite of an apple. "These tables. What are they about?"

"Battle games, of course," Lucius said. "Then again, you must have figured that out."

"I told you we're training Lucius to become the greatest military commander the world has ever seen," Silvanus said. "Now, my dear wife, we'll show you how we do it."

Battle Games

Frida set her plate down and followed Silvanus and his friends as they stepped toward the table showing Dragos Castle. This was going to be interesting.

"We fight seven battles every day," he said. "Some from history, and some that will teach us how to win upcoming clashes. This one shows the giants storming the vampire capital."

"There are rules, of course," Farus added.

Frida glanced over her shoulder. Gunnar had remained near the food table and was pouring himself a glass of orange juice.

"Rules," she said. "Tell me more."

"Each piece represents a unit of soldiers," Farus said. "This is one hundred." He lifted a small gray piece: a man armed with a spear, no doubt representing a unit of serfs from the Vampire Kingdom. "This is three hundred, and this is five hundred, and the big one over there is one thousand." Each of the pieces he pointed to was slightly larger than the previous one. "The unit sizes are smaller for the giants, of course. But don't let that bother you, not today. Let's move on to your table."

My table? Frida wondered.

She followed Farus to a miniature battlefield that had a green army and a blue army facing each other on hilly terrain. More blue pieces and green pieces lay in two baskets that hung from the sides of the table.

Farus spread his hands wide. "This is the battle that the great pirate

Bjorn Ulfsson, the Shark Slayer, fought in Lysennia forty-two years ago, against the Lady's followers. He was more than twenty miles inland, far from his ships; and he was outnumbered, with his three thousand warriors facing almost four thousand. Still, he won a crushing victory. We had our artisans reconstruct the land and the two forces from various descriptions of the battle."

"Lothar should see this," Frida said. Bjorn the Shark Slayer was Ulf's son, but he was also Lothar's father.

Four years earlier, she'd seen Old Bjorn's lifeless body tossed into the sea for its final swim. He'd died of old age, surrounded by his loved ones, exactly how he'd wanted to go.

"Not today," Lucius said.

Farus pointed to a blue figurine holding a spear. "Standard Islander infantry. That one next to it is veteran infantry." It was a darker shade of blue, and armed with an axe and a large shield. "That's an Islander archer, and that's a Verdant archer." The latter piece was green. "Light cavalry and heavy cavalry." Those were both green pieces showing mounted men, and the second sported a long lance and had a more streamlined shape, as if both horse and rider wore armor. "Verdant spearmen. Verdant swordsmen."

"What about cannons?" Frida asked.

"Oh, we have those, too," Farus replied. "And ballistae, horse archers, camel riders, crossbows, giants, and vampire nobles. Not for this battle, though. Bjorn's cannons were back on his ships, out of reach."

"And wizards? What about those?"

Farus shook his head. "There aren't enough of those to make a difference in a large battle. We just think of them as part of the infantry, or cavalry, or ranged units."

"I see. So, you're going to show me how Lothar's father won the battle."

"Oh, that would be boring," Farus said. "You're going to fight the battle yourself. Against your dear husband. You're going to act as the Islander general, and lead your troops to victory or defeat."

Silvanus punched him in the shoulder. "I was supposed to tell her myself, you big oaf!"

"*Small* oaf," Gunnar said. He picked up a lamb sausage, sniffed it, wrinkled his nose, and dropped it back onto the plate, opting for a piece of salted fish instead.

Silvanus grinned. "Small oaf. I like it."

He turned to Frida. "Forty-two years ago, Sir Ferdinand charged Bjorn's shield wall with his knights. When they didn't break through, as he thought they would, he sent in most of his foot soldiers as well. But the Islanders were stronger, and cut them to pieces; and then Sir Ferdinand wisely had his archers perform a strategic withdrawal, rather than suffer the same fate."

"They ran from the battlefield," Lucius added. "Sir Ferdinand hanged himself a week later. His family still bears the shame of the defeat."

She understood. "But I'm not fighting Sir Ferdinand, am I?"

"You're fighting me," Silvanus said. "And I'll use some of the tricks I've learned from the dozens of battles I've fought already, against my two dear friends."

"This is the timekeeper," Farus said, placing his hand on an hourglass that stood on a corner of the table. "We turn it over when the game begins, and it marks the speed of battle. Here, on this table, time passes five times faster than in real life; a minute is five minutes, and a dozen minutes is an hour. This helps us decide how fast the troops can move."

"We usually play at ten times the real speed," Silvanus said. "But since this is your first game, we'll just do five."

"We can stop time," Farus added, and pointed to a lever that jutted out from the side of the hourglass. "But we only do this when we need to perform complex maneuvers." He smiled. "The pieces don't move by themselves, you know."

Frida understood. "We're the ones to move them, or have them stay in place." She picked up one of the blue pieces and examined it closely: an axe-and-shield man, his hair neatly braided. "And what happens when two forces clash?"

"That's where the number books come into play," Farus said.

He reached under the table and pulled out a thin book. Its cover was painted half green, half blue. He opened it onto a page that contained row upon row of neatly arranged numbers.

"This takes some getting used to," Farus said, "so I'll help you. Look here. This tells you what happens if three hundred of the green infantry engage two hundred of your veterans."

"My veterans win," Frida said.

"Exactly. You're left with one hundred veterans, and the Green are left with one hundred as well, and they withdraw. If you pursue them and catch them, you destroy them completely. Of course, full battles are not that simple. Those three hundred may have another hundred supporting them, or your veterans may be under arrow fire. And then the result changes."

"I see. And who came up with these numbers?"

Farus stood straighter than before, if that were possible. It would have been impressive, except for Frida being much taller than he was.

"The god of war," he said. "Ares himself."

"He instructed our scribes to write these books," Lucius said. "The numbers in them reflect what the gods have seen happen in past clashes between various forces, over the centuries. Even better, they take into account the improvements in weapons and armor since those battles were fought, and the landscape as well, though we won't worry about that today. This book deals with the Verdant Kingdom fighting the Islanders. We have twenty-one such books."

Each kingdom fighting another, Frida thought. *Seven kingdoms, six opponents for each kingdom, that's forty-two. But you only need each pair once.*

"Twenty-one seems right," she said. "But how do you get Islanders-versus-orcs? Or Julians versus vampires?" The lay of the land had prevented such confrontations.

"What a great question!" Farus exclaimed. He turned to Silvanus. "You should marry this one. She's clever."

"Already done," Silvanus shot back.

Frida smiled at the exchange. *Children. All of them.* But these were no ordinary younglings. Together, they ruled an empire — and seemed to be up to the task.

Lucius smiled as well. "The numbers in those books are based on guesswork, and on calculations from more viable matchups. Even so, I trust them. It was Athina who did the guesswork, and the calculations as well."

"And you've memorized all these books?"

"We could only wish," Lucius said. "Your husband has the best memory among the three of us, and he makes good decisions using these numbers, given enough time." Silvanus smiled at that. "Farus is impetuous and has good intuition about when to strike and when to defend. And I'm the best strategist of the three."

"That he is," Silvanus agreed.

"Less talking, more fighting," Farus said. "Generals. Take your places."

Frida moved to stand behind her army of blue figurines, while Silvanus faced her.

"Generals, survey your armies," Farus said.

Frida did. She had ten figurines, each representing three hundred warriors. Two archers, four standard infantry units, and four veteran infantry.

"Survey the enemy army," Farus said.

Instantly, Frida saw the difference. "You have cavalry. And more archers."

"More troops overall," Silvanus said. He had four swordsmen, three pikemen, one light cavalry unit, one heavy cavalry, and four archers. Each of his pieces represented three hundred men. "Yet it was Bjorn Ulfsson who won the field that day. Can you do the same?"

Farus reached for the hourglass — the timekeeper — and turned it over. "Generals. Begin."

"Wait," Silvanus said.

Farus pulled the timekeeper's lever and the grains of sand stopped falling. "What?"

"We've told her about time, but not about distance."

"Ah, yes. Of course." Farus pointed to four black lines painted onto the side of the table, two of them much longer than the others. "Walking distance for infantry in a minute. Running distance. Galloping camels and galloping horses. When the cavalry is walking or trotting, we use the same speed as for the infantry's walking or running. Ready now?"

Frida took a deep breath and scanned the battlefield once more.

Her infantry was arrayed in a line, with the archers to the front. The terrain was higher to her right. Ahead of her, the green figurines of Silvanus's army held the higher ground.

His army was split in two, with a wide gap in the center. The pikemen opposed her right flank, supported by two units of archers and his heavy cavalry. The swordsmen opposed her left, with the other two archer units and his light cavalry.

"Ready," she said.

"Begin," Farus said, and moved the lever again, allowing the grains of sand to fall.

Frida advanced her forces. Silvanus moved his two armies toward her at an angle, sending them even farther apart, as if he tried to flank her. His cavalry led the way.

"Gallop," he said, and moved his light cavalry toward Frida's archers. With his other hand, he pushed his heavy cavalry further away from her right flank. The rest of his left wing claimed the high ground to her right, while his right wing took a defensive position.

He's doing too many things at once, Frida thought. She moved her archers away from the light cavalry's charge and pushed two units of infantry forward to intercept it.

The heavy cavalry was circling, getting closer to her right wing. Luckily, she had two of her veteran units bracing to meet them. *I'll beat them, if that number book is fair.*

Silvanus withdrew his light cavalry just before her infantry reached it, and pushed his heavy cavalry onward, passing her veterans.

He pointed to one of her veteran units. "These men are in range of my archers. What do you do, attack or pull back?"

She pushed her figurine forward, toward his army. It would be one unit of three hundred veterans against three spear units and two archers, but she'd bring more of her army to support it soon.

"I attack," she said. She pushed the bulk of her army forward. She moved another of her veteran units toward Silvanus's knights, keeping them away from her main force.

"Interesting," Silvanus said. "Farus?"

Farus leafed through the number book. "Her shield wall is strong. Your arrows are doing some damage, but not enough to matter. Not yet."

Emboldened, Frida pushed on. Most of her troops would strike at Silvanus's left flank, reinforcing her veterans as they charged. She moved three units to engage his other flank and sent one more to intercept his heavy cavalry.

"First mistake," Silvanus said, and turned his light cavalry to the right. They'd crash into her veterans just as they reached his left flank. "Lost that one, I'm afraid."

Farus raised his eyes from the number book. "Frida, drop your unit to one hundred. They're hemmed in by his infantry, and they're taking a cavalry charge to the rear, and they got pelted with arrows, too. One hundred is me being generous."

"Fine," Frida growled. She replaced her three-hundred veteran piece with a one-hundred piece from the basket hanging from her side of the table. She still had two units of spearmen charging toward Silvanus's flank, and those would turn the tide.

Just then, his heavy cavalry charged into the bulk of her forces. Then he moved it away.

"That's going to cost you one hundred knights," Farus said. "And Frida's archers are firing after your knights as they retreat."

Silvanus nodded and replaced his three-hundred-knights piece with two one-hundred pieces. "It bought me time." The majority of Frida's army hadn't reached his troops yet.

"A little," she said. She pushed those two spearmen forward, both engaging one of Silvanus's spear units. "These should destroy him, yes?"

"They will," Farus agreed. "But it will take them a while. They're strong men, but they're sailors, not warriors. In the meantime, your veterans are getting annihilated." With two units of spearmen and two units of archers focusing on them, and having taken that cavalry charge to the rear, Frida was not surprised.

She pushed the bulk of her forces forward, but three units were lagging behind, having followed Silvanus's heavy cavalry. Which had, of course, escaped their grasp.

One of her units rushed her opponents' right flank. Then Silvanus said, "Charge," and sent his light cavalry onto their backs.

Frida sighed. "Second mistake?"

"It only costs you one hundred," Farus said, and she replaced her three-hundred piece with two one-hundred pieces. "So far."

She nodded and pushed three of her units forward to reinforce the attack on that flank. Even so, they'd be outnumbered.

Silvanus pushed her units back slightly. "Go slower. They're only human."

She waited a few heartbeats and pushed them forward again. Now they were right against his troops.

Farus looked at the timekeeper and pulled the lever that stopped time. "You lose this unit, and that one." He removed Frida's first two units that had made contact with Silvanus's infantry. "But your veterans sold their skins dearly." He took away one of the green three-hundred-spearmen pieces from Silvanus's army and replaced it with two one-hundred pieces. "Your two-against-one attack is working as well. Your left flank, though, is failing." He moved the lever again, restarting time.

Frida nodded. She didn't have enough troops there, and Silvanus's light cavalry had outrun her laggards and was crashing into the archers on her left flank.

"These veterans are surrounded and fighting against three-to-one odds, and under arrow fire," Farus said, pointing to one of her units. "They'll be destroyed soon."

She hurried the last of her troops onward, but they were too slow, and too far away. After a few more cavalry charges and some sustained arrow fire, her left flank was in tatters.

Her two-against-one attack fell apart next. It had turned into two-against-three, and Silvanus's knights charged into her troops from behind, and his archers were targeting her men as well.

She looked up from the battlefield and into Silvanus's eyes. "It's over, isn't it?"

Silvanus nodded. "Even so, dear wife. Fight me to the end."

She did. The last of her troops reached his left flank, and the strength of the Islanders showed. Soon, Silvanus was left with only one hundred knights and one hundred light cavalry, and half of his spearmen were gone as well. His archers, though, were untouched, and his other flank was completely dominating her troops. He brought his swordsmen to join the battle on his left, and though Frida's last two units made short work of most of his spearmen, they were overwhelmed.

"A great victory for the Verdant Kingdom," Farus said. "And though they've lost a lot of troops, at least the archers and some of the swordsmen will get to go home to their wives. Or mothers, or whatever. And Sir Ferdinand will die of old age. Unlike poor Bjorn, who's getting trampled by horsemen before the battle is done. Or perhaps pincushioned with arrows."

"And that's why you didn't invite Lothar today," Frida said. "You didn't want him to see this. To watch me lose the battle his father won."

"Exactly," said Lucius, who'd been following the game without speaking.

She turned to him. "I had fewer troops, and Silvanus had cavalry, and more archers, too. I couldn't win, could I? Not against a competent general."

"I beat him yesterday, with your troops," Lucius said.

"How did you do it?"

"You have the stronger warriors. Every moment your men are exchanging blows with their enemies on equal terms gets you closer to victory. Every moment you're taking arrow fire, or chasing his cavalry, or having your troops fight against much higher numbers, brings you closer to defeat."

"So, I should have just charged him."

"Yes. With a long battle line, so that some of your units could get past his swords and spears, and rush his archers. And with a couple of units screening the rest from his cavalry. You'd change the ones that would be doing the screening over time, depending on where he moved his knights; and if they finally engaged your troops, you'd converge upon them and destroy them. That's what I did, and the numbers in the book did the rest."

"It's only a game, Lucius," Frida said. "It doesn't mean as much as you think."

"A game designed by the gods," Lucius replied. "A game where a competent general who outthinks his opponent can make the difference between a devastating defeat and a crushing victory. Just like in a real battle."

"Have you *been* in a real battle?" she asked him.

"Not yet, no."

"When you stand in the shield wall with your men, you don't get to see the whole battlefield from above. And here, on this table, you don't have your men getting tired, and officers giving conflicting orders, and fresh-blooded men-at-arms pissing themselves and screaming for their mothers as they see their comrades fall."

Silvanus smiled. "Oh, believe me, dear wife, if our artisans could make our little soldiers piss themselves in battle, I'd love to see that. With clean water, of course."

"We know it's not real, Frida," Lucius said. "But it's the best we have. And as long as our troops are disciplined and obey their officers, this will teach us how to win battles we'd otherwise lose. Battles that our forces and yours will fight, side by side, against the orcs and the desert men and whoever else comes next. Trust me, we'll do better after learning from this game than if we were to go without it."

"You assume that each of your units will follow your orders," Frida said.

"In real life, we assume that our officers are competent and that they know the battle plan. As generals, we play to the strengths of our forces when planning the battle, and prepare for what our opponents might do. And if the enemy still manages to surprise us, our decisions in the heat of battle may well make the difference between victory and defeat."

"And you think you can make better decisions than your generals."

Lucius nodded. "And draw better battle plans as well. That's what we're training for. See for yourself."

He walked to another table, where orange figurines faced red ones across a grassy field.

"Farus will play the orcs," Lucius said. "I'll take the Julians. And these."

He took out four one-thousand infantry pieces from his basket and placed them on the table, on his left flank. They were blue.

"A quarter of your army," he said. "No cannons, not yet. You'll see cannons in two of tomorrow's battles."

"I'd love to see what the number books say about those," said Gunnar from behind Frida. He'd approached the table soundlessly.

"I'm sure you'll like it, old sea wolf," Lucius said.

"Dear wife," Silvanus said, walking over to Frida's side.

She turned. "Yes?"

"I hope you're not upset with me for defeating you."

She shook her head. "It was my first game. I'll beat you next time."

"Perhaps," he said, though his tone said otherwise. "After this battle, let us speak alone for a while."

She nodded.

"Very well," Silvanus said. He turned toward the miniature battlefield, reached under the table, and pulled out a number book. "Generals. Take your places."

They did. A look of concentration was etched on Farus's face. As for

Lucius, he seemed relaxed.

"Generals," Silvanus said. "Survey your armies. Survey the enemy army."

He reached for the hourglass and turned it over. "Generals. Begin."

A Great Fighting Force

Standing on the side of the arena, surrounded by hundreds of Augustian Guards, Lucius smiled as the Islander queen's people entered the Imperial Stadium.

Queen Frida led the group, with Silvanus and Gunnar at her sides. She'd donned her new armor, its pauldrons decorated with Njord's trident and Augustus's lightning bolt. She held her husband's hand, and Lucius appreciated that.

Lothar Bjornsson followed her, as did her bodyguards Torsten and Arne. After them came three sea witches, Astrid, Ingrid, and Helga. Lucius recognized them from the royal wedding the night before. A dozen Islander warriors followed, all tall and bulky, armed with swords, axes, and spears, and carrying heavy shields.

She chose them well, Lucius thought. They were fierce, and if their skill with weapons matched their strength, they'd each be worth three Augustian Guards, if not more.

More than half of the men were sweating heavily in the afternoon sun, and Lucius could not blame them. They were used to the harsh, cold weather of Hemland and to the gentle breezes of the mainland's northern shores. Here, in the heart of the empire, the climate was warmer, especially now, in the middle of summer.

"Let our guests through," he said, and the sea of guards parted in front of him.

Frida bowed as she reached him. "Emperor Lucius. Thank you for inviting us here."

It was for the benefit of his guards, of course. There was no need for formalities between him and Frida, and he'd made sure she knew it.

"May I present my followers to you?" she continued.

"I know many of them from yesterday's wedding," Lucius said. "Except for these fine men."

"They're my brothers in arms," Frida said. "They stood with me in the shield wall against Queen Marion's army and kept me safe from her knights."

Of course, it had been Gunnar and his cannons that had won the battle. Lucius shot Gunnar a look, half expecting him to say something. The man winked at him, but kept quiet.

Frida recited the men's names. "Axel, Sverre, Olof, Bjarke, Findal, Karl, Magnus, Sander, Arvid, Nils, Gustav, and Ivar."

Lucius nodded at the men. "I've invited you all here to show you the skills of our warriors, and to witness those of yours. It will be the next step in forging our armies into a great fighting force."

He paused for a moment, then continued. "Let us begin. Sound the trumpets."

He turned around as two of his guards answered his command. They blew the notes in unison; three low, short ones followed by a high, longer note. The Augustian Guards parted in front of him as the gate to his far left opened.

Two dozen horse archers, led by Farus, entered the stadium. They rode through the gate in a column three wide, and fanned out into two neat rows as they passed into the arena proper.

"Look, Queen Frida." Lucius pointed to the opposite side. A dozen archery targets stood there, each of them over six feet tall and fashioned in the shape of an orc warrior, complete with sword and shield.

"Your craftsmen are impressive, Your Majesty," Frida said. Lucius turned to her and saw a spyglass in her hand. "They even got the tusks right."

"They did," Lucius said. "Have you ever faced the orcs, Queen Frida?"

"Not in battle. My father hired four of them into his crew, back when he was young. Best hunters he'd ever seen, he used to say, though poor fishers and worse sailors. They used to tell me stories when I was a child." She looked into the distance, as if savoring a memory. "The last of those orcs died of old age before I turned twelve."

"You were fond of him," Lucius guessed.

"Aye. He taught me how to wrestle. I used his tricks countless times. But now his kind are our enemies."

"And we'll defeat them. Together. Watch this."

He signaled, and the trumpets sounded again. Farus and his riders spurred their horses into a trot, then into a gallop. They raised their bows, and when they were less than forty paces from the line of targets, they let their arrows fly.

They pulled their horses up short and stopped just ahead of the targets.

Lucius turned to Frida. "How did they do?"

She handed him the spyglass. "Better than I expected."

Lucius surveyed the targets. Two arrows had hit each one, as Farus had promised him. At least eight of the shots could have been lethal.

"Of course, your targets didn't raise their shields to protect their faces," Lothar grumbled. "Let's see what your men can do against moving targets."

"Indeed, let's see," Lucius said. He raised his hand, and the trumpets sounded again. This time, four svelte and very frightened deer darted into the arena.

"Dinner," Silvanus said.

"Dinner," Lucius agreed as four of the riders turned their horses about.

They broke into a charge as the deer scattered, and shot one arrow each, and four deer went down. Then three of the riders returned to their ranks, while the fourth — Farus himself — rode toward Lucius and his retinue.

In mid-charge, he nocked an arrow, turned in the saddle, and put it through the throat of the closest deer, which was still twitching. It went still, and Farus pulled his horse up and dismounted.

Show-off, Lucius thought. "Impressive demonstration, Princeps Farus," he said.

"As promised, Your Majesty," Farus replied.

"So, this is how you plan to counter the desert men," said Gunnar. "How many of these horse archers do you have?"

"Princeps Farus is training seven thousand," Lucius said, "though they're not all as skilled as these men. Not yet."

"They'll ride to the frontline with us," Farus said. "I'll bring three infantry legions as well, and our regular cavalry, and even a few thousands of Emperor Lucius's Augustian Guards. Over forty thousand men in all. More troops from the provinces will join us later."

"General Patricius and General Justinian will be waiting for you," Lucius said. "I expect that they still have over eighty thousand men. With Princeps Farus's warriors and yours joining them, we'll form a powerful army. One more than capable of defeating the orcs and the desert men. Especially since we have your cannons."

"We can't drag *those* through the desert," Gunnar cautioned.

Lucius gave him a conspiratorial wink. "Perhaps we won't need to. I have a plan for dealing with the desert men after we smash the orcs. But we'll talk about that later. For now, let us move on to part two."

The trumpets called again, and a long column of soldiers entered the arena, all wearing armor. Two ox-drawn carts followed, and Lucius smiled. He knew what they carried.

At an unseen signal, the men broke ranks and darted to the carts. Moments later, a hundred sarissas rose toward the sky. A sharp intake of breath came from behind Lucius.

"By Njord," Lothar murmured. "Those things are *long*."

The men formed into ranks ten deep. Then, at once, they lowered their long spears and advanced. They stopped, and stabbed their weapons forward against an imaginary enemy, and advanced, and stopped, and stabbed, again and again, like a relentless machine of death.

Though he'd watched the men twice before as they trained, Lucius found himself smiling. With battle formations such as this one, supported by cavalry and by an impeccable logistics system, a young warrior king had conquered a large swathe of his world. His name was Alexander the Great, and according to Augustus, his battle tactics were still studied centuries later. Lucius had learned a lot from them himself.

He turned to the Islanders. "I wonder how well your shield wall would do against these men, Lothar Bjornsson. If you didn't have your cannons, that is."

"Not too well," Lothar replied, shaking his head.

"Neither will the orcs," Farus said.

Gunnar grinned. "I bet you've never seen such a big, bad hedgehog before, lad." He grunted. "*Prince Lothar*, I mean." Ahead, the formation continued its advance.

"They're two for each spear," observed Ivar, one of Frida's warriors. "I bet I could handle one by myself." He was a mountain of muscle, and Lucius did not doubt his words.

"Then go forth, Ivar, and show us," he said. "Take your best warriors with you. Our men have been told to welcome you."

At once, a dozen Islanders rushed forward. Only Lothar, Gunnar, the bodyguards Torsten and Arne, and the three sea witches remained at Frida's side.

"New toys for our big boys," Gunnar said as the Islanders joined the Julian ranks and started practicing the maneuver. "I wonder what other tricks you have up your sleeve, Your Majesty."

"I have a few. You'll see. And you'll show me what your cannons can do, yes?"

"Aye," Gunnar replied. "Tonight, if you wish."

"He does," Silvanus said before Lucius could answer. "If only to please a dear friend."

"Two dear friends," Farus said.

Lucius nodded. "Tonight it is. And tomorrow, we'll meet your army on the training grounds outside the city. Princeps Farus and Queen Frida will lead the training. We'll bring some of our wizards as well."

"We need to learn how to lead battles with this combined army," Frida said.

"You have Farus for that," Lucius said. "He and I have been fighting three battles per day with this army ever since our alliance was forged. He'll teach you what he knows. And maybe your men won't listen to him at first, but they'll listen to you."

"We'll have a great fighting force," Farus added. "The strongest in the world."

That is, Lucius thought, *if the orcs and the desert men don't thin our numbers too much, and if Queen Marion manages to whittle down Queen Elena's forces before they spill into our lands.*

After Anders's betrayal, the vampires had cannons as well. Each of their nobles would be a great threat, and though their serfs were no match for the Islanders one-on-one, they were many, and they were bigger and stronger than the Julian soldiers.

Even so, Lucius felt confident. He had the Augustian Wall, the sarissas, and his cavalry; he had bows and crossbows in untold numbers; he had the Islanders, the strongest human fighters in all the lands; he had their cannons and his ballistae; he had the sea witches and the Julian wizards. He had Farus, and Silvanus, and Frida, and Gunnar, and thousands of trained warriors who would fight and die for them. He had the knowledge he'd gained from countless books, and from speaking with his generals, and from fighting the miniature battles against Farus and Silvanus — and they had that knowledge as well. His army was growing every day, as new troops arrived from the northern provinces. And best of all, he had the support of the Julian gods, and the visions from another world that Augustus was still giving him.

We're the strongest in this war, he thought. *And so, we're going to win it.*

He sighed inwardly as he caught himself. *Yesterday I thought victory was far from certain. Today, I am more optimistic than I have the right to be. And nothing changed.*

I get excited too easily. And perhaps this is normal. I'm still a boy, after all.

Yet Augustus says I am wise beyond my years. And I've played my cards well so far. As long as I keep doing that, our chances are good.

He turned to Frida, who was watching the sarissa formation, now led by her own men. "Would you like to try one of those pointy sticks, Queen Frida?"

She smiled. "I thought you'd never ask."

"I'll go with her," Farus said. "If Your Majesty allows it."

Lucius nodded and watched them go. *They'll become friends*, he thought. *And together, they'll lead our armies well.*

The World's Making

Squinting his eyes against the roaring flames, Hagor the Sniffer took a deep breath. His lungs filled with smoke, but that only lifted his spirits higher.

He raised his jug of ale to his mouth and took another gulp. "A good feast with a fiery lass. And tomorrow we take the city." The Julian province capital lay less than half a mile from his campfire. "A juicy prize, ripe for the taking."

At his side, Tarkanna grunted. "That she is. But I don't think she'll give up her riches easily."

"She won't," Hagor agreed. "Those ballistae will pick off many of our warriors as we charge. Then we'll have to cross the ditch, and climb the wall, and smash the Julian spearmen, and their crossbowmen, and their wizards, and Grok-knows-what-else they throw at us."

"Even so, we'll win, yes?"

"We will." With the Great Horde still numbering over forty-five thousand warriors, the outcome was certain. "It will be a great victory. We'll sing about it for centuries."

"Some of the songs will be yours, yes?"

He nodded and took another bite of the eagle's chest. "Yes. Did I tell you how much I'm enjoying this bird?"

"Only three times so far." She'd shot down the eagle earlier in the day, with a single well-placed arrow. "I used Grandmother Kaia's recipe.

My favorite, when I have all the herbs I need."

"You'll have to teach it to me one day." He'd tasted wild garlic, black pepper, thyme, rosemary, and something he didn't recognize.

She snorted. "As if you'd ever *cook*, shaman."

"You'd be surprised. Besides, I'd enjoy watching you."

She smiled, but did not answer.

She's warming up to me, Hagor thought. It was the third meal they were sharing in as many days, alone at their own campfire. This time, she'd invited him. And though he hadn't touched her yet, that would come, and soon.

She looked past the fire, toward the enemy walls. "You think they'll try to flee in the middle of the night?"

"They won't. They're not that stupid." King Ghark had spread his forces to surround the city, and many of his warriors had lit five fires each, to make their numbers seem bigger than they were. Only the south-eastern side was shrouded in darkness, but there was no escape that way. Just beyond the edge of the forest, the Great War Chief Syrkka lay in wait with her six thousand braves, and Hagor knew they'd set traps as well. If the Julians fled that way, it would be a massacre.

Tarkanna picked out a morsel from between her teeth. "Uncle Zordo says they might try."

"Your uncle thirsts for blood. But just wishing for them to move won't make it so."

She leaned against him, her presence warm, and rested her head on his right shoulder. He braced his left arm against the ground to support her weight. The scent of her hair was intoxicating.

"Tell me a story, Hagor," she whispered.

He wrapped his right arm around her waist, then slid his hand higher, caressing her torso.

She pushed his hand away. "No. Not yet. Tell me a story, I said. Tell me about the world's making."

"You're teasing me."

"I like to take things slow." She took another bite of eagle meat and threw the bone over her shoulder. "The story, then."

"You know it." Her clan was renowned for its bards, and she was a great chief's niece and a fire witch's daughter. "You must have heard it a dozen times already."

"More than a dozen. But not from you, Hagor." She laughed and pushed herself against him. "Take what I'm giving you."

"Fine," he grunted. He wasn't used to taking it slow. With his renown, his deep voice, and his good looks, he could have most of the females he desired, and *had*, though none had held his interest for long. But this one lass was different.

If anyone's worth the wait, it's her, he thought.

He took a deep breath, tilted his head back, and blew the smoke out through his nostrils, up toward the sky.

"The world's making," he began. "No one knows how our world was created, not even the All-Father. What we do know, is that our world is but one of many, all basking in the Supreme One's infinite wisdom."

The Supreme One himself — for it was known it was a *he* — was a mystery. No one but the gods themselves had felt his presence, yet his power was magnificent. He could summon entire worlds into existence, and he *had*, many times. Perhaps he could destroy them as well, if he wished.

Why he wouldn't stop the Vengeful One himself, Hagor did not know. The Supreme One had left that task to the gods, and now the whole world was at war because of it.

"Two thousand years ago," he continued, "the first of our ancestors appeared. A small clan, only two hundred strong, led by Grok the All-Father himself."

"That's not how it started," Tarkanna said.

Hagor grunted. "I'll get to the giants later. Who's telling the story, you or me?"

"You are."

He pulled her closer, and she did not object.

"Two hundred young braves, all in their prime," he continued. "They awoke into being at the break of day, high up on the World's Peak, with no memories of anything before their time. They were fierce and proud, they had their language and their bond with each other, and they knew greatness awaited them. And what they didn't know, Grok taught them."

He laughed. "Five of the first orcs challenged the All-Father during the first week. He beat them easily, yet he did not kill them, nor did he shame them in front of the others. 'You are strong, my children,' he told them. 'Let us take this world, for we are its masters, if only for a while.'

"He did not tell them what he meant. They'd find out, in time.

"At first, the food was plentiful, and the hunts were easy. The wild beasts hadn't learned to fear our kind yet. But learn they did, and fast, and then Grok took the clan north.

"Down from the mountain they came, until they emerged from the forest, onto a vast plain. And there, a herd of great lizards grazed. The long-necked ones, as tall as forty feet from the ground to the tops of their heads.

"Grok's followers gasped in awe at the creatures, and made their plans, and retreated into the forest. For three nights and three days, they prepared. They sharpened their spears, and readied their torches, and then they left the forest again, and went on the greatest hunt of their lives. Until then, at least.

"On that night, a great fire burned on the plain, and our ancestors tasted great lizard meat for the first time, and it was good. A dozen braves died in the hunt, and a dozen new ones were made that night, to emerge from their mother's wombs a year later."

He breathed in Tarkanna's scent. "Once this war is done, we can make one of our own."

Tarkanna slapped his arm. "You know you just said that out loud."

Hagor smirked. "It was the All-Father himself speaking through me," he said in his deepest voice.

"Tell the All-Father I'll think about it," she said, and Hagor's heart beat faster. "But for now, the story."

"When the feast was over, Grok the All-Father raised his hands, and pulled the ores of the earth with his might, and fashioned a great cauldron. He placed it on top of the burning fire and asked for the bravest of the braves to climb inside."

"And only three of the lasses raised their hands."

"Aye. They did, and climbed into the cauldron; but the fire did not hurt them, and neither did the heat. And when they came out, a new force was coursing through their veins."

"Magic."

"Magic, aye. And so, the three became the first of the fire witches. Fyrra could shoot fireballs the farthest, Korta was the greatest healer, and Magra used her power to sculpt metal into weapons and armor. In time, they taught each other. Many of their daughters followed in their footsteps."

"Until me," Tarkanna said. Unlike her mother, she had no magic.

"You don't know that," Hagor said. "The gift may come back, if you have daughters." The ability to use magic did die off in some bloodlines; but in others, it merely skipped a generation or two.

She sighed, but did not reply.

"On that night," he continued, "after giving his followers the gift, Grok left them, though he promised to return. And return he did, once in a while; and every time, the braves held a feast in his honor and told him of their adventures.

"So now Grok's followers had weapons, and they had magic. They had the mountain, and the great plains, and the clean, fresh water of the rivers. They hunted the great lizards, and the smaller, meat-eating ones, which were still bigger than the orcs themselves, and the fierce many-toothed birds that darted at them from the sky at night. But they were still alone.

"And so they were for a while, until all the first orcs were gone from this world.

"When that was done, the All-Father told their grandchildren to scatter into the four winds. They obeyed him, and it did not take long for them to run into other clans, many in number, and all of them telling the same story.

"They'd all been brought into being at the top of the mountain, or at least their grandparents had been. The All-Father had been there at their beginning. He feasted with them in their early days, and taught them things, and hunted the great lizards with them, and left them after a while. But he'd only given the gift of magic to the first of the clans.

"The clans had all started the same way, but as decades passed, they'd grown different. Some were great hunters; others kept herds of goats and sheep; and yet others plowed the fields, planted their grains, and baked that bread that King Ghark despises. Over time, they traded food and weapons, stories and wisdom, and husbands and wives as well. The trades spread across the clans, as did the working of metal and the gift of magic.

"Some of the clans fought each other, and Grok let them. He knew the wars would make them stronger; and stronger they had to become, for great perils awaited them. Other clans merged, but none became too big; the age of kings was far into the future. A few of the clans moved farther and farther from the World's Peak, to less crowded lands, where the hunting was better. The world was smaller back then, and over the centuries, the great race of orcs spread far and wide across the land, and hunted the great lizards to their last.

"Then, five hundred years after Grok's first coming, the ground trembled and shook, and the giants emerged from their slumber caves. They'd been asleep for a thousand years, as had their god; and as they awoke, they found that the world had changed. The great lizards were gone, and the clans of orcs ruled over the land. And that... Well, that made the giants angry.

"They were fewer in number than the orcs. But they were bigger than our kind, and stronger, and smarter than the great lizards. For a century, the two great races warred, and countless died on both sides. Until Grok and Malleon, the god of the giants, met high up on the World's Peak and decided to share our lands. We took the south, and the giants took the north. And then there was peace."

"But not for long," Tarkanna intervened.

Hagor nodded. "Peace never lasts long for our kind. Sometimes I wish it did."

She pushed against him. "The story, Hagor."

"Our clans grew and prospered," he continued. "They gave our lands their names. Grok's Lair, Shattered Fang, the Hills of Spite, the Howling Rocks, and Mother's Cauldron were all named during those years, as were the rivers and the valleys that hadn't been named yet. And centuries later, with the giants' permission, Ghraz the Explorer was the first of the orcs to set foot on every cliff and every beach that bordered the great ocean. Or at least that's how his story goes.

"He traveled all around the world, or what the world was at the time. Everywhere he went, he told the story of his travels, and he told it well. And so, even the grumpiest of the giants came to love him. He liked the far northern lands the most, and the giants allowed him and his clan to settle there for the rest of his life, though it was on their side of the world.

"And then, one thousand years after Grok's first coming, the ground trembled and shook again. And Ghraz the Explorer saw the great ocean retreat from the beach he stood on, as tall blades of grass sprang from the seabed.

"A strange creature stood in front of him. She was smaller, and thin, and green from head to toe, and she called him a brute, and so, Ghraz charged her."

"And the Lady put her arrow through his heart."

"Aye. His clansmates took his body and burned it with the honors he deserved, and then they journeyed south, over the mountains and back to their homeland. Only to be told of the change that had happened everywhere.

"The great ocean had retreated on all sides, for hundreds of miles. Strange four-legged beasts roamed the new desert to the south, and two-legged creatures rode them. Winged creatures scoured the western skies, and the little men we now call the Julians emerged from the east. The world had grown bigger. The ocean had pulled back, its shores far away from our lands, perhaps forever out of reach, and the great races of orcs and giants were no longer alone. The men and the vampires had arrived."

Tarkanna ran her fingers through her hair, her elbow gently brushing Hagor's chest. "And so, we fought them."

"We did, as is our nature. They were not united, but neither was our kind. We lost some battles, and won more, and got to know the rest of the new gods. Even Njord, the Islander God, when he chose to travel inland. Then the giants invaded from the north, and our clans had to fight them as well."

"And so, we fought war after war," Tarkanna said. She yawned. "And now we're fighting the greatest of them all."

"Aye. It is said that the Vengeful One will arrive two thousand years after Grok's first coming." Which was a thousand years after the arrival of the other gods, not counting Malleon, the oldest of them all. "And only the last of the gods, taking the strength of all the others, can stop the Vengeful One."

"What is this Vengeful One?"

"I don't know. The All-Father wouldn't say. But whatever it is, Grok is certain he can beat it. First, of course, we have to win this war."

Tarkanna yawned again. "We will. Thank you for the story, Hagor. Now tell me about your clan."

Hagor puffed out his chest. "My clan is strong and proud. We've birthed great warriors over the centuries, and great bards as well, and some who were both. Let me tell you the saga of Yurko the Stout, who slew three vampire nobles and five of the desert men's assassins, and that in a single year."

He held her closer, and spoke softly as her breaths became deeper, and it didn't take long until she was snoring gently, her head pressed against his shoulder.

He sat with her for a while, careful not to disturb her sleep. Then he picked her up, carried her to her tent, and covered her with a thick blanket. He left the tent and stretched himself on the bare ground, a few paces from the entrance.

He wouldn't spend the night inside; she hadn't invited him. But there would be more nights like this one. And though Hagor was not a patient orc, he'd wait for Tarkanna.

Her bloodline was strong, as was his own, and her scent was the sweetest he'd ever sniffed. She'd give him sons, and daughters, too; fire witches, blessed with the All-Father's magic.

I'll sing them the songs of how we won this war, was his last thought before sleep took him.

The Gathering Storm

The eastern wind carried the scent of rain and the promise of blood.

General Patricius stood atop Praetorium's western wall, his hands resting on the weathered stone parapet, his gaze focused on the plain ahead.

The orcs' Great Horde stretched out like a living sea, red-skinned warriors clustering in endless ranks, their banners fluttering in the wind. Thousands of fires still burned in their camp, sending their smoke into the gray morning sky. Even at this distance, the orcs' howls and roars reached the walls — a rumble of menace that seeped into the bones.

"By the gods," muttered General Justinian from his place at Patricius's right. The younger general's fists clenched tightly at his sides. "There must be twenty thousand warriors on this side alone. More, perhaps."

Patricius didn't answer. He'd fought the orcs many times before, and he held a grudging respect for their prowess in battle. Orc warriors were over a head taller than the average Julian soldier. They were much stronger than his men, and they fought well. But this time, the Horde was starving. Desperate. And desperate warriors made mistakes.

"They won't break us," Justinian said, but Patricius did not miss the edge of doubt in his voice.

"They'll try," he replied, his tone calm as always. "And we'll hold."

The city's defenders were as ready as they could be. Ballistae and the catapults lined the walls, with spare bolts and stones stacked high behind them. Barrels of oil waited nearby, ready to be set aflame. Every able-bodied soldier had been assigned to a post, while the engineers reinforced the gates with iron braces. Archers filled the watchtowers, their bows strung and arrows at the ready.

Discipline, preparation, order. Patricius valued these things above all else. Today, King Ghark's orcs would put them to the test.

Justinian paced like a restless wolf. "We should have hit them with our cavalry and thinned their numbers further, before —"

"No," Patricius said sharply. "My strategy was correct. The walls are our strength. Let Ghark and his horde crash against them. We'll thin their numbers here."

Justinian huffed and looked back toward the plain. "He's a crafty one, this Ghark Bloodaxe."

And today he'll meet his match, Patricius thought, though he would not say it out loud. Such a remark straddled the line between confidence and vanity. And vanity was not something he'd show among the empire's foremost officers.

Instead, he nodded. "He is. But we're ready for him, and we outnumber his forces two to one. We'll beat him, Justinian. Now go and defend the southern wall. The gods are watching us."

"As you command, General," Justinian said.

Patricius nodded, though the younger officer had already turned away.

He still has much to learn, he thought. Less than a year after his promotion to general, Justinian still regarded Patricius as his superior — a notion Patricius had done nothing to correct. Stopping a few of the desert men's border raids over the past decade wasn't enough to earn his respect. But the War of the Seven would surely provide the younger general plenty of opportunities to prove his worth.

As long as he survives this day, Patricius mused.

He was still watching Justinian's departing form when a soldier spoke to him. "General. Look!"

Patricius turned his gaze toward the plain. A fireball shot out into the sky, then another, and the orcs began to advance. They formed into columns, their war drums pounding.

He watched them come, a tide of steel and muscle that swept toward the city. The ground trembled under their feet. His fingers gripped the stone of the parapet, steady and firm.

"Archers ready!" he shouted.

Flags waved. Trumpets passed on his command. Thousands of archers raised their bows, the arrowheads glinting in the weak sunlight.

"Catapults ready?"

"Ready!" an officer shouted back.

Patricius raised his voice, letting it carry to every soldier who could hear. "The orcs have come to destroy us. But today, the red tide will shatter against our walls. Today, we shall send them to their deaths. For the empire!"

"For the empire!" thousands of voices answered.

Patricius turned and strode toward the nearest watchtower, his six guards and two signal men following close behind. From there, he would oversee the battle, directing the defenders with precision.

Our men will hold, he told himself. But deep in his heart, a glimmer of doubt remained.

To the Death

Ghark Bloodaxe climbed atop a boulder at the edge of the encampment, with Krakkar the Fist at his side. The Julian city loomed ahead, its walls black against the gray sky. Above them, thousands of Julian soldiers waited, with their bows and shields and spears and war machines.

We'll scale the walls and crush them, Ghark thought. *And then, finally, we'll have a proper feast.*

Krakkar growled. "Our warriors are ready, Ghark. They just need your word."

"Good." Ghark turned to face the Horde. Thousands of orcs waited with weapons in hand, their breaths steaming in the cold morning air.

Ghark's gaze swept over his warriors — tired, hungry, but still fierce. Many of them would die on this day, fighting for Grok the All-Father, but their sacrifice would not be in vain. The orcs *needed* this victory, and they needed to replenish their supplies. And taking the city would deal a crushing blow to the Julian Empire.

He stepped to the edge of the boulder, raising his axe high. The warriors around him fell silent, their eyes fixed on him. The hush rippled outward like a wave until the entire Horde stood still. Silent. Waiting.

"My brave warriors!" Ghark shouted. His voice carried across the plain, loud, deep, and clear. "We stand before the walls of Praetorium, the richest city of this wretched province. Behind those walls, they have food.

They have ale and wine. They have gold and silver, steel and horses, and plenty of warriors for us to kill!"

The orcs roared in answer. Some pounded their weapons against their shields.

"They think they've broken us!" Ghark thundered, his voice rising. "But we shall never be broken! We are the Horde! We are strong, fierce, and proud! We are the fire that will burn their empire to ash!"

More roars. A drum began to pound, slow and steady, matching the cadence of Ghark's words.

"Today, we'll take this city! Then, the empire! And after that, the world! They're all ours for the taking!"

"Take them! Take them! Take them!" the warriors shouted.

Krakkar nodded, a fierce grin on his face.

Ghark raised his axe higher. "I see you, my braves! I see you standing here before me, and though you haven't eaten well in weeks, you do not falter. You do not turn back. You fight! Because that's what warriors do! And if we must die today, we shall die fighting, with blood on our blades and fire in our hearts!"

The Horde erupted in howls, their voices echoing across the plain.

"To the death!" Ghark bellowed.

"To the death! To the death! To the death!" the warriors roared back.

"The death of our enemies!" Ghark shouted.

"Kill them!" Krakkar added.

"Kill them! Kill them! Kill them!" the warriors chanted.

Ghark turned to Krakkar and nodded.

Krakkar raised his swords in the air. "We'll smash 'em and bash 'em and slice 'em to bits! For the All-Father! For King Ghark Bloodaxe! For the Horde, and for our people!"

The Horde answered with a deafening roar.

When the warriors were silent again, Ghark raised his axe one last time and pointed it at the walls of Praetorium. "Go! Take this city! Bring me their heads!"

The Horde surged forward, and Ghark watched them go.

Krakkar's Charge

Krakkar sprinted across the Julian plain, his boots trampling the tall grass. Thousands of braves ran with him, their battle cries cutting through the air. Praetorium's walls loomed ahead, bristling with soldiers and war machines.

Krakkar grinned. *The Julians think their walls will save them. They think their stone and iron will hold back the red tide.*

Today, we'll show them how wrong they are.

"Faster!" he bellowed, his voice carrying above the roar of the charge.

Atop the wall, a ballista fired, then three more. Massive iron bolts tore through red-skinned warriors. The charge did not slow.

The Julian archers released their arrows, darkening the sky. Krakkar growled as the arrows thudded into shields, armor, and flesh. To his left, an orc collapsed, an arrow buried in his throat. Krakkar sprinted forward, his axe banging against his armor with every stride.

The catapults struck next. lusters of stones, each missile bigger than a man's fist, flew through the air. One crashed into an orc's head, and the warrior fell, as if Grok the All-Father himself had struck him with his mighty fist. Krakkar kept running.

He reached the ditch at full stride, leaped over two spikes, and halted. A tall, wide-eyed warrior dashed to his side and raised a large wooden shield above their heads, protecting them both.

Krakkar turned back toward the warriors surging behind him.

"Ladders! Shields! Move!" he roared.

The first ranks scrambled to set the ladders, carrying them forward through the hail of missiles. Some of the warriors fell, struck by arrows or pierced by falling stones. Others arrived at the walls and raised their ladders, the hooks finding purchase against the battlements.

Krakkar nudged the shieldbearer, and together they headed to the nearest ladder, while arrows rained from above. He grabbed the side rails and began to climb, three warriors ahead of him, all three leading with their shields. Arrows slammed into the wood, but the warriors pressed on.

With a scream, the leading orc fell off the ladder. Whether by chance or accident, he fell to the side and did not drag the other warriors down with him. Krakkar growled and kept climbing. *I'll avenge you, my battle brother*, he vowed to himself.

He scaled the last few rungs and leaped onto the wall. The two braves that had climbed ahead of him stood side by side, their shields raised, their weapons thrusting.

Dozens of enemy soldiers swarmed them, the tips of their spears peeking above their shields. Farther away, others raised their bows, taking aim. They let their arrows fly, and one of the orcs howled as an arrow sliced through his arm, but he did not falter.

Twenty paces to his left, Krakkar spotted another orc reaching the top of his own ladder. Three Julian soldiers met him with their spears, and one of their thrusts went past his guard. The orc fell from the wall, and other warriors rushed up the ladder to take his place.

A Julian soldier lunged at Krakkar, his spear darting forward. Krakkar sidestepped the attack, kicked at the man's shield, and sent him stumbling into the men behind him. The soldier regained his footing and raised his spear, preparing for another strike.

We must gain a proper foothold, Krakkar thought. Soon, more braves would join him atop the wall and push the Julians back. After that, the killing would begin in earnest, and the Julian walls would run slick with blood.

Then again, this would not be an easy fight. The Horde was tired and hungry, and this time they weren't attacking a small Julian fort along the empire's border. The walled city was well-defended, and judging by the number of soldiers on this section of the wall, Krakkar expected the Julians to vastly outnumber Ghark's force. Two to one, if not more.

He shrugged. *Only one thing to be done about it.*

He roared, unhooked his axe and his mace from his belt, and began to kill.

The General

From the watchtower's heights, Patricius saw everything — the city, the walls, the Horde.

The orcs had reached the battlements, their ladders slamming into stone, hooks digging into mortar. They climbed fast, howling their fury. On the walls, his soldiers fought fiercely, spears thrusting, shields locked tight.

Patricius didn't allow his focus to linger upon individual clashes. If he looked too long, he'd see a man stumble, hear a scream, catch the arc of blood flung into the air. No. He focused on the whole. The lines, the movement, the flow of the battle.

"Signal the western wall," he said, his voice calm despite the din of war below. "Reinforcements to Sector Three."

The signaler beside him raised a green flag, waving it in sharp, practiced arcs. Moments later, a trumpet echoed from the courtyard. Soldiers hurried to obey Patricius's command, rushing toward the troubled section of the wall.

"The catapults?" Patricius asked.

"The engines to the left are still firing, General," an engineer replied.

"The ballistae too."

Patricius nodded and returned his attention to the battle.

The catapults hurled clusters of stones over the walls, crushing warriors and slowing the Horde's progress. Still, more enemies came, placing their ladders against the walls and scaling them. In the end, the battle would be won or lost on Praetorium's walls.

The ballistae fired again, their cords propelling their missiles forward with great speed. Patricius watched an iron bolt smash into a ladder, splintering it before it reached the wall. Another bolt speared through a cluster of warriors.

But too many ladders had already arrived. Too many orcs were on the walls. And more were coming with each passing moment.

Patricius turned to the signaler. "Burn them. Now."

The man nodded and raised a yellow flag, waving it in two wide arcs. Across the walls, men tipped barrels of boiling oil over the battlements. The scalding liquid splashed down onto the ladders. Flaming arrows followed, setting orcs ablaze. Their screams cut through the clash of weapons.

"Steady," Patricius murmured to himself. "Steady now. Hold your lines."

From his vantage point, he spotted another group of orcs that had gained a foothold on the western wall. Their leader—a massive warrior wielding a mace and an axe—smashed and bashed his way forward like a whirlwind of death.

Patricius's jaw tightened. *That one will be trouble.*

"Send another unit to Sector Three," he commanded.

The signaler raised the green flag again, and the trumpets answered with a chorus of sharp, urgent notes. Patricius watched as another column of soldiers rushed to the wall's defense.

His men would hold. They had to hold.

"General!" shouted a voice nearby. "The ram is near the gates!"

Through the smoke and chaos, Patricius spotted a massive battering ram, brought forth by a score of orcs. Arrows and stones rained down on them, but the orcs pushed forward, shields raised above their heads.

"Archers, stop that ram!" he shouted, though he doubted his men would succeed. The orcs could endure what his warriors could not. And when an orc fell, another would take his place.

The gates wouldn't hold forever.

Another horn sounded, deep and guttural. Patricius turned his attention back to the walls. Near his tower, a ladder had been pushed off, toppling orcs to their deaths. But less than twenty paces away, the orcs had gained another foothold on the wall, their weapons flashing as they pushed the defenders back.

"Reinforcements there," Patricius ordered, pointing to the troubled section.

The signaler raised a flag, and the orders were sent.

Patricius ground his teeth and clenched his fists at his sides. "Steady. Steady now."

Fighting on the Walls

Krakkar swung hard with his mace, crumpling the helmet of the nearest Julian soldier.

The soldier fell. The men at his sides raised their shields, and Krakkar growled as his next blow failed to punch through. A sword sliced the air, aiming for his face. Krakkar twisted away, denying the Julian soldier his prize.

We're beating them, he thought. Two dozen braves were already at his side, and more were coming, ready to take the city in the name of Grok the All-Father.

The orc at his side shoved against the massed defenders with his heavy shield, creating a small gap in their formation. A bald, heavyset warrior hurled his axe into the gap, and a Julian soldier screamed. But a blast of blinding light erupted from the left, and the bald warrior raised his arm to cover his eyes, and a well-aimed spear thrust opened a gash in his throat. He fell, and Krakkar knew he wouldn't rise again.

Those bloody wizards, he thought. *They'll distract us with their tricks, but that won't save them. We'll have them screaming before the day is done.*

He fought on, killing foe after foe. More warriors joined him, and slowly they pushed the defenders back. An orc fell to his knees, and a Julian soldier stabbed him in the face.

Krakkar snarled. *They're better than I thought.*

He hung his axe onto his belt and pulled Right Fang out of its sheath.

His foes fought well together, swords and spears thrusting from behind their shields. Orcs roared and struck at them with swords, axes, and maces, but too few of their blows went through. Bodies lay everywhere, orcs and men alike, some still twitching. Blood flowed onto the stones, making every step treacherous.

A soldier lunged, his spear aimed at Krakkar's throat. Krakkar knocked the spear aside with his mace, twisted to the side, and drove Right Fang past the man's shield and into his gut. The soldier crumpled to the ground. He screamed, dropping his spear and clutching at his spilling insides.

Another man came at Krakkar, sword in hand, shield raised high. Krakkar swung low, his mace crashing into the man's knee with a satisfying crunch. The man toppled forward, and Krakkar ended him with a slash across the back of the neck.

To Krakkar's right, an orc howled in pain. Krakkar took a quick glance and saw him impaled by a long iron bolt. Another glance showed Krakkar the ballista atop the tower, its crew straining as they loaded another missile. A wave of arrows struck down two more braves.

Krakkar snarled. *Too many are falling.*

"Push forward!" he shouted. "To the tower!"

His warriors roared in reply, and together they smashed into the Julian defenders. An orc with a great hammer shattered a soldier's shield, sending the man stumbling backward. Another orc seized a screaming Julian and hurled him off the wall.

But still, the defenders held. They fought with discipline, their shields overlapping, their swords and spears stabbing through the gaps. Even now, they weren't breaking.

The ballista fired again, the massive bolt tearing through two orcs at once. The archers kept on firing as well. Brave red-skinned warriors fell, shouting their pain and rage as they died.

For the first time since the attack began, a shadow of worry crept into Krakkar's mind. *Are we going to lose?*

He shook his head. *No. We'll smash 'em and bash 'em and slice 'em to bits. For the All-Father.*

"Kill! Kill! Kill!" he bellowed.

His battle brothers answered with a deafening roar, and together they cut and smashed their way through their foes with newfound strength.

We'll Hold Them Back

The clash raged on. The smoke from burning oil mixed with the stench of sweat and blood. Archers on the southern wall ran out of arrows, and the runners resupplied them. The ballistae reloaded slower now, their crews exhausted. Some were overrun, and the orcs shattered them into pieces or hurled them off the wall.

But the Julian defenders held.

Battered and bloodied, their shields dented and their armor streaked with gore, the soldiers stood resolute. Their lines, though frayed in places, did not shatter. Thousands of orcs lay dead, and all along the wall, save for a few pockets, the assault was faltering.

Patricius took a deep breath, long and steady. He turned to the signaler. "Send a message to all units: we are winning."

The man nodded and raised a flag. Several trumpets passed the message further. Across the battlements, the soldiers roared in response, their voices rising above the din.

"We'll hold them back!" Patricius shouted. "For the empire!"

"For the empire!" his soldiers took up his call, strong and defiant.

For the first time that day, Patricius allowed himself a smile.

The red tide had crashed against his walls. And the walls, and the men above them, were about to turn it back.

We Can't Break Them

This can't be happening, Krakkar thought.

He fought on, mace and axe in hand, his arms growing heavy with the effort. He'd lost Left Fang in the fighting, the blade stuck in the chest of a dying foe. His eyes were clouded with weariness and rage, and his hands were slick with Julian blood.

Around him, brave orcs fought and died. The warrior to his left struck at his foes with the rim of his shield, his sword arm hanging uselessly at his side. Another warrior limped forward and swung his axe, severing a Julian soldier's head. A lucky spear thrust through his armpit brought the orc down, and Krakkar groaned as the warrior took his final breath.

He roared and fought on, striking and parrying, doing his best to protect the warriors at his sides. A few spear thrusts went past his guard, but Krakkar's armor turned them aside. The defenders took many of his blows on their shields, and when one man fell, another took his place.

They're too many, Krakkar thought. *We can't break them.*

He deflected a spear that was meant to skewer the orc to his left. He kicked at the Julian soldier's shield, unbalancing him. From behind Krakkar, a small throwing axe flew past him and struck the soldier in the face.

The man fell. But it wasn't enough.

A trumpet sounded, then another. More foes rushed onto the walls.

I'm not dying here, swarmed by these bloody Julians! Krakkar thought. "Hold them back!" he shouted. "Defend yourselves! For the All-Father!"

The orcs roared and rallied around him, but Krakkar knew the battle was lost.

He struck again and again, his mace crushing a soldier's arm, his axe cleaving into another's thigh. Blood sprayed, men died, but the Julian line did not falter.

At least the ladders are still standing, Krakkar thought. Many warriors could escape and live to fight another day, though some of their battle brothers would give their lives covering their retreat. But even now, Krakkar would not flee from battle.

We go back when Ghark calls us back. Not before.

Tarkanna

"This isn't how it was supposed to go, Mother," Tarkanna said.

They stood at the edge of the forest, three hundred paces from the Julian wall, with the rest of Uncle Zordo's reserves. Ahead, the battle had turned into a nightmare.

The defenders were as many as the stars in the night sky. They had ballistae, and catapults, and too many bows and crossbows that rained death upon Uncle Zordo's braves as they stormed the walls. Those who made the climb were met by a forest of spears, and though they fought hard, they hadn't broken the defenders yet. Many had already been pushed off the wall, shouting their defiance as they fell.

Already, wounded warriors were returning to the cover of the forest, where the shamans and the fire witches tended to them as well as they could. Other warriors lay on the ground beneath the walls, and Tarkanna knew few of them would rise again.

"There's still hope," her mother said. At thirty-nine, Olkha was a powerful fire witch and one of the well-respected warriors of the clan, yet Zordo had left her with the reserves. "Maybe the defense is weaker elsewhere. Or maybe King Ghark has some cunning tricks left to play."

A young orc warrior rushed toward them, coming from the walls. Tarkanna did not recognize him. His right arm ended in a hastily bandaged stump.

"Great Chief Zordo," he said between breaths. "He's in trouble. Over there." He pointed to a section of the wall, where three of the orcs' great ladders still stood. Two more had been shoved off the walls by the defenders.

"What trouble?" Tarkanna asked.

"He's on a fighting platform," the warrior said, "with two dozen braves. Fewer by now, I reckon. They're surrounded. I tried to get to him, but —" he raised his stump to the level of Tarkanna's eyes.

"We must save him," Olkha said, fierce determination in her voice. "You, go to the shamans and have that arm taken care of. Tarkanna, you stay here."

Tarkanna did not protest. There was no time for argument, not when Uncle Zordo's life was at risk. "Go, Mother."

"With me, warriors!" Olkha shouted. "For the All-Father!"

She dashed toward the wall. Hundreds of braves followed her, howling their battle cries.

Tarkanna grabbed her spear and ran with them, turning slightly to her left and dropping a few ranks behind, so her mother wouldn't see her.

Arrows whistled through the air. A rock flew in an arc and landed on a warrior who ran at Tarkanna's side, crushing him. She ran onward, leaped over two fallen warriors, and in moments, she was at the bottom of a ladder. Three other warriors had already started their climb, the one at the top holding a large, round shield above his head.

She climbed, holding onto the rungs with her left hand, her spear angled to the right so she wouldn't skewer the orc ahead of her. Above them, the air rang with the clang of weapons and the screams of wounded orcs and men.

A yell, and the warrior above her lost his footing. He fell, and Tarkanna barely had the time to shift out of the way. She hurriedly climbed the last few steps, her head peeking above the edge of the wall, where orcs and Julian soldiers were locked in deadly battle. She took another step — and something slammed into the side of her neck.

She lost her hold on the ladder and fell, crashing onto her back, the impact drawing the air out of her lungs. Her back hurt, and she hoped it wasn't broken.

She raised a hand to her neck and found that something was sticking there. A shaft, slick with blood.

"Don't touch it!" an orc warrior yelled.

She jerked her hand away, drew in a breath, and coughed blood.

"Take her to safety!" the warrior shouted.

Another warrior lifted her onto his back and ran toward the forest, where the healers awaited. A great horn sounded, then another.

We're retreating, Tarkanna thought. *King Ghark gave the order.*

Uncle Zordo. Mother. Are you still with us?

The warrior carrying her ran on, jolting her with every step. She felt tired, so tired.

Don't close your eyes, she remembered her mother saying. *If you're badly wounded, whatever you do, don't close your eyes. Not until the healers tell you to.*

Her eyelids were heavy, yet she forced them to stay open. Blood poured out of her neck wound, her own life essence leaving her.

No. I can't think like that. The healers will save me.

She was being laid down, as in a dream. Three orc females knelt at her side, their faces blurry. One of them shook her head. Another raised her hands to cover her face.

An icy chill washed over her. She tried to move her right hand, but it did not obey her.

"Hagor," she tried to whisper, but nothing came out. Then another orc was here, holding her hand, and she knew it was him.

She sighed and closed her eyes.

Heroes of the Empire

Patricius leaned against the battlements and watched the cavalry scouts riding back toward the city. Below him, the ditch stretched out like a vast graveyard of broken bodies, discarded weapons, and fallen ladders.

We'll clean it up tomorrow, he thought. For now, his soldiers enjoyed a well-deserved rest, though many of them remained alert, their weapons at the ready. They'd collected their own dead, dispatched the wounded orcs, and thrown the dead orcs from the battlements into the ditch. Everything else could wait.

Patricius tilted his head and watched the setting sun, until a young attendant rushed to his side. "General. The scouts have given their reports."

"And?"

"The Horde is pulling back."

"Good. Send six cavalry squads to shadow them from a distance."

"As you command, General." The attendant hesitated. "Do you think the orcs will try again?"

Patricius shook his head. "They know they're beaten. Perhaps they'll come back, but not anytime soon." He kept his voice steady, his satisfaction carefully masked. "Now go and relay my orders."

The attendant bowed and retreated, stepping aside as General Justinian approached. The younger officer's polished armor gleamed even in the dim light, and his face was flushed with victory.

Patricius waited for Justinian to reach him. "Do you have the numbers?" he asked.

"Six thousand dead."

Patricius raised an eyebrow.

"Six thousand and ninety-five, General," Justinian corrected quickly. "Many more wounded. Eighteen thousand, at least." He smiled, a triumphant gleam in his eyes. "But we held, didn't we? Just as you said we would."

Many good men died today, Patricius thought. They'd died well, fighting for the empire, but that wouldn't ease the pain of those they'd left behind: mothers and fathers, loving wives, sons and daughters, and comrades in arms. A bleak tide of grief would sweep over the empire, and it wouldn't be the last one, for many more soldiers would have to die before the war was over.

"They'll be back," Patricius said, his voice low.

"And we'll beat them again," Justinian replied, his tone brimming with confidence. "As many times as we have to."

"They'll be better prepared next time."

"And yet it won't matter." Justinian smiled again. "We should celebrate, General. We're heroes of the empire!"

"*You* should lead the celebration, Justinian. The men love you, and I heard you've done well on the southern wall. I'll stay here a little longer."

The younger officer strode away with a spring in his step, and Patricius watched him go. *Let him celebrate*, he thought. The men needed to see his joy, his enthusiasm. It would raise their spirits.

He gazed into the distance, alone with his own thoughts. When the sun finally set, he summoned his guards and headed to the quarters where the gravely wounded were being treated.

The buildings were quiet, save for the muffled groans of injured men and the low voices of the healers. The air was heavy with the smells of poultices, blood, and death.

Despite the healers' efforts, some of the men would die in the hours to come. Others would lose limbs or be rendered unfit for combat, and

Patricius would send them back to their homes. But he needed the rest to recover quickly, for the War of the Seven was far from over.

He moved among the wounded, pausing at each bedside to offer a word of comfort or a brief touch of his hand. These men had borne the brunt of the Horde's fury, and Patricius would not forget their sacrifice.

The Long Way Home

It was a sad and defeated Horde that Ghark Bloodaxe led across the Julian plain. The assault against the province capital had been a disaster.

He'd lost five thousand orcs, a great war chief among them — and gained nothing.

"We should have pressed on," Krakkar the Fist said at his side. "A few more days and you would have found a weakness. And then the city would be ours."

He'd lost one of his swords in the fighting, the one he'd called Left Fang. Ghark knew Krakkar wouldn't miss it for long. The smiths would fashion him another just like it.

Ghark shook his head. "I didn't have a few more days, Krakkar. We barely have enough food for the journey home. Even with five thousand fewer mouths to feed."

They could eat their dead if they had to, but that wouldn't help much. They'd left most of their fallen behind as they retreated.

"There was plenty of food in that city, Ghark," Krakkar said. "I'm sure of it."

"Aye. And maybe we could have taken it. Or maybe they would have pushed us back, again and again, until we starved to death outside those walls. I couldn't take that chance."

"Even so, some say we should turn back and try again."

You among them, perhaps, Ghark thought. "But they'll obey me, yes?"

"They will. And before you ask, I'm with you to the end."

"Good." Ghark kicked at a stone in his path and sent it spinning. "We need to watch out for infighting. When the food runs low, the strong will prey upon the weak."

"If they do, we'll bash some sense into them. Better yet, tell them that whoever starts the infighting gets eaten first. That'll keep them in line."

"Aye. That could work." Ghark would not eat his fellow orcs, but perhaps the threat of it was enough. "I'll spread the word among the clans."

Krakkar gnashed his teeth. "Tell them it was *my* idea, if that helps. And that I'll take the first bite myself. *Before* killing whoever's to blame."

Ghark nodded. "It's good to have you by my side, friend." He picked at a scab on his arm. "How fares Hagor?"

Krakkar looked away. "He still carries her, the poor lass. Hasn't set her down for a moment."

"We'll burn her with full honors when we stop to rest."

Tarkanna. One of Ghark's second cousins had told him of her fate. She'd taken a crossbow bolt through the throat, only moments before Ghark sounded the retreat — and neither the witches, nor Hagor himself, had been able to save her. With her final breath, she'd whispered Hagor's name.

"Her clansmates tried to take her body," Krakkar said. "But Hagor wouldn't let her go. He roared and raged at them, and said she was his mate in the All-Father's eyes, though the words of the marriage bond were never spoken. When two of her friends drew steel, I had to put them in their place."

"And?"

"I didn't kill them, if that's what you're asking. Just made them go away."

"Good. They've suffered too much today." The Great War Chief Zordo, Tarkanna's uncle, had perished in the fighting as well. As had her mother. "I'll speak to them myself, and make sure no bad blood comes out of this."

"They'll need someone to lead them."

"Aye. Rekto the Sour is next in line, yes?"

"He was," Krakkar replied.

"Good. My father fostered him for a year, back when Rekto and I were boys. We were brothers in all but name. I'll make him their war chief, and gladly so."

Krakkar shook his head. "Rekto lost his right hand on the wall, and one of his ears, too."

"Nooo!" Ghark roared, but Krakkar wouldn't lie to him. His guards rushed toward him, and he waved them off.

"They won't follow him now," Krakkar said. "You must choose someone else."

Ghark growled. "Those bloody Julians. When we return, we'll burn them all."

He'd bring the great herds along with his army. There was plenty of grass on the Julian plains, and the goats and the sheep would give the Horde the meat they needed. He'd take more of the younglings, too, to replenish his numbers, though his heart ached at the thought. And he'd visit such a terrible vengeance upon the Julian Empire that they'd remember the name of King Ghark Bloodaxe until the end of time.

Sigurd Larsson

On the deck of his ship, Sigurd Larsson, once a powerful fleet captain and the richest man in Hemland, gazed into the distance.

They've gone to war without me, he thought. *They've left me here to rot.*

Two weeks earlier, Frida and Gunnar had led the bulk of the Islander force toward the Julian Empire's capital, to join with the Boy Emperor's army and march against the orcs. They'd left Sigurd behind, here at Verrano, the closest port to the capital, along with their ships, a hundred and fifty-two cannons, and two thousand loyal men.

He'd beaten the local nobles at cards half a dozen times, and he'd set his eyes on buying an estate near the harbor from its aging owner. But those were the pastimes of idle men, and would get him no closer to recovering his fortune, nor would they help his god in the War of the Seven.

A heavy hand lay on his shoulder. He turned, and dropped to one knee. Njord, the sea god, was facing him.

"Rise, Sigurd," he said. "I hear you long for adventure, my friend."

Sigurd stood. "I only wish to serve you, my god."

"Then get ready to sail. You'll leave in the morning, and travel farther south, then west, to the port of Silvestria. Soon after that, you'll be sailing up the desert men's river."

"We can't sail up the Karim. Our ships would scrape its bottom before we're a mile upriver, if not sooner." They were made for the ocean, after all.

The sea god nodded. "*These* ships would indeed. But the Boy Emperor has a plan, and his carpenters are hard at work already. They'll need your shipwrights to guide them, of course."

"Of course," Sigurd said as understanding began to form. "And the floodgates?"

"The Boy Emperor has a plan for those, too." Njord smiled. "Do this for me, Sigurd. Take the desert men's capital, and many of its riches will be yours."

"I would, my god." It was an audacious plan. "But I need more men."

"You'll have them soon enough."

"Then I'll do this." Sigurd stood taller and raised a hand to his heart. "For you, and for our people."

"Very well. And before I forget, Sigurd. I place great faith in the Boy Emperor and in his two young princes, Farus and Silvanus. You'll obey their commands as if they were my own."

"Aye," Sigurd said. He did not relish the thought of answering to boys less than half his age, but if this was Njord's will, he would not question it.

"Then my work here is done," Njord said, and leaped into the sea.

He didn't shift into his sea serpent aspect, not so close to the shore. But Sigurd watched the water carefully, and soon he saw a long blue shape dart across the waves, turn to the east, and disappear into the distance.

I'll do my part, he thought. *I'll fight for Njord and for his Julian allies. And one day, perhaps I'll get to fight Anders the betrayer, and strike his head from his shoulders myself.*

Full Strength

Marion descended the steps toward the stateroom of Godric's Keep with a heavy heart.

The Keep was the birthplace of Milton, her dearest Companion. But Milton was gone now, slain in the battle against the Islanders, only days after his twenty-eighth birthday. He'd led the first charge, riding straight for Queen Frida, and one of her sea witches had put an ice spear through his eye before he could reach her. Two of his closest friends had seen him fall and had told Marion of his fate.

He was a true knight, strong and honorable, Marion thought. *He would have made Sir Godric proud.*

She could have loved Milton, if she'd allowed herself. Not his twin brother Nelson; there was a darkness to that one, and it was as strong as was the light in Milton's eyes.

I could have taken him for my husband, if I had a choice. But the families had decided otherwise. They'd given her a worthless King Consort: Lord Simon, a weakling and a drunkard who hid behind his mother's skirts on his best days, and found every excuse under the sky to stay away from the marital bed.

She hadn't let herself think of Milton as more than a friend, at least not for long. It would have led her to betraying her husband; a dishonorable deed, unworthy of the Verdant queen. Yet his passing affected her more than she let on. She still woke in the middle of the night with tears in her eyes, whispering his name, more than once a week.

She sighed. *No time to think of him now.* The war council was about to begin — and she had arrived. The large wooden door of the stateroom, with the Verdant Cross painted upon it, loomed in front of her.

She nodded at the two guards, and one of them pushed it open.

Five high chairs stood around the great stone table. The Lady sat facing the door, and smiled at Marion as she entered. On her left, the wizard Eugene the Trickster was half-turned from the table and studied a tapestry depicting the second fight between Sir Godric and King Dragos of the vampires. Sir Galahad, the Paladin, sat thoughtfully, his left hand cupping his chin.

At least I'm not late, Marion thought. Sandra hadn't arrived yet — and Sandra was always on time.

She returned the Lady's smile and took the empty seat to her right. Then the door opened again, and Sandra joined her at the table, walking with hurried steps. They both turned to the Lady.

The goddess spoke first. "Now that we're all here, we can begin. Queen Marion, you can go first."

"Most of our men have gathered," Marion said. "Eight thousand mounted knights and seventy thousand infantrymen." They were encamped around the fortress, a great sea of tents covering the field. "It will take less than a week for the laggards to join us. They'll swell our numbers with another ten thousand, or perhaps eleven. Then we'll march with our full strength, and put our enemies to the sword." The battle against Queen Elena's army could well decide the fate of the world.

Sir Galahad raised his hand, and the Lady motioned him to speak.

"I still believe that you should let me fight this war for you, my queen," he said. "I advise that you and High Priestess Sandra stay behind and seek the safety of Hearthstone. Let the Verdant army follow me."

They wouldn't, Marion thought. But that was not the only problem with his request, which she'd heard — and had rebuked gently — half a dozen times already.

She stood, her hands pressed onto the edge of the table. "And what would that make me, Sir Galahad? The Verdant queen who dared not face Queen Elena and her monsters, and bravely ran away?"

"Courageously she turned and fled," Eugene the Trickster added.

She nodded at him. *At least Eugene sees things as I do.*

"No," she said, cold steel in her voice. "I will not have that. I'll lead my army into battle, fighting side by side with my Companions. I'll do this for my people, and for our Lady, and for our ideals of honor and chivalry. We'll vanquish the vampires and anyone else who dares to invade our lands."

They were fearsome, the vampires. But Marion had her enchanted armor and her training, and she'd have brave knights and wizards at her side.

"There's still a problem, my queen," Eugene said as Marion took her seat again. "I heard a rumor about one of their champions, the wizard Zoltan Barko. It is said that he can use magic to strike fear and terror into the hearts of men. And women, too, I'd imagine. If he targets you, perhaps you'll flee from battle, against your better judgment."

Marion shuddered at the thought. She turned to the Lady. "Would my armor protect me from such magic?"

"The Godly Pact forbids me to answer this," the Lady replied.

Marion nodded. "It's a risk I'll have to take, then. Besides, if this Zoltan Barko moves against me, my Companions' crossbows will pluck him from the sky." She turned to Sandra. "What news do you bring, sister?"

"The wizard Alphonse has sent me a message from the lands of the giants. It was reading his letter that made me late for this meeting."

"You don't have to explain your tardiness, High Priestess," the Lady intervened. "Everyone at this table knows full well that all your thoughts and actions are in service of the greater good of our realm."

She'd rarely lavished such praise upon Marion. Yet if a small part of Marion resented the Lady for it, she'd never find fault with her sister. Perfection had been part of Sandra's nature from the moment of her birth, and it had never left her.

If only she hadn't lost her eye. She should have been the queen, not me. But after the accident, the families wouldn't have accepted Sandra as queen. And so, Lady Anne had been forced to change her plans and train Marion as her candidate instead.

"Thank you, Lady," Sandra said. "Alphonse's letter confirms that the giants are marching east. He expects them to cross into the Vampire Kingdom a week from today and head straight to Dragos Castle."

"Can they take it?" Marion asked.

"Alphonse thinks they can. Many of the vampires' war-trained nobles have invaded our lands, so their defenses will be weak. And once the giants take the castle, the vampires must retake it in a month, or their god will die."

Marion nodded. It was one of the rules of the Godly Pact forged at the war's beginning. Without it, the vampires could have simply flown away from battles, and their champions would have survived until the end.

"Can the giants hold the castle?" Sir Galahad asked.

"It would be difficult," Sandra said. "They marched with all the strength they could muster, but awakenings take time. Perhaps longer than they used to. Most of their priests have stayed behind in the slumber caves. They're raising more of their warriors from their centuries-long sleep, and sending them west when they gather large enough groups. Even so, if the vampires bring their whole army to the fight, it would be a near thing."

Marion sat straighter in her chair. "Not if we can help them, sister."

"And how are we going to do that, my queen?" Sir Galahad asked. "We can't reach Dragos Castle fast enough, not with the vampires harassing us and striking at our supply lines as we advance into their lands."

"Perhaps we don't have to."

"Then?"

"Think, my friend. If we smash the vampires here, on our lands, they won't be strong enough to retake the castle from the giants. And then Serya Krov dies."

"And if their nobles flee from battle and rush to Dragos Castle's defense?"

"Then we destroy their army. They'd be weaker without their nobles, and we'll be at full strength. Even if the vampire nobles rally more serfs and defeat the giants, they'll take heavy losses. They'll be no match for us after that, and we'll march into their lands and finish them. If they flee from our advance again, we'll take Dragos Castle ourselves."

Eugene the Trickster ran his fingers through his beard. "Yes. That could work."

"Even better," Marion continued as a new thought struck her. "You'll have a part to play, Eugene, and it will be glorious."

"I'm listening."

"I'll send you and your Rangers ahead of our army. You'll target Queen Elena from a distance. Strike down the head of the serpent and the body will wither and die. But Queen Elena's nobles will be watching from the sky, and you must find a way to do it without putting your own life at risk. I won't lose one of the Lady's champions in this. Nor another friend." If the Lady knew how hard she'd taken Milton's death, she hadn't thought to comfort her.

"I know you mourn Sir Milton," the Lady said in a gentle voice.

Marion turned toward her. "Lady?"

"We all do," the Lady said, "and more so here. This castle was his birthplace, after all. But you must let go of the past and focus on the future. You must be strong."

Marion nodded. "As you say, Lady. Forgive me for my weakness."

"And you *are* strong, Queen Marion," the Lady continued. "Right here and now, your decisions are sealing the fates of our enemies. Your ancestor, the great Queen Lysenna, would be proud of you."

Marion tilted her head. "Thank you, Lady."

The Lady smiled and turned her gaze to Eugene. "Judging by the look on your face, I think you've thought of a way to accomplish your mission."

The old wizard beamed. "The escape tunnel of Wallis Castle. The one that's collapsed halfway through. You all know the one I speak of, yes?"

Marion did. "Will you get there before the vampires take the castle?" With their cannons, and with the Verdant army too far away to stop them, taking it was a question of *when*, not *if*.

"I will, if I leave at once," Eugene replied.

"Then do so, my friend. But before you do, hear this, and rejoice. We know the vampires have the Islanders' cannons and are using them to take our castles."

Eugene nodded.

"Which means Anders Svensson's fleet is poorly armed."

"You plan to send our own fleet against his," Eugene said.

"I've already sent the orders. Our ships will scour the shores to the west, and once they find the Islander ships, they'll send a small advance party to test their strength. If we find that the pirates have sent most of their cannons to the vampire army, our fleet will engage them with its full might. We'll take their ships, or send them to the bottom of the sea."

"I like it, my queen," Eugene said.

"And I," added Sir Galahad.

"And I," Sandra said.

"The vampires drink their followers' blood," Marion said. "But we have our own noble blood, and it is stronger. We have the wisdom of the ages, and the strength of honor and chivalry. We have noble knights, enchanted armor, and wizards of great skill, such as you, Eugene. We have the giants striking for our enemies' capital. All of our four champions still live. And we have you, Lady. We shall prevail. I am certain of it."

"And I," Sandra, Eugene, and Sir Galahad said at once.

Eugene rose from his seat. "I shall take my leave now. The road calls to me."

"You should ask Sir Sebastian's men to provide you with supplies," Sir Galahad said.

The wizard shook his head. "They'd only slow us down. My Rangers and I will hunt along the way. The forest is my friend, and it will give us everything we need."

"That it will," the Lady said. "Go swiftly, Eugene, and may your men's arrows fly true, as if I guided them myself."

She couldn't, of course. The Godly Pact forbade it.

Even so, Marion felt a newfound strength coursing through her veins. Her plans were good, and they were set in motion, and a great victory against the vampires was in her grasp.

Now she only had to reach out and take it.

Blood Ties

Leticia Alba smiled as Lucius entered her room. "You came, Your Majesty. Thank you."

"Of course I did," Lucius said. "For you, Leticia, I'll always make time. You look tired."

She sighed and sat down on one of her comfortable chairs, facing the door. "It has been a long day." She'd been blessing the orchards of the Orchard of the Gods, the northernmost province of the empire. As many as she could reach in one day, from this distance, with the goddess Demetra's help.

Lucius took the chair facing her, his elbows resting on the small table that separated them. "You should rest and preserve your strength."

"I use the strength Demetra gives me. This body is only a vessel." In truth, the magic she'd been channeling had taken a toll on her. And she wasn't getting any younger.

Lucius nodded. "Even so, I am your emperor and I command you to rest." He said it kindly.

She bowed. "Then I will do as you command. You've come far, my boy."

He frowned, but did not protest. Vesperus had raised him well.

"It's hard to believe that we're the last," she continued. "That the fates of our gods rest upon our bloodline."

"Bloodlines," he replied.

She shook her head. "I know what I said."

"Then explain yourself." He'd used the commanding voice this time.

She pulled the letter from her pocket and handed it to him. It was encrypted with the secret cipher and bore Vesperus's signature.

Lucius's eyes grew wider. "A letter from my father. What does it say?"

"I couldn't read it," Leticia answered. "But I expect it confirms the truth of what I'm about to tell you. That I am your grandmother, and Vesperus's mother."

"Empress Olivia was my father's mother."

"Empress Olivia couldn't give Emperor Tiberius a son for the first five years of their marriage. So, he came to me, following Augustus's advice. I was young and favored by the gods, and I obliged. Then I invited Olivia to my country estate, away from the imperial court, so that I could take care of her during her so-called pregnancy. Eight months later, your father was born."

"But... your servants must have known of the deception."

"Only two of them. Both sworn to secrecy in front of Augustus himself."

"And Aquila, my uncle? Was he yours, too?"

"He was not. Five years later, Olivia was able to conceive. Whether it was the will of the gods or simply her being fertile at the right time, I do not know."

"So, my father was born out of wedlock, and Aquila was the true heir to the throne. And his rebellion was him claiming his birthright."

Leticia shook her head. "You can't think of it this way, my boy. Empress Olivia loved your father like a son, though he was not her own, and she never revealed the secret. Demetra herself assured me of it. Besides, what's done is done." Both Vesperus and Aquila were dead, and the latter had no offspring.

"What's done is done," Lucius agreed.

"I know this is a lot to take in."

"It is. And I know you speak the truth. You wouldn't lie about something like this. And I'll have confirmation as soon as I decrypt my father's letter."

"You will." She didn't know the cipher, but Vesperus had told her what the letter said.

"Why tell me now?" Lucius asked. "Why not earlier? Or… why at all?"

"Earlier, it didn't seem necessary. As for why at all — if something happens to me, I want you to know."

"Nothing will happen to you. You're guarded day and night."

"As was Selenius."

"I can move you into my quarters, if you wish."

Leticia smiled. "I'd like that very much, and not just for my safety. I want to be close to you, my boy. I want us to face the challenges that are to come, side by side. If you'll have me."

Lucius nodded. "As you say, Grandmother."

"I'll still call you 'Your Majesty'. For the guards."

"For the guards," Lucius agreed.

She leaned forward and took his hands in hers, and he did not pull back. "I am proud of you, Lucius. You are truly your father's son. The War of the Seven is a great challenge, but I hear you've done well so far, from Augustus himself."

"As have you."

She smiled. "I have great faith in you, my boy. The fates of our gods are in good hands."

There was one more secret, a greater one. But not even Vesperus had known of it. She'd take it to her grave.

The Gods and their Champions

Aljin: King Ammon, Nasir bin Fatih, Achmad bin Fayzal, Al-Khanjar

Augustus: Emperor Lucius, ~~Marcus Severus~~, Leticia Alba, ~~Selenius Gracchus~~

Grok the All-Father: King Ghark, Hagor the shaman, ~~Rorra Fireborn~~, Krakkar the Fist

The Lady: Queen Marion, High Priestess Sandra, Eugene the Trickster, Sir Galahad

Malleon: King Tassadar, Paeren, Neressia, Eldris the Duelist

Njord: ~~King Knut~~, Queen Frida, ~~Ursula~~, Gunnar

Serya Krov: Queen Elena, Duke Zoltan Barko, Kirill Skromnik, Katrina

Bonus Content

Congratulations! You've finished Part Six.

To explore the bonus content, visit https://bradtowers.com/wots-bonus-6/ or scan this QR code:

Part 7: Surprise Attacks

The Chase

General Justinian leaned forward in his saddle and spurred his horse onward.

Ever since the war's beginning, he and General Patricius had led the Julian defenses. They'd burned the villages and the crops of their own people, and helped them flee to the eastern provinces. They'd harassed the orcs and slowed their advance, and Justinian's cavalry had clashed with the desert men's mounted parties more than two dozen times. They'd defended the province capital against the orcs, winning a glorious victory and sending the Great Horde back to their realm. And now, after a day and a half of hard riding, a grand prize was in Justinian's grasp.

With him rode two hundred and ninety-four elite cavalrymen, the pride of his legions. They were chasing a much smaller raiding party of desert men across the Julian plain, and they were gaining ground.

He smiled to himself as he rode. *Another hour, perhaps two, and King Ammon will fall.*

The day before, one of his scouting parties had spotted the desert men's raiders as they burned down an abandoned Julian village. The scout leader, who carried a spyglass, had seen King Ammon in their midst. He'd galloped to Justinian's camp with the news, and Justinian had rushed to seize the chance of killing or capturing the enemy king.

He'd lost a dozen men in the initial clash, and his forces had killed at least forty of the desert men as they covered their king's retreat. And now he was chasing the survivors, fewer than four dozen in all, into the heart of the Julian Empire.

Their desert horses were black as night, and blazingly fast over short distances. But this was an endurance race, and Justinian knew he'd win it. Five of the enemies' horses had foundered since midday, their riders dispatched quickly by his cavalrymen. More would follow soon.

He looked over his shoulder. The laggards in his group had fallen farther behind, yet more than half of his cavalrymen rode together at the front of his force, arrayed in five neat lines. Six of Justinian's bodyguards flanked him, three on each side, and four more followed in the second line.

Ahead, the enemy force was losing its formation. The last two of their riders were less than a hundred paces away. The rest had lost cohesion, and half a dozen enemies angled to the left, pulling away from the main group. Justinian pointed at them with his sword, and the sergeant on his far left took off in pursuit, his horse leaving a cloud of dust in its wake.

With a satisfied grunt, Justinian sheathed his sword and reached for the trumpet at his waist. *We crush them now.*

He sounded the signal to attack. His riders sped up, just as the enemy force did a curious thing.

They split in two, to the left and right, and wheeled their horses around.

They're charging us, he thought, sword in hand again. *Forty against three hundred.*

The two enemy riders who had fallen behind turned in their saddles and spread out their hands — and a cloud of dust and smoke rose from the grass, obscuring Justinian's vision as he galloped toward his foes.

He raised his left hand to protect his face — and felt his horse slip under him.

Instinct took over. He dropped his sword, threw himself out of the saddle, and rolled, taking the fall on his right shoulder. He winced at the impact and hoped his own troops wouldn't trample him.

On his right, two more horses fell, taking their riders down with them.

Others galloped past, toward the enemy forces. He could barely see them through the thick gray smoke surrounding him.

He rose to his feet, his movements slow. His head was ringing, and dust entered his nostrils as he breathed. Only a few heartbeats had passed, yet he felt as if he'd been down for an eternity.

He spat. *Those bloody wizards! I'll put their heads on spikes when this is over.*

Farther ahead, he could make out the silhouettes of men and horses crashing against one another. Horses whinnied, men screamed, and steel clanged on steel. Arrows whistled through the air.

More of his cavalrymen passed him, heading to the fight. Then a rider pulled up short. He leaped out of the saddle, a dark figure in the cloud of smoke. Justinian reached for his sword.

It wasn't there. He'd had it in his hand and dropped it in the fall.

"General!" the man shouted. "Take my horse. Hurry!"

Justinian recognized his voice. Albius, one of his veteran sergeants. The urgency of his words made him follow the sergeant's command without questioning him.

"What's happening?" he shouted back as he mounted.

"We're beaten," the sergeant replied. "You must flee sou—" Then an arrow pierced him through the throat, and it had come *from behind*.

There was no time to think. Justinian spurred his horse before Albius's body hit the ground, and took the direction he hoped was south. As he emerged out of the cloud of smoke, he finally understood the magnitude of the disaster.

To his left, the grass was littered with the corpses of horses and men. Most of the fallen men's outfits were orange, and most of the dead horses were brown and white, instead of the black steeds of the desert men. A few of Justinian's soldiers still fought, but they were heavily outnumbered. As for the enemies, they'd been forty only moments earlier, yet now they numbered in the hundreds.

To his right, a long line of riders advanced toward his position. Their outfits were light gray, the color of the desert men.

He thought he'd been hunting King Ammon. But King Ammon had been the bait, and it was he, Justinian, who had been hunted. How his enemies had been able to coordinate so well across such a long distance, he did not know.

I can still escape, he thought, until the first arrow struck him in the small of his back. His armor stopped it, but he knew they'd target his horse after that.

Moments later, he threw himself off as his mount fell. He landed on his right shoulder again and cried out in pain.

He staggered to his feet, facing his enemies, and reached for the hunting knife at his belt. Ahead, half a dozen riders readied their arrows and took aim.

They wouldn't even give him the honor of making a final stand. They'd just kill him from afar, shoot him until he stopped twitching. He gritted his teeth.

At least I'm going out my own way, he thought as he drew the knife across his throat.

Head of the Serpent

Deep inside the escape tunnel of Wallis Castle, the wizard Eugene the Trickster smiled as he heard the familiar patter of small feet upon stone. His fox had come back from her scouting adventure.

He turned to the Head Ranger. "It's time, Robert. Get your men ready."

"They've been ready for hours, Master," Robert said.

"Even so. Check on them again. This will be the most important mission of their lives."

The Ranger nodded and disappeared deeper into the tunnel, taking his torch with him. That left Eugene and Vixen in darkness — and *that* was fine, for darkness was their friend.

He crouched and patted her head, as he always did. *Did you find her?* he thought.

Yes, Master.

Where? He didn't need to speak the words out loud, not with Vixen.

Middle of camp. Big red tent. She's not there.

Then where?

Monster queen behind big red tent. Forty paces back, sixty-two paces right. Smaller tent, round, six paces across. Been there for hours.

Is she alone?

No. Bald man with her. Old, shorter than her, gray-skinned. No weapons.

Any monster guards?

Monster guards up in sky. Almost saw me. Very scary.

Any patrols outside?

Not here. Halfway to the camp, yes.

Eugene scratched the back of her neck. *Well done, Vixen. Monster queen dies tonight. You know what to do.*

He stood, just in time, for Robert was returning, along with his men.

"I have your target, Robert. And it's not the command tent. Just as I thought."

He told Robert what he'd learned, and the Head Ranger nodded. "Aye. We can hit that."

"Then you may just win this war for us," Eugene said. He remembered Queen Marion's words. *Strike down the head of the serpent and the body will wither and die.* "How far do we have to walk?"

"Two hundred and fifty paces from the tunnel's mouth."

Eugene nodded. "Let's go. Lead the way, Robert."

He followed the Head Ranger, as did his men, all two dozen of them. They left their torches behind and emerged out of the tunnel on a steep incline, deep in the forest, under the roots of an ancient tree. Vixen rubbed herself against his leg; then she scurried off and disappeared into the trees.

The night was dark and quiet. The bombardment had ceased hours earlier, but Eugene had no doubt that Wallis Castle was about to fall.

Unless our strike makes the vampires turn tail and run.

He followed in Robert's footsteps as the Head Ranger advanced soundlessly through the forest. He'd use a simple spell to take care of the tracks on the way back to the hideout.

The ancient escape tunnel was three centuries old and half a mile long. It had collapsed halfway a hundred years earlier, and no one had bothered to repair it. On this night, and on the nights to come, it would serve Eugene well.

An owl hooted somewhere to his right, but that did not worry Eugene. In fact, it was a good sign. If there were any vampires around, the bird would have had the good sense to keep quiet.

He walked on until Robert motioned him to stop. In moments, all his archers had gathered around him.

"Remember to use the green-tipped arrows," Eugene told them, as he always did. A few of the men answered with nods.

Robert lined them up in five rows of five, whispering his final instructions into their ears before taking his position in the center of the formation. He nocked an arrow and raised his bow at a high angle, and his men did the same.

They drew as one, and let their arrows fly.

They'd fly for half a mile. Eugene's spell would give them the speed they needed. And they'd land right where he'd wanted them to.

When that was done, the archers followed Robert as he sped through the forest, back toward the tunnel's mouth. Eugene trailed them at a slower pace, muttering the spell that erased their tracks.

Ten paces past the threshold, he stopped.

He turned around, raised his hands high, and cast another spell. The ground shook and trembled, and in moments, a great pile of earth and stone blocked the entrance. He cast yet another spell, and knew that earth would gather above the tunnel's mouth, and grass would grow, matching the surrounding landscape. To an outsider, it would seem that the tunnel's collapse had happened years earlier.

They were safe now. No one would think to look inside.

Eugene breathed in deeply as his shoulders sagged, and sat himself down on the ground. He'd sleep for days, after using so much magic — and he'd be weak as a kitten when he woke. But on a mission like this one, it was worth the effort.

He and his Rangers would cluster around the three small air holes they'd dug farther from the entrance, and feed on their two weeks' worth of supplies, and wait. And after the enemy moved on, Vixen would come to one of the air holes and signal them.

They'd dig their way out after that. And if all had gone well, they'd emerge into a world free of Queen Elena's tyranny.

The Face of Death

Queen Elena paced Kirill Skromnik's tent. The priest slept on a thin mattress at her feet, his gentle snoring the only sound on an otherwise quiet night. A single candle placed on a low table gave off a dim light.

She'd taken to spending the night in his tent, and that accomplished two things at once. It kept her away from a surprise attack on her command tent, and it kept Kirill safe. For there was no safer place for him than at the side of the vampire queen.

The war was going well so far, except for Katrina's earlier defiance — and Elena had to admit that her Islander allies had proven their worth. With their cannons, she'd taken castle after castle, with much fewer losses than she'd expected. Yet all this was merely a prelude to the upcoming clash.

She'd sent scouts ahead, flying high above the Verdant lands, and knew that Queen Marion was gathering her armies. Soon, they'd meet on the field of battle — and the Verdant knights were formidable. Especially those who wore enchanted armor. Yet Elena was not worried.

Cannons had beaten Marion once, and they'd do so again. And Elena's serfs were more than a match for Marion's infantry.

We'll crush them and hunt down the survivors, she thought. *And then—*

"Arrows!" a shrill warning came from above.

Elena leaped toward Kirill and landed on top of him, wings

outstretched. Hot fire seared her chest and her left thigh, and a hail of arrows punched into the ground around her.

Poison. Under her, Kirill grunted; he was waking.

She tried to roll off him — and tore a deep gash into her right wing, where a third arrow had struck her. She snarled and pulled it out with her left hand.

"Arrows," she said. "Stay low."

"My queen!" Kirill exclaimed. "Your face!"

She snapped her head to the mirror to her right, and it shattered, but not before she could get a glimpse. For an instant, the face of death stared back at her.

Her once beautiful skin was wrinkled and leathery, and ghostly pale. Her hair was straw-like and dirty white. Her eyes had sunk deep into their sockets. Her fangs were chipped, and her upper teeth were gray. Her once elegant nose was anything but. A black vein pulsed in the middle of her forehead.

In an instant, she'd aged five hundred years.

The waterskin, she realized. The arrow that had struck her in the back had burst it open.

The flapping of wings told her Vladimir was coming. "Stay away!" she shrieked.

She hissed at Kirill, and he shrank under her glare.

She pulled out the arrow from her leg, and winced in pain. The one in her back, she didn't dare to touch. No blood was pouring out, but that would come as soon as she pulled out the arrow. Or simply *moved*.

Even so, I can't stay here. Her enemies knew where she was, and another strike could come at any time.

She tore off a wide strip from Kirill's shirt and wrapped it around her face, leaving only her eyes visible. Then she grabbed the priest under his arms and burst through the side of the tent and into the air.

"Away!" she shouted, knowing her nobles would obey her command. No doubt, a few were already scouring the surroundings for the archers who had dared to target her.

She flapped her wings wildly, each move sending new stabs of pain into her chest and back. Every moment she grew weaker.

She gritted her teeth. *I must get help, and fast.*

She landed roughly in front of a serfs' tent near the edge of the camp, letting go of Kirill just before her feet touched the ground. She pulled him into the tent, and he did not resist.

Inside, four serfs were rising from their sleep. Four of her throwing knives took care of them, and suddenly she and Kirill were alone in the darkness.

"My queen…" he whispered.

"Wait." She lit a candle and pointed at her face, still hidden by the strip she'd torn from his shirt. "This. This stays between us. I've been poisoned, Kirill."

He paled a little. "Are you dying, my queen?"

"Not today. I'll get better, and soon. With your help."

"You saved my life."

She had no doubt. The arrow that was still in her would have struck him in the heart. It would have struck *her* in the heart, if she had one.

"I'm not worthy," Kirill continued. "I'm just a servant."

"You're one of Serya Krov's champions." She pointed to the bodies of the dead serfs. "These deaths were necessary. I couldn't trust them. You'll keep my secret, yes?"

He nodded. "I swear it."

"I believe you. Here's what you must do. Send for Vladimir and tell him to stand guard outside this tent. No one comes inside but you. No one. And have Nikolay guard you at all times, when you're not here with me."

"As you wish."

He made toward the entrance, and Elena grabbed his arm. "Not yet. Look at me, Kirill."

She unwrapped the fabric that hid her hideous face. This time, he forced himself to gaze at her without flinching. She appreciated him even more for it.

She winced as another hot flash of pain lanced through her chest. "The poison is strong, Kirill. And it is killing me. But noble blood is stronger than poison. I need lots of it, and soon."

"But you won't go and take it yourself."

"I can't let them see me like this." It wasn't just her face; it was her weakness that she didn't dare let them see. Not when Katrina had already challenged her.

"Then, how?"

"Get Duke Zoltan. Tell him I've been hurt, and that I need ten pints of blood. One from each of my strongest nobles. Starting with him. Ask him to get the blood to you. He'll find a way. Not Katrina's blood, though." That would only make things worse.

"He'll wonder why you're not taking their blood yourself, my queen."

"Find an excuse. Now go, Kirill, and be swift. I'm dying." She'd need a lot more blood over the next few days, but she wouldn't tell him that, not yet.

He walked out into the night, barking orders. Soon, the flapping of wings, followed by a soft thud, told Elena that a vampire had landed in front of the tent.

"My queen." It was Vladimir.

"Stay outside," she said. "Guard me. Follow Kirill's orders; he speaks with my voice tonight. No one enters this tent but him."

"As you wish, my queen."

She hissed as pain struck her again. Even so, she did not dare pull out the arrow.

She pushed one of the dead serfs off his blanket and took his place, lying on her side. "Tell him to pour it down my throat, Vladimir. He'll understand."

She'd been through this once before. Two hundred and fifteen years earlier, the desert men's assassins had made an attempt on her life as she visited the Bloodriver province. A suicide mission, of course — but the head assassin's blade had struck deep, before her talons had opened his throat.

She'd aged then as well, though not as much. Serya Krov had helped her recover, as had one of her servants — and two weeks of rest, along with five pints of blood per day, had been enough to restore her. But this was worse. And this time, the vampire god was not allowed to intervene.

She closed her eyes. If she was to survive this, she had to conserve every bit of strength she had left.

The Verdant queen will pay for this, was her last conscious thought.

The Giants' March

Storm clouds gathered in the sky as Eldris the Duelist strode into the Vampire Kingdom, with King Tassadar and Neressia at his side.

With them came a great army of over ten thousand giants. White-haired and purple-skinned they were, and bare-footed, and long-lived. Many of them were over five giant feet tall, or twice that in human feet.

They carried weapons of war; great hammers, heavy maces and flails, axes that could fell a young oak in a single blow, and swords and spears of legend, which a man could barely lift. They had ranged weapons as well; long javelins, powerful slings, and war bows that shot heavy arrows across great distances when needed. Only the wizards were unarmed. Their powers were vast, and weapons would only slow them down.

They'd gathered the first eight thousand at the Slumber Gates, the capital, after awakening many of their greatest warriors from their centuries-long sleep. They'd passed through the Winterlands province before descending into the Western Lowlands, their forces swelling as they marched. More warriors had joined them from the Rockfalls province. And now they'd crossed into Bloodriver, the largest province of the Vampire Kingdom, leaving behind their own realm's hills and mountains for the vampires' grassy plains.

They wouldn't stay long in Bloodriver. Their path took them straight toward Dragos Castle, the vampire capital.

Conquer the castle and hold it for a month, and the vampire god will die. Those had been Malleon's words, and that was their mission. A mission that Eldris would fight for, without regret.

On his right, King Tassadar whistled as he marched, balancing his hammer on his shoulder. Besides his belt and his loincloth, his only other garment was the royal cape, which hung over his back. His armor bearer, a young giant in his second hundred years who marched three ranks behind, carried his battle outfit.

Tassadar's eyes sparkled, and often he looked far into the distance, as if he knew that a great fate awaited him.

He was born at night, during an eclipse, Eldris remembered. *A sign of a magnificent destiny. He's our king and one of our best warriors. Perhaps he's meant to win this war for us.* Yet, in his dream, Eldris had been wearing the royal cape himself.

He hadn't mentioned that to Tassadar, nor to any of the others.

Tassadar tapped him on the shoulder, pulling him from his thoughts. "A good day for a stroll into enemy lands, eh?"

Eldris pointed to the darkening sky above. "Not if those clouds start pouring down. I'll sink to my ankles with every step." The ground was soft under his feet, and heavy rain would turn it into mud.

Tassadar nodded. "Aye. You should travel light, as I do."

"I prefer to travel ready." Unlike his king, Eldris wore his ancient armor, properly oiled and mended. In his left hand, he carried a heavy shield that sported five long, forward-facing spikes, which he'd use with devastating effect. The Reaping Blade, the only weapon in existence that could kill a god, hung in its harness on his back.

"As you always did," Tassadar said. "It's been a long time since we marched together, friend. Too long."

"Four hundred and fifty-nine years." In truth, the centuries of slumber had restored much of Eldris's strength from his early days, and he felt at least two decades younger than before.

Then again, not having to murder Grok the All-Father with the Reaping Blade, at least not anytime soon, had lifted a great weight off his shoulders. After asking the orcs for an alliance and waiting in vain for their reply, Malleon and King Tassadar had chosen the vampires as their next target.

Eldris smiled. If he had to kill a god, he could think of no better choice than Serya Krov. Though how he'd get close enough to the vampire god, he did not know.

Only a handful of giants knew of the weapon's true nature, and they were all sworn to secrecy. For the others, it was just a big sword, worthy of their greatest warrior.

At Eldris's side, Tassadar grunted. "I wish Paeren was here with us. Then again, he has the most important mission of all." He was back at the slumber caves, along with most of Malleon's priests, performing the awakening rituals — and every day, more and more giants rose from their centuries-long sleep, some of them heroes of legend. Once enough of them took arms, they'd be unstoppable.

Of course, the longer the giants' sleep had been, the longer the awakenings took. And only a hundred priests were skilled enough to perform them. Ten of those traveled with the army, while the others had remained at the caves.

Eldris nodded. "I'm glad you had him start with me."

"You were Malleon's choice, and mine," Tassadar said.

"Look." Neressia pointed ahead.

Far in the distance, Eldris thought he could see the outline of a settlement.

"The way forward is right through Bleakhall," she said. It was one of the Vampire Kingdom's frontier towns. "Shall we go around it, or…?"

Eldris shook his head. "I think our king would like to test our enemies' strength."

"You're right, friend." Tassadar's voice boomed, his words as hard as stone. He raised his hammer high. "We march right through that town. We knock their stone walls down. And we slaughter anyone who gets in our way."

The Storming of Bleakhall

The young vampire Sveta leaned against the parapet, her hands flat on the cold stone of Bleakhall's wall. The wind whipped her hair around her face as she gazed into the distance. The giants' army was drawing near, a long line of purple-skinned, white-haired warriors, their war cries rumbling like thunder. Their weapons and armor gleamed faintly in the dim light beneath the storm-heavy clouds.

"How many?" Sveta asked, her voice steady despite the tightness in her chest.

"Too many," replied Baron Miklos, the commander of Bleakhall's garrison. He stood at her side, his talons outstretched, his eyes scanning the enemy ranks. His gray skin seemed paler than usual, though his face betrayed no fear. "At least ten thousand."

"They won't stop here," Sveta said. "They're headed for Dragos Castle."

Miklos nodded. "They'll try to take it before Queen Elena returns." He placed his hand on the pommel of his sword. "We must delay them as long as we can."

Sveta bit her lip. There was no doubt in her mind: Bleakhall would fall. The giants were too many and too powerful. The town's garrison of four thousand serfs could not hold against such overwhelming force.

"I'll do my part," she said, fully aware of the tremor in her voice.

Miklos shook his head. "No. Watch the battle from the sky, and when it's over, take the news to Queen Elena. She must know what's coming."

"And my uncle?"

"He'll take the news to Dragos Castle. I'll give him the order myself."

Relief washed over Sveta. "Thank you, Miklos." Her uncle, Baron Laszlo, would have laid down his life for Bleakhall, but he wouldn't disobey his commander's orders.

Miklos gave her a thin smile, tinged with sadness. "If only Queen Elena's peace had lasted another decade. I would have liked to…" He trailed off and shook his head. "It doesn't matter. Go. Take to the sky."

"As you wish." Sveta unfurled her wings. "Farewell, Miklos. Fight well today."

He lowered his gaze. "Remember me, Sveta."

Her heart clenched as she watched him turn away, his shoulders heavy but his steps resolute.

With one last look at his retreating figure, his cape swelling in the wind, Sveta burned the image into her memory.

If only I could protect them all, she thought. But there was nothing she could do but obey Miklos's command. She flapped her wings and soared into the sky, high enough so that the giants' arrows wouldn't reach her.

The town looked small from up here, its stone walls thin and fragile, as if a mere gust of wind could tear them down. Archers rushed onto the walls and strung their bows. More serfs came forth from the nearby buildings, swords and spears in hand.

Her uncle, Baron Laszlo, took to the sky. He waved at her, then sped west toward Dragos Castle, his wings cutting through the air with purpose.

Below, the giants drew near, forming themselves into ranks. Time seemed to stretch as they stood silent, and Sveta's heart beat faster in her chest. Then, with a mighty roar, they charged. On the walls, the archers nocked arrows to their bows.

The giants neared the walls, and a few screamed as they fell into deep holes hidden in the ground, impaling themselves into the sharpened stakes that waited at the bottom. Most of the giants surged onward.

The defenders fired their arrows. Some struck armor and shields, while others found their targets, but too few of the giants fell.

A dozen vampires took to the air. They hurled javelins at the charging giants or darted in to strike them with swords and axes. Sveta spotted Miklos among them, flying fast, spilling purple blood with powerful swings of his sword.

The giants fired stones and arrows, striking three vampires from the sky. Sveta flinched as their bodies vanished into the mass of purple-skinned warriors. Two other vampires dove into the crowd, their blades flashing before they were overwhelmed. The others retreated, landing atop the walls to command the serfs in their defense of the city.

The giants brought no ladders, but six of them carried a massive battering ram. Others marched alongside them with their shields raised high, protecting them from the defenders' arrows.

Giants scaled the walls, climbing over each other in a brutal frenzy. Those who reached the parapets struck the defenders with their massive weapons or hurled them to their deaths. Men screamed as they fell, their screams cut short as they crashed onto the cobblestones below.

A giant fell, impaled by a lucky spear thrust. Another sank to his knees as a vampire struck his leg with an axe.

The ram slammed into the gates with a deafening noise. It was matched by a thunderous boom further along the wall. Sveta's gaze snapped southward, where a massive giant wielded a great hammer. He struck the wall again with immense strength, no doubt amplified by magic. The wall shuddered and cracked under the impact, and a section began to crumble, the serfs above screaming as they fell with the collapsing structure.

The wind howled, and the first drops of rain began to fall.

Lightning split the sky. Thunder roared, drowning out the sounds of battle. The rain grew stronger, pelting Sveta's wings, soaking her to the bone. Below, a few giants slipped onto the slick ground, but most of them fought on.

Through the chaos of battle, Sveta spotted Miklos diving toward an enemy, his sword driving cleanly through the giant's skull. The giant fell, but a massive javelin struck Miklos through the chest, punching through his armor. Blood sprayed as his body arced through the air, crashing onto the roof of a nearby house. The roof gave way, and Miklos fell into the building.

I could swoop down and save him, Sveta thought. But it was too late. From atop the wall, four giants leaped into the town and rushed toward the house, swords and axes in hand.

Her heart twisted with guilt, but what could she do against so many? Besides, Miklos had told her to stay away from the battle.

She snarled. *I must try.*

She folded her wings and dove from the sky, her eyes fixed on the crack that Miklos had disappeared into. As she neared the ground, she opened her wings and flapped them hard, slowing her fall.

Below, the two leading giants crashed through the building's wall and disappeared inside.

She darted through the gap in the roof, wincing as her thigh struck something sharp. She turned through the air and landed in a crouch.

The giants were already there. One headed toward her, his sword slick with blood. The other pinned Miklos beneath his foot, his axe raised, ready to strike.

"Go," Miklos groaned. Then the axe fell, hitting the floor with a loud thump, severing Miklos's head from his body.

"No!" Sveta screamed, but the other giant was swinging at her with his sword. She leaped to the side, flapped her wings, and took to the air. A javelin flew at her, tearing a narrow gap through her right wing.

I must rise! She beat her wings furiously, veering to avoid other missiles. Finally, she rose out of range, the heavy rain pelting her wings and face.

Below, Bleakhall's gates split apart with a loud crash. Giants poured through, roaring their triumph, smashing their way through the defenders. Screams echoed through the streets as vampires and serfs fought and died.

The town was lost, and there was nothing Sveta could do.

She didn't need to see the end. With a frustrated scream, she turned north, her wings beating against the storm.

I must find Queen Elena before it's too late. If Dragos Castle falls, all will be lost.

A Difficult Mission

When his hawk's screech pierced the quiet night, Al-Khanjar, the Black Blade of the desert men's assassins, opened the door of the pantry and advanced into the castle's great kitchen.

For two days, he'd waited. Hidden behind the large sacks of grains, he and his two men had remained unnoticed, even as the kitchen maids bustled to-and-fro, preparing the night's feast. And now, hours after the castle's most important guests had retired to their chambers for the night, the time to strike had finally arrived.

The kitchen was deserted. Dim light peered in from the window facing the stables, and Al-Khanjar ducked as he passed the opening. If the guards outside saw him, his mission would be over before it began. But only a novice would let himself be seen, and Al-Khanjar hadn't been a novice for over two decades.

With him came Khaled, the last of his disciples; a skilled shot with the crossbow, who fought with sword and whip when he needed to get close. He'd been Al-Khanjar's second for the killing of that half-breed Julian diplomat. But tonight's mission was harder; and so, despite his better judgment, Al-Khanjar had brought along a wizard as well.

Usman was the boy's name, and he was only seventeen. A half-breed with a rich merchant for a father and a Verdant prostitute for a mother, he'd been trained by Al-Khanjar's own mentor, the Old Man himself, in the years before his passing. His training complete, the boy had been placed as a spy in Lysennia, the easternmost province of the Verdant Kingdom. And there he'd waited for three years, serving as a blacksmith's apprentice, until Al-Khanjar had collected him on the way to his target.

The three assassins crossed the kitchen with quiet steps. A wide hallway lay behind the door, and it would be lit by torches. From there, they'd take the spiral staircase, climb three flights of steps, and reach their target's chamber.

Though he'd been hiding in the pantry during her arrival, Al-Khanjar knew he'd find her there. For it was the local Noble Dame's chamber, and the Dame had fled for the safety of Hearthstone weeks earlier, and *of course* tonight's guest of honor would claim her room. After all, the people of this land were all about following protocol.

Entry through the window was not an option. It was barred, and dozens of guards patrolled the courtyard below. Crossbowmen dotted the rooftops as well, just in case the vampires decided to send an advance party and spoil their enemy's rest. So, Al-Khanjar and his men would take the inner staircase instead. They'd reach their target, kill her in her sleep, and escape before her men sounded the alarm.

As he neared the kitchen door, Al-Khanjar stopped and listened. On the other side, four pairs of steps patrolled the hallway, two teams of two men each. Two pairs of footsteps were heavier and walked side by side, the clink of armor accompanying them.

First targets, Al-Khanjar thought. The others would be easier to kill from a distance.

He reached behind him, found Khaled's arm, and squeezed it twice, then twice again. Khaled would relay the message to Usman as well.

Khaled answered with three light taps on his right shoulder, and Al-Khanjar tapped once in agreement. Then he moved to the side of the door, giving Usman the leading position. The boy began muttering a spell, quietly enough that the guards wouldn't hear his words.

When Usman was done, Al-Khanjar pulled out his sword and waited until the armored men were in line with the door. Then he grunted.

The boy opened the door with a swift motion and spoke a final word, triggering the spell as Al-Khanjar burst into action.

He took the closest man through the roof of his mouth with his sword as Khaled stabbed the next man through the eye. Then Al-Khanjar whirled around and threw one of his daggers into the neck of one of the unarmored men before he could react. The man fell, just as a crossbow bolt took his companion through the back of the neck. There was no sound as the bodies hit the wooden floor, and with that, Usman the boy wizard had proven his worth.

Al-Khanjar pulled out his sword from his first victim. He nodded at Khaled, who was doing the same. *Four down. Now, up the stairs.*

He took the lead and his men followed him, Khaled reloading his crossbow as Usman muttered his spell again. Two guards waited on the next landing, and they fell as easily and soundlessly as the others.

The second landing was empty. A stroke of luck, or perhaps a sign that more formidable opponents would be waiting at the top.

He'd heard of them. The Queen's Companions: sons of noble families, trained from childhood in the arts of war, some of them wearing enchanted suits of armor forged by the god Malleon himself. But not even those would stop Al-Khanjar from accomplishing his mission.

In a fight, they'd be real threats. But he wasn't about to give them one.

Up the stairs he went again, keeping close to the wall. He paused midway until Usman ceased his muttering, and advanced again.

The first of the Companions was indeed clad in a green suit of armor — and he spotted Al-Khanjar first. He opened his mouth, but his scream was cut short by Khaled's crossbow bolt. It struck his front teeth loose before lodging farther inward, just as Al-Khanjar darted forward, sword in hand.

He parried the second Companion's sword blow, his arm shaking upon the impact, and buried a black-bladed dagger in his eye.

Amateurs, he thought dispassionately as the bodies landed soundlessly on the floor. Then again, not even the Queen's Companions would lower their visors on a routine guard assignment, in a castle they thought their own.

They'd been twins. And now their charge was moments away from death.

Al-Khanjar recovered his dagger, placed it in its sheath, and pointed to the torch that lit the hallway. Two whispered words from Usman extinguished it. Al-Khanjar grabbed the doorknob and turned it ever so slowly.

He pushed the door inward.

The vast room was dark, save for a faint light peering from behind a curtain. A shadow waited inside, facing the door. She sat on the edge of her bed, her long hair flowing down her shoulders — and, clearly, she was awake.

Quick as a snake, Al-Khanjar threw his black-bladed dagger, still slick with the blood of the man he'd just murdered.

The shadow snatched it from the air, her hand moving with inhuman speed. There was a faint clink of metal as her fingers grabbed the weapon. She threw it back in a swift motion. Al-Khanjar ducked to his left and heard the thud as the blade pierced flesh.

He glanced over his shoulder. Usman was sinking to his knees, clutching his throat as blood gurgled from the deadly wound.

Al-Khanjar's head snapped back to his target. She was now standing, a longsword in hand. At least her hair was loose, which meant she hadn't had time to don her helmet.

"Guards!" she shouted. There was no doubt she'd be heard. In less than a minute, the whole castle would wake.

There was no turning back. Al-Khanjar, the Black Blade, would die tonight. But first, he'd accomplish his mission. And in a fight in the darkness, two against one, he had the upper hand. Enchanted armor or not.

"Bar the door, Khaled," he said as he advanced farther into the room, sword in hand. "Well met, Queen Marion."

Aljin's Followers

"Well met, assassins," Marion said. The name Khaled belonged to Aljin's followers. Besides, none but the desert men's trained killers could have gotten to her on this night.

She kept her eyes on the taller man, who was clearly in command, by his words and his tone of voice. Her suspicion was confirmed when the other assassin remained by the door.

"My guards outside?" she asked.

"Dead," said the leader.

He rushed forward and attacked with a lunge, the tip of his sword aiming for her throat. She parried it and darted to the left before he could follow. The shorter man was uncoiling something — a whip?

I'll kill him first, she thought. *When I have the chance.*

The man lashed out with the whip just as she reached for her helmet, which she'd left on the nightstand. The tip of the whip struck the helmet with a clang of metal and it clattered to the floor.

She scurried back and parried the flurry of blows the leader rained upon her. She'd been training since childhood, and the enchanted armor gave her strength and speed. But the assassin was lightning quick, and she couldn't sneak in a blow of her own. Not yet.

The man stepped back — and, with a flick, Khaled's whip lashed at her face. She caught it with her armored left hand, tugged at it to pull the man off balance, and let go before he could do the same to her.

She parried the leader's next strike, and the one after that.

"Is this the best you can do?" she shouted. For Aljin's followers would loathe being bested by a woman, and taunting them could provoke them to act rashly. And one mistake was all that Marion needed.

"We're just playing cat and mouse," the man shot back. His second had pulled out his own curved sword and was advancing, trying to flank her.

She let him. She had to take his measure first, and then his life.

"On three," the leader said. "You go high, I go low."

Marion did not put any trust in his words. Most likely, they were meant to distract her; the assassins could as well do the opposite. Then again, she wouldn't play their game.

"One," the first man said. "Two," and they came at her at once, but she pivoted out of the line of attack. She parried the second man's strike, shoved him in the shoulder with her left hand, and leaped across the room. In the hallway, men were shouting and pounding against the door.

They were her knights, and they were strong, and yet the door would hold.

My sister, she thought. *She'd open it in moments.* After all, Sandra was one of the strongest wizards in the kingdom.

"You fight well," the tall assassin said as he and his second moved to flank her again.

"You too," she replied. "I thought you people only killed your victims as they slept."

She rushed the leader before he moved in. *Always do the unexpected.* A dagger had appeared in his left hand, and he stabbed at her side as she blocked his sword, but the smaller weapon scraped uselessly against her armor. The man stepped back, and a glance in the mirror that stood in the corner of the room told Marion that his second was creeping up behind her.

"The face," she said. "You must go for—" She reversed her grip on her sword and stabbed behind her as she dropped to one knee. The second man grunted in pain as his cut, meant to take her head off her shoulders, passed harmlessly above her. "The face."

She pulled her sword from his stomach and held it in a high guard as the man toppled to his side, clutching his wound.

The leader nodded. "The face, yes. Though it would be bad luck for your family to lose another eye before I kill you."

His mention of Sandra's accident stung Marion, but only for an instant. She gritted her teeth. *He's taunting me. I can't lose focus.*

She stepped back, keeping her eyes on her opponent, and stomped hard on the fallen man's face with her armored boot. Something cracked under her foot. She leaped to the side, without wasting a moment, and the leader's cut missed her cheek by inches.

"It's just you and me, dear," she taunted him. "And I'm the cat, not you. How does it feel to be the mouse?"

Outside, her guards were throwing themselves against the door. To reach it and open it, she'd have to get past her opponent.

She pressed him, striking high, then low, then high again — and it was he who was defending now. When he stabbed at her face after a quick parry, Marion was ready, and dodged to the side. She lashed out with a low cut, and the man hissed as her sword sliced his trouser leg, and the flesh beneath it.

"My blade's poisoned, too," she lied. His own had to be, of course. "Be quick now. You don't have much time."

He rushed her, and his moves betrayed his intention. Marion parried his attack with her armored left arm and stabbed him under his ribcage, angling her sword upward to pierce his heart.

She pulled her sword back and pivoted to the side, before he could match her deadly stab with one of his own. Outside, a bird shrieked.

The man sank to his knees, and his head tilted back toward the sky.

"Aljin," he whispered.

A flash of light blinded Marion for an instant. She blinked twice, slashing with her sword from side to side, but no attack came. Instead, all sounds ceased. The pounding on the door stopped, and suddenly the whole room was inundated with yellow light, and an otherworldly being stood before her.

He was taller than Marion, and his head had strange proportions. It was bigger than a man's head; not exaggeratedly so, but enough for her to notice. His mouth was lower on his face than it should have been, the upper part of his nose stretched to the middle of his forehead, and his cheekbones were sunken inward. His eyes were wider apart, had no pupils, and brimmed with golden light. His long hair was golden as well, and combed toward the back of his head.

He wore a splendid golden suit of armor that left his face and his muscular arms free, and Marion had no doubt of his identity. The sun god had answered his follower's call.

She pointed her sword at him, then thought better of it. No weapon could harm a god.

"You can't be here," she said. "The Godly Pact forbids it."

Aljin regarded her with a look of amusement on his face. "Do not be afraid, Queen Marion. I only came to congratulate you for defeating my champion. The Lady herself has allowed it."

"Why is everything so quiet?" The banging on the door had ceased, and the shriek of the bird outside had cut abruptly at the sun god's arrival.

"I stopped the sands of time from flowing," Aljin said. "But only for a little while."

He wants something, Marion realized. "So, this was your champion. Is he —"

"Dead," Aljin replied.

She couldn't see the man, not with the bright aura that emanated from the sun god.

"See for yourself," Aljin continued.

He stepped aside. Behind him, the assassin lay unmoving, blood pooling under his chest. His face was painted in a dark gray color, and the blade of his sword was black.

"He died with your name on his lips," she said, then scowled inwardly. The sun god must have witnessed it.

Aljin nodded. "My men underestimated you. That was a mistake. And now there are a few things I would ask of you, Queen Marion."

"Speak."

He tilted his head slightly to the side, the light in his eyes intensifying, and instantly she knew why. She'd used the commanding voice, out of habit. With the *sun god*.

It did not matter. He couldn't harm her, and she'd just killed one of his champions. And in all likelihood, by the time the War of the Seven was over, at least one of them would be dead. Perhaps both.

"You'll forgive me if I don't bow to you," she pressed on.

He smiled. "That's not what I ask of you. If you win this war, Queen Marion, I'll have you treat my people kindly. Even though they are so different from everything you know."

They were indeed. The desert men viewed women as inferior to men and treated them as such. In the Verdant Kingdom, women thrived and ruled. But that was not all. Their clothes, their habits, the food they ate — almost everything about them was different.

A harsh people, born from a harsh land, Sandra had told her once.

"So, you think we have a good chance to win this," she said.

"Enough to have you marked for death." Aljin pointed to the lifeless body of the assassin. "Just as you targeted Queen Elena of the vampires, and Ursula the sea witch before her."

"Queen Elena invaded my lands. As did the sea witch and her people."

"Yes. And if you live long enough, you'll invade mine. But let us set this unpleasantness aside for now. I ask you not to seek revenge on my people for what happened here tonight."

He's worried, Marion realized. *The sun god is worried about what I might do.*

She nodded. Vengeance would be an act unworthy of the Verdant queen. "I won't act unjustly toward your people if I win. At least not by my own will. With that said, I will do as the Lady commands. Now and always."

"That is acceptable," Aljin said.

"In return," she pressed on.

Aljin tilted his head to the side again.

"In return, I ask that your followers do not target my people. At least not while the vampire god still lives."

"You have my word," Aljin said. "And you'll give me one more thing. I would have your permission to take my champion's body, so that he can be burned with the proper honors."

Marion frowned. "And I must trust that this is not a trick."

"He's well and truly gone from this world. And I can't bring back the dead. Only the vampire god could do that, and only once."

She knelt next to the assassin's body. There was no sign of life, and enough of his blood had poured out that she had no reason to doubt his passing. *Besides*, she thought, *if the sun god tried to trick me, the Lady would intervene.*

"Done," she said. "What of the other two?"

"Those you can keep. And now I must go. Thank you for being agreeable, Queen Marion." His light was dimming. "You should have asked for more."

"Wait," Marion said. But the room was dark again, and her men were banging on the door. She stepped forward and unbarred it. A throng of armored men crowded the hallway, all of them bristling with weapons.

"I'm fine!" she shouted. "Not a scratch." Then she noticed the blood at her feet, and though she couldn't see the bodies through the press of men, she realized that Gilles and Jacques, her Companions on guard duty, had perished in the assassins' attack.

"Let me pass." Sandra's voice came from the stairway, loud but calm, as always.

Marion smiled. Finally, the night's ordeal was at an end.

"Clear the hall, men," she commanded. "Leave a dozen knights to guard us. And hand me a torch. I need to speak with my sister."

The Accident

Sandra's heartbeats returned to normal as she strode toward Marion. Her sister had survived. She followed Marion into her room, closing the door behind her.

Marion placed the torch in a stand at the side of the door.

Sandra wrapped her arms around Marion and held her close. Marion returned the embrace, though she was the first to let go.

"Little sister," Sandra said. "I feared for your life."

"I'm fine," Marion said. Her breathing was faster than usual, the only sign that she'd been fighting a dangerous enemy only moments earlier. "Just like I told the guards."

"I came as fast as I could."

"I know, big sister. It's all over now. My armor saved my life."

Sandra's eyes fell upon the motionless, black-clad body of a man. "An assassin."

"Three of them. I killed one before he could enter the room, and two in here."

"I only see one body."

"Aljin came and took the other with him. He was one of his champions."

That took Sandra by surprise. "The sun god was here? How? And more importantly, why?"

"He wants us to be kind to his people, if we win. I'll tell you everything. Sit with me, sister."

They sat on the edge of Marion's bed, and Sandra listened intently as Marion recounted the quick and brutal struggle with Aljin's followers and her short conversation with the sun god.

"You were right," Sandra said in the end. "Your armor saved your life. How did you know to wear it tonight, of all nights?"

"I've been wearing it every night since I sent Eugene against the vampire queen. I figured her nobles would try something. I wasn't expecting the assassins, though."

"Aljin said you should have asked for more. I wonder what he meant. What you could have gotten out of him."

"Perhaps we'll never find out. Because, as you know…"

"Aljin works in mysterious ways," they both said at once.

They shared a smile.

"You did well in taunting his assassins," Sandra said. "Maybe that gave you an edge as well."

Marion nodded. "It must have. Though I didn't like it when the leader mentioned your eye. I made him pay for it."

"The *accident*, yes," Sandra said. "It brings me no joy to think of it. Yet I will speak of it now." After all those years, it was time for Marion to learn the truth of what had happened that day.

#

Sandra was a girl of nine back then, and wise beyond her years. "You'll be queen one day," Mother told her more than once a week.

On that evening, she'd been in her study, seated on a comfortable sofa and poring through an old trade agreement with the Julian Empire. Sir Galahad sat at her side, keeping her company; a dashing knight in his prime, clad in his enchanted armor. He hadn't yet earned the title of the Lady's Paladin, but many thought of him as the best choice when the position would open again.

A knock on the door made Sandra raise her eyes from the parchment. "Enter," she said.

The door opened slowly, and a servant passed the threshold, carrying a tray laden with sweets. She was young and slender, and Sandra did not recognize her.

"You're not Joanna," she said.

The servant bowed. "She wasn't feeling well, my lady. They sent me in her stead. I bring you treats from the kitchen, along with Master Antoine's regards."

"Your name?" Sir Galahad asked.

"Katrina, if it pleases you, sir."

Sandra raised an eyebrow. "That's an unusual name."

"My father escaped from the Vampire Kingdom two decades ago," the servant Katrina replied. "The noble Lord Seamus received him well and gave him work in his stables. He met my mother, and they fell in love, and nine months later, I was born." She blushed. "Thank you for taking an interest, my lady. I recommend the honey cake, if I may."

Sandra set the parchment aside and stood. "I'll have one of those." The honey cake had been her favorite, until that night.

She stepped forward.

"Wait," Sir Galahad growled.

She stopped — and in that moment, it was as if time itself had slowed down.

The servant dropped her tray and dashed toward her. Her skin turned gray, and dark wings sprouted from her back. A claw-like hand darted toward Sandra's face, each red talon an instrument of death.

Something tugged at her left arm, yanking her away. Sir Galahad. But he was slow. Too slow. Pain exploded on the right side of her face, and the light of her eye went out.

She fell to the floor, clutching her face and screaming. Sir Galahad barreled into the monster, knocking her down. They struggled for an instant, then the vampire spread her wings and flew through the open window, into the night.

#

"It was Mother's idea to call it an accident," Sandra said as she finished her story. "And that was only to make sure you didn't grow up fearing that the monsters would come for you as well. Though she did double the guards from that day onward. But now, as we're about to face our mortal enemies in battle for the fates of our gods, I thought you should know."

Marion nodded. "Who else knows the truth?"

"Only Mother and Sir Galahad. And now you, sister."

"And Father?"

Sandra shook her head. "Not even him." On that day, he'd been away, riding through the forest with Marion. She'd always been his favorite. "We'll keep it that way, yes?"

"As you wish." Marion took Sandra's hands in hers. "You had to bear this burden for so long, big sister. I am so sorry. And if it wasn't for this, you would have been queen."

"Perhaps it was for the best," Sandra forced herself to say. "I took to magic more than you did. It is part of me now, as much as your swordplay is part of you."

"And by my sword," Marion said, "I will avenge you, big sister. I'll find this Katrina, or whatever her true name is. And I'll make her pay for what she's done."

Sandra shook her head. "I prayed to the Lady for revenge that night, and she came to me. 'I can't touch Katrina,' she told me. 'She's protected. And I can't give you your eye back. But you'll have my love, my dear Sandra, and you will have my counsel. Now and always.'" She'd kept her promise, and that was a greater gift than Sandra could have hoped for.

"Perhaps she won't be protected anymore after the vampire god dies," Marion said. "We'll strike his champions from this world, and when Serya Krov is dead, I'll ask the Lady to avenge you. She'll do it, if it's within her power."

"It doesn't matter," Sandra lied with a straight face. "I struck vengeance from my mind after that." She sighed inwardly. She wasn't as perfect as Marion thought, but she could keep up appearances. After all, she'd had plenty of practice.

A heavy knock made her turn to the door. "Yes?"

The door opened. It was Nelson, Milton's twin. *The dark side of the family,* Marion called him, though not without affection.

He bowed. "My queen. High Priestess. I was wondering what to do with the assassins' bodies."

"Burn them," Sandra said, "as it is their custom. If my sister agrees."

"I do," Marion said.

"And what about this?" Nelson raised his gloved right hand. It held a dagger, its blade painted black. "It's the weapon that killed the man in the hallway."

"I know," Marion said. "I threw it myself, after the leader threw it at me."

"It's poisoned, no doubt." Nelson frowned. "I hope the blade didn't touch you."

"I caught it in mid-air." Marion raised her own gloved hand. "Not a scratch, just as I said. Call it good reflexes, or a stroke of luck, or perhaps both."

A flash of inspiration struck Sandra. "If it was luck, then you should keep it, sister."

Marion smiled. "I will. I'll keep poisoning the blade as well, though I'll use our own brews. I'll make good use of it when we face the vampire army on the field of battle."

That day will come soon, Sandra thought. *And many will die.* But with the giants striking for Dragos Castle, the Verdant army would find their enemy weakened. Marion would drive them from the field and take their cannons. And that, perhaps, would be enough to turn the tide of war.

The Right Decision

"My queen!"

Elena leaped to her feet at the urgency in Vladimir's voice. *I've been postponing this for far too long.*

She strode out of the tent for the first time in a week, and blinked rapidly as her eyes adjusted to the morning light. Two dozen of her nobles had gathered outside, Serya Krov's champions among them.

Zoltan Barko spoke first. "You look radiant, my queen."

She nodded. The ten pints of blood that she'd drunk every day since the attack had helped restore her beauty, along with some of her strength. She'd charged Zoltan with collecting the blood and passing it on to Kirill, and she'd only allowed Kirill to enter the tent.

None of her nobles had seen her weakness.

"A bit pale, though," Katrina said, her face betraying no emotion. "I trust it won't take long until you're fully recovered. My queen."

Elena shot her an icy glare. "I've recovered well enough, Katrina," she lied. "Thank you for your concern."

Her wounds still gave her pain at times, yet she was confident she could hide it from the others. She'd practiced for hours over the past two days, with Kirill as her only witness.

Just another week or two, she thought, *with plenty of rest and ten pints of blood each day. Then I'll be back to my full strength, as if this had never happened. And I'll make Queen Marion pay for this attack.*

Her gaze panned over the others, and it was then that she noticed Sveta, a young noble she'd left behind at Dragos Castle.

She turned to her. "Sveta. You've come a long way. Tell me why."

The noble bowed deeply. "We've been invaded, my queen. I came as fast as I could."

"The giants," Elena said through clenched teeth. It had to be them. The desert men wouldn't dare, and the Great Horde of the orcs had marched against the Julians. "How far did they get?"

"They smashed Bleakhall to pieces. I was there, visiting my uncle. He took the news of the defeat to Dragos Castle, and I came to you. We think they're marching straight for the capital."

"We must go back and defend it," Sergey said. "Before it falls to those savages. Will you give the order to march, my queen?"

Elena raised her right hand. "Wait, Sergey. How many, Sveta?"

"At least ten thousand. Too many for us to defeat without the main army."

Elena clenched her fists, her talons digging into her flesh. Most of the forces she'd left behind in the Bloodriver province were stationed farther south, to defend her lands against the orcs and the desert men. Then again, perhaps that was for the best. Without a large enough army and a strong core of nobles to lead it, stopping ten thousand giants was a task doomed to failure.

"Our nobles are conscripting more serfs to defend Dragos Castle," Sveta said. "Yet I fear it won't be enough. I beseech you to come to the capital's rescue, my queen."

Elena weighed her options. None of them were good.

If I do nothing, we are lost. The giants will take Dragos Castle, and we'll be too far away to take it back in time.

If we march now, it will be a race between our forces and theirs. They'll reach the capital first, but perhaps our defenders can hold them back until we arrive. Even so, we'll have to leave our cannons behind — and Queen Marion will be quick to seize them.

I can fly ahead with my nobles and defend Dragos Castle. But then

Marion will smash my army and take our cannons. Her forces will cross into our lands after that, and slaughter our people. We'll be doomed, regardless.

This is a disaster. She'd almost lost her life, and now she was about to lose the war.

"Your orders, my queen?" Sergey asked.

She snarled at him, and he shrank back.

"Let her think, Sergey," Zoltan spoke for her.

She closed her eyes and sought the strength and wisdom of noble blood.

I should have foreseen this. But what's done is done. Of course, Serya Krov couldn't have told her of the giants' movements. The Godly Pact forbade it.

She was stuck between the Verdant knights' lances and the giants' hammers. If she attended to one of the threats, the other would destroy her.

Even worse, Queen Marion had to know of the giants' plan. If Elena rushed to defeat her first, she'd simply pull back her forces, and shy from battle — and give the giants more time to advance. She'd only attack once Elena gave her the upper hand.

And so, I have to fight both threats at once, and win.

It was the only way. She opened her eyes.

"We need to stop the giants' invasion, and we will. But we're not retreating. I'll stay here and face Queen Marion on the field of battle."

"And what of our lands?" Sergey asked. "What of Dragos Castle?"

"You'll fly back to protect them, Sergey. Along with most of our nobles. Duke Zoltan will lead you."

"It would be my honor," Zoltan added. "Even so, we'll be hundreds against thousands, and most of our war-trained serfs are here. I don't think I can raise a strong enough army from the ones we've left behind. Not with the little time we've got left."

"You'll find a way, Duke Zoltan. You're one of Serya Krov's champions. Make our god proud."

Katrina smiled. "I'll go with him. I'll find a way to make myself useful."

"Then go." In truth, Katrina's departure would be a relief. And with Marion's army closing in, Elena didn't need yet another thorn in her side. "Your husband will stay, of course. We need him to lead his men."

Katrina nodded. "He'll serve you well, my queen. He'll do his duty. I'll make sure of it."

She'll find a way to emerge stronger from this, Elena thought. *And perhaps to make me look weaker.* But that was a problem for another day. For now, they had to fight on both fronts and survive.

"Summon King Anders here, Katrina," she said. "I'll speak with him after I confer with Zoltan. Everyone else, make preparations. You'll have your orders within the hour, and most of you will fly to our homeland's defense. Not you, Vladimir. I need you by my side."

The guard nodded. "As you wish, my queen."

"Duke Zoltan, with me," Elena said, and retreated into the tent. Zoltan followed her with heavy steps. Behind, the flapping of wings told her that the rest of her nobles were taking flight. Vladimir would guard the tent, as he'd done for the past week; but this time he'd do it from high in the air, out of earshot.

She turned to Zoltan. "Did I make the right decision?"

"You made the only one you could. Yet I fear its outcome."

She gave him a practiced smile. "You're the one who instills fear in others, Zoltan. I didn't think you could feel it yourself."

His face was serious. "You must promise me something, my queen."

"I'm listening."

"If the Verdant queen gains the upper hand in battle, you must fly away. Return to Dragos Castle, and take Kirill the priest with you. We'll find a way to survive and keep fighting for our god."

She shook her head. "I won't let it come to that." A jolt of pain stabbed through her chest and she snarled, trying to mask her suffering. "I'll win this battle, Zoltan. Whatever it takes."

If Zoltan had noticed anything was amiss, he did not show it.

"Our serfs will obey you," he said, "and they'll do their best. They're disciplined, and they are brave. We've drilled them well, and Kirill's words and those of the other priests have inspired them. They'll stand against the charge of the Verdant knights, and they won't break easily. Yet I fear they are no match for Queen Marion's shock troops. And her archers are second to none."

"I'm aware of that." Her troops hadn't managed to catch the archers who'd targeted her, though they'd scoured the countryside for days. "And yet I must win. And so must you."

"Then I hope the Islanders will live up to their renown. How many nobles would you keep at your side?"

"Two dozen."

Zoltan frowned. "It is too few, my queen."

"Keeping more would weaken your force. If you are to beat the giants back, you need all the help you can get. Do you have a plan for it already?"

The wizard shook his head. "I'll think of one along the way. I'll do my best to make it swift and return to your side. Still, wouldn't it be more prudent to defeat Queen Marion first?"

"I've thought of that. She must know of the giants' invasion. She'll only give battle if she's properly enticed. It must be why she hasn't moved against us yet."

"Except for the attempt on your life."

"I've survived worse than this." In truth, she hadn't. "Do your duty, Zoltan. I'll do mine."

"As you command. Which of our nobles would you retain?"

"I'll give you a list." She wrote the names on a sheet of paper and handed it to him. "Tell them to meet me here after I speak to the Islander king. Gather the others and fly, Zoltan. And return swiftly, with news of our victory."

He bowed and strode out of the tent, leaving Elena alone with her thoughts.

She wouldn't meet Queen Marion's army here, in the shadow of

Wallis Castle. It was a fortified position, but the Verdant queen and her strategists must have already drawn their battle plans. She had to find a place they were not prepared for — and it came to her in an instant.

I'll take the army ten miles north, into that valley. She'd scouted the place eight days earlier, before the archers' cowardly strike had brought her to the brink of death. *I'll watch the battle from the air and swoop in when the situation demands it. And I'll make Queen Marion pay for the attempt on my life.*

The Gods and their Champions

Aljin: King Ammon, Nasir bin Fatih, Achmad bin Fayzal, ~~Al Khanjar~~

Augustus: Emperor Lucius, ~~Marcus Severus~~, Leticia Alba, ~~Selenius Gracchus~~

Grok the All-Father: King Ghark, Hagor the shaman, ~~Rorra Fireborn~~, Krakkar the Fist

The Lady: Queen Marion, High Priestess Sandra, Eugene the Trickster, Sir Galahad

Malleon: King Tassadar, Paeren, Neressia, Eldris the Duelist

Njord: ~~King Knut~~, Queen Frida, ~~Ursula~~, Gunnar

Serya Krov: Queen Elena, Duke Zoltan Barko, Kirill Skromnik, Katrina

Bonus Content

Congratulations! You've finished Part Seven.

To explore the bonus content, visit https://bradtowers.com/wots-bonus-7/ or scan this QR code:

Part 8: Of Love and War

Unexpected Love

Leaning over a large wooden table, Lucius wiped the sweat off his brow and studied the battlefield one last time. He was alone in the throne room, waiting for Silvanus to join him for the first battle of the day.

Lucius's troops were all mounted and would attack from three sides. He had split his two thousand horse archers and one thousand heavy camel riders into small units, to allow for more complex maneuvers, while his eight hundred lancers would charge the rear of Silvanus's forces. The figurines were all painted a bright yellow, the color of the desert men.

They'd ambush Silvanus's column as it advanced through a river valley, surrounded by forested hills. And while Lucius had studied Silvanus's troops for the better part of an hour, his friend wouldn't know the size and the placement of the attacking forces until Lucius called him to the table and began the attack.

A decisive win for Lucius's desert men was out of the question, for the orange and blue forces severely outnumbered his own. What mattered was how many losses he could inflict before retreating, and how fast Silvanus could repel him, with both of them trying their best.

As King Ammon would, when they met him in the field.

It wouldn't be Silvanus leading the Julian forces when that happened. Farus would have that task, or perhaps Lucius himself. But Lucius judged that putting himself in the mind of his opponent was a good step toward defeating him when the time came.

I hope we can beat him on Julian lands, he thought. Chasing King Ammon through the desert would be a far more difficult endeavor.

A knock on the door made him raise his eyes from the table. "Yes?"

"Princeps Silvanus, Your Majesty," came the guard's reply.

"Send him in."

Lucius strode from the table and clasped arms with his friend, blocking his path to the table. "Are you ready to be ambushed, General Silvanus?"

Silvanus huffed. "You won't even let me get a peek at your troops first, will you?"

"Neither would King Ammon. So, shall we begin?"

"Not yet. My throat is parched. Besides, I have something to tell you." A mischievous look set upon Silvanus's face.

"Fine." Lucius led him to the refreshments table. He poured two glasses of orange juice and handed the first one to Silvanus; a gesture reserved for such moments, when no servants and no stone-faced Augustian Guards surrounded them.

He took a sip and waited as Silvanus drained his cup in a few long gulps. "The weather's gotten warmer than usual these days, hasn't it?"

Silvanus nodded. "I was about to say the same."

"So, what is it you wanted to tell me?"

A wide smile appeared on Silvanus's face. "I am in love, Lucius."

Lucius raised an eyebrow. "You can't be in love. Not now. You're a married man!"

"That's just it." Silvanus's eyes were gleaming. "I'm in love. With my wife!"

Lucius couldn't believe his ears. "What?"

"You heard me."

"But — she's so unlike you. You like books and cats, and she stands in the shield wall and leads men into battle. She prefers women to men and has one waiting for her back home. She's *twice your size*, for Augustus's sake!"

Silvanus grimaced. "You wound me, Your Imperial Majesty. I'm not *that* supple. Maybe twice *your* size."

"You've only known her for a week." She'd left the capital eleven days earlier, with Farus and the rest of the army. "Wait. Is she... is she *that* good in bed?"

"It's not that. I slept on my sofa, every single night. We haven't even touched."

Lucius raised an eyebrow for the second time that day.

"I stand corrected," Silvanus said. "She held my hand a few times, but only in public."

"Then what is it?"

"I'm *smitten* with Frida. Not with her body, with *her*. I've seen her strength, and her intelligence, and how she treats her men, and her sense of duty and loyalty. I know we're not exactly made for each other, and I know that she prefers women, and that she may die before this war is over. And yet this is how I feel."

"Does she know about it?"

Silvanus shook his head. "Do you take me for a fool?"

"You must know she doesn't feel the same. This was a political match. For the alliance."

"I know it, yes. And it doesn't matter."

"You'll still do your duty, yes?"

Silvanus sighed. "Of course I will. In this, she and I are alike. I know this is unexpected, Lucius. But you can't tell people how they should feel."

Perhaps the gods can, Lucius thought. *Perhaps it was Njord who did this. A move to strengthen the alliance, and to give Frida a better chance of survival.* Though Lucius hadn't expected Njord to be that crafty, nor for Augustus to allow it.

"I can speak to Afrodisia if you want me to," he said. "I can ask her to put an end to your infatuation."

"Don't!" Silvanus gripped his arm — and released it quickly. "Not yet, at least. I've never truly been in love before. Not like this. And if it is the gods who wanted me to feel this, which *of course* I've considered already," he tilted his head and gave Lucius a smug smile, "they must have had a reason."

"Fine," Lucius relented. "I won't do it yet. And not without asking you first." He paused. "You know you could have had your pick. Before Augustus married you off to Frida, that is. Any of our young noble ladies would have been lucky to have you."

Silvanus shrugged. "So they told me. Airheads, the lot of them. Except for the cunning ones, who only wanted me for my wealth."

"There was Flavia."

Silvanus looked into the distance. "Yes. And we would have been a good match. But what's done is done. Flavia married General Justinian's son two years ago."

You were too slow, Lucius thought, but he remained silent. At the time, both he and Silvanus were recovering from the deaths of their parents in Aquila's insurrection.

"You're right, Silvanus," he said. "What's done is done. Keep this love of yours, for now. But don't let it make you do anything stupid." He punched him in the shoulder. "Not more than usual, at least."

Silvanus returned the punch. "Someday, Your Imperial Majesty, you'll fall in love as well. And then you'll know how I feel. Though I do hope you'll find a more suitable match than mine."

Lucius nodded. "I'll let you know when that happens."

He hadn't had time for love, not with the responsibility of ruling the empire being thrust upon him at the age of thirteen. And he wasn't about to get distracted any time soon.

For now, he had to win the War of the Seven. That was the hand he'd been dealt.

He pointed to the table where his yellow figurines waited, ready to spring into action. "My desert men are about to ambush your dear wife, and your Julian forces as well. Come and defend them, General Silvanus. I'll start the sands of time."

With that, he dashed toward the table, and Silvanus raced after him.

At the Temple

The Lady strode forward, her bare footsteps moving gently across the marble floor of Augustus's temple.

It's warm, she realized. *As is the air. More so than usual.* Then again, it was late in the afternoon, and the midsummer sun shone brightly in the cloudless sky.

She remembered her last visit. She'd been angry at Augustus for his alliance with Njord, and for the *other* thing, too — and yet he'd pacified her, and quickly.

Much had changed since then.

"You were right," she said when she reached him.

"About what?" Augustus asked. He'd come as himself; his favorite aspect, and hers as well. The taste of his lips from that day in her own temple was fresh in her thoughts, as was everything that *that* had led to.

She pushed the memory away. "About Malleon. He's marching his giants toward Dragos Castle. Queen Elena had to split her forces, and Marion is going to crush her."

"That is good news," Augustus said. "For us both."

So he didn't know. "You haven't traveled to that side of the world in a while, have you?"

"I am everywhere," he said, his voice echoing from the far corners of the room.

She smiled. "A nice trick. What have you been up to?"

"Nothing much," Augustus replied. "Two weddings between my people and Njord's, helping Lucius and Leticia with their tasks, and watching our generals defeat the orcs and send them back to their homes, and General Justinian falling prey to the desert men's cunning tricks. Oh, and giving Lucius some nice visions from another world, since the Godly Pact does not forbid it. Don't tell the others."

"Speaking of visions," the Lady said. "I wanted to thank you for your help with Marion's training all those years ago. She just bested Al-Khanjar the assassin, and two of his men as well."

Augustus nodded. "Aljin told me. She still thinks those visions came from you, yes?"

"She has no reason to suspect otherwise." Augustus had come to her at night, wearing Artemisia's aspect, which matched the Lady perfectly. He'd imitated her voice as well — and, in the dark, ten-year-old Marion hadn't been able to see that the goddess giving her the visions was orange instead of green. After watching Idrissa the Vixen, a skilled young fighter from another world, as she trained with her master, she'd put more effort into her own training.

"Aljin said she threw a knife," Augustus said.

"She did. She held her own in the sword fight, too. Malleon's armor helped."

"And now she'll break Queen Elena's army, and Lucius will crush the orcs and the desert men. And then it's between the two of us, Njord, and Malleon."

"You're the one I'll miss the most, Augustus. You know that."

"Of course I do," he said. "You're even wearing your glamor for me. But first, you'll have to beat me."

She hadn't let go of her glamor in a while, and for good reason. But that was a discussion for another day. "I didn't come here for our verbal sparring, Augustus. I came to celebrate. To share a moment of joy."

His smile was so bright, it could have lit the darkest night.

Then, suddenly, it faltered. "Something's wrong," he said.

"What?" she asked. But Augustus had already vanished.

The Heatwave

In her room at the Imperial Palace, Leticia Alba finished her glass of water and stretched on her bed.

She was — tired. Unusually tired, so early in the afternoon.

It's the heatwave, she thought. Even for the peak of the Julian summer, the past two days had been hotter than any she could remember, at least here in the capital. Even so, she'd been blessing the harvest for hours, though she'd been channeling less magic since her move into Lucius's quarters.

I should rest for a day or two. I'm not getting any younger.

A jolt of pain lanced through her chest.

This isn't normal. She sat up, feeling weak, short of breath. She tried to stand and slumped back onto her bed. Pain struck her through her heart again.

"Help," she moaned, but no one would hear her.

She rolled off the bed, hitting the leg of her bedside table as she fell. Her empty glass crashed onto the marble floor, as did her nighttime candle, and a moment later two guards dashed into the room.

She took a few quick breaths, and heard one of them shout for a healer. Then everything went black.

The First to Fall

Will he come back? the Lady wondered as she paced Augustus's hall.

"I'm dying." His voice came first.

He appeared just where he'd stood only moments earlier. His face was grim.

The Lady's mouth fell open. "You're— What? How?"

"Leticia. My third champion. Her heart is giving out, and I'm not allowed to interfere. It's the heatwave."

"Aljin," the Lady said instantly, and the magnitude of it hit her. Aljin's assassin had murdered two of the Julian champions, and now Aljin was killing the third. He'd destroyed Augustus all by himself.

Augustus nodded. "Aljin, yes. He *tricked* me. Me, the trickster god."

"But — how was this not against the Pact?"

"It wasn't a direct attack. He turned up the heat, but that is not what's killing Leticia. Her exertion in this weather *is*. Her use of magic, beyond what her mortal body could handle. And that, she brought upon herself." He slapped his forehead. "She and my stupidity. I should have foreseen this."

"What can I do?"

"Nothing. You can't interfere. Her fate is sealed, and so is mine."

"How — how much time do you have?" Her voice was breaking.

"An hour. Perhaps less. I must use it well. I have to go, Lady."

She grabbed his arm. "Wait."

She focused, let go of her glamor, and let him see her true form. Her rounder belly, which she'd been hiding from him, and from Aljin, and from her followers as well.

His eyes widened. "You're pregnant." He reached for her belly.

She pressed his hand upon it. "Twins, Augustus. Yours. *Ours*. The family you've always wanted."

His mouth fell open. It moved, as if he tried to speak, but no sound came out. Joy and despair warred across his face. Then, in an instant, he steeled himself and looked her in the eye.

"You have to win this war, Lady," he said. "And you must keep them safe, and the world as well. I'll meet them in a thousand years."

She took his hands in hers. "Stay with me."

"I can't. There's work to do. But let this not be our final kiss."

He pressed his lips against hers. She kissed him back, with a hunger she'd never felt before.

He pulled away. "About the war. My people's alliance with Njord still stands. Even so, they'll help you, if they can. Speak to Lucius if you need help, and to Njord as well. Stay away from Malleon's champions. I can't tell you more without betraying Njord, and you *know* I can't do that, since we're bound in Godly Pact. But you do have a good chance to win this. I'll see you again in a thousand years."

"Goodbye," she whispered.

"Farewell, Lady."

He placed a hand on his heart. And then he was gone.

She roared and sank to her knees, yet there was nothing she could do.

The Fate of the World

Alone in the throne room, Lucius surveyed the last battlefield of the day. The remnants of his forces lay scattered, with the last of his elite infantry surrounded by a sea of red figurines. Silvanus and his orcs had dealt him a stinging defeat.

His friend had kept a large warband in reserve, hidden in a narrow valley at the side of the table. A feigned retreat had pulled the bulk of Lucius's forces away to the west, and then the warband had charged his cannons, overwhelming their defenders before Lucius could reinforce them. They'd used the cannons against the Julian forces, and the battle had quickly become one-sided after that.

I should have done better, Lucius thought. In a real battle, a defeat like this would cost tens of thousands of lives. And the generals' messages from the frontline had said that Ghark Bloodaxe, the orc king who led the Great Horde, was a skilled battle commander.

He exhaled, loudly. *I'll write to Farus about this, and to Queen Frida. They won't make the same mistake when it matters.*

"I'm dying," Augustus's voice came.

Lucius raised his eyes and saw him standing on the other side of the table.

He shook his head. "No. I'd flee from the battle, and I'd be mounted, and surrounded by cataphracts. The orcs wouldn't catch me."

Augustus gave him a thin smile. "Fine, you'd probably escape. But you're not paying attention. I. Am. Dying. Now."

Lucius's heart skipped a beat. "How?"

"Leticia's heart is failing. I don't have long. Listen, Lucius."

Lucius's knees weakened, and he pressed his hands heavily against the table. The moment he'd feared the most had come — and it wasn't just Augustus who would die. All the Julian gods would perish with him, and be gone from the world for a thousand years, until the Supreme One brought them back.

If there will even be a world to come back to.

Suddenly, it was hard to breathe.

In an instant, Augustus was at his side. He placed his hand on Lucius's arm. "Take deep breaths. I need you to be strong now. This is not the end, not for you. And I've prepared you for this." He pointed to the throne. "If you need to sit, there's a good chair over there."

Lucius steeled himself. "I'm fine here. As much as I can be. I'm listening."

"Njord is your god now. You will do his bidding, and he'll be kind to our people if he remains the last of the gods. But remember, he's impulsive, and wisdom is not among his greatest strengths. I told him to place his trust in you, and in the lessons I've taught you. I hope he'll follow my advice."

Lucius nodded. "I'll do my best to win. For Njord, and for our people."

"I blame Aljin for Leticia's death, though he didn't kill her directly. He must have caused the heatwave, and your grandmother couldn't bear it. Not after using as much magic as she did."

Lucius bowed his head. "It's my fault. I should have stopped her."

"And I as well. But what's done is done. Aljin must die, and you will see to it. I've just spoken to Njord, and he agrees. You'll do what it takes, and you won't shy from it."

"I will."

"Good. If Njord falls, fight for the Lady, then for Malleon. Bend your knee to Serya Krov if you have to; he's not my favorite choice, but at least he won't tear down everything I've built, and I'll restore the balance when I return. Aljin and Grok, you must destroy."

"As you say." Augustus had given him the same instructions after forging the alliance with the Islanders.

Augustus placed a hand on his shoulder. "I know this is hard, Lucius. But you are ready. The war is not over, and you are fighting for the fate of the world. It is a heavy burden, especially for one as young as you. And yet you must carry it."

Lucius straightened his back and looked Augustus in the eye. "I won't disappoint you."

"I expect I'll read about your deeds in the history books." Augustus's smile returned to his face, if only for a moment.

"Any last-minute advice?" Lucius asked.

"I've given you all the advice I could give. Let us go now. Leticia should have us both at her side in her final moments."

"Augustus?"

"Yes?"

"I…" Lucius's voice was breaking. "After I lost my parents, I… There was a void in my life."

"Until I came and filled it," Augustus said. "Along with my *family*." There was a sour note in his voice, no doubt from the pain of having all the Julian gods perish with him. "If I had ever sired a mortal son, Lucius, I couldn't think of a better one than you."

Tears welled in Lucius's eyes.

Augustus flicked his hand, and the tears dried in an instant. "Cry for me when I'm gone, in private. Not now. The emperor must be strong."

He was right. They'd pass over a hundred guards between the throne room and Leticia's room.

Augustian Guards, Lucius thought. *I'll keep the name. Even after this.*

He took a deep breath, then another. "I am ready."

"Then walk with me," Augustus said, and they strode out of the throne room side by side, on their final journey together.

The Gods and their Champions

Aljin: King Ammon, Nasir bin Fatih, Achmad bin Fayzal, ~~Al Khanjar~~

Augustus: Emperor Lucius, ~~Marcus Severus~~, Leticia Alba, ~~Selenius Gracchus~~

Grok the All-Father: King Ghark, Hagor the shaman, ~~Rorra Fireborn~~, Krakkar the Fist

The Lady: Queen Marion, High Priestess Sandra, Eugene the Trickster, Sir Galahad

Malleon: King Tassadar, Paeren, Neressia, Eldris the Duelist

Njord: ~~King Knut~~, Queen Frida, ~~Ursula~~, Gunnar

Serya Krov: Queen Elena, Duke Zoltan Barko, Kirill Skromnik, Katrina

Bonus Content

Congratulations! You've finished Part Eight. We're getting close to the end of the book!

To explore the bonus content, visit https://bradtowers.com/wots-bonus-8/ or scan this QR code:

Epilogue

Four Times Over

Seated on a tree stump on the bank of a river, Frida touched the marks the bear's claws had left on her chest. "I didn't think it would come to this. Not so soon, at least."

Gunnar stretched out his legs in front of him. "Neither did I, Little Frida."

Njord had just disappeared into the river's waters, having told her and Gunnar of the coming death of the Julian gods. For the moment, she and Gunnar were the only ones in the army who knew. He'd found them at the edge of the camp, and had commanded Frida's guards to wait at a respectful distance, out of earshot, until she'd summoned them.

"*Go to Prince Farus's tent when you're done here,*" he'd told them before leaping into the river. "*Bring Lothar, too. Send everyone else away.*"

It was the right move. They'd plan their next steps away from prying eyes, and decide how to share the news with the rest of the army.

Frida picked up a flat stone, threw it, and watched it skip across the water. "And yet here we are."

"You've accomplished much," Gunnar said. "When King Knut died, you stepped up to lead our people, since there was no one better. You weathered Ursula's death and Anders's betrayal and kept our people strong. You asked Queen Marion for an alliance, and when she came at you with steel, you defeated her."

"*We* defeated her," she corrected him.

"Aye, my cannons did their part. And then we sailed east—"

"—which was Lothar's idea," she intervened, though she'd considered it herself as well.

Gunnar nodded. "You joined us in alliance with the Julians, and you got us fair terms. You married one of their princes. And now, they'll all fight for you. Look at them!"

Frida glanced over her shoulder. The camp stretched as far as she could see; a sprawling city of tents, orange mixed together with blue, two armies learning to march and fight together. Former enemies becoming friends.

"They'll all follow you, if you lead them," Gunnar said. "The Julians, too."

She shook her head. "Not yet. I'll let Prince Farus lead the war effort. And the Boy Emperor, when he comes. They've trained for it with their battle games, and they know how to run the supply lines. I'll stay at your side, with the cannons."

"Good," Gunnar said. "I'll keep you safe, Little Frida."

"And I you." She sighed. "I didn't ask for this, Gunnar."

"I know. And yet you'll do your duty. And with some luck, when this is done, you'll be the queen of the world."

"First, we must win." Gunnar was right, of course. When Njord became the last of the gods, he wouldn't let the Boy Emperor rule above her. But she wouldn't think of that, not now.

"What's your beef with Njord?" she asked instead.

Gunnar ran a hand through his hair, which he hadn't dyed blue in more than a decade. "Ah. *That.* I was wondering when you'd ask."

She had, years earlier, but he'd changed the subject. Abruptly.

"I thought you'd tell me when the time was right. And there's no better time than now." She paused. "You can keep it to yourself if you choose to."

He stared into the distance. "No. You should know. I've kept it from you for too long."

She waited for him to continue.

"It's that bloody prophecy," Gunnar said. "That, and all the friends Njord took from me. All those who died in my stead."

"What do you mean?"

"Remember Harald Gustavsson, who took an arrow for me?"

"Aye." He'd told her the story when she was eight.

"And One-Eye Olof, who went home for more coins and got knifed in that alley behind the tavern? I should have gone myself, but I was too deep in my cups."

"I remember him."

"And Jorg, who stumbled and fell as those woodsmen were chasing us?"

Frida nodded.

"And Big Greta, whom I loved as a sister? We tossed a coin to decide which of us got to go on that raid. She won the toss, and sailed into that storm, and I lost her."

"As did I."

"It was Njord's doing, all of it. He was protecting *me*. Keeping me safe because of the bloody prophecy. Because he knew that one of my bloodline would save him from destruction."

Njord sent my mother to her death. Suddenly Frida was a ship driven by the storm, crashing against the rocks.

"You're certain of it," she said.

"He told me himself. He thought he was doing me a favor — and he murdered all my closest friends. He sacrificed them, when I should have died instead. Four times over."

"Aaaargh!" Frida roared as she leaped to her feet. She clenched her fists, her nails digging into her palms. Her guards rushed toward her and she waved them away.

She whirled toward Gunnar, who had stood as well. "Why? Why would you tell me this?"

"I thought you should know who you're fighting for. It is only fair." He kept his voice low.

"I am fighting for our people!" She lowered her voice to match Gunnar's. "For Hemland. For our future. If we lose this war, there'll be scores to settle."

"I know," Gunnar said. "And I fight for you, Little Frida. You and no one else."

She waved toward the camp. "Look at them, Gunnar. Our people and the Julians. If Njord dies, they'll turn against each other."

"They might, yes." He paused. "I wish we could just run from this."

"We can't, and we won't. I'll fight for my people. *Our* people, Gunnar. You won't abandon them."

"I won't abandon *you*."

"And I won't abandon Njord, Gunnar. Njord is the future. In a hundred years, your bones and mine will be resting on the bottom of the sea. And the last of the gods will rule our people's fates for a thousand years." She paused. "I choose Njord, with all his flaws. Though I wish he had saved you and Mother both."

"Fine," Gunnar said. "I'll follow you. As will our men."

She nodded. "Get Lothar and go to Farus's tent. I'll join you shortly. And, Gunnar?"

"Yes?"

"No more secrets."

"Aye." He walked away, and six of her guards followed him. After all, he was one of Njord's champions.

She stood and watched the river for a while.

I'll set this aside, Njord, she thought at last. *As I must, for now.* She couldn't do her duty to her people if she didn't.

But when this war is over, you and I will have words.

Final Moments

High above the Imperial Palace, he flew. High above the city. High above the world.

He soared, and swooped, and shifted, over and over. Athina, then Ares, then Fortuna, then Afrodisia, then Ares again. Demetra. Athina. Augustus.

When faced with oblivion, he thought, *I'd better enjoy my final moments.* For that was all he had left, for a thousand years.

Up he went, higher and higher, shifting from one aspect to the next. Then, as Athina, he had another thought.

There was no better place for him to die than at the top of the world. Upon the highest mountain.

It was far away, and getting there quickly would take an enormous effort. Then again, he had no need to save his strength.

He focused, and suddenly he was *there*, on the World's Peak, standing between two enormous flags blowing in the wind. Grok's and Malleon's. And he was not alone.

Aljin waited there. As did Serya Krov.

He sighed and shifted from Athina into Augustus. "I didn't think I'd find you two here."

"I knew you'd come," Aljin said. "Tell me I played this well."

"You did. And the Boy Emperor will destroy you."

"I warned you when this started." Aljin's voice was level.

"And I'm warning you now. I *will* have my vengeance, even after I'm gone. And we'll speak about it in a thousand years. If we return."

"I'll keep the world safe for the two of you," Serya Krov intervened. "I have no fight with you, Augustus."

"Nor I with you." The Vampire Kingdom lay in the west, far from the Julian Empire. Four realms separated them: the Verdant Kingdom in the north, the giants' kingdom and the lands of the orcs in the center, and the great desert in the south.

Serya Krov flapped his wings. "You know I'll go for the boy. Within the limits of the Godly Pact, of course." Which meant he wouldn't harm him, not directly, though his followers were allowed to. More likely, he'd try to get him as an ally.

"I know," Augustus said. "He has my instructions."

"And those are?"

Augustus chuckled. "You'll find out soon enough. For now, let us enjoy my final moments together. In silence."

They obeyed him in that, as he knew they would, and his thoughts drifted to the Lady.

She has to win, and to keep the world safe when the Vengeful One comes. And in a thousand years, when I return, I'll meet our children for the first time.

We'll be a family, if they'll have me.

And that was the thing he wanted the most.

Bonus Content

Here we are, Dear Reader. We've reached the end of this book, and Augustus was the first of the gods to die. He and his people underestimated Aljin, and he paid the ultimate price. With some luck, he'll meet his children for the first time in a thousand years.

The story continues in Book 2, **Songs of the Heroes**. Queen Marion's army will clash with Queen Elena's diminished forces. Zoltan and Katrina will lead the vampire nobles against King Tassadar's giants. And Emperor Lucius will ride to war, ready to put his training to the test. For some of these champions, their next battle will be their last.

Songs of the Heroes is faster, more epic, and more intense than **War of the Seven**. Since you're now familiar with Ethasar's factions and heroes, it's time for large-scale battles, heartfelt character moments, and more awesome bonus content. You'll see.

The final Bonus Content page for **War of the Seven** includes links to all the campaign maps, a vast image gallery, all the nine songs, and other bonus materials.

Before we get to that, I have a quick — and important — request:

If you enjoyed this book, please leave a review and help other readers discover War of the Seven! This is very important for the success of the series. Star ratings and reviews encourage the right readers to check out the book, and every single review matters.

Leaving a star rating and writing a short review will take less than two minutes of your time.

To do this, simply visit https://bradtowers.com/review-wots and choose your Amazon domain, and write your review. Or scan the following QR code:

Now, to explore the bonus content, visit https://bradtowers.com/wots-bonus-9/ or scan this QR code:

Thanks a lot for your support!

Printed in Great Britain
by Amazon

WAR OF THE SEVEN
By
BRAD TOWERS
bradtowers.com

Copyright 2024 Brad Towers
All rights reserved.